LIGHTSABERS

Luke Skywalker has come to a grim conclusion. The Shadow Academy has become very powerful, and the New Republic needs all the warriors it can muster. It is time for the young Jedi Knights to build their weapons . . .

DARKEST KNIGHT

The Dark Jedi student Zekk has been given his rite of passage. Finally he will fulfill his awesome potential. But first he must face his old friends Jacen and Jaina—once and for all . . .

JEDI UNDER SIEGE

The day of reckoning is at hand for the young Jedi Knights. The Shadow Academy—with its army of Dark Jedi and Imperial stormtroopers—has appeared in the sky over Yavin 4. And when a commando raid destroys the shield generator protecting the Jedi academy, there is only one option: to fight . . .

D0937353

YOUNG JEDI KNIGHTS

JEDI SUNRISE

KEVIN J. ANDERSON
and REBECCA MOESTA

BERKLEY JAM BOOKS, NEW YORK

These are works of fiction. Names, characters, places, and incidents either are the product of the authors' imaginations or are used fictitiously, and any resemblance to actual persons, living or dead, business establishments, events, or locales is entirely coincidental.

STAR WARS: YOUNG JEDI KNIGHTS: JEDI SUNRISE

A Berkley Jam Book / published by arrangement with Lucasfilm Ltd.

PRINTING HISTORY
Berkley Jam edition / December 2003

For information address: The Berkley Publishing Group,
a division of Penguin Group (USA) Inc.,
375 Hudson Street, New York, New York 10014.

ISBN: 0-425-18684-9

BERKLEY JAM BOOKS®
Berkley Jam Books are published by The Berkley Publishing Group,
a division of Penguin Group (USA) Inc.,
375 Hudson Street, New York, New York 10014.
BERKLEY JAM and its logo
are trademarks belonging to Penguin Group (USA) Inc.

PRINTED IN THE UNITED STATES OF AMERICA

10 9 8 7 6 5 4 3 2 1

CONTENTS

Lightsabers

To Jonathan MacGregor Cowan,
whose love, intelligence, imagination, sense of humor,
and sense of wonder constantly inspire us—
and challenge us.

acknowledgments

We would like to thank Lillie E. Mitchell for her spectac-ular typing and her love of the books, Dave Wolverton for his input on the Hapes Cluster, Lucy Wilson and Sue Rostoni at Lucasfilm for their constructive comments and their vision, Ginjer Buchanan and Lou Aronica at Berkley/Boulevard for their wholehearted support and encouragement, and Skip and Cheryl Shayotovich for being some of our most faithful cheerleaders.

1

DAYBREAK AT LAST spilled across the treetops on Yavin 4, where Luke Skywalker, Jedi Master, listened to the stirring, rustling sounds of the awakening jungle. The looming stone blocks of the ancient temple had absorbed the deep night's chill, and now glistened with dew.

As the morning brightened, he wished his spirits could lift as easily.

Cool and stiff, Luke had been atop the Great Temple for a long time already, sitting patiently in the primeval darkness and thinking. He had used Jedi relaxation techniques to dispense with sleep; in fact, he had not rested thoroughly for some time, so great was his concern over the growing Imperial threat to the New Republic.

Jungle birds cried out and took wing, searching for a breakfast of flying insects. The enormous gas giant Yavin hung overhead, luminous with reflected light, but Luke stared beyond it with his imagination, envisioning all of the galaxy's dark and secret corners where the Second Imperium might lie hidden. . . .

Finally Luke stood and stretched. It was time for his morning exercises. Perhaps the exertion would help him think more clearly, get his heart beating harder, tune his reflexes.

At the top of the pyramid, he went to the sheer edge of the enormous, vine-covered blocks that formed the sides of the towering temple. It was a long drop to the next level, where the ziggurat widened toward its base. Each squared-off set of blocks displayed decorative etchings and crenellations,

7

carved into the stone thousands of years earlier during the building of the ancient structure, weathered by scorching attack and passing time. The dense jungle encroached at the rear of the temple pyramid, embellishing the massive stones with thick vines and overspreading Massassi tree branches.

Luke paused for a moment at the edge, took a deep breath, and closed his eyes to center his concentration. Then he leaped out into space.

He felt himself falling and rotated in midair, executing a backward somersault that brought him into position, feet down, just in time to see the cracked old stones rushing up at him. Using the Force to slow himself just enough for a hard landing, he rebounded and pushed off toward the nearest vine. Allowing himself a brief laugh of exhilaration, Luke snagged the rough jungle creeper and swung up onto the lichen-flaked branch of a Massassi tree. He landed smoothly and ran along the branch without pausing. Next he jumped across a gap in the jungle canopy and grabbed a small branch overhead, hauling himself higher, climbing, running.

Each day Luke challenged himself, finding more difficult routines in order to continue honing his skills. Even during times of peace, a Jedi Knight could never allow himself to relax and grow weak.

But these were not quiet times, and Luke Skywalker had plenty of challenges to face.

Years ago, a student named Brakiss had been planted in Luke's academy as an Imperial spy to learn the ways of the Jedi and twist them to evil uses. Luke had seen through the disguise, however, and had tried unsuccessfully to turn Brakiss to the light side. After the dark trainee had fled, Luke had not heard from Brakiss again—until recently, when Jacen, Jaina, and the young Wookiee Lowbacca had been kidnapped. Brakiss had teamed up with one of the evil new Nightsisters—Tamith Kai—to form a Shadow Academy for training Dark Jedi in the service of the Empire.

Panting from his workout, Luke continued to climb through the trees, startling a nest of ravenous stintarils. The rodents turned on him, flashing bright teeth, but when he nudged their attack instincts in a new direction, they forgot their intended target and scattered through the leafy branches.

He swung himself up and finally reached the jungle canopy. Sunshine burst upon him as he pushed his head above the leafy treetops. Humid air filled his burning lungs, and he blinked again in the morning light. The lush world around him seemed very bright after the filtered dimness of the thick underlevels. Looking back toward the stepped pyramid of the Great Temple that housed his Jedi students, Luke considered both the new group of fighters he had brought here to help protect the New Republic and the trainees at the Shadow Academy. . . .

In the past few months, the Shadow Academy had begun recruiting candidates among the disadvantaged young men and women of Coruscant, taking these "lost ones" to serve the Second Imperium. One of these had been the teenager named Zekk, a dark-haired, green-eyed scamp who had been a good friend to the twins, especially Jaina. In addition, the TIE pilot Qorl—who had spent over two decades hiding on Yavin 4 after the first Death Star was destroyed—had led a raid to steal hyperdrive cores and turbolaser batteries from an incoming New Republic supply ship.

All this and more had led Luke Skywalker to the conclusion that the Shadow Academy was gearing up for a major battle against the New Republic. Since the death of Emperor Palpatine, there had been many warlords and leaders who had attempted to rekindle the Imperial way—but Luke sensed through the Force that this new leader was something more evil than just another pretender. . . .

Bright sunlight fell across Luke, warming his hands. Brilliantly colored insects flitted about, buzzing in the new day. He shifted against the rough branches and drew a deep breath of the fresh air, catching mingled scents from the lush jungle all around him.

The Shadow Academy was still out there, still training Dark Jedi. Luke hated to rush his training of those who studied the ways of the light side—but circumstances forced him to attempt to bring out powerful defenders faster than the Shadow Academy could create new enemies. A fight was brewing, and they had to be prepared.

Luke grabbed a loose vine and let himself drop, drop, *drop* until, landing with a jarring thump against a wide Massassi tree branch, he set off, running at top speed back to the academy.

The workout had awakened him fully, and now he was ready for action.

It was time for another gathering of students at the Jedi academy—and Jacen Solo knew that meant his uncle, Luke Skywalker, had something important to say.

Life at the academy was not a constant series of lectures and classes, as he had experienced during tutoring sessions back on Coruscant. The Jedi academy was designed primarily for independent study in a place where Force-sensitive individuals could delve into their minds, test their abilities, and work at their own pace.

Each potential Jedi Knight had a range of skills. Jacen himself had a knack for understanding animals, calling them to him, and knowing their thoughts and feelings. His sister Jaina, on the other hand, had a genius for mechanical things and electronic circuits, and possessed engineering intuition.

Lowbacca, their Wookiee friend, had an eerie rapport with computers, which allowed him to decipher and program complex electronic circuits. Their athletic friend Tenel Ka was physically strong and self-trained, but she usually avoided relying on the Force as the easiest solution to a problem. Tenel Ka depended on her own wits and strength first.

In his quarters Jacen's exotic pets rustled in their cages along the stone wall. He hurried to feed them and then ran his fingers through his unruly brown curls to remove any stray bits of moss or fodder he might have picked up from the cages. He poked his head into his twin sister Jaina's chambers as she, too, prepared for the big meeting. She quickly combed her straight brown hair and scrubbed her face clean so that her skin looked pink and fresh.

"Any idea what Uncle Luke's going to talk about?" she asked, drying drips of water from her chin and nose.

"I was hoping you'd know," Jacen said.

One of the other young Jedi trainees, Raynar, emerged from his room dressed in garishly colored robes with an eye-popping display of intense primary blues, yellows, and reds. He seemed terribly flustered as he brushed his hands down the fabric of his robe, let out a sigh of dismay, and ducked back into his rooms.

"Bet the meeting has something to do with that trip Uncle Luke just took to Coruscant," Jaina said. Jacen remembered that their uncle had recently flown off in the *Shadow Chaser*—a sleek ship they had appropriated from the Shadow Academy in order to make good their escape—to discuss the threat of the Second Imperium with Chief of State Leia Organa Solo, Luke's sister and the twins' mother.

"Only one way to find out," Jacen said. "Most of the other students should be in the grand audience chamber already."

"Well then, what are we waiting for?" Jaina said, and took off with her brother at a brisk clip down the corridor.

Behind them, Raynar emerged from his quarters again, looking much more satisfied now that he had managed to find a robe that was, if anything, even more dazzlingly bright than the first one—enough to cause tension headaches in anyone who looked too long. Raynar cinched the robe around his waist with a green and orange patterned sash, then bustled after Jacen and Jaina.

When they stepped out of the turbolift into the grand audience chamber, the twins looked at the restless crowd of human and alien students, some with two arms and two legs, others with many times that. Some had fur, others had feathers, scales, or slick damp skin . . . but all had a talent for the Force, the potential—if they trained and studied diligently—to eventually become members of a new order of Jedi Knights that was growing stronger with each passing year.

Over the background chatter they heard a resounding Wookiee bellow, and Jacen pointed. "There's Lowie! He's with Tenel Ka already."

They hurried down the central aisle, passing other students and slipping between rows of stone benches to reach their two friends. Jaina held back and waited while her brother took a seat next to Tenel Ka, as he always did.

Jacen wondered if his twin sister had noticed how much he liked being with Tenel Ka, how he always chose a place beside the young warrior girl. Then he realized that Jaina would never miss anything of that sort—but he didn't really care.

Tenel Ka didn't seem to object to Jacen spending his time next to her. The two of them were an odd mix. Jacen always wore an impish grin and enjoyed joking around. Ever since they had met, one of his main goals had been to make Tenel Ka laugh by telling her silly jokes. But despite his best efforts, the strong girl with reddish-gold hair remained serious, almost grim, though he knew she was intelligent, quick to act, and profoundly loyal.

"Greetings, Jacen," Tenel Ka said.

"How are you doing, Tenel Ka? Hey, I've got another joke for you."

Lowbacca groaned, and Jacen shot him a wounded look.

"There is no time," Tenel Ka said, pointing toward the speaker's platform. "Master Skywalker is about to address us."

Indeed, Luke had come out onto the stage and stood in his Jedi robe. His face deeply serious, he folded his hands in front of him, and the audience quickly grew quiet.

"A time of great darkness is upon us," Master Skywalker said. The silence grew even deeper. Jacen sat straight and looked around in alarm.

"Not only does the Empire continue its struggles to reclaim the galaxy, but this time it is using the Force in an unprecedented manner. With its Shadow Academy, the leaders of the Second Imperium are creating their own army of dark side Force-wielders. And *we*, my friends, are the only ones who can stand against it." He paused as that news sank in. Jacen swallowed hard.

"Though the Emperor has been dead for nineteen years, still the New Republic struggles to bring the worlds of the galaxy into an alliance. Palpatine did not take so long to squeeze his iron fist around star systems—but the New Republic is a different kind of government. We aren't willing to use the Emperor's tactics. The Chief of State will not send armed fleets to crush planets into submission or execute dissidents. Unfortunately, though, because we use peaceful democratic means, we are more vulnerable to a threat like the Empire."

Jacen felt warm inside at the mention of his mother and what she was doing with the New Republic.

"In days long past," Luke said, walking from side to side on the stage so that he seemed to be talking to each one of them in turn, "a Jedi Master spent years looking for a single student to teach and guide along the path of the Jedi." Luke's voice became graver. "Now, though, our need is too great for such caution. The Empire nearly succeeded in obliterating the Jedi Knights of old, and we don't have the luxury of such patience. Instead, I'm going to have to ask you to learn a little faster, to grow strong a little sooner. I must accelerate your training, *because the New Republic needs more Jedi Knights.*"

From one of the front rows, where he always sat, Raynar spoke up. Jacen had to blink to clear the spots of bright color from his vision when the sandy-haired boy raised his hand. "We're ready, Master Skywalker! We're all willing to fight for you."

Luke looked intently at the boy who had interrupted him. "I'm not asking you to fight for *me*, Raynar," Luke said in a calm voice. "I need your help to fight *for* the New Republic, and *against* the evil ways we thought were behind us. Not for any one person."

The students stirred. Their minds churned with a determination they didn't know how to direct.

Master Skywalker continued to pace. "Each of you must

work individually to stretch your abilities. I'll help as I can. I want to meet with you in small groups to plan strategy, discuss ways to help each other. We must be strong, because I believe with all my heart that we face dark times ahead."

Down in the echoing hangar bay beneath the temple, Jacen crouched in a cool corner, extending his mind into a crack between blocks where he sensed a rare red and green stinger lizard. He sent a tendril of thought to it, imaginary enticements of food—dismissing reptilian concerns of danger. Jacen very much wanted to add the lizard to his collection of unusual pets.

Lowbacca and Jaina tinkered with Lowie's T-23 skyhopper, the flying craft that his uncle Chewbacca had given him when he'd brought the young Wookiee to the Jedi academy. Jacen knew his sister was a bit jealous of Lowie for having his own flying machine. In fact, that had been one of the reasons Jaina had so badly wanted to repair the crashed TIE fighter they'd found out in the jungle.

Tenel Ka stood outside the upraised horizontal door of the hangar bay. She held a forked wooden spear that she used for target practice, throwing it with exceptional skill toward a tiny mark on the landing pad. The teenaged warrior could strike her target with either hand. She stared at her goal with cool, granite-gray eyes, focused her concentration, and then let the sharpened stick fly.

Tenel Ka could have nudged the spear with the Force, guiding it where she wished it to go—but Jacen knew from long experience that she would probably tackle him to the ground if he dared suggest such a thing. Tenel Ka had gained her physical skill through faithful practice and was reluctant to use the Force in a way that she considered to be cheating. She was very proud of her skills.

In the rear of the hangar bay, the turbolift hummed. Master Luke Skywalker emerged and looked around. Jacen gave up his designs on the stinger lizard and stood. His knees cracked, and his ankles were sore, which made him realize how long he had crouched motionless. "Hi, Uncle Luke," he said.

Tenel Ka threw her spear one last time, then retrieved it and turned to meet Luke. She and the Jedi Master had shared a special bond from the time the two of them had spent together searching for the kidnapped twins and Lowie and rescuing them from the Shadow Academy . . . though Jacen sensed that Tenel Ka and Uncle Luke shared other secrets as well.

"Greetings, Master Skywalker," Tenel Ka said.

The tinny voice of Em Teedee, the miniaturized translator droid hanging from a clip on Lowbacca's belt, chimed out, "Master Lowbacca, we have a guest. If you're quite finished fussing with those controls, I believe Master Skywalker wishes to converse with you."

Lowie grunted and raised his shaggy head, scratching the remarkable black streak of fur that rose over one eyebrow and curved down his back.

Jaina scrambled up beside him. "What is it? Oh, hi, Uncle Luke."

"I'm glad you're all here," Luke said. "I wanted to discuss your training. You four have been in closer contact with the Second Imperium than my other students, so you know the danger better than they do. You also all have extraordinarily strong Jedi potential, and I think perhaps you're ready for a greater challenge than the others."

"Like what?" Jacen asked eagerly.

"Like taking the next step toward becoming full Jedi Knights," Luke said.

Jacen's mind spun, trying to figure out what his uncle meant, but Jaina exclaimed, "You want us to build our own lightsabers, don't you?"

"Yes," Luke nodded. "I normally wouldn't suggest this so early, especially for such young students. But I think we're in for a battle so difficult that I want you to be prepared to use every weapon at your disposal."

Jacen felt a surge of delight, followed by sudden uneasiness. Not long ago he had desperately wanted his own lightsaber, but he had been forced to train with one at the Shadow Academy . . . and he and his sister had come close to killing each other in a deceptive test. "But, Uncle Luke, I thought you said it was too dangerous for us."

Luke nodded soberly. "It *is* dangerous. As I recall, I once caught you playing with my weapon because you wanted one so much—but I think you've learned an important lesson since then about taking lightsabers seriously."

Jacen agreed. "Yeah, I don't think I'll ever again think of a lightsaber as a toy."

Luke smiled back at him. "Good. That's an important start," he said. "These weapons are not playthings. A lightsaber is a dangerous and destructive instrument, a powerful blade that can strike down an opponent—or a friend, if you're not careful."

"We'll be careful, Uncle Luke," Jaina assured him with an earnest nod.

Luke still seemed skeptical. "This isn't a reward. It's an obligation, a difficult new set of lessons for you. Perhaps the work involved in building your own lightsaber will teach you to respect it as a tool, as you learn how the Jedi created their own personal weapons, each with its special characteristics."

"Always wanted to know how a lightsaber worked. Can I take yours apart, Uncle Luke?" Jaina asked, her brandy-brown eyes pleading.

Now Luke let a smile cross his face. "I don't think so, Jaina—but you'll learn about them soon enough." He looked at the four young Jedi Knights. "I want you to begin without delay."

2

JAINA PAID ATTENTION to her uncle Luke's words with only half a mind, the rest of her concentration focusing on the problem of where to get the precious components for building her very own lightsaber.

She and her brother, along with Lowie and Tenel Ka, were in one of the upper solariums in the Great Temple, a room made of polished marble slabs inset with semiprecious stones. Bright light streamed through tall, narrow windows that had been chiseled into the stone blocks by ancient Massassi tribesmen.

Luke Skywalker sat nearby on a deep window ledge, uncharacteristically relaxed and boyish. He enjoyed being with a small group of trainees, especially his niece and nephew and their friends, talking about things that interested him.

"You may have heard about Jedi Masters during the Clone Wars who were able to fashion lightsabers in only a day or two, using whatever raw materials were at hand," Luke said. "But don't get the idea that your weapon is a quick little project to be slapped together. Ideally, a Jedi took many months to construct a single perfect weapon that he or she would keep and use for a lifetime. Once you build it, the lightsaber will become your constant companion, your tool, and a ready means of defense."

He stood up from his seat on the window ledge. "The components are fairly simple. Every lightsaber has a standard power source, the same type used in small blasters, even in glowpanels. They last a long time, though, because Jedi should rarely use their lightsabers."

"Got some of those power sources in my room," Jaina said. "Spare parts, you know."

"One of the other crucial pieces," Luke continued, "is a focusing crystal. The most powerful and sought-after gems are rare kaiburr crystals. However, though lightsabers are powerful weapons, their design is so flexible that practically any kind of crystal can be used. And, since I don't happen to have a stash of kaiburr crystals"—he smiled—"you'll have to make do with something else, of your own choosing."

Luke held out the handle of his own lightsaber, sliding his palm over the smooth grip, then igniting it with a startling snap-hiss. The brilliant yellow-green blade drowned out even the bright sunlight in the room.

"This is not my first lightsaber." Luke drew it back and forth through the empty air so that its hum changed frequency. "Note the color of its blade. I lost my first lightsaber years ago . . . my father's lightsaber." He swallowed and seemed to struggle against a dark memory from his past. Jaina knew the story of how Luke had lost his other lightsaber during a duel with Darth Vader on Cloud City. In that terrible fight Luke Skywalker had lost not only his lightsaber, but his hand as well.

"My first weapon had a pale blue beam. The colors vary, according to the frequencies of the crystals used. Darth Vader's lightsaber"—he drew a deep breath—"*my father's* lightsaber was a deep scarlet."

Jaina nodded solemnly. She remembered fighting Vader's holographic image on the Shadow Academy—though it had actually been her own brother Jacen in disguise. Her lightsaber experiences had not been pleasant on the Imperial station . . . and now her feelings about the energy blades were even more confused. Her friend Zekk had also been taken by Brakiss and the Second Imperium. Jaina knew she would have to fight to get him back.

Luke continued, "One of my students, Cilghal, a Calamarian like Admiral Aekbar, made her lightsaber with smooth curves and protrusions, as if the handle had been grown from metallic coral. Inside, she used a rare ultima-pearl, one of the treasures found in the seabeds of her watery planet.

"My first true failure as a teacher was another student named Gantoris. He built his lightsaber in only a few intense days, following instructions given to him by the evil spirit of

Exar Kun. Gantoris thought he was ready, and my mistake was not seeing what he was up to.

"You, my young Jedi Knights, must be different. I can't wait any longer to train you. You must learn how to build your lightsabers—and how to use them—in the right way. The galaxy has changed, and you must meet the challenge. A true Jedi is forced to adapt or be destroyed."

Tenel Ka spoke up. "Where will we find these crystals to build our weapons, Master Skywalker?" she asked. "Are they lying on the ground?"

Luke smiled. "Perhaps. Or it's possible they could be scavenged from old equipment left here from when this place was a Rebel base. Or maybe you already have resources you haven't yet realized." He shot a quick look at Jacen, but Jaina couldn't decipher what the glance meant.

"I'd like you to start on your lightsabers immediately." Luke switched off his throbbing weapon and looked down at its handle. "But I hope you'll need to use your weapons only rarely . . . if ever."

A few days later, Jaina sat hunched over her worktable inside her quarters. She had strung up extra glowpanels to allow her sufficient illumination to work through the night. Dozens of tools and pieces of equipment lay on the tabletop, arranged in a careful order so that she knew where every component, every wire and circuit might be found.

After Jaina had given each of her friends an appropriate power source to build their own lightsabers, the young Jedi Knights had split up to search for the precious crystals and other components that would make their new weapons function. Jaina, though, wanted to make the lightsaber particularly *hers*, a symbolic extension of her unique personality. She would make it from scratch in a way that the others would never attempt. She smiled at her own ingenuity.

Dark smoke rose from the portable furnace she had brought in, and she blinked to clear the chemical fumes from her eyes as she bent over it. Carefully, she added the next batch of powdered elements in the precise mixture her data-pad suggested. She drew on her Force powers, amplifying her vision to observe the chemicals interacting, to watch them bond into a tight, organized lattice.

The precisely pure crystals began to grow. . . .

She adjusted the temperature, watching intently, though the process of crystalline growth took hours. She focused her mind on shaping the facets as they emerged from the molten mixture in the furnace, making the planes tilt at appropriate angles. The growing crystals gobbled up and stored the extra energy pumped into the mixture by the furnace.

Finally, by morning, her eyes bloodshot and gritty from lack of sleep, Jaina shut down the system. She let the furnace cool until she could reach in and take out her beautiful, sparkling crystals.

They were a rich purplish blue, shimmering with inner energy. They had formed perfectly, as she had expected, guided by her own mental skills. She held them in her palm and smiled. Now for the next step.

The tip of Jacen's tongue stuck out between his lips as he focused with unaccustomed concentration on the mechanical task at hand. It had already taken him a week to get this far.

He wanted to rush through the project, jam the components into place, connect the power, and turn on his lightsaber—his *own* lightsaber—but he took Uncle Luke's words seriously. This was a weapon he would use for the rest of his life, the weapon of a Jedi. A few weeks didn't seem so long to invest in creating it.

Much as it went against his nature to do so, Jacen forced himself to be meticulous and patient, knowing that he had to make sure everything fit together *just so* in the precise configuration required.

He had the power source Jaina had given him, and it was easy to find pieces of metal in the right shape and size to form the casing. He used Jaina's tools to cut the pieces into interlocking configurations and file down the rough edges. After a few days of doing that, he installed the power source, connecting all the leads. Then he added the control buttons.

Jaina could have whipped the casing together in just a few minutes, but it took him days to gather all the parts. Now, even though his scavenger hunt was over, it still seemed to take forever to assemble the thing.

Jacen would rather have been outside hunting for more specimens to add to his menagerie—or better yet, playing with the ones that cheerfully bounced about in their cages, often housed mere centimeters from other creatures that would gladly have had them for breakfast.

He heard the crystal snake rustling in its repaired cage, and then one of the reptile birds began to chirrup—but Jacen steeled himself, focusing on the project at hand. The lightsaber was almost finished, almost finished! He would be the first to complete his, and Master Luke would be very proud.

With the handle mostly assembled, he wrapped special grip-textured bindings around it so that he could hold and wield the blade with the gentle ease of a Jedi swordsman. Now Jacen was ready to install the powerful crystal.

He went to the personal locker box where he kept his valuable possessions and withdrew a small, glittering object—a Corusca gem. He had snared the gem during a mining demonstration at Lando Calrissian's GemDiver Station, and had later used it to cut himself free from his locked quarters in the Shadow Academy. He had offered the jewel to his mother as a special gift—but she had persuaded Jacen to keep the gem, to find a special use for it.

And what could be more special than using it in his own lightsaber?

Lowbacca prowled through the clutter in the former Rebel control room, left over from when the Great Temple had been used as a base in the struggle against the Empire. The soldiers had left most of their old equipment here when they fled the small jungle moon. In the years since, most of the machinery

and computers had been gutted for other purposes, since Luke
Skywalker's Jedi academy did not rely heavily on gadgets and
technology. Although Jaina had already scavenged these rooms,
Lowie knew that a great deal of equipment still remained to be
picked through.

Poking his snout into shadowy corners, the Wookiee snuffled
and rumbled thoughtfully to himself. He lifted metal coverings
to look around, rummaging through wires and circuit boards,
taking apart flat-screen displays.

"Master Lowbacca, I simply cannot imagine what you
think you're accomplishing," Em Teedee said from the clip at
his waist. "You've been prodding around here for hours, and
you've found nothing."

Lowie let out a short growl.

"Well, really! No, I don't believe you can sniff them out
with your nose. What an absurd notion! How could anyone
possibly sniff out a crystal?" Em Teedee's temper seemed to
be getting short and Lowie wondered if perhaps the little
translating droid's batteries were running low.

"Anyway, I doubt you'll ever locate any kind of crystal in
here. I'm sure the entire control room was thoroughly ran-
sacked years ago."

Lowie barked a comment as he continued his search.

"Quite the contrary," Em Teedee said. "I am not a pes-
simist—I'm simply being realistic. I don't know why Master
Skywalker should expect everyone to simply *find* appropriate
crystals here or there. What if one of you created an inferior
lightsaber? What good would that do? I daresay it's a possibility. I really think you should give up the search."

With a sudden bellow of triumph, Lowie reached into the
cluttered interior of a small, high-resolution projection system
and withdrew two glittering components: a flat focusing lens
and a spherical enhancement jewel. The items had been used
in the high-res display, and Lowie knew instinctively that they
could be applied to the same general purpose inside his new
lightsaber.

With great delight, he held them in his long hairy fingers

in front of Em Teedee's optical sensors. He growled with pleasure, and a hint of smugness.

Em Teedee replied with some degree of petulance, "Well, of course I could be wrong."

3

DAYBREAK FOUND TENEL Ka atop the Great Temple limbering up in preparation for her new exercise routine. After tying back her wavy red-gold hair with a few simple braids, she stretched each muscle slowly, deliberately, efficiently. Her lizard-skin bodysuit was even more abbreviated than her usual reptilian armor, so as not to restrict her movement. The sparkling blue scales rippled with every flexing of her muscles.

Standing barefoot on the ancient weathered stone of the temple, Tenel Ka reached toward the sky, stretching first with one arm, then the other. She felt her body begin to loosen up, as the jungle around her blossomed with the scents and sounds of the dawning day. A light breeze stirred the leaves, and Tenel Ka took in deep breaths, letting her mind focus on what she needed to do. She would make her new routine as rigorous as the calisthenics Master Skywalker himself performed each morning.

She had been surprised by her reaction to the Jedi teacher's instruction for them to build their own lightsabers. Despite her fierce pride at knowing she would soon begin earnest training for real battles, Tenel Ka had resented the implication that she would somehow be judged on the basis of the *weapon* with which she would fight.

Earlier, she had scaled the Great Temple using nothing more than her grappling hook, her fibercord, and her own muscles. Wasn't the warrior who wielded the weapon much more important than the weapon itself? she asked herself.

Even holding a simple stick instead of a dazzling lightsaber, Tenel Ka was capable of defeating an enemy.

When she felt truly limbered up, Tenel Ka hefted the meter-long wooden staff she had carried to the top of the temple. For half an hour she practiced throwing the stick into the air and catching it, alternating between her left hand and her right, first with eyes open, then closed. Next, she practiced twirling the wooden rod over her head and jumping over it as she swung it beneath her feet.

Perspiration glistened on Tenel Ka's neck and forehead, and was trickling down her spine by the time she moved on to the next challenge. Finally, once Tenel Ka was satisfied that her reflexes were as finely tuned as she could wish, she grasped one end of the staff with both hands as if it were a lightsaber and began sword drills.

After an hour of that, Tenel Ka was ready for more exacting physical activity. Taking a deep breath, she sprinted down the steep outer stairs of the pyramid to ground level and began her ten-kilometer run for the day.

The breeze felt cool against her face as she ran. Glancing down at herself, she assessed her lean muscular arms and long sturdy legs, reveling in the unrestricted motion and complete control. She sped up, pleased to note that her muscles were more than equal to the demands she made on them.

Yes, she decided, the *warrior* was what mattered, not the weapon.

After her fifth day of intensive drilling to hone her skills as sharp as any weapon, Tenel Ka felt ready to begin fashioning the handle of her personal lightsaber. Still glowing with perspiration from her morning workout, she decided to swim in the warm jungle river while she considered her next task.

She thought of the many materials available for her lightsaber handle, as she stripped off her exercise suit and dove with easy confidence into the swift current. Tenel Ka was a strong swimmer, trained on both Hapes and Dathomir, at the insistence of both grandmothers. It was one of the few times she could remember that her parents' mothers had ever agreed on anything.

Augwynne Djo, mother of Teneniel Djo, Tenel Ka's mother, had taught her to swim, saying that the strongest hunters and warriors were those who could not be stopped by a mere lake or river. Ta'a Chume, on the other hand, matriarch of the Royal House of Hapes and mother of Tenel Ka's father, Princee Isolder, had taught swimming as a defense against assassins or kidnappers. In fact, her grandmother had once escaped an attempt on her life by jumping from a wavespeeder into a lake and swimming for shore underwater, so that the would-be assassins assumed she had drowned.

Tenel Ka surfaced from the river, drew a deep lungful of air, and struck out upstream against the current. It was difficult swimming, but she used the added strength she had gained in her recent lightsaber training . . . which brought her back to the task at hand.

She supposed she could fashion her lightsaber handle from a piece of metal pipe, or even carve one from hardwood, since a lightsaber gave off little heat. But somehow those did not seem right for her.

Tenel Ka propelled herself forward with long smooth strokes, keeping a steady rhythm. Left. Right. Left. Right.

Stone would be too difficult to shape, and too heavy for her purposes. Tenel Ka needed something that would suit the *image* of a warrior from Dathomir. She pictured Augwynne Djo's proud form clad in reptile skin, a ceremonial helm on her head, riding a domesticated rancor. The taming of these ferocious beasts was an appropriate symbol of the courage of her rugged people, since the huge beasts were powerful and their sharp claws deadly.

Tenel Ka allowed herself to sink below the surface of the river and changed to a new stroke, recalling that she had kept two teeth from her grandmother's favorite rancor when it had died a few years ago. They were not the rancor's largest teeth by far, but each *was* the perfect size and shape to be a lightsaber handle. . . .

A week later, Tenel Ka studied her handiwork with justifi-
able pride and etched another groove into the pattern she had
carved on her rancor tooth.

Lowie, sitting ahead of her in the tiny cockpit of the T-23
skyhopper, turned and roared a question at her. She waited for
a moment for Em Teedee's translation. "Master Lowbacca
wishes to inquire whether you have any preference as to the
volcano in which you hope to search for crystals."

Tenel Ka glanced out at the rich green jungle canopy rushing beneath them. "You may choose," she said.

Lowbacca gave a short bark. "It makes little difference to
Master Lowbacca," Em Teedee told her. "He has already assembled the components he intends to use for his lightsaber.
The primary construction on his instrument is complete, and
he has only to tune it now."

Tenel Ka blinked in surprise, not only at the length of Em
Teedee's translation after Lowbacca's short reply, but also at
the thought that Lowbacca—and perhaps Jacen or Jaina—was
so far ahead of her. Well then, she would have to make her
search quickly and assemble her lightsaber without delay.

"The closest volcano," she said, reaching forward and
pointing. "There." Then, gruffly, because she felt foolish for
having asked Lowbacca to take her out on this errand, she
said, "I apologize. I would not bave troubled you with my request had I known your lightsaber was almost complete."

The Wookiee growled and dismissed this with a motion of
one ginger-furred hand. "Master Lowbacca wishes to assure
you that you have not inconvenienced him in the slightest,"
Em Teedee supplied. "It has been many days since he enjoyed
solitude and meditation out in the jungle, and he delights in
the opportunity to assist you in this manner."

The Wookiee snorted and gave the little translator droid a
flick with one finger. "Oh—that is to say," Em Teedee
amended, "it was Master Lowbacca's intention to take a break
anyway, and he's pleased he could help."

The young Wookiee sniffed loudly, but accepted this translation. He brought the T-23 skyhopper down on a patch of

hard-packed volcanic sand between the jungle's edge and the base of a small volcano. After Lowbacca woofed a few words, Em Teedee said, "When you have completed your search, successful or not, simply return here to the T-23. Master Lowbacca and I will watch for you from the treetops."

Tenel Ka nodded curtly. "Understood. Thank you." Without further ado, she turned and hurried up the slope toward the volcano.

Though none of the volcanoes near the Jedi academy had erupted in quite some time, tendrils of white steam still curled from this one's peak. Skirting the sharp black rocks on the perimeter, Tenel Ka soon found a gaping lava tube leading in toward the core of the volcano, as she had hoped.

A pungent sulfurous odor filled the warm tunnel. Tenel Ka pulled the finger-sized glowrod from a pouch at her belt and ignited it to light her way. Black crystalline sand crunched under her feet and glittered like thousands of fiery sparks, throwing back the light of her glowrod. As she trudged farther in, the sandy floor became hard rock, glassy like obsidian. Ahead of her the rocky corridor radiated an eerie red light, and the heat grew stifling.

Occasionally she heard a rumbling, rushing roar, as if the volcano itself were breathing deeply in its sleep. The stony walls around her took on a cracked, broken look. Some of the larger fissures ran from floor to ceiling and leaked puffs of acrid white steam. But she saw no embedded crystals.

The lava tube wound on and on. Losing patience, Tenel Ka had just about decided to turn back when she rounded one last corner and encountered a wave of searing heat. She had found what she was looking for.

"Ah," she said. "Aha."

She wouldn't be able to bear the heat for long, but she had to risk it. On the floor of the tunnel lay a huge slab of glossy black rock that had broken free from a crack on the tunnel wall. Ripples of scorching air danced before her in the dimness. Rivulets of perspiration ran down her forehead and into her eyes, blurring her vision. Even so, she could not mistake the chunks of spiky crystals that grew on the broken slab, glittering and hazy.

The rock surrounding her was too hot to touch, so Tenel Ka worked quickly. Holding her glowrod in her teeth, she pulled a small scrap of lizard hide from a pouch at her belt, wrapped it around a clump of the crystals, used her grappling hook to chip away at a few of the crystals, then pried them loose.

Tenel Ka tucked the crystals, still wrapped in their protective lizard hide, into her belt pouch, then headed back up the tunnel at a trot. Holding the glowrod high above her head, she raised her voice in a loud ululating cry of triumph that echoed down the length of the lava tube.

Back in her quarters, Tenel Ka sat at a low wooden table with the components of her future lightsaber spread in front of her. Everything she needed for assembling her weapon was here: switches, crystals, the covering plate, a power source, a focusing lens, and the rancor-tooth hilt.

She ran a light fingertip over the intricate battle etchings she had carved on the ivory lightsaber handle. The markings had turned out even better than she had hoped.

After returning from her crystal hunt, she had applied to the rancor tooth a paste made of dampened black sand from the floor of the lava tube. When she polished the tooth to a soft luster, pigment from the dark sand had stained every crevice of her carving to bring each etched line into sharp relief. The decorated rancor tooth was a beautiful piece, worthy of a warrior.

A yawn of contented weariness escaped her lips as Tenel Ka began to piece the components together according to Master Skywalker's directions. She frowned when she realized that the hollow inside the rancor's tooth was not quite large enough to contain the arrangement of crystals she had hoped for. She frowned again when she noticed on close inspection that each of her hazy crystals contained a tiny flaw. She suppressed another yawn and shook her head in resignation. Well, she didn't have much choice. There hadn't been time to examine the crystals more carefully in the searing lava tube, and now it was too late to search for more.

Tenel Ka thought back over the past two weeks, the drills and exercises she had put herself through. Her reflexes were lightning-fast, her skills and senses sharp as a laser. She shrugged, trying to loosen the knot of weary tension that had crept into her shoulders. She would have to make do. After all, in the long run it was the warrior and not the weapon that determined victory.

She nodded to herself as she picked up the lightsaber handle and began placing the components inside.

4

THE JUNGLE CLEARING was alive with thousands—no, millions!—of living creatures and interesting plants, strangely colorful mushrooms and droning insects, all of which offered great distractions to Jacen. He had to work very hard to keep his mind from wandering. At the moment it was far more important to pay attention to Luke Skywalker as he set up the first lightsaber dueling exercise for the young Jedi Knights.

During the construction of their weapons, the trainees had sparred with dueling droids and with each other, using sticks the same length as a lightsaber blade. After completing their lightsabers, they had spent a week practicing with their real weapons against stationary targets, accustoming themselves to the feel of the energy blades.

Now, though, Master Skywalker had deemed them ready to move on to the next step.

The clearing was a burned-out spot where lightning had sparked a brief but intense forest fire. The jungle dampness and lush foliage had quickly smothered the blaze, but a huge Massassi tree—its trunk charred and weakened by the searing flames—had toppled over, taking with it several smaller trees and bushes. The rest of the clearing was a matted maze of pale green undergrowth—weeds and grasses and flowers attempting to reclaim the burned and crumbly soil.

Because today's exercises would be both mental and physical, Uncle Luke wore a comfortable flight suit, as did Jacen and Jaina. Tenel Ka's ever-present reptilian armor left her arms and legs bare, giving her complete freedom of movement. Her long reddish-gold hair had been plaited into intricate braids, with special ornamentation on each one. Lowbacca wore no garment other than his belt, woven of strands he had harvested from a deadly syren plant in the deep forests on Kashyyyk. Em Teedee hung in his accustomed place at the Wookiee's waist.

All of the young Jedi Knights carried something new and special this time, though—their own lightsabers, completed after weeks of delicate construction.

While Jacen stood with his friends, flicking occasional glances in the direction of rustling leaves that hinted at the presence of strange creatures, Luke Skywalker took a seat on the massive fallen trunk. At last he unslung the mysterious pack he had lugged all the way from the Great Temple.

"What's in there, Uncle Luke?" Jacen asked, unable to restrain his curiosity. Since he couldn't investigate the interesting insects and plants, he needed to focus his mind on something else.

Luke gave a secretive smile and withdrew a scarlet sphere the size of a large ball, perfectly smooth except for tiny covered openings that might have been repulsorjets or small targeting lasers. Luke set the ball on the slanted, burned trunk; miraculously, it did not roll down the slope, but remained exactly where he had placed it. He withdrew another of the scarlet spheres, and another, and another.

"Remotes!" Jaina cried, guessing what they were. "Those *are* remotes, aren't they, Uncle Luke? What are they for?"

"Target practice," he said. All four remotes sat balanced on the burned Massassi trunk, refusing to roll, as if they could ignore gravity.

Lowbacca grunted with surprise, and Tenel Ka straightened. "We are going to shoot at them?"

"No," Luke said. "They're going to shoot at *you*."

"And we deflect the shots with our lightsabers?" Jacen asked.

"Yes," Luke said, "but it's not as easy as you might think."

"I never said I thought it would be *easy*," Jacen muttered.

Tenel Ka nodded. "A lesson to sharpen our reflexes and concentration. We must react quickly to intercept each burst from the remotes."

"Ah, but it gets harder," Luke said. He reached into the sack again, removed a flexible helmet with a transparisteel visor tinted a deep red, and handed it to Tenel Ka. "You'll each wear these." He withdrew another pair of helmets for the twins, but the last one consisted of only a red visor fastened with crude tie-straps. "Sorry, Lowbacca, but I couldn't find a helmet big enough for your head. This will have to do."

Jacen slipped the helmet over his perpetually tousled brown hair and suddenly saw the jungle through a scarlet filter. The thick forest held a more primeval quality now, as if backlit with smoldering fires. The details were duller, darker, and Jacen wondered what the helmet and visor were supposed to do—protect them against stray shots from the remotes? He looked over at where the bright red remotes had rested on the burned tree trunk . . . or rather where they should have been.

Jacen blinked. "Hey, they're gone!"

"Not gone," Luke said. "Just invisible. When you look at the remotes through the red filters, you can't see them anymore." Luke smiled. "That's the point. When Obi-Wan Kenobi taught me, he made me fight using a helmet with the blast shield down. I couldn't see a thing. You'll at least be able to see your surroundings . . . but not the remotes."

Jacen wanted to ask how he was supposed to fight what he couldn't see, but he knew what Uncle Luke would say.

"I didn't want you totally blind," Luke continued, "because all four of you will be training here in the clearing with different remotes. This way you'll be able to see *each other*. I don't want anyone getting too enthusiastic and causing injuries instead of just deflecting laser bolts."

This brought a small chuckle from Jacen and Jaina, but Master Skywalker looked at all of the trainees sternly. "I wasn't kidding," he said. "A lightsaber can cut through practically any substance known—and that includes people. Remember this warning: lightsabers are not toys. They are dangerous weapons. Treat them with the utmost care and respect. I hope that the time you each spent building your lightsaber has taught you more about its power and its risks."

Luke picked up a set of controls. "Now let's see how well you work with the Force and your own energy blades."

He flipped a switch, and Jacen heard a hissing, whirring sound. But he saw nothing until he pushed up the scarlet visor. The four remotes drifted into the air, spinning around and scanning the vicinity.

"These lasers are low power," Luke said, "but don't think they won't sting if you get hit by one."

Jacen muttered to his sister, "At least he's not throwing rocks or knives at us, like at the Shadow Academy."

"Visors down," Luke said. "Take your positions."

The companions spread out in the clearing, tramping down the weedy underbrush.

"Ignite your lightsabers," Luke said, then sat back. He seemed to be enjoying himself.

As one, the four Jedi trainees held out the handles of their new weapons and depressed the power studs. Brilliant beams sprang out in the red dimness, bright slashes the length of a sword blade burning through the thick crimson in front of Jacen's eyes. The tinted masks drained all other color from their lightsabers, transforming them into glowing red rods. It reminded Jacen of Darth Vader's weapon.

"The remotes are circling now," Luke said. "In the next thirty seconds they'll begin to fire at random. Reach out with the Force. *Feel* them. Sense the impending attack—then use your lightsaber blade to deflect it. A lot of your training has been leading up to this. Let's see how well you do."

Jacen tensed, holding his lightsaber ready. Much as he hated to admit it, he drew upon some of the skills Brakiss had taught him at the Shadow Academy. He felt the energy blade humming in his hand, pulsing with power. The sharpness of ozone reached his nostrils. He heard his friends moving about, preparing for an attack that could come from any direction.

The buzzing lightsabers muted all other sounds, just as the red filter drowned all other colors. Suddenly Jacen heard a snapping shot, though he saw nothing. A loud Wookiee yowl preceded the vibrating hum of a lightsaber blade sweeping sideways and hitting nothing. Lowie roared again.

"Dear me, Master Lowbacca, that wasn't even close," Em Teedee exclaimed. "I do hope you'll improve significantly with practice."

Lowie snarled, sounding hurt, and Em TeeDee responded in a somewhat cowed fashion, "Well, all right. I understand it's more difficult since you can't *see* anything. . . . Even so, I should think it inadvisable to allow it to strike you again."

Jacen's interest in the conversation vanished when a sizzling bolt shot out from behind and struck him squarely on the backside. He yelped with pain. The tiny wound burned as badly as if a stinger lizard had zapped him. He whirled, slashing with the lightsaber, but by then it was too late.

From across the clearing another bolt shot out, followed by a crash of underbrush. Through the visor he saw Tenel Ka leap to one side. A branch snapped in two as the invisible laser struck it where Tenel Ka had stood only seconds before. The warrior girl crouched, holding her lightsaber up, her head cocked in concentration.

Jacen reached out with his mind, trying to sense through the Force where his remote would shoot next. He heard two more laser blasts and then a *spang* as Jaina successfully deflected one of the bolts. Jacen focused on the pain at the spot where he had been struck by the laser, using it to intensify his determination. He didn't want to be stung again.

Another laser beam shot out. He swiped the lightsaber at it, barely missing—though his motion was enough to shift him out of its path so that the beam sizzled past. He felt the warmth of its passage, but could not see it.

"That was close," he said, then instinctively swung to strike again as the remote fired once more.

Jaina parried a flurry of bolts as her remote attacked mercilessly, firing five times in rapid succession. One of her bolts ricocheted off the glowing edge of her lightsaber directly toward Jacen. He responded without conscious thought, using the Force and flowing with it, somehow knowing what to do as he shifted his own blade sideways just enough to catch the diverted bolt. The deflected blast bounced up into the trees, where it fried a fistful of leaves.

In a single follow-through motion, Jacen spun, reaching up with the lightsaber blade to ward off a second bolt fired from the other remote hovering in front of them.

Lowbacca bellowed with triumph as he, too, got the hang of defending himself.

Except for her heavy breathing, Tenel Ka was quiet, thoughtful. Through the red filter Jacen watched as she parried one of the lasers and leaped upward with all her might, using her lightsaber like a cleaver. A shower of sparks erupted and a smoking hole appeared in midair. Jacen heard a *thunk* as pieces of Tenel Ka's remote fell useless to the jungle floor.

"All right. That's enough for now," Luke Skywalker said.

Tenel Ka switched off her weapon and stood with her hands on her hips, her elbows spread. Jacen flipped up his red visor to discover his own remote hovering barely at arm's length in front of his face. He stepped back, startled.

Tenel Ka's remote lay on the ground sliced in two, its circuits flickering and sparking. Jaina and Lowie also shut off their weapons and stood panting and grinning. Jacen rubbed the burning pain in his backside and grimaced sheepishly, hoping none of the others would notice.

"Excellent, all of you—except now it looks as if I'll need a new remote," Luke said, smiling wryly at Tenel Ka. "You did very well with the Force."

"Not only with the Force," she said, thrusting her chin upward and squaring her shoulders. "I also used my ears to track the remote. When I concentrated, I could hear it even above the sound of the lightsabers."

Luke chuckled. "Good. A Jedi *should* use all available skills and resources."

Jaina gripped the lightsaber in both hands and positioned the brilliant, electric-violet blade in front of her. She looked past the searing line of controlled fire at Lowbacca, her opponent, who stood opposite her, a lightsaber in his hairy grasp. He growled his readiness.

Jaina looked into the young Wookiee's golden eyes, saw the dark streak of black fur swirling up from his eyebrow and around his head. She swallowed and tensed. Though lanky, Lowbacca was much taller than she, and Jaina knew he was about three times as strong. But in his furry expression she saw an uncertainty, a genuine discomfort that mirrored her own.

"Do I really *have* to fight Lowie, Uncle—uh, Master Skywalker?" Jaina asked.

Luke Skywalker stood. "You're not fighting him. Jaina. You're *fencing* with him. Test your opponent. Gauge each other's skills. Learn to judge reactions. Explore strategies. But be careful."

Jaina thought of her training at the Shadow Academy and how she and Jacen had dueled with lightsabers, not realizing that they had fought each other in holographic disguise.

"Remember," Luke cautioned, "a Jedi fights only as a last resort. If you are forced to draw your lightsaber, you have already forfeited much of your advantage. A Jedi trusts the Force and at first seeks other ways to resolve problems: patience, logic, tolerance, attentive listening, negotiation, persuasion, calming techniques.

"But there are times when a Jedi *must* fight. Knowing that the Shadow Academy is out there, I fear those times will come all too often for us. And so you must learn how to wield your lightsabers."

He stepped back and motioned to Jacen and Tenel Ka, who waited on the edge of the clearing, sitting next to each other on the burned tree trunk. "You two will be next. Jaina, don't worry about Lowie being so much bigger and stronger than you are. Dueling with a lightsaber is primarily skill, and I think you're equally matched in that. Your one true disadvantage is that his reach is much longer than yours. Unfortunately," Luke said with a sigh, "circumstances don't always pit us against equal opponents. As for you, Lowie, be careful not to underestimate Jaina."

He dropped back to watch. "Now, show me what you can do."

"Well?" Jaina stepped forward, keeping her gaze locked with Lowie's. "What are we waiting for?"

The Wookiee shifted his lightsaber, bringing its molten-bronze blade into position. Jaina moved hers up to meet it, crossing her blade against his. She felt the pressure, the sizzling of sparks, and the discharge as the powerful beams drove against each other. She saw the muscles bulging in Lowie's long arms as he strained against her—but Jaina held her own.

"All right, let's try something else." Jaina withdrew her lightsaber, then swung it at her Wookiee friend slowly, cautiously—and Lowbacca met it with another crackle of released energy.

Swinging to strike again, she said, "This isn't so bad."

Lowie defended himself. He seemed reluctant to do battle.

Knowing that Lowie had endured horrifying struggles at the Shadow Academy—and remembering again that she had been forced to fight her own brother—Jaina realized that Brakiss and the violet-eyed Tamith Kai would stop at nothing to bring down the New Republic. She and Lowie would both be needed to defend against the Dark Jedi. She decided now that the best way to rid Lowie of his reservations would be to go on the offensive.

And this time she did not feel strangled by darkness. Today Jaina fought with full willingness, learning to be a defender of the light side, a champion of the Force. Uncle Luke had been correct in his speech in front of the Jedi trainees. She knew in her heart that the Shadow Academy had only begun to cause trouble, and she would have to fight to get her friend Zekk freed.

But first she had to learn how.

Lowbacca responded with greater strength, a better show of his abilities, as he parried her blows and struck back with his own. She had to move quickly to cross blades with him again. They clashed and struck. Sparks flew.

Lowie spun and chopped down, but she met his lightsaber with hers, smiling, intently focused. She heard Jacen cheering from the side.

"Excellent, Master Lowbacca!" Em Teedee said. "Now do be careful—you wouldn't want a flying spark to damage me."

Jaina felt the Force flowing through her; Lowbacca wore an expression of exhilaration on his furry face. He opened his mouth, showing fangs and letting out a bellow of challenge—not mean or angry, simply an outpouring of excitement.

Lowie grasped the handle of his large lightsaber with both hands and swept sideways, attempting to catch Jaina by surprise—but she turned the tables on him. Summoning a burst of energy, she astonished the Wookiee by leaping high into the air up to the level of Lowie's head. His lightsaber swept harmlessly beneath her, and she landed lightly on the weed-covered ground behind him, laughing and panting.

"Oh my! That was *most* unexpected," Em Teedee said. "Splendid work, Mistress Jaina."

"Hey, that was great, Jaina!" her twin brother called.

Lowie raised his lightsaber in salute. Jaina grinned, her eyes gleaming.

"Most impressive," Luke said, turning to Jacen and Tenel Ka. "Next, let's see how well our spectators can do."

TENEL KA HESITATED, rubbing her fingers along the ivory surface of the rancor-tooth lightsaber handle. She held the de-activated weapon in front of her, drawing deep breaths. Intent on her body, her surroundings, she tightened her muscles and brought them to full readiness. Jungle sounds filled the clearing: the whisper of breezes ruffling leaves, the song of insects, the flutter of birds in the canopy.

She centered her thoughts, making sure her reflexes were primed and ready for action. Tenel Ka relied on her body and pressed it to its limits, but she always knew how far she could take it. So far, her muscles had never let her down.

Slowly, she opened her cool, granite-gray eyes and looked at the young man who stood in front of her, ready for the next duel.

He grinned at her. "Good against remotes is one thing, Tenel Ka," Jacen said, "but good against a real opponent? That's something else."

"This is a fact."

Depressing a button, Jacen switched on his lightsaber. The emerald-green blade sprang forth, snapping and glittering with power. "Hey, I'll try not to be too hard on you."

Tenel Ka's fingers found the recessed power button on the rancor-tooth handle. A shimmering gray-white blade extended like crackling electric fog shot through with golden sparks. The lightsaber's color reminded her of the hazy crystals she had taken from the lava tube.

"And I will try not to be too hard on you, my Jacen," she said. Tenel Ka tested the weapon by turning her wrist, flicking the blade from side to side. The beam sparked and sizzled as it encountered moisture in the air.

"Be careful," Master Skywalker said from his vantage point on the burned tree trunk. "Don't get cocky. You both have a great deal to learn."

"Don't worry, Uncle Luke," Jacen said. "I know it was a bad time for me, but I *did* have some training at the Shadow Academy." He grinned. "Fighting Tenel Ka will be more of a challenge than battling holographic monsters, though."

Jaina cleared her throat and spoke from where she sat, sweating and worn out after her session with Lowbacca. "And better than fighting your own sister in disguise?"

"That too," Jacen said.

Tenel Ka flicked her lightsaber back and forth again, taking a step closer to Jacen. She squared her shoulders, knowing that she stood taller than her good-humored friend. The lightsaber thrummed with power in her hand. "Are we going to talk all day, Jacen?" she said. "Or will you leave time for me to defeat you before the morning is over?"

Jacen laughed. "Hey, we're not supposed to be enemies, Tenel Ka. It's just a practice session."

She nodded. "This is a fact. Even so, we *are* opponents."

She swung her lightsaber slowly enough that he wouldn't perceive it as a real attack, but instinctively Jacen brought up his own weapon. Their blades intersected with sizzling force.

Jacen blinked in surprise, then drew back and struck against her nebulous gold-shot blade, testing. "All right then—let's go, Tenel Ka!"

She deftly sidestepped the thrust and returned with a parry of her own as he stumbled to regain his balance. Had he been a real enemy, she could have finished him then, but she pulled her blade aside for a split second, just to demonstrate that Jacen had let his guard drop—a lesson a Jedi Knight would need to learn to avoid defeat.

Unexpectedly, Jacen whirled and came up with a backhanded strike that forced her to retaliate. "I figure we should do something about that lack of confidence you've got, Tenel Ka," Jacen said, still grinning.

"I have no such lack," she said, and found that perspiration had broken out on her forehead. She swung, and Jacen caught her blow on his blade, laughing. She noted the degree of strength he used, the speed with which she maneuvered his weapon. They clashed again. Her cheerful friend, usually so scattered and disorganized, was giving her a surprisingly difficult workout.

"Hey, Tenel Ka," Jacen said as he struck twice more, as if he always held conversations while fighting with a lightsaber, "you know why a wampa snow monster has such long arms?" He paused for just a beat. "Because his hands are so far away from his body!"

Lowbacca groaned with miserable laughter, prompting the little droid at his waist to speak up in a tinny voice. "I fail to perceive the amusement value in Jacen's explanation of a zoological anomaly," Em Teedee said.

"Your jokes cannot distract me, Jacen," Tenel Ka said, swinging her lightsaber once more. Did he really think he could break her concentration so easily? "I do not find them humorous."

Jacen sighed as he met her blade with his own. "I know. I've been trying to get you to laugh ever since I've known you."

Tenel Ka watched her opponent closely, trying to judge from the tension in his muscles how soon he intended to make a surprise move, in which direction he would react, when the motion of his blade was a genuine attack and when it was merely a feint.

"Good," Master Skywalker said from where he watched. "Feel the Force. The lightsaber is not just a weapon. It is an extension of yourself."

Jacen pressed Tenel Ka hard, and she skipped backward a couple of paces. It was obvious he was trying to drive her toward an outcropping of broken boulders at the edge of the clearing. Jacen must have thought she had forgotten about them, but Tenel Ka filed away every detail of her surroundings in her mind.

Just as she reached the rocks, Jacen gave away his plans even more clearly with a broad grin. He pushed forward abruptly, no doubt expecting her to trip. But Tenel Ka leaped lightly backward over the boulders and landed on the other side, her legs planted firmly in a fighting stance. Suddenly foiled, Jacen stumbled and fell toward her, almost hitting the rocks himself. He came up sputtering in disbelief.

"Hey," he said, then smiled. "Good one!"

Tenel Ka stood waiting for him, her braided hair dangling about her head, drenched with sweat. Allowing herself a brief moment of self-indulgence, she switched the lightsaber to her left hand to prove she could fight just as well with either arm. She had practiced equally with her left and right hands, knowing it might prove a useful skill sometime.

"Show-off," Jacen said. After a heartbeat of hesitation, he switched his own blade to his left hand and charged at her, swinging hard with the emerald-green lightsaber. She raised her own misty-white and gold blade, struck at him, then struck again. Sparks flew as the blades met.

When Jacen laughed with exhilaration, she allowed herself a satisfied grin as well. "You are a good opponent, Jacen Solo," she said.

"You bet I am," he answered.

Tenel Ka knew that her skill was based on her prowess, her physical ability. Though she had constructed a fine lightsaber, she would become a great warrior because of her *fighting abilities*, not because of the strength of any weapon, no matter how powerful.

Jacen's lightsaber pressed against hers, and she took a step back. They stood deadlocked, slamming energy blade against impenetrable energy blade. Fiery electricity crackled, and the air thickened with the sharp scent of ozone. Tenel Ka pushed with all her strength, but Jacen countered with equal force.

Her palm was sweaty, but her hand maintained its grip on the rancor-tooth handle. Inside, the components of her lightsaber vibrated, as if struggling to maintain the full energy of the blade while Tenel Ka pressed so furiously against an equally powerful weapon. She pushed harder. The handle rattled.

Jacen grinned at her. "Hope you don't expect me to surrender too easily."

"Perhaps you should," she panted, and pressed harder, ignoring the strange, unsettling sensations from her weapon. She gritted her teeth. Her arm strained. The lightsabers whined and buzzed. Jacen shoved back with all his might. His eyes glittered with the effort.

Over by the edge of the clearing, Master Skywalker stood watching the tense battle, as did Lowbacca and Jaina.

Tenel Ka narrowed her gray eyes, not easing up for an instant, wondering how best she could defeat Jacen and end this match.

Suddenly, something changed inside her lightsaber. She heard a sharp crack and then a loud hissing sizzle.

Jacen pressed harder with his emerald-green blade. For the briefest instant, the golden sparks that shot through her white pulsating energy beam flickered wildly. Her blade blurred with static, grew less focused.

Intent on the battle, Jacen gave a final, extra push with all his strength.

It happened all at once.

The power source in Tenel Ka's lightsaber gave a shriek of electrical overload—and the blade winked out like a snuffed candle. Sparks and smoke poured from the end of the handle where an energy blade should have glowed.

Suddenly, encountering no resistance as Jacen thrust with his last reserves of strength, the emerald-green lightsaber sliced through the opening where Tenel Ka's own blade had been just a moment before—plunging down to the only thing that stood in its way.

Tenel Ka felt a line of blazing agony sweep across her arm just above the elbow. It *burned* . . . and yet below the burn she felt only a sickening, horrible coldness—a bone-deep chill like none she had ever felt before.

Somehow her lightsaber thumped on the ground with a soft *thud*. Impossibly, she saw her hand clenching the carved rancor's tooth. Sparks the size of lightning bolts flashed around the handle as her weapon exploded in a burst of blinding light.

Bright. So very bright . . .

Tenel Ka felt a dizzying haze swirling up to engulf her. Everything was so confusing. Jacen screamed something she couldn't understand. Tenel Ka hoped intensely that she had not hurt him.

Jaina, Lowbacca, and Master Skywalker all ran toward her, shouting, but Tenel Ka couldn't find the energy to stay upright any longer. Just as Jacen reached a hand out toward her, she felt herself falling to the ground.

Then the pain and shock were completely swallowed up in blackness.

6

ON THE FRINGES of the unmapped heart of the galaxy, the Shadow Academy found a new hiding place near the flaming shells of two stars that had been dying for the last five thousand years.

Without its cloaking device, the dark Imperial training center hung like a circlet of thorns, washed in the blaze of solar radiation. The whispering of thrown-off star gas would camouflage the station from prying Rebel eyes.

Zekk stood before the broad windowports of the tallest observation tower, staring into the dazzling maelstrom of starfire. The darkened transparisteel of the viewport filtered out the deadly radiation—but even dimmed to a fraction of its true power, the fury of the universe left Zekk breathless.

Beside him stood Brakiss, Master of the Shadow Academy, a tall and statue-handsome Jedi. As an Imperial spy, Brakiss had once studied at the New Republic's Jedi academy; when Master Skywalker had tried to turn him away from the dark side of the Force, however, Brakiss had fled back to the Empire. There he gathered a group of Dark Jedi trainees and conditioned them to serve the great leader of the Second Imperium, the resurrected Emperor Palpatine himself.

Brakiss lifted his serene face, drinking in the view of the double suns. "This reality makes the image in my office seem like a pale glimmer by comparison, doesn't it, Zekk?"

Zekk nodded, but found himself without words.

"More than five millennia ago the Denarii Nova exploded, ripping through these stars and reducing them to cinders," Brakiss said. "The powerful Sith sorcerer Naga Sadow caused this cataclysmic event to gain his freedom from pursuing Republic warships. With the extravagant power of the dark side, Naga Sadow tore these two stars apart and used giant flares like two slapping hands to crush the fleet behind him."

Zekk nodded again and finally found words. "Another example of the power of the dark side."

Brakiss smiled proudly at him. "It is a power your friends Jacen and Jaina would never have shown you—much less taught you."

"No," Zekk agreed. "They never would have." For years, he had been friends with the twin children of Han Solo and Leia Organa Solo. Zekk was just a street kid, though—a nobody, who lived by his wits scavenging items in the dangerous underlevels of the city-covered world of Coruscant. His hopes for a better life had been little more than dreams until the Nightsister Tamith Kai snatched him and brought him to the Shadow Academy as part of a new recruitment drive.

In an earlier attempt to gain talented candidates, Brakiss had made an error by kidnapping the high-profile trainees Jacen, Jaina, and Lowbacca. When that failed, he had decided the Shadow Academy might do better with a different sort of person: downtrodden young ones who wouldn't be missed, yet had just as much potential to acquire Jedi powers—and more to gain by swearing allegiance to the Second Imperium.

Zekk had resisted the transformation at first, fighting to stay loyal to his friends. But gradually Brakiss lured him, showing Zekk how to use the Force for one small thing, then another. Zekk discovered that he was strong in the Force, and he learned quickly.

The experience altered his feelings toward the twins from friendship to resentment. Jaina and Jacen had never thought to include him in Jedi testing, though he felt he had as much innate talent as any of their highborn friends. Zekk's main regret in leaving his old life was that he missed his companion, old Peckhum. But now he had much more of a future. Zekk was beginning to understand Jedi powers, and he had already done things he'd never dreamed of.

Gazing at the stormy suns, Brakiss raised his arms to each side, spreading his fingers. His silvery robe flowed around him as if knit from silken spiderwebs. He stared into the swirling flares of the Denarii Nova. "Observe, Zekk—and learn."

Closing his eyes, the Master of the Shadow Academy began to move his hands. Zekk watched through the observation port, his green eyes widening.

The ocean of rarefied incandescent gases between the dying stars started to swirl like arms of fire . . . writhing, changing shape, dancing in time with the hand motions Brakiss made. The dark teacher was manipulating the starfire itself!

He whispered to Zekk without opening his eyes, without observing the effect of his work. "The Force is in all things," Brakiss said, "from the smallest pebble to the largest star. This is just a glimmer of how Naga Sadow reached out to the stars and delivered a mortal wound five thousand years ago."

"Could you make the sun explode?" Zekk asked in awe.

Brakiss opened his eyes and looked at his young student. His smooth, perfect forehead creased. "I don't know," he said. "And I don't believe I ever want to try."

Zekk remembered the way Brakiss had first enticed him to experiment with his innate Jedi powers, by giving him a flarestick and showing how simple it was to draw shapes in the flames with the Force. Here in the Denarii Nova, Brakiss had done the same thing—only on a scale the size of a star system.

"Could I try it?" Zekk said eagerly, leaning forward. He touched his fingertips to the light-filtering viewport, looking out at the double star and its brilliant corona, which rippled like a barely contained inferno.

Brakiss smiled again. "You're ambitious as always, young Zekk." He placed a firm hand on his prize student's shoulder. "But do not be impatient. There is more you must learn, much more. You've been such a voracious learner, surpassing my greatest expectations about how capable you are of using the power you were born with. You easily accomplish the exercises I set for you—but there comes a time when every Jedi trainee must be tested to the limit." Brakiss raised his eyebrows. "Tamith Kai continues to flaunt her greatest student, Vilas, who has been training here for more than a year. But you are learning so much faster. I believe you have reached that stage, Zekk."

He reached into his silvery robes and grasped something there, but hesitated, meeting the dark-haired boy's steady gaze. "I know you are ready for this. Do not disappoint me."

"What is it, Master Brakiss?" Zekk asked.

From the folds of his robe Brakiss removed a dark, ornate cylinder. "The time has come for you to have your own lightsaber."

Zekk took the ancient Jedi weapon and stared at it in wonder. Even deactivated, it felt powerful in his hand. He squeezed the grip and swung the handle back and forth, imagining a crackling energy blade. It felt good. Very good.

"Normally," Brakiss said, "I would have suggested that you build your own weapon. But it takes time and intense concentration to assemble the components, understand the workings. And we have not the time. Through the dark side, many things are easier, more efficient. Take this lightsaber as my gift to you; wield it well in the service of the Second Imperium."

"May I turn on the power?" Zekk whispered, still in awe.

"Of course."

Brakiss stood back as Zekk activated the lightsaber. A scarlet beam lanced outward, glowing like lava. "This is a masterful weapon," Brakiss said. "It has already been attuned for use by the dark side."

Zekk swiveled his wrist left and right, listening to the hum of the powerful cutting edge.

"In fact, this lightsaber is very similar to the one Darth Vader used," Brakiss pointed out.

Zekk struck out against the air. "When can I train with it?" he said. "How will I learn?"

Brakiss led the young man out of the observation tower. "We have simulation rooms," he said. "A while ago, I spent some time training your friends Jacen and Jaina. Very disappointing. They did learn how to use lightsabers, but they resisted me each step of the way.

"I expect you, on the other hand, to excel in every routine. *You*, Zekk, will quickly surpass anything your friends accomplished. And I know Master Skywalker and his fears—he is too nervous to train his precious younger students with their own lightsabers. He considers the energy blades too dangerous." Brakiss laughed. "His fears are misplaced. The most truly dangerous thing is a Dark Jedi *wielding* such a weapon."

As Zekk accompanied his teacher down the corridor, he switched off the lightsaber and held its sturdy handle in his grip. He looked down at the legendary Jedi weapon and ran his finger over its case.

The lightsaber felt warm, ready . . . begging to be used. The afterimage of the scarlet blade still blazed across his vision.

Zekk tried to blink it away, but the bright line remained. At last he said, "Yes, I can see how such a weapon could be very dangerous indeed."

JACEN COULDN'T HELP brooding as he wandered aimlessly through the halls of the Jedi academy, keeping to the shadowy corridors that were least used by other students. Jaina walked beside him in stunned silence, as she had for the past two hours. She seemed to need her brother's company as much as he needed hers, though neither of them knew quite what to say.

Jacen still couldn't understand why Uncle Luke hadn't allowed anyone else to stay with the unconscious Tenel Ka while the medical droid tended her. Neither had he allowed anyone to be present when he went to the Comm Center to contact Tenel Ka's family and inform them of the accident.

Uncle Luke himself had scooped up Tenel Ka's limp form and rushed her back to the Great Temple. As the twins hurried behind, Jacen had sensed the Jedi Master drawing on the Force to help the injured young woman maintain her strength, as well as to move faster and to keep from jarring her. At the same time, he had sent a continuous stream of soothing thoughts toward Tenel Ka's unconscious mind, thoughts of peace and healing.

Jacen had known he should try to do the same, to help his friend in any way he could, but his thoughts were in such a turmoil that he was afraid his attempts would only make things worse. Perhaps that was why Master Skywalker hadn't let any of them stay with the warrior girl once they returned to the Great Temple. He had assured the friends that he would call instantly if Tenel Ka asked for them.

Since then, the twins had roamed up and down stairways and dim passages, both of them alone with their private thoughts. When Lowie joined them without a word, neither asked where he had been. After all, he often went out to the tall trees alone, to sit and think about his home on Kashyyyk, his parents, his younger sister. . . . Now he was ready to be with friends again. But Jacen was not surprised to note, when he glanced down at Em Teedee, that the little droid had been shut off.

They were all disturbed by what had happened—no one more so than Jacen. He replayed the scene over and over in his mind as they walked: the sizzling, popping sound of the lightsabers as they clashed, the look of challenge in Tenel Ka's eyes, the glowing green of his own energy blade passing *through* hers. . . . He squeezed his eyes shut in an effort to block the rest from his mind, but that was a mistake. The scene was too vivid in his memory. His eyes flew open again.

"I can't wait any longer," he choked. "I have to see Tenel Ka to make sure she's all right—and to apologize to her."

"We'll go with you," Jaina said. Lowie purred his agreement.

When the three Jedi trainees reached the room where their friend had been treated, they saw Luke Skywalker emerging, Artoo-Detoo at his side.

"How's Tenel Ka?" Jacen asked immediately. "Is she awake? Can we see her?"

Luke Skywalker hesitated, and Jacen could see the concern written on his face. "She's still recovering from the . . . shock," he said. "She *is* awake now, but she's not quite ready to see you yet."

"But a time like this is when she needs her friends most," Jaina said.

Artoo-Detoo swiveled the top of his domed head back and forth once and buzzed an emphatic negative.

"But I have to see her," Jacen objected. "I need to do *something* for her—tell her jokes, hold her hand. . . . Blaster bolts! She only *has* one hand now, and I'm the one who's responsible."

Artoo gave a low mournful whistle, and Luke looked at his nephew in sympathy. "I know this is hard for you," he said, "but it's even harder for Tenel Ka. I remember the thoughts that went through my head when I lost my own hand on Cloud City, fighting with Darth Vader. I had just learned that he was my father. It felt as if I had lost a part of myself, a part of who I was . . . and then I lost my hand, too."

"But hands can be fixed," Jaina pointed out. "They can be reattached and healed in bacta tanks."

Luke shook his head. "My hand was gone. There was nothing to reattach."

"But your synthetic hand works just as well as your old one did," Jacen said.

"Perhaps," Luke said, flexing his lifelike prosthetic and running the artificial thumb along his fingertips, "but it was a difficult decision to make. I remember thinking that maybe I had just taken another step toward becoming more like my father, like Darth Vader—partly alive, but partly a machine. Tenel Ka will have to face the same decision herself. When her lightsaber exploded, it destroyed any chance we had of reattaching that arm."

"Uncle Luke, I need to see her," Jacen pleaded. "I *have* to apologize."

Luke squeezed his shoulder. "I promise to call you the moment she's ready to talk. Try to get some rest now."

Jacen slept fitfully, tossing and turning as images of a wounded Tenel Ka haunted his dreams.

"We are opponents," he heard her say.

"No. I'm your friend," Jacen tried to answer, but his voice was trapped in his throat; he could make no sound. He felt again the sickening jolt as her lightsaber dissolved beneath his and the sizzling green energy blade sliced through her arm.

The smell of singed flesh clawed at his nostrils. The sound of her exploding rancor-tooth weapon crashed against his eardrums, and his vision filled with the image of Tenel Ka's cool gray eyes, clouded with accusation.

"We are opponents. . . ."

Jacen felt something push at his mind, and he woke drenched in sweat, his single light blanket damp and tangled around his legs. He wasn't quite certain what had awakened him, but he knew it was somehow urgent. *It's Tenel Ka. She needs us.* The thought came unbidden to his mind. Through his open window, from the direction of the jungle he heard the faint ululating howl of a Wookiee.

Jumping from his sleeping pallet, he hurriedly fastened the front of the rumpled orange flight suit he had never quite bothered to take off when he'd lain on his bed. The distant howl came again, and Jacen could sense that Lowie, meditating at the top of a high Massassi tree, must be trying to tell him something. Without bothering to put on a pair of boots, he bolted out of his room and called at his sister's doorway.

"Jaina, wake up. Something's wrong." He raced on down the hallway, not waiting for her reply. But something—perhaps Lowie's call—had already wakened his sister, because he hadn't even turned the corner before he heard Jaina running down the hall after him. He didn't slow, though. Bare feet slapping against the cold flagstones, he rushed out the nearest exit and down one of the Great Temple's external stairways, taking the torchlit steps three at a time. He felt the nudge against his mind again and headed in the direction it had come from: the landing pad.

As he rounded the corner of the temple, with Jaina hard on his heels, he was surprised to see Lowie coming toward them from the jungle, where eerie night mists blanketed the ground with translucent white. On the landing field, though, Jacen saw something that surprised him even more.

A small, sleek shuttle, about half the size of the *Millennium Falcon*, lifted off the grassy stubble of the landing pad, blasting away wisps of ground fog. And there, bathed in the blue glow from the landing lights, his hair whipping wildly in the breeze, stood Luke Skywalker.

The Jedi Master was facing the shuttle, one arm raised as if in farewell, as the three young Jedi Knights raced up to him. Jacen and Jaina spoke at the same moment.

"Who was that?"

"What's going on?"

The tall, gangly Wookiee added a questioning bark of his own.

Luke Skywalker lowered his eyes to look at his Jedi students.

"It was Tenel Ka, wasn't it?" Jacen persisted, without really needing to hear the answer. In the dimness, his gaze locked with his uncle's, and the Jedi Master nodded.

"Her family insisted on coming immediately to pick her up. She should be in good hands now—don't worry."

Jacen felt as if a bantha had just stepped on his chest. He struggled for enough breath to speak. He felt betrayed. "She's gone! You said you'd call us when Tenel Ka was ready to see us."

Luke Skywalker cleared his throat. "She wasn't ready."

Lowie gave a despairing groan.

"But we didn't even get a chance to say good-bye," Jaina said.

Her uncle sighed. "I know. But she's with family now. They'll take care of her."

Jacen saw his sister shake her head in confusion. "But how can that be true?" Her question made no sense to him, and he looked at her, waiting for her to explain. "What I mean is," she went on, "why would Tenel Ka's family from Dathomir come for her in *that* shuttle?"

Jacen shrugged, feeling as if she expected him to understand. He didn't. "What's so strange about it?" he asked finally.

"That was an *Express*-class ambassadorial shuttle," she said. "And it had the markings of the Royal House of Hapes."

Three pairs of questioning eyes turned toward Luke Skywalker.

THE PASSENGER'S QUARTERS aboard the Hapan royal shuttle *Thunder Wraith* were spacious and equipped with every convenience a space traveler could desire. The elegant appointments of the cabin fell just short of ostentation; the chief adornment on each wall consisted of an ornate gilt frame surrounding a massive viewscreen.

Tenel Ka took no notice of the spectacular view, however. She had seen hyperspace before. She had no desire to see anything. Or anyone.

Or to *feel* anything. Numb. That was what she felt. Mind, emotions . . . even her arm. All numb.

The thought crossed her mind briefly that perhaps she ought to eat something. She'd had no food since before . . . since *before*.

No, she decided. No food. She could not work up enthusiasm for eating, or anything else, for that matter.

Her reddish-gold braids hung in tangled disarray around her face. Though the medical droid had done a serviceable job of washing her body and disinfecting the wound before cauterizing it, the droid had no programming on what to do with hair. It had kindly offered to shave Tenel Ka's head for her, but she had declined. One of the twins might have been willing to help her comb through the mess and rebraid it. But she'd been too proud to let her friends see her in her current condition, afraid of the disgust she might see on their faces— or worse yet, pity.

At least that was one good thing about having been spirited away from Yavin 4 in the middle of the night, Tenel Ka thought: she didn't have to see anyone, and so would be spared both sympathy and derision.

As if to dispel Tenel Ka's only comforting thought, Ambassador Yfra chose that moment to appear. Her grandmother's aging henchwoman, for all her kindly smiles and refined features, was still cut from the same cloth as the former queen—power-hungry and more than willing to do whatever it took to add to her personal power. Not long ago, Yfra had tried to visit Yavin 4, but when her friends were kidnapped by the Shadow Academy, Tenel Ka had gone with Master Skywalker to rescue them. Tenel Ka had not been disappointed to miss the ambassador, who had canceled the visit. She had never trusted the woman and disliked her instinctively.

"Are you feeling any better, my dear?" the ambassador said with nauseating insincerity. "Would you like to talk?"

"No," Tenel Ka said stubbornly. "Thank you." Then curiosity began to tickle her numbed brain, and she asked, "Why were you the one chosen to bring me home?"

"Actually," Yfra said, not meeting Tenel Ka's eyes, "I wasn't so much *chosen* as I was . . . convenient. I was in a nearby star system on business, you see, when your grandmother received word of your . . . unfortunate accident.

"Now, my dear," she continued, "we'll be coming out of hyperspace in a few hours, so if there's anything I can do in the meantime—"

"Yes, there is," Tenel Ka interrupted in her usual forthright manner. "I wish to be left alone."

If the ambassador was put off by the abrupt answer, she covered it well. "Why, of course you do, my dear," she said with gracious insincerity. "You've been through *such* an ordeal." She looked meaningfully at Tenel Ka's arm and artfully pretended to suppress a shudder of revulsion. "You must feel simply terrible."

With that, Yfra withdrew, managing to leave Tenel Ka feeling even worse than she had before—which might actually have been what the ambassador wanted. The ruthless henchwoman was a skilled manipulator.

Tenel Ka looked at her left arm—what remained of it, after her faulty lightsaber had exploded. There had been no chance of salvaging the limb and allowing it to heal in a bacta tank. She was no longer complete.

How could she be a true warrior now? She could not even claim her wound as the honorable result of battle. Her injury had, in fact, been caused by her own pride. And haste. And stupidity. If only she had taken more care in choosing her lightsaber components. If only she had been more meticulous in assembling the weapon. . . .

Certain that her success or failure in battle would depend on her physical skills, she had not bothered to use her best talents when constructing her weapon. Even during her Jedi training, Tenel Ka had always proudly tried to rely solely on her natural abilities, refusing to use the Force unless there was no other way to accomplish her goals.

But now what had become of her fighting prowess? How could she ever again climb a building using nothing but her fibercord, her grappling hook, and her own wits? How would she climb a tree? Or hunt? Or swim? Why, she couldn't even braid her own hair! And who would respect a Jedi with only one arm?

Lost in such grim thoughts, Tenel Ka drifted into sleep. The next thing she heard was a tapping on the door to her stateroom.

"My dear, are you resting?" Ambassador Yfra called in her cultured voice. "Time to come out now. We're almost home. We're near Hapes."

Tenel Ka shook herself awake, stood, and looked at the viewscreens around her. The *Thunder Wraith* was no longer traveling in hyperspace. The stars and planets of the Hapes Cluster lay all about her, like handfuls of rainbow gems from Gallinore scattered on rich black velvet.

"Did you hear me, my dear?" the ambassador's voice came through the door again. "You're home."

"Home," Tenel Ka repeated. The dread she had feeling congealed into a ball of ice in the pit of her stomach, as she considered that this place might indeed be her home from now on.

* * *

Immense warships, Hapan Battle Dragons, appeared as if out of nowhere to escort the tiny shuttle to its landing area. When the *Thunder Wraith* finally landed and Tenel Ka disembarked, she looked around with the first trace of eagerness she had felt since the lightsaber accident, searching for her parents. She was surprised, however, to find that her grandmother, Ta'a Chume, was the only relative present.

The former queen, accompanied by a large honor guard in full ceremonial garb, stepped forward to greet her granddaughter. Tenel Ka endured an embrace and a showy display of affection—although her grandmother *never* hugged her in private—and asked, "Why did my parents not come?"

"They were called away," Ta'a Chume answered smoothly, "on an urgent and top-secret diplomatic . . . matter. Only I and my most trusted confidant know their whereabouts." She motioned to one of her retainers, who strode forward to drape a royal robe across Tenel Ka's shoulders. Its thick, soft folds hid Tenel Ka's arms, and she did not have the energy to object. "But," her grandmother continued, "I assure you that your parents will return as quickly as they are able."

Four pairs of scantily clad male servants appeared, bringing cushioned seats for the princess and her grandmother. Tenel Ka sat, and only then noticed that at least two dozen more handsome servants had filed onto the landing pad. She closed her eyes and sighed. She might have known. It seemed that in her parents' absence, Ta'a Chume had decided to receive Tenel Ka with as much spectacle and fanfare as possible—perhaps to prove to her aspiring-Jedi granddaughter how wonderful it was to be a member of the royal family.

Tenel Ka was not thrilled.

Three brawny young men, dressed only in loincloths, moved to the center of the landing pad and began a rhythmic display of their gymnastic abilities. Other servants along the sidelines produced stringed instruments and flutes and began a musical accompaniment. During their performance, the former queen leaned toward her granddaughter and murmured, "You are so fortunate."

Tenel Ka blinked in surprise.

Her grandmother made an all-encompassing gesture. "Everything you see—Hapes and its sixty-three worlds—is yours to command." Her voice took on a persuasive tone. "Not many who fail to become Jedi Knights have such a pleasant alternative. After all, unlike the weapons of battle, wielding political power does not require the use of both arms."

Tenel Ka grimaced, not only at her grandmother's unfair assertion that she had failed in her Jedi training, but also because one of the acrobats had performed a double handspring—an act she had done countless times herself, and one she'd always assumed she'd go right on doing. She had even included flips, cartwheels, and handsprings in her daily exercises at the Jedi academy. The Jedi academy . . . she missed it already.

When the gymnasts finished, a young man stepped forward and began to juggle with phenomenal agility. Tenel Ka grew more uncomfortable as she watched him pass fire crystals, hoops, and blazing torches from hand to hand, tossing them high into the air with ever-increasing speed.

Another thing I will never be able to do, Tenel Ka thought, pressing her lips into a grim line.

She tried to concentrate on the juggler's face instead. The young man was indeed beautiful, but right then Tenel Ka would have traded every servant and guard on the landing platform for just a glimpse of a face that was friendly: Jacen, Jaina, Lowbacca, even Master Skywalker. . . .

"You know," her grandmother said, leaning toward her again, as if a thought had just occurred to her, "perhaps your injury was the Force's way of showing you that you were never meant to be a Jedi Knight—that your destiny has always been to rule Hapes."

Tenel Ka's breath left her in a rush, as if a rancor had stepped on her stomach. She wondered if perhaps, for once, her grandmother might not be right.

THE ACOUSTICS IN the grand audience chamber on Yavin 4 could carry even a whispered word from the stage to every seat in the hall. But today no lecturer stood at the far end of the long chamber, and Jaina's steps were so slow and hesitant that her booted feet made no sound. With the exception of Jacen and Lowie, who sat on stone benches near the front, the audience chamber remained completely empty.

No, not quite empty. Images of a confident young warrior from Dathomir filled Jaina's vision: Tenel Ka raising her cup in a pledge of friendship, Tenel Ka braiding her long hair in preparation for Jedi training exercises, Tenel Ka scaling the outer walls of the Great Temple, pulling herself up easily hand-over-hand. Jaina could sense through their connection in the Force that similar thoughts troubled her twin brother.

Just moments after Jaina took a seat near Jacen, the Jedi historian and instructor Tionne appeared through a side door and came to stand near the three trainees. Jaina felt her brother's mood brighten at the sight of the silvery-haired Jedi woman. Tionne had taught them to look for multiple solutions to any problem, to find choices, fresh perspectives, new alternatives. As always, Jaina was struck by the wisdom in the mother-of-pearl eyes, wisdom gained from years of studying the tales and lore of ancient Jedi.

Tionne's voice was soft and melodious. "Master Skywalker has asked me to . . . help you to move forward in your lightsaber training."

Jaina shifted uncomfortably, not wanting to think about the deadly weapon she wore clipped to a utility loop on her orange jumpsuit.

Tionne motioned to the three seated trainees. "Please. Come up on the platform where we have more room to work."

Jacen and Lowie mounted the steps, but Jaina hung back, not sure if she could express her reluctance. But when Tionne beckoned again, smiling at her with kind patience, Jaina found herself moving to join the others.

With each step, her lightsaber bumped against her leg, a grim reminder of its deadly presence. Her heart began to pound with dread, and a cold sweat broke out on her neck and forehead. Continuing with her lightsaber training, she could see now, was going to be even more difficult than she had expected, and Jaina could tell from the set of Jacen's jaw that her brother was also struggling to control his own anxiety. He must have sensed her difficulty too, because he turned to her with a shaky smile. "Want to hear a joke?"

She forced a laugh. "Why not?"

This took her brother by surprise, and he paused a moment to think. "Okay, why is a droid mechanic never lonely?"

Jaina shrugged, knowing better than to attempt an answer.

"Because he's always making new friends!"

Jaina giggled in spite of herself, grateful for the release in tension. Lowie let loose a bark of laughter as well. A dimple appeared in Tionne's cheek, and the approving glow in her alien eyes showed that she understood how hard this must be for all of them.

Then, spacing the trainees two meters apart, each facing the same direction, Tionne took them through a series of exercises, using only the hilts of their lightsabers. Clearing her mind of all else, Jaina echoed the instructor's strong, fluid movements as if she were performing a dance.

Apparently satisfied with their progress, Tionne ended the exercise and came to stand in front of Lowie. Gesturing for Jaina to take a position beside her, facing Jacen, Tionne pressed a stud on the handle of her weapon and a shimmering silver beam sprang from it, coruscating with energy.

"Please ignite your lightsabers," she said.

Though a frown of doubt crossed Jacen's face, he soon held a glowing emerald blade. With a snap-hiss, Lowie's blade appeared too, blazing a deep gold, like molten bronze. He held it at his side.

"Oh, *do* be careful, Master Lowbacca," Em Teedee said

from the Wookiee's waist. "You know how delicate my circuitry is."

Biting her lower lip, Jaina closed her eyes and touched a button on her lightsaber. Her weapon whooshed to life; the flare of its electric-violet beam and the light of the three other energy blades penetrated even through her shut eyelids, bringing with them a flood of vivid memories.

Violet. The color of the evil Nightsister Tamith Kai's eyes.

Silver. Brakiss's flowing robes. The Shadow Academy. Jacen and Jaina dueling with each other in holographic disguise. A mistake by either of them could have meant death.

Bronze. Almost the reddish gold of Tenel Ka's hair. Tenel Ka's severed arm, still holding the handle of the failed lightsaber as it exploded. The shock on Tenel Ka's face as an emerald blade sliced through her arm.

Emerald green. The color of Zekk's eyes, surrounded by a dark corona. Zekk, who was even now being trained at the Shadow Academy, learning to serve the Second Imperium and using the dark side of the Force. And if the Second Imperium attacked the New Republic as planned—the New Republic that Jaina and Jacen and Luke Skywalker's other Jedi Knights had sworn to protect—she would be forced to fight. How could she not *defend the New Republic, when her mother was its leader?*

Would she have to face Zekk with a lightsaber to protect her own mother?

With a cry, Jaina switched off her weapon and dropped it to the flagstones, backing away from it as if it had turned into a krayt dragon. An instant later all lightsabers were extinguished, and Jaina shuddered with relief.

Tionne's pearly eyes were grave as she looked at her three young charges. Picking up Jaina's discarded lightsaber, she seated herself on the cool stone of the raised platform and said, "Please, make yourselves comfortable. I need to tell you a story."

Jaina, Jacen, and Lowie settled in a tight half-circle around her, crowding close, needing the contact. Tionne sat straighter and held her delicate hands before her, moving them as she wove her tale like an invisible tapestry before their eyes.

"Thousands of years ago, in a time of great evil and great good," Tionne began in her rich musical voice, "there lived a woman named Nomi Sunrider with her husband, Andur, who was training to be a Jedi Knight.

"When Nomi and her husband traveled to take a gift of precious Adegan crystals to Andur's new Jedi Master, they were stopped by a group of greedy bandits, who killed Nomi's husband and tried to steal the crystals. But when Nomi saw her husband lying dead, she snatched up his lightsaber and took a deadly revenge on his murderers. Afterward, seeing what she had done, Nomi was so filled with revulsion that she vowed never to touch a lightsaber again.

"To fulfill the dying wish of her husband, Nomi carried the crystals to his Jedi Master, Thon. There she stayed with her baby daughter, Vima, and began her own training to become a Jedi. She learned and grew in wisdom and the Force, but still she refused to touch a lightsaber, although it was the weapon of the Jedi.

"Eventually, however, there came a day when she discovered that her power with the Force alone could not protect the ones she loved. To save her beloved Jedi Master and to guard her daughter, Nomi once again took up a lightsaber and fought for what she knew was right.

"But by this time Nomi understood the purpose and meaning of the lightsaber—and from that day forward she fought with all the power of the light side of the Force. She was never eager to use her lightsaber, but she knew it was occasionally necessary. By learning to accept this, she became a great Jedi Master and a great warrior."

As the story ended, Jaina drew a deep refreshing breath, coming out of the near trance she entered whenever listening to Tionne's tales. Jaina sensed that much of the horror she had felt earlier had already drained away, though her muscles were as sore and weary as if she herself had fought all of Nomi Sunrider's lightsaber battles.

Jaina felt something heavy and solid slide into her hand. She glanced down to see the handle of her lightsaber. Tionne had slipped it to her.

"No need to turn it on for now," the Jedi instructor said gently, looking directly into Jaina's brown eyes. "I think we've come far enough for today."

10

DOCTORS WERE BORN meddlers, Tenel Ka decided with annoyance.

The fifth court physician in as many hours continued explaining in a calm, patronizing voice that, although Tenel Ka was perfectly correct in not desiring a crude droid arm, she could have *no* objection to a lifelike biomechanical prosthetic replacement. (Apparently they thought they knew her better than she knew herself.) Tenel Ka finally raised the stump of her arm in exasperated surrender and let the doctor have her way. The physician looked satisfied and not at all surprised that Tenel Ka had agreed. After all, it had been the only reasonable choice.

The doctor beckoned to one of her nurses, and the man came forward to begin taking measurements of the stump of Tenel Ka's left arm. Next, an engineer placed electrodes against her scarred skin and sent intermittent jolts of electricity into the flesh—to measure the nerve conduction, she explained.

Meanwhile, the nurse placed Tenel Ka's right arm in a holographic imaging chamber. Each time the engineer administered a jolt to Tenel Ka's stump, the nurse patted her shoulder comfortingly and asked her to hold still. The man took great pride in telling her how the holographic image would be reversed to make a pattern that could be used as the mold for her new biosynthetic left arm.

Like children let loose at a sweets bazaar, physicians buzzed around the room snapping orders, conferring with each other, and making preparations. Allowing the poking and prodding and the chaos of voices to fade into the background, Tenel Ka sank into her own thoughts.

As the daughter of two strong ruling families, one from Hapes and one from Dathomir, Tenel Ka had long known who and what she was. Her philosophy of life had been as clear in her mind as her views on lineage, loyalty, friendships, and even her own physical abilities and limitations.

If one of those components changed, did everything else change as well?

From childhood, Tenel Ka's parents had taught her to make her own decisions based in equal part on reason, fact, and personal belief. Therefore, she had never been one to sit passively while others made choices for her. Yet, since the loss of her arm, hadn't she done just that?

She had hardly given it a thought when Ambassador Yfra appeared in the middle of the night to whisk her away from Yavin 4 in secret. In these last few days on Hapes, Tenel Ka had allowed her grandmother to control her movements and communications, tell her when to sleep, bring all her meals, and select appropriate clothing for her. And now Tenel Ka, who had always relied on her own mind and body, was allowing herself to be fitted for a biomechanical arm.

Had she truly changed so much?

The Force was a part of her, flowing through her just as the blood of her parents flowed through her veins. But this artificial arm was no part of her. If she accepted it, then she was allowing the loss of her limb to change her in ways that reached deeper than the eye could see. She didn't object to changing—but this change was not for the better. If she allowed herself to be transformed, it should be in the direction of becoming stronger or wiser.

Tenel Ka's reverie was cut short by the sound of whirring servomotors. The doctor and an engineer stood before her holding a grotesque metallic arm. A droid arm. It reminded

Tenel Ka of the unwieldly contraption she had heard the former TIE pilot Qorl now wore since going back to serve the Second Imperium. Tenel Ka shook her head in wordless denial.

"Now this is only temporary, of course," the doctor said with the same infuriating condescension she had used before. "Just accustom yourself to it while we're synthesizing the biomechanical arm."

Tenel Ka decided then and there that she had not, in fact, changed that much. If she needed to use the Force from now on to assist her in small ways, then so be it. But she refused to become dependent on a machine that masqueraded as part of herself.

"No," she managed to croak when the doctor moved to attach the mechanical arm to her severed limb. The engineer backed away uneasily, but the doctor continued as if Tenel Ka had not spoken.

"This is all part of the process of making you whole again," the doctor said in her maddening voice, "and that is exactly what you want."

"No," Tenel Ka repeated, setting her jaw stubbornly. Anger seethed inside her at the doctor's confident presumption that she knew what was best.

The doctor shook her head and bent down, as if chiding a young child, "Now, you agreed to be fitted for this new arm and—"

"I've changed my mind," Tenel Ka gritted, clamping down on her temper to hold it in check.

The doctor's lips were still smiling, but grim determination shone in her eyes, indicating she would never take no for an answer—not from any patient of *hers*. The woman kept up a steady stream of talk and motioned for the engineer to help her position the droid prosthetic against the stump of Tenel Ka's arm, as if the doctor thought that by forging ahead she could overwhelm her patient's determination with her own.

"Now, there's no disgrace in having a biomechanical arm,

you know. Even your great Jedi Master Skywalker has a prosthetic hand."

Tenel Ka acknowledged inwardly that there had been no weakness in Master Skywalker's choice. It made him no more or less than what he was. He had wrestled with his own decisions and made his own choices, just as she must make hers. The Jedi Master would not ask her to do otherwise—as the people who surrounded her here on Hapes seemed intent on doing.

"Your new arm will look quite natural," the doctor went on in her exasperating, soothing voice, "and your grandmother has spared no expense."

When the cold metal of the mechanical limb touched Tenel Ka's arm, she lost the last vestiges of control over her anger.

"No!" Tenel Ka cried, unconsciously using the Force to give the engineer and the doctor a backward shove. The droid arm was already clamped in place against her skin, however, like a protruding cancerous growth.

"I said NO!" Tenel Ka quite consciously used the Force to yank the contraption free and fling it with blinding speed against the nearest wall. It hit the stones with a clang and a crunch and fell in pieces to the cold tile floor.

Gasps went up from all around the room, and a dozen pairs of eyes regarded her with shock and apprehension.

Having vented her fury, Tenel Ka's voice was now quite calm. "And I meant no."

11

THE BUZZING VIBRATION of the T-23 skyhopper both soothed and unsettled Jacen for some reason be could not define.

Up in the cockpit with Lowie, Em Teedee amplified his speaker volume to be heard above the whine of the engines.

"Really, Master Lowbacca, I don't see what the point of all this flying about could be, without even so much as a destination in mind."

At Lowie's soft growl, the little droid replied, "Therapeutic? For what? And in any case, I should think that performing some sort of physical exercise would be far more beneficial than flying aimlessly over the treetops."

Jaina sat pensively beside Jacen in the skyhopper's cramped passenger seat, toying with her lightsaber. "We actually tried that, Em Teedee, but lately it seems like any exercise we do only reminds us of the things we were trying to get our minds off of in the first place."

Jacen was surprised to hear Jaina answering the pesky little droid just as Lowie had addressed it a moment earlier without annoyance, and as a friend. In fact, a full day had passed since any of them had had the heart to switch Em Teedee off. It was as if they hoped the little translator's chatter might fill the void that none of them wished to think about.

But something *was* missing, Jacen thought. Different. Under normal circumstances he probably would have been crowded into the tiny cargo well behind the passenger seat . . . and he would have happily endured that discomfort, if it meant that Tenel Ka could have been with them, sitting where he now sat.

"Oh, dear me!" Em Teedee said in a much subdued voice. "How terribly insensitive my processor can be. You've all been thinking of Mistress Tenel Ka, haven't you? I *am* dreadfully sorry."

Jacen saw Lowie reach down to give the little droid what looked like a comforting pat. Now that Em Teedee had brought up the subject the friends had been avoiding, Jacen felt Tenel Ka's absence all the more keenly.

"It's okay, Em Teedee," Jaina said. "We all miss her."

Jacen sighed. "I wish I could just talk to her."

Jacen, Lowie, and Em Teedee voiced agreement. Then, as though they had discussed it and come to a unanimous decision, Lowie turned the T-23 about and headed back to the Jedi academy.

Master Luke Skywalker looked down at his small barrel-shaped astromech droid as they entered the hangar bay at the base of the Great Temple. "I'm fine, Artoo," he said, answering the droid's questioning whistle. "I just have an important decision to make."

Luke frowned and thought back on the direct communication he had just sent to the Fountain Palace on Hapes. He had been unable to get hold of Prince Isolder and Teneniel Djo, Tenel Ka's parents. Instead, Ta'a Chume, the matriarch of the Royal House, had come onscreen and told him in no uncertain terms that Tenel Ka's parents were traveling outside the Hapes Cluster and could not be reached, and that the princess herself had already endured enough trauma because of her Jedi training. Under no circumstances would the young woman be allowed to speak with Master Skywalker. With that, the former queen had abruptly terminated the connection, leaving Luke with an entirely new set of concerns.

Tenel Ka's grandmother had never approved of the direction the girl had chosen for her own life. The harsh old woman had always wanted to mold her granddaughter into a scheming politician of whom she could be proud—someone just like herself.

What if, Luke wondered, instead of supporting and comforting Tenel Ka during this time of turbulence, her grandmother chose to use Tenel Ka's weakness to her own advantage? Without Isolder and Teneniel Djo to support their daughter emotionally, Tenel Ka might be too despondent or confused to make her own choices. It was possible she would blindly accept any decision the matriarch might make on her behalf.

Luke shook his head. Political considerations aside, Tenel Ka would not find the comfort she needed from her grandmother. He thought of the close bond the four young Jedi Knights had developed from working and training together at the academy. Tenel Ka needed that kind of closeness right now. She needed the unselfish caring that Jacen, Jaina, and Lowie could provide.

Luke had no wish to influence Tenel Ka's decision about whether or not to return to Yavin 4; that would have to be her choice, and hers alone. And certainly any competent medical droid could be trusted to tend Tenel Ka's physical wound. But she needed the warmth and support of friends in order to heal her emotional wounds and come to her own decision.

Luke smiled as he saw Lowbacca maneuver the T-23 sky-hopper onto its pad in the hangar bay. Those Jedi trainees needed to have their emotional wounds healed as well. He straightened and walked toward the T-23. "I think we'd better do a preflight check on the *Shadow Chaser*, Artoo. Let's get ready to fly."

Artoo warbled and beeped, asking a question.

"Yes," Luke Skywalker said. "I've made my decision."

From the moment her uncle announced he would take them to see Tenel Ka after all, adrenaline began to rush through Jaina's veins. She made a mad dash for her chambers, snatched a fresh jumpsuit, a robe, and a few other odds and ends, then stuffed them along with her lightsaber into a small flight duffel. By the time she raced back out of her quarters, down the echoing stone stairs and hallways, and out onto the landing pad, where their ship waited, she no longer had any idea what she had packed.

Jacen arrived ahead of her, running up the ramp of the sleek *Shadow Chaser*, a disordered pile of clean clothes tucked under one arm, his lightsaber under the other. Jaina didn't slow as she followed him up the ramp, marveling as she always did at the powerful ship and its glossy quantum armor. The ship had once been the finest craft created by the Second Imperium. After Master Luke Skywalker and Tenel Ka had used it to rescue the twins and Lowie from the Shadow Academy, the New Republic had given the *Shadow Chaser* to the Jedi Master for his own use.

Once Lowie had scrambled aboard with Em Teedee, his lightsaber clipped to the webbed belt at his waist, Luke instructed Artoo-Detoo to raise the boarding ramp, and the *Shadow Chaser* lifted off.

Jaina felt a thrill as the *Shadow Chaser*'s repulsorlifts boosted them off the landing field; sublight engines kicked in, launching them away from the jungle moon. The last few minutes of rushed preparation were a blur in her mind, and she looked around for something else to speed them on their way.

Lowie rumbled a question from the navigation console, and Em Teedee answered. "No, I'm certain Master Luke doesn't need our assistance in plotting the most efficient route."

Her uncle smiled down at the Wookiee. "We'll be going to lightspeed in just a few minutes. Why don't you all try to relax, get some rest."

Jaina took a deep breath and watched the stars through the viewports—like glittering gems sinking in a depthless black sea—until each pinprick of light elongated into a starline and the *Shadow Chaser* made a smooth jump into hyperspace.

The three Jedi trainees found they were too excited to rest, though. They spent the remainder of the journey trying to distract themselves aboard the tiny ship. Jaina and Lowie were just about to remove an access panel to the rear thruster stabilizers to study how they worked when Luke announced their final approach to Tenel Ka's home planet.

The three friends rushed to the cockpit. As they took their seats behind the Jedi Master, Lowie squinted and scanned the star system around them. When she saw his ginger-furred face register surprise, Jaina looked around, seeing no nearby planet that could have been Dathomir.

"That's odd," she said at last. "From the descriptions I've heard and the star charts I've studied, I could swear we were in the Hapes Cluster."

Her uncle swiveled in the pilot seat and met each pair of eyes in turn.

"We *are* in the Hapes system," Luke said gravely. "It's time I explained to you that Tenel Ka is more than just a simple warrior from a backward planet."

12

BROAD-SHOULDERED NORYS, FORMER leader of the Lost Ones gang and new stormtrooper trainee, spread his white armor on the bunk in front of him. He studied the pieces carefully, then began to assemble the glossy outfit, donning the components one at a time—and enjoying every minute of it.

The boots went on first, stiff and sturdy. Then the greaves, the shin armor, the leg plates, body armor, arm plates, and finally the flexible but tough gloves. He felt as if he had been transplanted into the body of an assassin droid, a fighting machine encased in an impenetrable shell.

Norys allowed himself a satisfied smile. This was much more impressive than anything his gang members had ever scrounged deep in the decaying alleys of Coruscant's underworld. He had been the toughest, meanest, angriest young brute of all the gang members. But being a stormtrooper was better . . . so much better.

All of his former companions were also soldier recruits undergoing training. Norys fully expected to be the best among the new troops, just as he had been toughest among the Lost Ones.

On the downside, he was no longer his own boss, free to do as he wished. He had to follow the orders of the Second Imperium. But with armor such as this and the military might of those who followed their Emperor, it was all worth it. Besides, if Norys proved himself valuable enough, his rank would increase, and he'd be placed in command of more soldiers, maybe even fly a TIE fighter. Without a doubt, he would have more power and cause much more damage than he'd ever imagined when he was just a gang leader.

Things were looking up.

The last piece of his stormtrooper outfit was the hard white helmet with black eye goggles and mouth speakers. He slipped the helmet over his head and locked it into place at the neck joint. At last he stood totally encased, completely protected—no longer a disreputable bully with a grimy outfit and stolen scraps as his only possessions.

Now he was someone to be reckoned with: a *stormtrooper*.

Norys marched down the corridor, taking care to clomp loudly on the deck plates with his armored boots. They made such a satisfying sound.

He had memorized the layout of the Shadow Academy station and knew exactly how to get to the private training room where old Qorl, the former TIE pilot, had ordered him to report. Standing outside the sealed door, he keyed in the access code—he'd felt a private thrill when Qorl had given him the secret numbers—and waited for the computer to process his entry request.

With a hiss like an angry serpent, the door slid aside. Norys marched boldly into the shielded room, and the door sealed itself behind him.

Qorl stood inside the training chamber holding a wicked-looking spear in his black-wrapped left hand. His droid replacement arm gripped the gleaming shaft with enough force to dent the metal. The serrated head of the spear had a long central prong with two side spikes curving up like a dragon's barbed tail.

"You're late," Qorl said. He cocked his droid arm back— and hurled the deadly weapon at Norys with all the strength in his robotic servomotors!

Norys stood astonished as the deadly spearpoint hurtled toward his chest plate. He just had time to cry "Hey!" in a panicked voice amplified by his helmet speakers before the barbed tip impacted squarely with enough force to smash him backward.

Norys slammed into the wall, his helmet ringing against the hard metal bulkhead. His vision sparkled with impending unconsciousness. He expected to see a spear sprouting from his heart and waited for his nerves to send shouts of mortal pain. He wanted to scream that Qorl, his supposed teacher, had betrayed him, murdered him—

But a split second later his thoughts cleared enough to hear the clatter as the spear shaft fell harmlessly to the floor. He looked down at his chest in amazement and saw only a nick in the white armor where the spear had struck.

"What did you do that for?" Norys shouted

Qorl answered in a gruff but calm voice. "To teach you respect for your stormtrooper armor, Norys," he said, "but also to warn you not to become overconfident. Yes, that armor is powerful enough to stop many weapons, such as this crude spear." The TIE pilot nodded toward the jagged weapon on the floor plates.

Norys bent down to grab the spear, narrowing his eyes in rage as he looked at his teacher. The old pilot had made a fool out of him. He felt a dangerous anger boiling through his veins. He had a good mind to take the triple-pronged spear and attack the pompous old man with it.

"But don't think your armor is invincible." Qorl reached inside his uniform, pulled out a deadly blaster pistol, and pointed it directly at Norys. "For instance, this blaster could slice through that armor as if you were wearing nothing at all."

Norys stiffened, looking into the ominous snub barrel of the pistol. His mind raced. What had he gotten himself into? Why was Qorl so upset with him? He wondered whether he could swing the spear, knock the blaster away, and strike down the TIE pilot. That would serve the old man right. . . .

Qorl turned the blaster pistol around and extended it toward Norys, butt end first. "Here. This will be your personal weapon," he said.

Norys dropped the spear to the floor and tentatively took

the blaster. The pistol felt very good in his gloved grip. Qorl nodded at him. "For target practice," he said, then went over to the controls by the door.

The gray light-absorbing walls of the windowless room shimmered.

Suddenly Norys found himself standing in a dank, dim cave with fanged stalactites dripping from the walls and ceiling. Long spikes of stalagmites rose like blunt knives from the floor. Unseen water trickled somewhere, and a pallid light seemed to ooze from the pale rock itself. Despite the room's visible transformation, Norys could detect no change in the smell of the air through his helmet filters.

"The walls of this chamber will absorb blaster bolts," Qorl said. "Your weapon has already been set to full power. There won't be much recoil, but you must become accustomed to how it feels to aim and shoot and hit a target. Pay attention now. Watch for them as they attack."

"Watch for what?" Norys said, looking around from right to left. "What's going to attack me?"

The cave seemed more sinister now. The eye goggles distorted his vision, and he tried to compensate. Strange creature noises burbled and hummed from every direction. He couldn't tell if they were insects or rodents, but they sounded vicious to him, as if everything within this chamber might be a predator.

Norys had hunted in the lower alleys of Coruscant, tracking giant granite slugs, multifanged spider-roaches, mutated feral rats—and his intuition told him this was simply a testing chamber on the Shadow Academy. He didn't think there could be any real danger. Not really.

However, this cave certainly seemed real enough. . . .

With a squalling cry, a leathery-winged creature dropped out of its hiding place in the ceiling and swooped toward him. Its eyes were huge and slitted, and Norys could see pointy ears or antennae on top of its head and razor claws at the ends of its flapping wings as it swept down.

A mynock. They weren't supposed to be terrible predators—but from the wicked fangs and claws as it swooped toward him, Norys decided this was one mynock with a bad attitude.

He pointed the blaster and squeezed off an energy bolt, but the beam went wide, striking a stalactite and startling up four more of the angry flying creatures. The new batch of mynocks also attacked, annoyed at him for disturbing their dark slumber.

Norys squeezed the firing button again and again, adjusting his aim as he watched the bright bolts streak through the dimness. The brilliant spears of light dazzled his eyes, and he could barely see through his filtered goggles.

The devilish mynocks swooped and avoided the deadly beams.

This wasn't fair! It was supposed to be target practice. He should have been able to point at a bantha's-eye or hide behind a window while shooting at an unsuspecting target in the streets below, as he had often done on Coruscant.

The blaster missed again and again as mynocks swirled around him, flapping their wings and assailing his ears with skull-splitting screeches. Norys wondered if Qorl had intentionally adjusted the blaster's aimpoint to throw the beam off.

He suddenly realized that he had been aiming wrong. It was his own fault. Reacting wildly to his sudden fear, he had overcompensated.

As the first mynock came toward him again, claws outstretched and long fangs ready to tear him to shreds, he took a second to aim and squeezed off a long bolt that sizzled through the creature's body. The mynock gurgled and fell to the floor, where it was impaled by one of the stalagmites.

"Yes!" Norys shouted in triumph—but three new mynocks swirled around him, attracted by his shout. He fired again and missed. The creatures came at him from the front, side, and behind. Norys turned, remembering to *think*, point, aim, and shoot. He eliminated another creature.

Two more emerged from the ceiling, but Norys swiveled at the waist and forced himself to concentrate. One of the two struck from behind, though its claws skittered off Norys's white stormtrooper armor. He ignored it as he set the second mynock firmly in his sights and shot it.

"Gotcha!" He turned and carefully targeted the remaining creatures, one after another. Gradually, his shooting improved. He learned how to aim. He had learned how to be deadly.

Finally, his blaster pack winking from low charge, Norys stood still and waited—but no more of the creatures emerged from the illusionary cave. He squinted through his goggles, alert for a new attack.

The walls of the cave shimmered and vanished, leaving only the flat metal shell of the training chamber. He allowed himself to relax.

"Good," Qorl said.

Norys turned to see the old TIE pilot standing next to the controls. In the excitement of the exercise, he had forgotten entirely about the military instructor.

"That was fun," Norys said. "I'm getting good at it." He looked down at the blaster, wondering when he'd be able to use it next, when he'd be allowed to practice against a real target.

"You did well enough, Norys," Qorl said again, "but you must remember—*mynocks don't shoot back.*"

Qorl pushed another button on the controls, and the door to the training chamber opened. "Come, we must go to the assembly rooms. Everyone will be there." The old TIE pilot waited for Norys to march ahead of him. "Our Great Leader is planning to address the Shadow Academy."

Zekk sat smothered in his private shell of self-confidence as dozens of Dark Jedi students gathered in the confined room where Master Brakiss and Tamith Kai lectured them in the ways of the dark side.

Zekk wore his padded suit of dark leather armor and sat straight and proud, shoulders squared. His lightsaber hung comfortably at his side. After weeks of training, he had grown fully comfortable with it. It was like a part of him, an extension of his body. That, more than anything else, convinced him he was destined to be a Jedi Knight. He was a loner, but he was also the most powerful of Brakiss's students. The other trainees flashed him occasional glances. Zekk had rapidly surpassed all of them, even those who had been at the Shadow Academy for months and months.

But then, Zekk had the greatest motivation. He wanted to be strong. He wanted everything the Force could give him.

Among those gathered in the assembly hall he noticed Vilas, the Nightsister Tamith Kai's dark-haired and brooding trainee. Vilas, who was from Dathomir, was arrogant and smug, always looking down at him, never letting him forget that it was *he* who had stunned Zekk when he'd resisted capture on Coruscant. Zekk wasn't about to forget. He felt a rivalry with this swarthy young man who talked too often about how he had ridden rancors and summoned storms on Dathomir—as if Zekk was supposed to be impressed.

The ominous Tamith Kai stood next to her protégé Vilas. She and the new Nightsisters had begun training Vilas during the Shadow Academy's construction. They therefore considered him the first of the new Dark Jedi, stronger than the others. For now.

Zekk crossed his arms over his leather-armored chest, knowing that they were wrong. And one day, Zekk told himself, he would prove it.

Burly Norys and the Lost Ones—new stormtrooper recruits taken under the wing of military commander Qorl—stood at attention. The other senior-ranking stormtroopers seemed at ease, while the Lost Ones appeared restless and uncomfortable in their new body armor.

But everyone listened intently to the Great Leader's speech.

In the center of the chamber the overwhelming and awesome image of Emperor Palpatine filled the open space in the confined room. The glowing hologram towered taller than any person present, a paternal figure and stern watchman.

Crackling from transmission static, the image of the cowled Emperor addressed them from his hideout somewhere in the Core Systems. Yellow reptilian eyes under hooded brows watched the gathered students. The eye of Palpatine was always on them.

"Our plans for the Second Imperium are close to completion," the Emperor said. "All beings are doing their part to return a New Order to our galaxy. Each of you will help my Second Imperium become powerful. Each of you is an important part of a great machine that will crush the Rebellion and put an end to their so-called New Republic."

The holographic image pivoted, giving the impression that Palpatine's gaze was sweeping across each and every person there.

"Our space fleet grows day by day, thanks to the hyperdrive cores and turbolaser batteries stolen in a recent brilliant military ambush. That equipment is helping us create our own battle fleet. Our ships will at first be smaller than the behemoths the New Republic can bring against us—but we shall fight, and we shall win. Our army of Dark Jedi is nearly complete."

The Emperor seemed to grow larger, his image swelling to loom above them. The rippling hood around Palpatine's shriveled face seemed to blow in an unseen wind. His eyes widened, blazing with the light of twin white suns.

The Emperor's voice boomed out, raised to such a volume that Zekk flinched. "Hear me, my Jedi Knights and stormtroopers. The Force does not favor weaklings. *We* have the strength. The Force is with *us*—to victory!"

Then the transmission ended, and the Emperor's cowled silhouette dissolved into sparkles and static.

The entire assembly set up a deafening cheer, in which Zekk joined wholeheartedly.

FLANKED BY A pair of Hapan Stinger security escort vehi-
cles, the *Shadow Chaser* touched down lightly on the main
landing pad of the Fountain Palace. In the cockpit, Luke Skywalker gave a small sigh of relief. Letting his eyes fall closed
for a moment, he reached deep within himself, found the calm
core of Force at his center, and then focused outward.

Artoo-Detoo gave a short warble, and Luke opened his
eyes to find all three young Jedi Knights already unbuckled
from their crash webbing and scrambling toward the exit
hatch, barely able to restrain their impatience. Jacen bounced
nervously from one foot to another, while Lowie raked fingers through his ginger fur in an effort to smooth it down.
Jaina shrugged and looked at him. "Well, what are we waiting
for, Uncle Luke?"

Chuckling, Luke released the flight interlocks, and the
three Jedi trainees tumbled down the ramp as soon as it began
to extend. Ta'a Chume, in the customary half-veil she wore
for public appearances, was already waiting on the landing
pad with a retinue of guards and attendants. Luke was pleased
to see the twins and Lowie greet the old matriarch with cour-
tesy and respect.

The former queen looked coldly at Luke as he began his
greeting. "I'm sorry, but your journey here has been a complete waste, Jedi Master. You see, my granddaughter will not
be able to speak with—"

Just then Jaina gave a delighted cry, and Jacen yelled,
"Hey, Tenel Ka, are we ever glad to see you!" Lowie bellowed a loud Wookiee greeting. The three young visitors
rushed across the landing platform to embrace their friend,
who had emerged from the sparkling palace. Snatches of the
excited conversation drifted to where Luke stood.

"Master Lowbacca wishes to compliment you on how, er,
well-rested you look."

"Thought we'd never see you again."

"I am glad you came."

"Want to hear a joke?"

Luke's attention was drawn back to Ta'a Chume when she spoke to her nearest attendant. "I didn't call the princess. How could she possibly—"

"I called to her," Luke said simply.

Ta'a Chume shook her head. "Impossible. We would have picked up any transmission from your ship."

Luke allowed himself the barest smile at her mystification. "I didn't use a transmitter," he said. "I called her through the Force. You may wish it weren't true, but Tenel Ka is already more Jedi than you know."

The matriarch raised her brows, but her eyes were unreadable. "We shall see, Jedi Master. The princess may yet get over that foolish notion."

"Does it matter to you what your granddaughter wants for herself?" Luke asked bluntly. "I know it matters to her parents. When I let her leave my protection on Yavin 4 to return to Hapes, I thought her parents would be here for her. But maybe I shouldn't have sent her away so quickly. Where are Teneniel Djo and your son Isolder?"

Luke saw indecision cloud the matriarch's eyes, and he sensed that she was trying to decide whether she would be better served by the truth or a lie. At last she said, "Although I no longer rule the Hapes Cluster, I still have my sources of information. I learned that an attempt would be made on the lives of the royal family, so I urged my son and his wife to pay a visit of state to another system—to negotiate a liberalization of our trade agreements. The negotiations called for a royal touch, and so my son and his wife were easily persuaded. No one but myself and my most trusted advisor knew when they left or where they went.

"Tenel Ka's accident was an unexpected complication that, unfortunately, may put her in danger, drawing assassins to her, like piranha beetles swarming toward the scent of blood.

The princess will be safer here with me than at your primitive temple. She is no longer any of your business, Jedi."

Luke shook his head, unwilling to back down. "Whether or not she remains my business will be for Tenel Ka to decide, when *she* is ready."

Jacen looked around his assigned room and shook his head in amazement. It had been scarcely two hours since he had learned that Tenel Ka was a genuine princess, heir to the entire Hapes Cluster. He hadn't even adjusted to that idea yet. And now this.

His room was more luxurious than any in the Imperial Palace on Coruscant. Rich, exotic scents filled the air, along with the sounds of trickling water, faint music, and chirping avians. Decorative fountains spattered in every room, every corridor, every courtyard, striking musical water chimes.

This was where Tenel Ka had grown up? He still couldn't believe it. Why hadn't she told any of her friends? Uncle Luke had known, of course, but what possible reason could Tenel Ka have had for hiding the truth from her friends for so long? Jacen didn't understand that any more than he understood her refusal to speak to him after he had injured her with his lightsaber.

He cringed again at the thought of the harm he had caused his friend. Jacen had no idea how Uncle Luke had ever talked Tenel Ka's sharp-tongued grandmother into allowing the twins and Lowie to stay on Hapes for an entire month. He only knew that at the appointed time Luke would return to pick up three or—he hoped—four young Jedi Knights.

A whole month. He'd have to talk to Tenel Ka about the accident soon, to clear the air. But what would he say? She wasn't the same person he had known on the jungle moon. Not now. But then, she had never been the person he thought she was, had she? A real Hapan princess! What *could* he say to her?

"May I enter?" The voice startled him out of his reverie,

and Jacen turned to find Tenel Ka standing at the door to his chambers.

"Sure . . . I mean, um, of course," he said, blinking in surprise. "I was just thinking about you."

Tenel Ka nodded as if she had known this and swept into the room. Dressed in a long wine-colored gown topped by a rich cape in velvety silver-gray, hair flowing freely down her back in loose, golden-red ripples, Tenel Ka looked like a stranger to Jacen. He found himself tongue-tied.

She stared at him for a long moment, as if he too were a creature from some unknown world, but when she spoke it was the same Tenel Ka. "The room—it is acceptable?"

A thousand questions, apologies, and bits of news clamored in Jacen's mind, waiting to be spoken. But all he could manage to say was "Hey, it's a great room. This is an amazing place. All those fountains."

Tenel Ka nodded again. "This is a fact."

Jacen tingled with an odd pleasure at Tenel Ka's old familiar phrase. Looking into her cool gray eyes, Jacen struggled to collect himself and harness his racing thoughts. At last he managed to blurt out, "I'm really sorry I hurt you, Tenel Ka. It was all my fault."

"I was to blame."

"No," Jacen hurried to say, "I was being stupid. I was so busy trying to impress you with my dueling skills that I didn't even notice when your lightsaber blade started to fratz out!"

"This is not a fact," Tenel Ka said, frowning. "My own pride caused the accident. I believed my fighting prowess could compensate for any deficiency of my weapon. I foolishly believed that the quality of the energy blade was insignificant compared with the quality of the warrior. This was also not a fact."

Jacen shook his head. "Even so, it should never have happened. I should have—"

"The responsibility is *mine*," Tenel Ka broke in, stamping one foot adamantly, her face flushed with emotion. As if she suddenly felt too hot, she unclasped her cloak and tossed it over the back of a cushioned bench, leaving both of her arms bare.

With a stubborn lift of his chin, Jacen looked at the stump of her left arm. It made him feel sick, and he wanted to turn away. This was the first time he had really seen her injury. "I . . . I won't let you take all the blame. If I'd been letting the Force direct my movements, I would have sensed something was wrong." He pointed to where her arm ended so abruptly. "And *that* would never have happened."

Tenel Ka's eyes flashed with smoky gray fire and, using her right arm to hike up her gown to a comfortable thigh level, she plopped onto the cushioned bench. "And had *I* been using the Force," she argued, "I would already have known my lightsaber blade was inadequate."

"Well, I . . ." Jacen stopped, unable to dredge up a counter-argument to convince his infuriatingly proud friend. "I . . ." He cast about furiously for something else to say and finally finished, "Um, want to hear a joke?"

His mouth dropped open in amazement as Tenel Ka burst into peals of laughter. He could tell that this was neither po-lite amusement nor hysteria, but the laughter of enjoyment that sprang from the heart. It was a wonderful sound—one he had wanted to hear since the first day they met.

"But . . . Jacen shook his head in confusion. "I didn't even tell my joke."

"Ah," Tenel Ka gasped, and tears of merriment began to stream from her eyes. "Aha. I am so glad you're here."

Jacen shrugged as fresh waves of mirth assailed her. "I'm not objecting, mind you. I just don't get it. What's so funny?"

"We have often been in competition, you and I," she said. "I have missed that. Shall we now compete for the greater share of blame?"

Jacen gave her a lopsided grin. "Nah. I guess all I really need is for you to accept my apology."

Tenel Ka began to object but stopped herself. Her laughter faded and her expression turned sober. As if it took a great deal of effort, she said, "Apology accepted. I . . . forgive you, if that is what you desire." Her last words came out in a whisper: "Jacen, my friend."

Relief rushed through Jacen like a morning breeze clearing remnants of lingering fog. He had been holding his breath, and he nearly choked with emotion at her reply. There were no words to express the flood of feelings that welled up in him, so he sat beside Tenel Ka and put both arms around her.

Tenel Ka returned his hug, as best she could, with both arms. Shaking, she pressed a face wet with tears against his shoulder, and Jacen did not think that they were tears of laughter anymore.

When Tenel Ka and Jacen had both composed themselves, they went in search of Jaina and Lowbacca. Then Tenel Ka took the companions on a whirlwind tour of the Fountain Palace, ending at her own chambers. Because chattering went against her nature, the descriptions she provided were brief and succinct.

When they were alone in her rooms, Tenel Ka showed them her favorite—and most private—place in the Fountain Palace, a completely enclosed terrace garden at the center of her suite of rooms. The three-story-high ceiling was domed, and could be adjusted to simulate any kind of weather and any time of day or night.

The garden room was fifty meters across, its curved walls decorated with scenes from Dathomir. Terraced planters held bushes and trees, cunningly arranged to look as if they were part of the painted primitive landscapes.

At the middle of the garden, smooth stone benches surrounded a tiny artificial lake. Centered in the crystal-clear water, like a miniature volcano emerging from a primordial sea, stood a peaked island with a real waterfall flowing down one side.

"I come here when my heart is heavy, or whenever I miss my mother's homeworld."

"Beautiful," Jaina whispered.

Warmed by her friend's approval, Tenel Ka took a seat on

one of the stone benches and gestured for the others to join her. "We may speak freely here," she said, "and I will answer your questions."

And so the friends talked, more frankly than they had ever dared before, until Tenel Ka's grandmother arrived to summon them to evening meal.

"The banquet hall is ready," Ta'a Chume announced.

Tenel Ka's jaw took on a stubborn set. For the first time since her return to Hapes, she felt *alive*. How could her grandmother interrupt now? "We would prefer to eat in privacy," Tenel Ka said, knowing that she was displaying an appalling lack of courtly manners. But she didn't care.

The matriarch gave her granddaughter a smug smile. "I've already taken care of that," she said. "I sent away all my attendants and advisors for the evening."

This was an old game that she and her grandmother played—who could outmaneuver whom—and Tenel Ka took up the challenge. "Then it should be no problem if we choose to eat here."

"Oh, but the serving droids have already gone into the banquet hall," the former queen objected. "The meal will be served directly on the hour."

Tenel Ka saw Jaina glance at her chronometer. "But that's only five minutes from now," Jaina said, her eyes registering surprise. "I'll need some time to wash up first."

Lowie grunted his agreement, and Jacen said, "Hey, me too. I think we'd all be a lot more comfortable if we weren't so formal on our first night here." His grin, aimed at Ta'a Chume, was charming and infectious. "And we're all pretty tired from our travels."

Flashing Tenel Ka a look that said she would not give in so easily next time, the matriarch nodded. "Very well, then. I will have the serving droids sent in."

Ta'a Chume withdrew from Tenel Ka's private sanctuary, and they all relaxed, glad of the reprieve. Tenel Ka looked gratefully around at her friends and then said, "Let me show you to the refresher units before our meal arrives." She had just stood up to lead them to the door when suddenly the polished stone shook beneath her feet. An ear-splitting roar rent the air, along with a heavy blast, throwing Tenel Ka to her knees.

Lowbacca yelped with alarm, and Em Teedee replied, "Dear me, yes! Master Lowbacca wishes to inquire as to the origins of all this noise and commotion."

"Yeah," Jacen said, "you didn't warn us you had groundquakes."

Tenel Ka looked back to see the Wookiee scrambling to his feet and helping the twins back up as well. "That was no groundquake," she said, grimly launching herself toward the door. "Come with me."

Tenel Ka's heart raced, though not with exertion, as the four of them pelted down the corridor toward the private dining hall. Thick smoke billowed from the far end of the vaulted passageway. She felt her stomach clench.

Her dread lessened when a pair of guards emerged from the roiling, sooty clouds, supporting her grandmother. Emergency squads rushed to extinguish the fires still blazing inside the dining hall. Ta'a Chume coughed a few times and waved imperiously for the guards to allow her to walk on her own.

"No one hurt," she croaked.

"It was a bomb?" Tenel Ka asked.

Her grandmother motioned them all back the way they had come. "Yes. In the dining hall," she said. "Must leave immediately."

"*We* were all supposed to be in the dining hall!" Jaina blanched. "So that bomb—"

The matriarch nodded. "Was meant for the princess and me."

THE ROYAL YACHT, a Hapan Water Dragon, skimmed across the ocean waves at top speed, its repulsorjets kicking up spray. Bright sunlight shone through its transparisteel windowports, and the fresh smell of saltwater and rafts of seaweed filled the air.

Leaning against a windowport, eyes half shut, Tenel Ka watched the water dance and sparkle. She had always thought of Reef Fortress Island as her summer home, a place to enjoy the warm sun, the surf, and the ocean breezes. But in truth, it was a stronghold, a safe haven in time of danger.

"I feel ill," Jaina said. "Mentally and physically."

Tenel Ka, having been lulled by the yacht's rocking movement as it sped across the water, now straightened and blinked in surprise. "What is wrong, Jaina?"

"Do you realize that a few minutes one way or another, and we might all have been blown to bits by that bomb?" Jaina asked incredulously. "Or maybe I'm just a little seasick from these waves."

Tenel Ka looked at each of her friends in turn. Jaina did not look well. Her straight brown hair, dull with perspiration, clung in damp clumps to her pallid face and neck. Lowie, sitting beside Ta'a Chume as she steered the yacht with nonchalant confidence, seemed too interested in the navigational computer to be affected by the waves. Jacen, on the other hand, looked boyishly enthralled by the experience.

Tenel Ka said to Jaina. "You will recover."

Tenel Ka's grandmother spoke from her position at the helm. Although royal guards accompanied them, the former queen preferred to pilot the craft herself. "We're almost to the fortress now. You'll be safe there."

Tenel Ka's eyes narrowed shrewdly as she noted her grandmother's words. "Should you not have said *we* will be safe?"

"You and your friends will be safe, yes," her grandmother said evasively.

"Where will you be?" Tenel Ka asked.

"Much of the time I'll be with you, but I'm not sure I can trust the investigation of this bombing to anyone else. Until I get to the bottom of the plot against us, I may have to travel back and forth between Reef Fortress and the Fountain Palace."

Jaina looked startled. "And leave us on the island alone?"

"You will have a full complement of guards," Ta'a Chume said soothingly. "And Ambassador Yfra will stay with you whenever I'm away."

Lowbacca snuffled a question from the navigation station. "Master Lowbacca wishes to inquire whether that island up ahead is our final destination," Em Teedee elaborated.

Jacen and Jaina went to the front windowport to look out at the smear of darkness rising from the sun-dappled water.

"Yes," Tenel Ka's grandmother replied, "that is Reef Fortress."

Tenel Ka didn't move forward to look out at the island. She'd been there so many times, she already knew what she would see. It never changed. She closed her eyes, picturing the rocky spires jutting up from the foamy waters of the ocean. She envisioned the water-level entrance to the cave grotto, the steep stone walls of the fortress itself, the crystal-clear cove where she had once loved to swim, the dizzying heights from the parapets along the impenetrable walls where she could walk or run with the wind in her hair, the gently steaming thermal springs in the cellar that provided fresh water for bathing, cooking, and drinking.

Tenel Ka suddenly realized that she had felt homesick after all for this place that held so many of her happiest memories from her childhood, memories of carefree time spent with her parents. The corners of her mouth turned up slightly. Opening her eyes, she moved to stand beside Jacen. "I can't wait to show you my home."

*　　*　　*

Although the matriarch offered to select quarters for their guests, Tenel Ka insisted on personally choosing an appropriate room for each of the young Jedi Knights.

Lowbacca's chamber was massive, built at a corner where two of the fortress's protective walls met. The room's appointments were basic, its only decorations an ornamental spear on one of the inner walls and a threadbare tapestry on the other. But through the windows on the two outer walls, the room had a spectacular view of the sheer drop from the stone fortress down to the reef rocks and ocean below. Lowbacca stood by the window casement, staring through the force field screening with such rapt wonderment on his face that Tenel Ka knew she had chosen well for him.

"Do be careful, Master Lowbacca," Em Teedee squeaked in alarm. "If I were to fall down there, I'm sure the damage to my circuits would be irreparable."

For Jaina, Tenel Ka chose what she had always known as the "gadget room." It had belonged to Tenel Ka's great-grandfather, whose hobby had been inventing and tinkering with machines. Fully half of the chamber was filled with workbenches, adjustable-intensity glowpanels, power droids, electrical implements, and odd-looking equipment in various stages of assembly or disassembly. Jaina stayed behind to investigate the fascinating workshop while Tenel Ka showed Jacen the special room she had picked for him.

When they reached the arched doorway, Tenel Ka found herself assailed by an inexplicable bout of nervousness. What if she had judged wrong for her friend? What if Jacen found this room gloomy or dreary, instead of peaceful and soothing? Oh well, she finally decided, she might as well try for the whole effect.

"I would request," she said uncertainly, "that you close your eyes."

"Sure," Jacen said. "Need to clean it up a bit?" He squeezed his brandy-brown eyes shut.

Tenel Ka opened the door with her right hand and reached out to take his arm with her other—only to remember that she had no left hand. Even though Jacen could not have seen, she felt a flush of embarrassment creep into her cheeks as she grasped his arm with her good hand and led him into the room.

"Uh, if it'll make you more comfortable," Jacen quipped, "I can keep my eyes shut the whole time we're at the fortress."

"That will not be necessary." Tenel Ka shut the door behind her and adjusted the lighting. The room was still dim, but that was unavoidable. "You may look now."

She heard his quick intake of breath, and then a whispered exclamation. "Blaster bolts!"

"It is . . . to your liking?" Tenel Ka moved closer to observe Jacen's expression. In the glow of the violet lighting, his smile flashed a fluorescent white. She noted with great satisfaction the delight that lit his face as he used all of his senses to experience this special room.

Tenel Ka's own sense of wonder was renewed as she looked around with Jacen, as if for the first time. A four-meter-high curved aquarium lined the walls of the circular room, unbroken except for the arched doorway through which they had entered. The air tasted salty and tingled pleasantly in her nostrils. Almost hypnotic in its effect, the bubbling and whishing of recirculating water surrounded them. Colorful creatures of all shapes and sizes propelled themselves through the seawater, lit only by specially regulated glowpanels. Moist tropical warmth wrapped them like a blanket, and Tenel Ka stifled a contented yawn.

Jacen followed suit and then chuckled. "I don't think I'll have any problem sleeping in here," he said. "This is just perfect."

She felt him reach out, grope around for her hand, and then give it a squeeze. Tenel Ka sighed. This room was indeed filled with peace.

After they had had an opportunity to refresh themselves, Tenel Ka took her friends to one of her favorite places on the rocky shore of the island, a tiny cove with calm water in an amazing shade of living green. The four of them waded in the sparkling warm waters, joking and splashing, able to forget for a moment the dangers that had brought them to this place.

Jacen and Jaina wore only the undergarments from their flightsuits, which served admirably as swimming gear as well. Tenel Ka herself had changed into a brief lizard-hide exercise suit and felt more like herself than she had at any time since returning to Hapes.

"If you won't be requiring my services, Master Lowbacca," Em Teedee said, "might I stay on shore and shut down for a rest cycle? I have no idea what saltwater might do to my delicate circuitry."

Tenel Ka watched Lowbacca grumble a reply and splash out of the shallows to place Em Teedee high up on a dry rock. After the Wookiee returned, the friends waded out toward deeper water, enjoying one another's companionship, along with the feeling of the silky water around them.

When Jacen, Jaina, and Lowie turned onto their backs to float lazily on the surface while they conversed, Tenel Ka absently flipped over and floated as well. In that instant she remembered yet again that one of her arms was missing—but she also realized that, with only a slight adjustment of her posture and weight, she was able to float quite easily. By experimenting, she discovered she could propel herself at surprising speed, using nothing more than her strong legs.

Jacen, who had noticed her tentative attempts, swam over and favored her with what she could only interpret as a challenging grin. Starting to tread water, he raised his eyebrows at her. She met his gaze and began treading water as well—at first with little coordination, then finding her rhythm. When Jacen narrowed his liquid-brown eyes and moved to a sidestroke, Tenel Ka did the same.

Tenel Ka met one challenge after another with varying degrees of success. She found that she was able to do much more than she could ever have imagined. And even when her performance was less than stellar—as when she tried to perform an underwater somersault—she *enjoyed* herself.

When she resurfaced sputtering and coughing after one such attempt, she noticed a measuring look in Jacen's eyes, daring her to push herself to her limits. "Race you to the shore," he said.

Tenel Ka gave him a solemn warning look. "Only if you truly intend to beat me," she said.

Jacen's face was equally grave as he said, "I'll give it everything I've got."

She nodded. "Then—go!"

Tenel Ka drew on all of her strength, endurance, coordination, and ingenuity as she threw her body into the mad race for shore. Her entire consciousness was focused on one goal, and she drove forward with every bit of determination she possessed.

Before she even understood what had happened, she was standing on the shore being greeted by loud cheers from Jaina and a very bedraggled-looking, wet Lowbacca, who were already standing on the rocky beach.

Disoriented, Tenel Ka turned, looking for Jacen, and found him just emerging from the water behind her. From the surprised expression on his face, she knew their competition had been real: he had not "allowed" her to win.

Jaina ran forward to hug them both just as Lowbacca, with a loud Wookiee yell, shook himself dry, sending sprays of salty water in every direction. Jacen yelped, and Jaina gave a small shriek of surprise.

Tenel Ka was glad of the diversion, however, because some of the salty droplets glistening on her face were not seawater.

TWO DAYS LATER, the royal matriarch Ta'a Chume looked
sternly at her granddaughter as Tenel Ka defiantly tossed
aside the embroidered robe of state, as well as the glittering
and gaudy tiara.

The former queen was not pleased. "You must dress in a
manner befitting your station, child," she said in an indignant
tone. "And you might show a bit more respect for your heritage. Take your tiara. It is an heirloom, known throughout the
cluster." She held up the delicate crown studded with beautiful, iridescent jewels. "These are rainbow gems of Gallinore,
worth enough to buy five solar systems."

"Then buy five solar systems," Tenel Ka said. "I have no
use for such wealth."

"You can't avoid your duties by being impertinent. This is
not a carefree vacation. There is still work to do. We have an
important diplomatic meeting to conduct, and you must prepare yourself."

"I have no interest in your important meeting, Grandmother."

Jacen, Jaina, and Lowbacca stood uncomfortably, not sure
what to say as Tenel Ka argued with the matriarch.

"So long as you remain part of the Royal House of Hapes,
Tenel Ka, you will continue to receive diplomatic instruction
and learn how to become a useful member of our bloodline,"
her grandmother snapped.

Tenel Ka glared back, her one hand clenched into a fist.
"What makes you think I wish to stay here as part of the
Royal House? I am still in training as a Jedi Knight."

The matriarch laughed. "Spare me your fantasies, child,
and face reality. The Mairan ambassador is on his way to us
underwater right now, and we must go meet him at the shore.
Put on your robe. I promised him that *you* would be the one
to greet him."

"You didn't ask me," Tenel Ka said.

"There was no reason to," the matriarch answered. "You couldn't possibly have other plans, so I just told you."

"I have no need for diplomatic training. I am a fighter, not a politician," Tenel Ka said, indicating with a sweeping gesture the reptile-skin armor she had changed into to emphasize that her preferred heritage was from Dathomir.

"Hey, um, Tenel Ka?" Jacen said uncertainly, clearing his throat. "Uh, I mean, you've got to make up your own mind and everything . . . but remember what Master Skywalker says? Jedi ought to be open to all learning, to draw strength from knowledge—wherever they might find it? Seems to me that even though you're a good fighter, you might someday find a use for the skills your grandmother wants to teach you."

"I disagree with her politics," Tenel Ka said.

Jacen shrugged. "Nobody said you had to do everything the *way* she wants you to."

The matriarch scowled at the insolent young Jedi boy, and that made up Tenel Ka's mind. "Very well. I will do it," she said, "but I will do it my way. This is a fact."

"Oh, excellent!" Em Teedee said from Lowbacca's waist. "Might I take this opportunity to remind you, Mistress Tenel Ka, that a goodly portion of my programming was adapted from protocol droid subroutines? If I can be of any assistance in your political efforts, I gladly offer my services."

The old matriarch looked horrified.

Tenel Ka smiled inwardly. "Thank you, Em Teedee. I accept your offer. Lowbacca, I would like you at my side when I meet the Mairan ambassador."

Tenel Ka picked up the robe and with her one hand attempted to fling it about her shoulders, but the left side slid off, leaving the stump of her arm bare. When the matriarch moved to help her, Tenel Ka pulled away and quickly reached over to tug the garment into place.

"It is good to be an independent thinker, my granddaughter," the matriarch said. "Just have a care you don't do it to excess."

Royal guards had set out a plush chair on the outer edge of the reef, where curling whitecaps chewed against the rock. The damp air smelled of salt and freshness. The old matriarch stood back, observing.

Tenel Ka, in her rippling robe, marched to the chair without waiting for her grandmother to issue instructions. Adjusting the rainbow-gem tiara on her thick red-gold hair, she looked directly into the brisk wind that blew off the choppy waters.

Lowbacca, the breeze ruffling his ginger fur, stood beside Tenel Ka as she seated herself and looked out across the black rocks and the endless sea. She blinked against the bright sunlight and watched the waves for any motion.

The Mairans, a race of intelligent, tentacled, undersea dwellers, came from the ocean world of Maires, one of the planets in the Hapes Cluster. Their ambassadors had set up a consulate on the ocean floor of the Hapes central world. It seemed that, even from their undersea consulate, the Mairan ambassadors had managed to raise a political dispute with their traditional rivals from the planet Vergill.

The Mairans could leave the sea for short periods, but only if the tentacled creatures were periodically showered with a fine spray from bubbling tanks of filtered water they carried on their backs. By keeping their rubbery skin moist, the Mairans were able to spend hours on dry land, and the ambassadors had insisted on coming personally to the island fortress. They would allow the matter to be resolved by no one but the matriarch herself—or a member of the Royal House who was her designee.

The matriarch had designated Tenel Ka.

The princess sat waiting, watching the waves. She had not brought her chronometer along and wondered if the ambassador was late . . . or if she was just impatient for this ordeal to be over with.

Lowbacca stood watch at her side, tall and shaggy; Em Teedee gleamed silver in the sunlight. Jacen and Jaina, who hadn't been briefed, hung back.

"Uh, what are we doing here, exactly?" Jacen asked.

Tenel Ka turned to answer him, but Em Teedee chimed in first. "If I might be permitted to explain, Mistress Tenel Ka? I believe I can provide an appropriate summary." The little droid made a sound as if it were clearing its voice speaker. "Now, then. The Mairan underwater consulate—a domed structure built on their own planet and transported here to the Hapes homeworld—is perilously close to a subsurface mining project opened by the Vergills just after the Mairan consulate was established.

"Although the Vergill mining business is terribly productive, the Mairans have filed a formal complaint because of the noise and the silt stirred up by the drilling and excavation operations. They contend that, since the Mairans were there first, the Vergills should be required to clean up the muddied waters, cease their disruptive mining, and relocate to a place at least fifty kilometers from their consulate."

Tenel Ka nodded. "Yes, these are some of the facts. But not all."

Before she could elaborate, Tenel Ka saw a hulking shape rise out of the water and shamble in her direction, sloshing through the surf. Forty or so black tentacles—which Tenel Ka knew the Mairans let drift free underwater, to grasp any fish that might flit within reach—dangled from its slumped shoulders, and it weaved from side to side on two legs as it walked. The spherical discolored lumps on its sloping head must have been eye membranes. The entire creature looked dark and oily.

Tenel Ka's initial reaction upon seeing the alien ambassador was one of fear—a giant primeval monster nearly one and a half times her own height rising out of the surf and lumbering toward her—but she pushed the reaction away. Fear could only weaken her judgment right now.

Waves rippled around the Mairan's legs, which were like tree trunks clinging to the beach. Stopping in the low surf, the ambassador held a heavy convoluted shell, into which a pattern of holes had been drilled.

The Mairan ambassador spoke from a vibrating membrane beneath its tentacles in a resonant and burbling voice that was very difficult to understand. *"I am capable of speaking Basic if this is how we must proceed."*

Tenel Ka shook her head. "That will not be necessary. Use your native language." She cast a glance sideways at the silvery ovoid of Em Teedee at Lowie's side. "I have brought my own translating droid."

"Oh, my," said Em Teedee, who just an hour earlier had downloaded the Mairan language from the fortress databanks. "This is quite exciting!"

The tentacled hulk bowed once, then straightened. Placing the drilled side of the shell against its blowhole, it played a skirling, complicated series of flutelike notes.

"Ah, yes," Em Teedee said. "This musical language was indeed properly loaded into my memory banks. Thank the Maker! The Mairan ambassador formally greets you, Princess Tenel Ka."

The tentacled creature blew another series of notes. Teedee translated. "And he commends you on your capture of such a magnificent and well-trained pet, with its coat of silky brown seaweed—oh, dear!" the droid chirped. "I do believe he's referring to Master Lowbacca!"

Lowbacca growled and flashed his fangs. Tenel Ka stood, indignant, letting the robe fall away to reveal her reptile-hide armor and her arm stump. Behind them on the rocks, the matriarch frowned in disapproval at her granddaughter's performance.

"Wookiees are an intelligent species. They are *no one's* pets," Tenel Ka said. "This is my friend."

The Mairan appeared flustered, flailed his tentacles in agitation, and played another series of notes. "The ambassador offers his apologies for having misunderstood, Princess Tenel Ka. He grieves for your loss of one . . . tentacle—I believe he means your arm—and hopes that you exacted tenfold retribution on the fool responsible for your loss."

"How I have dealt with the loss of my 'tentacle' is not his

concern." Tenel Ka's voice was crisp and hard. "If he has a diplomatic matter to raise, he had better do so immediately. If he tries my patience, I will leave. I have other things to do."

The Mairan ambassador hesitated, its tentacles stirring uncertainly, then raised the shell flute again, drawing forth a long and tangled melody.

"The Mairan ambassador apologizes again and says that he understands the matriarch gave you this decision to make as part of your diplomatic training. Since it is to be your first ruling of major import, you will most assuredly want to give it the utmost time and consideration to choose the best course of action."

Tenel Ka did not back down. Her voice remained stern. "The ambassador is sorely misinformed. I have made *many* important decisions in my life. Although this may be the first one that affects *him* and his kind, he may rest assured that I am no stranger to making tough choices."

Some of those other choices flashed through her mind—particularly her decision to join Master Skywalker's Jedi academy, and her insistence on embracing the Dathomir side of her heritage as well as that of the Hapan Royal House.

"Please present your case without further digression," she said. Her one hand gripped the chair, but she remained standing to minimize the height differential between herself and the towering tentacled ambassador.

"Very well, Princess Tenel Ka Chume Ta' Djo. The Mairan ambassadorial delegation begs the intervention of the Royal House in a matter that has distressed us greatly." Em Teedee had a difficult time keeping up as he translated the fluting notes of the tentacled ambassador's speech.

"Our peaceful undersea settlement is our home on this world, set up by our first delegation no more than six months ago. We have been delighted with the beautiful and tranquil setting of our consulate under the sea. If only you air-breathers could come to see it, I'm certain you would agree that—"

"I'm not a tourist," Tenel Ka said. "What is your grievance?" She already knew, but she wanted him to spell it out.

"Only a month after we established our consulate," the ambassador whistled, "a mining crew of oafish, inconsiderate Vergills set up a floating platform and began drilling less than a kilometer from our settlement structures. The currents are now perpetually stirred up and dirty. The noise vibrates through the water, disturbing our concentration and frightening away fish. They have ruined our home."

The Mairan raised its tentacles beseechingly. "We had established our dwelling there first, most knowledgeable Princess. We beg you to order the despised Vergills to move their pollution away from our home. After all, they have the entire ocean. They need not disturb our peace."

"I understand," Tenel Ka said.

The tentacled ambassador bowed deeply in respect, but then Tenel Ka continued sharply, "I also understand that the Vergills conducted a mining survey of the oceans by satellite, well before you established your consulate city. When I consulted the access records, I learned that you Mairans received a copy of this mining report several months *before* you chose a location for your domed consulate. Finally, I have discovered that you identified the richest vein of ditanium picked up on the survey and chose to place your structure *exactly there*, knowing full well that the Vergills would eventually commence mining operations in the vicinity.

"Yes, Ambassador, the entire ocean *is* available," she said as the wind whipped her hair about like red-gold flames, "but it is you who chose to bring about this dispute. You erected your consulate *after* you knew for certain that the Vergills would desire to mine that very same spot."

She waited, but the Mairan said nothing. She continued. "The Vergills have also petitioned for our intervention. And so you may either change the location of your consulate—which is quite easily done, as I understand from the modular construction of your domes—or you may simply choose to tolerate the noise and disturbance."

After a moment of stung silence, the Mairan ambassador fluted stridently, waving his tentacles. "Don't even bother translating that," Tenel Ka said sharply to Em Teedee, then turned to face the hulking black creature. "You came to me asking for a decision, and I have made it. In the future perhaps you will attempt to work out your own problems instead of wasting our time with your petty squabbles. I have spoken."

She sat back down and shrugged into her robe again. After another moment the Mairan ambassador shuffled backward into the surf and disappeared beneath the waves.

"All right, Tenel Ka!" Jacen cried, running toward her. Lowbacca chuffed with laughter.

Tenel Ka felt her head spinning, exhilarated at what she had done. It surprised her that the speech had come easily after all. She adjusted the rainbow-gem tiara on her head.

She was actually startled, though, when she looked behind her to see her grandmother, the iron-hard and impossible-to-please matriarch, *smiling*.

"Perhaps your methods are a bit rough yet, child," her grandmother said, "but your judgment was sound."

16

REST AND SAFEKEEPING were all well and good, Jacen thought—but after several days staying at the Reef Fortress with no place to go but to the tiny cove to swim, he began to get restless. Terribly restless.

Tenel Ka, too, was a person of action—Jacen knew that better than anybody. She wanted to be out and around, having adventures, not coddled and sheltered like a pet. The injured warrior girl certainly didn't want to sit like an old woman, merely watching waves pound against the rocks.

Ta'a Chume had returned to the Fountain Palace to supervise the investigation of the bomb blast, leaving Tenel Ka and the young Jedi Knights under the questionable care of thin-lipped Ambassador Yfra. The ambassador was a hard woman, as if all the muscles in her body were made of durasteel rather than flesh . . . but then, everyone within the Hapan government lived a harsh life, trusting no one, always struggling for personal gain. Jacen supposed Ambassador Yfra was no worse than anyone else in this society. On the other hand, he could see why Tenel Ka preferred the honest ruggedness of her mother's world of Dathomir to the hypocritical and often poisonous dealings of Hapan politicians.

He found Tenel Ka outside the towering Reef Fortress standing on an outcropping of black rock. She was throwing stones with her good arm into the swirling pools of water that hissed around the outer reef. Deep in concentration, she took careful aim and was clearly pleased whenever she struck her imagined target. Reluctant to disrupt her reverie, Jacen stood behind her, content just to watch.

Jaina and Lowie, who had followed Jacen out of the fortress, also looked on as Tenel Ka threw stones. All of them seemed to feel the same restlessness—stuck on a minuscule island with no place to go.

After a few minutes, the balcony doors above them opened, and a flash of sunlight from polished transparisteel dazzled Jacen. Ambassador Yfra stepped out onto the high balcony, whip-thin, looking like a bird of prey as she scanned the rocks to find them. She waved, catching their attention. "Children, come here please."

Lowbacca sniffed the salty air and groaned a comment. Em Teedee made an electronic sound of disagreement. "I'm sure I don't know what you mean, Master Lowbacca! Whatever makes you think the air has changed for the worse? It still smells every bit as salty and refreshing to *me* as it has for the past hour."

Tenel Ka glanced behind her when Em Teede spoke and looked momentarily startled to find the others watching her. She clambered off the rock outcropping and joined her three friends. "Let us see what the ambassador wants," she said in a gruff voice, leading the way.

"Maybe it'll be something fun," Jacen suggested

Tenel Ka looked at him with her granite-gray gaze, raising her eyebrows. "Somehow the ideas of Ambassador Yfra and 'fun' do not go together in my mind."

Jacen snickered at that, wondering if Tenel Ka had purposely made a joke. By all outward appearances she had merely stated a fact.

Inside the fortress, the ambassador met them in the warmly lit balcony room with a surprise for them all. "My dears, I think it's time for you to have a little enjoyment!" she said, smiling with her face, but not with her mind. Jacen could sense it. Although she went through all the correct motions of being friendly and understanding, Jacen could tell that Yfra had no great love for children—or for anyone else who took up so much of her time and interfered with governmental business.

Tenel Ka placed her hand on her hip. "What would you suggest, Ambassador?"

"You children seem so bored," Yfra said. "I can understand that. Sometimes having no cares or worries *is* bothersome." She gave the briefest disapproving frown, then covered it with another false smile. "I've taken the liberty of reprogramming one of our wavespeeders so that you can get away for a while, cruise the ocean, and have a good time out in the sun."

"Are you planning to come along, Ambassador?" Jaina asked.

Yfra made a sour frown, then covered her expression with a cough. "I'm afraid not, young lady. I've terribly important work to attend to. My, you can't imagine the responsibilities I deal with. The Hapes Cluster has sixty-three worlds, with hundreds upon hundreds of different governments and thousands of cultures. Ta'a Chume is a very powerful woman, and we all have so much to do in the absence of Tenel Ka's parents." Yfra clasped her clawlike hands together. "You children ought to enjoy your younger years, while people like me take care of the difficult work."

She shooed them away. "Run along now. Down in the docking bay you'll find the speeder I programmed. It's completely safe, I assure you. I've input a simple loop course that will take you out beyond the reef into the open ocean and then back here by nightfall. I've even seen to it that you have a basket of food, so you can enjoy a meal together while you're out." She drew a deep breath and smiled her insincere smile. "I'm sure you'll have a wonderful time."

Jacen studied the ambassador, trying to determine whether or not to be suspicious. He certainly understood how time-consuming the demands of government could be, since his mother was a Chief of State herself. He also thought of how restless the four companions had been for the past day.

"Blaster bolts! Let's go out and have a good time," he said. "It'll be great to be away from the watching eyes of parents and escorts and ambassadors. I promise you we're going to have fun."

Tenel Ka nodded seriously. "This is a fact." Then she gave him one of the most remarkable gifts Jacen had ever received.

She smiled at him.

The wavespeeder roared across the sea, bouncing and thumping as it crossed the troughs and crests like a wheeled vehicle traveling at high speed across a heavily rutted road. Though the autopilot followed a predetermined course, Jaina and Lowie each took turns at the wheel guiding the rudder, seeing just how far the autopilot would let them deviate from its course. Lowbacca let out a happy-sounding bleat.

Em Teedee said, "Master Lowbacca observes that this vehicle bears some similarity to his own T-23 skyhopper."

Jaina looked at the ginger-furred Wookiee. "Reminds me more of the controls of the *Millennium Falcon*. You and I wouldn't have any problem piloting this thing, Lowie," she said. Lowbacca rumbled in agreement.

The wavespeeder took them away from the rough foamy

waters around the reef, on which the isolated fortress towered like a citadel overlooking the blue-green ocean of Hapes.

Jacen sat back and talked with Tenel Ka as they let themselves be lulled by the reflected sunlight and the hypnotic undulation of the waves. "Hey, Tenel Ka," he said tentatively. "I've got a great joke—listen. Which side of an Ewok has the most fur?"

Tenel Ka looked at him seriously. "I have never considered the question."

"The *outside*! Get it?"

"Jacen, why do you so often tell me jokes?" she asked. "I do not believe I ever laugh at them."

Jacen shrugged. "Hey, I was just trying to cheer you up."

Tenel Ka threw him an odd glance. "You think I need cheering up?"

When he answered her, Jacen noticed that he had a difficult time keeping his eyes away from the healed pinkish stump of her arm. "Well, you just seemed kind of quiet and serious."

Tenel Ka raised her eyebrows. "Am I not always quiet and serious?"

Jacen forced a laugh. "Yeah, I guess you're right."

Tenel Ka continued, "We have discussed this, Jacen. Please do not assume that I need cheering up, that I am helpless, or that I have somehow turned into a whimpering weakling. I am still a Jedi trainee, and I believe I will still become a Jedi Knight . . . as soon as I figure out how."

Jacen reached over tentatively to rest his fingers on her arm and slid them down until she caught his hand in her strong grip.

"If there's any way I can help you, let me know," he said.

She gave his hand a brief squeeze. "I will."

The wavespeeder cruised around a set of sharp rock points that thrust up from the water. The Dragon's Teeth, Tenel Ka called them. The jagged pinnacles hunched together, and the surging waters spurted between them with a slamming sound, regularly erupting in a geyser of white foam.

The engines roared as the craft turned to skirt the turbulence near the Dragon's Teeth, then picked up speed again, shooting out toward the open waves. Jaina and Lowie studied the course, each making calculations and trying to guess how far the craft might take them before they circled back.

"It's about time for lunch," Jacen said, rummaging through the food baskets and handing out meal packets.

When Lowie roared in agreement, Em Teedee said, "Well, of course, Master Lowbacca—aren't you *always* hungry?" The young Wookiee chuffed with laughter, but did not disagree.

The wind from their passage whipped spray in their faces, and the salty-fresh air made Jacen ravenous. He and his friends ate the self-warming meal packs and filled their cups from a thermal beverage container.

Jaina stared through the wavespeeder's transparisteel windscreen while she munched. She glanced at the course again. "I wonder how far this is going to take us."

Up ahead Jacen noted that the water seemed to have a different color and consistency . . . to be more greenish and rough-looking.

Lowie sniffed, sniffed more deeply, then growled a query. Em Teedee answered, "I couldn't tell you, Master Lowbacca—my scent analyzers can't seem to match this with the appropriate data to provide a clear answer. Salt, of course, iodine . . . and some sort of decomposing biological matter, perhaps?"

Jacen caught it too: a sick, sour stench that clogged the air and weighed it down. "Smells like dead fish."

Tenel Ka narrowed her eyes in concentration. "And rotting seaweed. Something very old is there. Something . . . not healthy."

Jaina scanned their course again. "Well, the wavespeeder's taking us right toward it."

Before anyone else could speak, they cruised into the strange, gelatinous area. The water was covered with leafy, floating seaweed as dense as jungle undergrowth. Thick, rubbery tentacles with long wet thorns glistened in the water. Huge, scarlet flowers as big as Jacen's head opened up in the thickest portions of the morass.

Jacen leaned over the edge of the wavespeeder to get a better look. The center of each fleshy-lipped flower held a cluster of moist blue fruits that made the entire blossom look like a wide-open eye. This impression was heightened when the wavespeeder's passing triggered some sort of reflex and the petals of the floating plants blinked closed like eye-lids squeezing shut.

"Weird," his sister said next to him.

"Interesting," he replied.

Ahead, the tangled mass of spiny seaweed extended as far as they could see. The wavespeeder continued automatically across the undulating surface of the water, and the foul smell grew stronger. The thick stems and fronds of weed twitched, as if moving by themselves, although Jacen decided it must be caused by swirling currents in the water underneath.

Some of the large eye-flowers rose on their stalks and turned in their direction, as if studying them. Jacen shivered and glanced at Jaina. "Uh, then again . . . maybe 'weird' *is* a better word for it," he agreed.

Lowie looked around, moaning uneasily. Jaina met the Wookiee's gaze and bit her lower lip. "Yeah, I've got a bad feeling about where this boat is taking us. I don't know if I want to go any deeper into this seaweed desert."

"But we're stuck with the autopilot, aren't we?" Jacen said. "If you shut it off, how'll we get back?"

The young Wookiee barked an answer at the same time as Jaina replied, "Been keeping an eye on the course. Lowie and I could probably find our way back home. Ought to be pretty easy."

Tenel Ka stood up, scanning the seaweed, as if to remember something. "Jaina is right," she said. "We should return now. To remain here would be unwise."

Jaina and Lowie took over the controls, throttling back while they disengaged the autopilot. As they eased the craft around to head back out of the seaweed, the engine sputtered to a stop.

Since he loved to investigate strange plants and animals, Jacen took the opportunity to lean over the side of the speeder again. He reached down to touch the rubbery, interesting-looking seaweed.

Suddenly, every red eye-flower swiveled to stare at him.

"Whoa!" Jacen said. He waved his hand experimentally, and the flowers turned, attracted by the motion.

Intrigued, he reached for the closest blossom—and a slick tentacle of seaweed whipped up to wrap around his wrist, capturing him in its barbed embrace.

"Hey!" he shouted. Thorns stung his arm. The seaweed began to pull. "Help!"

He grabbed the railing of the wavespeeder with his free hand to keep from being yanked into the mass of ravenous seaweed. The tentacles thrashed wildly now . . . *hungrily*. Other fronds reached up to slap the side of the boat, twining themselves about the rail.

Lowbacca leaped from the nearby pilot station and grabbed his friend's legs just as the tentacle, redoubling its efforts, gave a sharp jerk and pulled Jacen over the railing. He dangled over the water, struggling to free his arm from the seaweed.

Tenel Ka suddenly appeared beside them. Wrapping her legs around the deck rail, one of her throwing knives gripped tightly in her hand, she bent to slash at the tentacle that grasped Jacen's arm. The seaweed cut free with a snap, and in the recoil Lowbacca managed to yank Jacen back onto the deck.

"Blaster bolts!" Jacen cried, wiping blood from the oozing wounds on his hand. "That was close."

But it was just the beginning. With dread, he looked at the water all around them. The seaweed roiled angrily in every direction, as far as the eye could see. Large fronds thrashed into the air, grabbing the deck rails, as if intending to heave the wavespeeder down. The monster had tasted Jacen's blood, and now it had decided that Jedi Knights were exactly what it wanted for lunch.

Another writhing tentacle rose above the boat's side, searching for a target to skewer with its thorns. Tenel Ka leaped in front of the deadly frond, wielding her throwing dagger. She stabbed into the thick stem of seaweed, and a syrupy green ooze gushed out.

The seaweed recoiled, then lashed back, slapping Tenel Ka across the side of the head. A trickle of blood traced a scarlet line down her cheek. Rather than cry out in pain, Tenel Ka chose to respond with her knife, slashing through the coiled weed—and another fat tentacle thumped to the deck.

Jacen shook his injured arm to restore the feeling then grasped the lightsaber clipped at his side. He had not used it in some time, but there was no room for hesitation now—not if he ever intended to be a Jedi Knight . . . not if any of them wanted to get out of this mess alive. He flicked on the emerald-green blade. "I'm not letting some *weed* get the best of me!" he said.

The humming weapon sliced off one of the large tentacles twined around the rail. "Take that," Jacen said. Gray fumes burned his eyes as the chunk of severed seaweed fell away.

Out in the water the tentacles thrashed. Now they seemed to be in pain. The scarlet eye-flowers blinked and gyrated furiously. The smell of seared vegetables and saltwater filled the air.

"I'm getting us out of here," Jaina called from the controls, restarting the engines. But grasping tentacles held them in place, and the wavespeeder could not break loose.

Roaring, Lowbacca ignited his own blazing lightsaber and held it with both hands, a glowing bludgeon of molten-bronze light.

Larger stems rose now from the deeper water, each with a pair of serrated shells on the end, like vicious pincers ready to tear apart prey. The tentacles writhed and clacked their sharp edges together, looking for something to bite into.

Jaina pushed hard on the controls. The wavespeeder's engines whined as it strained against the grasping tentacles.

Lowie raced to the rail. Bellowing a warning, he swept down with his lightsaber blade again and again, slicing through the seaweed that still held their craft.

"Oh, do be careful, Master Lowbacca—here comes another one!"

Grunting a reply, Lowie slashed at the tentacle, and the little translating droid said, "Excellently done, Master Lowbacca! And it's *quite* a comfort to hear you would rather I didn't wind up as an appetizer for a mass of salivating seaweed."

Tenel Ka turned to fend off an attack from one of the sharp-shelled tentacles. She slashed with her knife, but one of the clamshell pincers clenched the point of her dagger with a loud click. The razor-edged shells clacked again, pushing to reach closer to her face.

Then Jacen was there, chopping the tentacle away with his brilliant green energy blade. He flashed Tenel Ka a roguish grin. "Just wanted to keep the score even!"

"My thanks, Jacen," she said.

Lowie hacked with his blade, severing the last of the seaweed tentacles holding the boat. The wavespeeder broke loose and lurched away while thorny fronds writhed and lashed out, struggling to recapture their prize.

As quickly as she could, Jaina pushed the wavespeeder to its highest velocity, roaring over the twisted weed. The malevolent eye-flowers stared at them. Other thrashing tentacles rose up, but the seaweed seemed unable to respond fast enough.

Jacen gripped his emerald-bladed lightsaber, ready. This thing was more than a plant. It was . . . something sentient, something that could *respond*. He used the Force, hoping to calm it, make it leave them alone. "I can't find its brain," he said. "It seems to be all reflexes. All I can sense is that it's hungry, *hungry*."

"Yeah, well it's going to stay hungry a while longer," Jaina said.

"Yes, indeed! I agree wholeheartedly," Em Teedee answered.

Moments later they were out into open water again. Jaina and Lowie plotted their new course, made the appropriate calculations, and manually set the wavespeeder's direction to take them back to the Reef Fortress.

Glancing over at Tenel Ka to make sure she wasn't hurt, Jacen was surprised to see her wearing a calm and satisfied expression as she slid her throwing dagger back into its sheath at her waist. She seemed more alive and confident now than he had seen her at any time since their fateful lightsaber duel on Yavin 4.

"We are fine warriors," Tenel Ka said. "There is nothing like a physical challenge to make the day more relaxing."

Lowbacca gave a low grunt. Em Teedee bleeped, but refrained from articulating a comment. Jaina looked at Tenel Ka in surprise, but Jacen laughed. "Yeah, we *are* quite a team, aren't we? Real young Jedi Knights."

Tenel Ka helped Jacen bind up the minor wounds on his arm, and he applied some salve from the wavespeeder's emergency medkit to the stinging cut on her cheek. "I do not believe Ambassador Yfra had this in mind when she sent us out for a day of recreation," she said, "but I found it enjoyable nevertheless."

Lowbacca growled and pointed toward the navigation console. "Oh, dear! Master Lowbacca suggests that it might, perhaps, be premature to feel safe and comfortable quite yet," Em Teedee translated. "You see, he hypothesizes that this wavespeeder was purposely sabotaged."

"What do you mean?" Jacen asked. "Those numbers don't mean anything to me."

"I think he means *this.*" Jaina nodded down at the console, indicating the preprogrammed course coordinates. "The autopilot was set to take us into the middle of that killer seaweed—with no return course!"

17

THE GURGLING, SHUSHING sound of gentle waves lapping against stone docks and anchored boats filled the cave grotto. With each breath, Tenel Ka drew comfort from the salty smells and the cool, solid rock around her. Sitting with bare, crossed legs, using a Jedi calming technique to help herself think clearly, she let her gaze drift across each of her friends.

Jaina, head under the control panel and feet high in the air, checked the wiring of the wavespeeder's directional controls. Lowbacca tinkered with the navigational computer from above, handing Jaina tools as she asked for them. Tenel Ka felt a pang of loss as she watched her two friends working with such confidence and agility, completely unconscious of how easy it was for them to use either one hand or the other.

Jacen lay stomach down on a ledge beside Tenel Ka, his right hand reaching deep into the water while the fingers of his left teased the surface, trying to lure a glowing amphibious creature close enough to grasp it.

"Hand me that hydrospanner, would you, Lowie?" Jaina said in a muffled voice. "I need to take this access plate off." Without looking up from his work, the Wookiee plucked the tool from the case behind him with one nimble-fingered hand and passed it to Jaina.

It is so simple with two arms, Tenel Ka thought. As quickly as the jealousy rose within her, she squelched it, chiding herself for being irrational. Even if she still had both hands, she might not have been able to do the things Lowbacca could do with his long, limber arms. He used everything he had, body and mind, to the best of his ability. Just as Jacen and Jaina did.

Just as Tenel Ka always had.

Was she still that same determined person, using her skills and abilities to their fullest, she wondered, or was that person gone now that she had lost her left arm?

She scowled at the thought. If the missing limb was the only thing that bothered her, then surely she could have accepted the biosynthetic replacement her grandmother offered. . . . So perhaps the injury itself was not her primary problem, after all.

Tenel Ka noticed then that Jacen had propped himself up on his elbows and had turned to look at her, his eyes serious. "Hey, you fought really well out there yesterday, against that killer seaweed."

"You mean for a girl with only one arm?" Tenel Ka said bitterly.

"I . . . no, I—" Jacen's cheeks turned crimson and he looked away. His voice was low when he spoke again. "Sorry. All I remembered was you fighting that plant. I didn't even think about your missing arm—it didn't slow you down a bit."

Tenel Ka flinched as if he had slapped her. He was right, she realized: she had not fought like some weak, pitiable invalid. Instinctively, she had battled with everything in her repertoire, drawing on all of her resources. She had truly been *herself*, using every weapon at her disposal.

"Do not be sorry, Jacen," she said. "Your words were meant kindly. It is I who must apologize." She thought again of the battle, musing over what she had accomplished. "I might have fought better, though, if I—"

"If you had had your other arm?" Jacen finished for her. "Hey, *I* might have fought better if I'd had a blaster cannon, but I didn't. I just did my best."

"No." Tenel Ka looked at him in surprise. "I meant to say, I might have fought better had I used a lightsaber."

With a hesitant smile, Jacen looked up at her again. "Yeah . . . you're pretty good with a lightsaber. Of course, you're pretty good at a lot of things."

This was a fact, she thought in wonderment. She was indeed good with a lightsaber. *Still*. And she was also still a good swimmer, fighter, runner. But she had stopped believing in herself, stopped using every portion of her body and mind

to their fullest ability. These things were an integral part of the
person Tenel Ka had always prided herself in being—and *that*
was what she had been missing since the accident.

"Thank you, my friend," she said. "I had begun to forget
who I was."

He dazzled her with one of his famous lopsided grins.
"Hey, if it was as dangerous to be *me* as it is to be *you*, I might
try to forget who I was, too."

"There, that ought to do it." Jaina's voice was loud and
clear as she climbed out of the wavespeeder. Lowbacca
growled and gesticulated.

"Yep," Jaina agreed. "Sabotage, no doubt about it." With
her usual directness, Jaina looked at Tenel Ka and asked,
"Any possibility your grandmother could be behind this?"

Jacen gulped. The thought had not occurred to him. "Your
grandmother? She wouldn't try—!"

Tenel Ka considered the question seriously. "No," she said
at last. "Had that been my grandmother's intention, she would
have . . . disposed of me long before you arrived." Lowbacca
gave an interrogative growl, and Tenel Ka continued. "Do not
misunderstand me. I believe her capable of murder—but I
also *sense* that her intention is to keep me from danger, to protect me, whether I become a queen or a Jedi."

Lowbacca growled a reply, and Em Teedee said, "Master
Lowbacca points out—and quite rightly, I might add—that
with Ta'a Chume traveling back and forth between here and
the Fountain Palace, as she did today, she can hardly be
counted on to provide protection."

"Well, she did leave some guards on duty," Jaina said.

"And Ambassador Yfra," Jacen added, rolling his eyes.
"Oh boy."

Jaina bit her lower lip. "Yfra's the one who suggested we
go out in the wavespeeder, you know."

Lowbacca barked a comment. "Not to mention the fact that
she claims to have programmed the wavespeeder herself,"
Em Teedee supplied. "Oh, my!"

Tenel Ka, who had never trusted Ambassador Yfra, made

no comment as her friends voiced their suspicions. In the distance she could hear the sound of the large Hapan Water Dragon approaching. "Perhaps it would be safest for the moment to trust no one," she suggested.

Jaina and Lowbacca agreed.

"And maybe we'd better stay as far away from Ambassador Yfra as possible," Jacen added.

Just then, the royal yacht floated into the grotto on a wafer-thin cushion of air. Tenel Ka's grandmother stood at the helm. Ta'a Chume brought the Hapan Water Dragon to a complete stop near one of the stone piers and climbed out onto the dock while her guards secured the craft.

Stepping forward to greet her grandmother, Tenel Ka tried to sense any harmful intentions the matriarch might have. The only emotions she picked up, however, were weariness, frustration, and a sense of grim determination.

"We had one of the bomb conspirators in our grasp today," her grandmother said in a tired voice, "but before I managed to question her, she was poisoned." Ta'a Chume shook her head. "She was under guard the entire time. I don't see how an assassin was able to get to her so quickly."

"You appear to require rest, Grandmother," Tenel Ka said, trying not to seem unduly concerned at the former queen's haggard appearance. "Perhaps you should not conduct this investigation yourself."

Ta'a Chume's eyes narrowed shrewdly. "For decades I ruled the entire Hapes Cluster by myself." The woman sighed and seemed to relent. "But perhaps you are right. I will send Ambassador Yfra back to the mainland to continue the search."

Tenel Ka bit her tongue to keep from voicing her suspicions that Yfra might sabotage the investigation rather than help it. But at least such an assignment would get the possibly murderous ambassador away from the Reef Fortress. Far away.

18

BY NOW ZEKK considered his lightsaber an old friend.

Though he had not taken the time or care to build his own weapon, he practically lived with the scarlet beam. He knew how to make it dance against imaginary enemies. He had fought and defeated every simulated monster the computers could portray in the training room. He had slain mynocks, Abyssins, krayt dragons, wampa ice monsters, piranha beetles, and hordes of angry Tusken Raiders.

In one battle he had even felled a ferocious rancor with his lightsaber. After that difficult victory, Zekk wished he could have watched the reaction of his rival Vilas, who seemed so enamored of the hideous beasts.

Now Zekk strode beside Brakiss as the Master of the Shadow Academy led him down corridors toward the station's central hub. Busy with his training, Zekk had never thought to venture here before. No longer an underconfident and overwhelmed trainee, Zekk walked in his full leather armor with ease, lightsaber at his side, as if he were almost Brakiss's equal.

The Shadow Academy Master seemed quiet and withdrawn, though. The perfectly chiseled features of his handsome face were set in an unreadable mask, his forehead showing just a trace of a frown.

Zekk cleared his throat, finally curious enough to speak. "Master Brakiss, I sense . . . uneasiness in you. You haven't told me about this next exercise. Is there something I should know?"

Brakiss paused and fixed the young man with a calm, piercing gaze. "You are about to face your most difficult trial, Zekk. Everything depends on this. You must demonstrate how talented you truly are."

Zekk lifted his chin and drew a deep breath, flaring his

nostrils. His hand moved instinctively to his lightsaber. "I'm ready for anything."

They reached a thick metal door, and Brakiss punched in a code that opened pneumatic locks. The heavy hatch opened slowly, revealing a small air-lock chamber and a second sealed metal door blocking the other side.

Brakiss said, "Trust in your abilities, Zekk. Feel the Force."

Zekk nodded solemnly. "As always, Master Brakiss. I will pass your test. But why is this so important? Why should you be so concerned?"

Brakiss gestured the young man inside the chamber. Zekk entered and stood waiting, but Brakiss remained outside. "Because it will be a fight to the death," he said, then slammed the door, locking Zekk inside.

Within the echoing airlock chamber, Zekk waited. Master Brakiss's words reverberated in his mind. The doors remained sealed, and he forced himself to breathe calmly, though he felt claustrophobic and trapped. Drawing his trusted lightsaber, he gripped it until his knuckles turned white, but he did not yet turn on the blade.

The seconds pounded by, and still the other door didn't open. Fear swelled within him, but he pushed it aside. A Jedi had no place for fear; no reason to fear. The Force was in all things, and the dark side was his ally.

Still, although Zekk had defeated ferocious creatures in the simulation chamber, those opponents had been mere phantoms. He knew that many more dangerous things might happen in a real battle with a real opponent.

He looked at the inner door, wondering if he should hack it open with his lightsaber and force his way free. He needed to see what lurked on the other side. Was this perhaps part of the test? How long should he wait?

Patience, he told himself. He began to count to a hundred—but before he reached ten, the automatic locks on the inner door gave a thump that vibrated through the metal wall. The door swung open by itself.

Zekk felt a disorienting lurch as he stepped out into well-lighted *nothingness*. . . . The floors and ceilings and walls spun about in a blur until he finally realized that he had tumbled into a chamber where the artificial gravity had been turned off—the zero-gravity arena at the hub of the Shadow Academy! He floated free in the open air of the spherical chamber, with no sense of down or up, with nothing to stop his motion.

Zekk's stomach gave a lurch, but he drew a deep breath and concentrated on not throwing up. He focused on the images around him, trying to snatch answers from the briefest glimpses. Grasping the hilt of his lightsaber, he slowed his weightless tumbling and balanced himself. Only then did he notice the seats and standing areas that studded the walls of the chamber, the dozens of noisy onlookers, the balconies pasted on at haphazard angles to accommodate spectators in zero gravity.

Stormtroopers stood in ranks, gripping the balcony rails. The other students at the Shadow Academy sat all around, ready to watch the spectacle. He stiffened, wondering just how difficult this test was going to be. What had Brakiss meant? What was Zekk supposed to do now?

Boulders like miniature asteroids floated in the center of the open arena, along with metal boxes, small cargo containers, and artificial geometrical constructions. Long durasteel pipes drifted free. Zekk could make no sense of the random mix of large and small objects.

Suddenly he understood: they were obstacles.

On the curved wall at the far side of the arena, Zekk saw the clear blister of an observation dome. With his sharp eyesight he spotted figures inside, figures he recognized: the silver-robed figure of Brakiss; the intimidating Nightsister Tamith Kai, with her voluminous ebony hair and her black-spined cape; and the black-armored figure of Qorl the TIE pilot.

Master Brakiss leaned forward and spoke into a voice amplifier. His words boomed through the amphitheater, and all background noise faded.

"You are all here to witness the selection of a leader for our new Dark Jedi trainees—a leader who shall be the first general of our Shadow Academy forces when the Second Imperium makes its grand foray to reclaim the galaxy. Here, before you, we will witness the great battle."

On the other side of the chamber, where the view was partially blocked by drifting obstacles, another air-lock opened, and a dark figure emerged. Because of the floating debris, Zekk couldn't see who it was.

Brakiss continued, "This will be a duel to the death between Zekk"—he paused, but none of the students cheered; they knew better, for they would have to follow whoever the victor of this contest might be—"and Vilas!"

Zekk turned, keeping his lightsaber handle in front of him as he faced the thick-browed young man from Dathomir, Tamith Kai's most powerful trainee. Vilas held his ignited lightsaber ready for the duel.

Vilas pushed off from the far wall and flew toward the obstacles at the center. Zekk switched on his weapon and did the same, moving to meet his opponent in the open space. Zekk's heart pounded, and he realized that despite his anxiety, this was a battle he had longed for. How many times since he'd come to the Shadow Academy had Vilas been his rival? After today there would be no question as to who the greater student was.

Vilas shouted in his mocking, oily voice, "If you surrender now, young trash collector, I may only cripple you." He laughed. Zekk felt himself flush. Norys or one of the other Lost Ones must have told Vilas their derogatory nickname for him. *Trash collector.*

Zekk reached the floating debris and found a pitted oblong stone, an iron-hard meteorite. He grasped it. "If you think victory is going to be *that* easy, Vilas, I'll defeat you before you can blink!"

Zekk hurled the stone with all his strength. In zero gravity the meteorite shot toward the other Dark Jedi—but the equal and opposite reaction after he threw the stone surprised Zekk, and he found himself tumbling backward from the momentum. He slammed headfirst into one of the floating metal cargo containers. A flash of bright pain burst inside his skull. His ears rang. He cleared his vision just in time to see Vilas easily nudge himself out of the path of the flying rock.

Vilas laughed. "Is that the best you can do, trash collector?"

Zekk realized he had been foolish. He concentrated, using the abilities he had recently acquired. Since Vilas was no longer looking at the stone, Zekk used the Force to yank it back toward his enemy. The rock didn't have enough distance to build up much speed, but it struck a sharp blow to Vilas's shoulder. The other young man cried out, rebounding from the impact.

Zekk found himself floating out of control, unable to move where he wanted. He couldn't swim through the air, and he felt entirely disoriented. The walls spun around him. Finally, his feet pressed against the side of a drifting cargo container, and he propelled himself toward Vilas again. His lightsaber drew a fiery streak through the air as he plunged forward.

Vilas was ready for him, though, his glowing energy blade held up as he spun forward. The two opponents approached like colliding cannon balls.

Zekk swung, and Vilas met his lightsaber with his own. The blades clashed and sparked. Bolts of electricity splashed off in random directions. Then Zekk shot past while Vilas scrambled in the empty air, trying to pursue.

Zekk tried to locate one of the floating obstacles for something else to bounce off of—but suddenly Jedi instinct warned him to twist out of the way. In that instant, Vilas came flying by, his lightsaber slashing and humming through the air. Zekk contorted as if leaping backward over a low fence—but not quite fast enough. His enemy's fiery weapon skimmed too close, nicking Zekk's prized leather armor and leaving a smoking gash.

When Vilas turned with a hoot of victory, Zekk felt anger boil up from the depths of his mind, allowing him to draw more strongly on the dark side of the Force. Reaching out into the floating debris, he grabbed a pyramidal greenhouse module and smashed the massive object into Vilas with enough force to shatter its transparisteel panes.

As Vilas reeled, he chopped with his lightsaber to cleave the greenhouse module in half. The two smoldering portions tumbled in opposite directions.

His face contorted with rage, Vilas kicked off of one of the floating segments and hurtled toward Zekk, who waited with his lightsaber held low. Vilas made ready to swipe his blade across the space where Zekk was. Zekk knew that if their blades clashed again, the momentum would send them both tumbling out of control. Just as Vilas drew back his lightsaber for a mighty blow, Zekk used the Force to give himself a sharp shove—*away*.

Vilas swept out with full force—and the energy blade buzzed through empty air. Because nothing had stopped the stroke of his sword, Vilas spun about like a slow tornado, tumbling and disoriented.

Zekk saw his opportunity to buy time. He shot up behind one of the larger meteoroids hanging in the center of the weightless arena and plastered himself to the rock surface, pressing his back against the rough stone.

He could hide here for a moment, and then come back fighting.

Inside the arena's observation blister, Qorl remained standing while Brakiss and Tamith Kai both sat in padded chairs, watching their respective champions and hoping for a personal victory. Qorl tried to hide his uneasiness, but could not divert his attention from the two talented young opponents fighting viciously out in the zero-gravity chamber.

Tamith Kai's eyes blazed with violet fire as she fixed upon

the battle. She spoke out of the corner of her wine-dark mouth, mocking Brakiss. "Your boy has no chance," she said. "Vilas is much more ruthless. I have trained him. Vonnda Ra has trained him. Even Garowyn has trained him. That young man is the culmination of our efforts on Dathomir. Why bother with this wasteful contest? Just give Vilas command of the new Dark Jedi."

Brakiss sat, exuding outward calm, though Qorl could tell from the subtle reflexive expressions on his face each time the battle reached a new peak that this duel had filled the Shadow Academy Master with tension.

"Ah, Tamith Kai," he said, "you forget that *I* trained young Zekk. That counts for more than all the schooling of all your Nightsisters put together."

Tamaith Kai tore her gaze away from the contest and glared at him. She gave a derisive snort.

"I think," Qorl said, "that Tamith Kai has a point. This type of contest is an utter waste—no matter what the outcome, we still lose our second-best trainee, someone far superior to any of the others we keep."

"This is a different kind of contest," Brakiss said, as if explaining to one of his students. "Those other trainees know their places and will follow orders without second thoughts. These two, though . . . each thinks he is best. But only one can command. Only one can be the greatest warrior. If we allowed the loser to live, he would always resent the rule of the other—perhaps even try to undermine his authority. No, it is better that we see who is the stronger."

Tamith Kai agreed. "Yes. It is good for the other Jedi trainees to see one of their number die. Only then will they understand the depth of our convictions . . . and realize that the Second Imperium may demand the supreme sacrifice of them, as well." Brakiss nodded.

Qorl made no answer. He did not wish to argue with his two superiors. Obviously, both Brakiss and Tamith Kai believed in the process; who was he to question it? And even if one of the two contestants out there were to forfeit the battle in hopes of saving his life, it would be a terrible blow to morale. *Surrender is betrayal*, after all. Qorl leaned forward to watch the struggle.

But he still thought it a wasteful exercise.

Zekk tried to catch his breath. He couldn't hide for long, of course—not in front of so many cheering spectators, who were growing more and more enthralled as the battle grew more vicious. His hands were slippery with sweat, and he knew he couldn't afford to lose his weapon at the wrong moment during this battle. He would have to be alert and aggressive. Just to be certain, he locked his lightsaber in the ON position and cast about in his mind for a plan that might let him take out Vilas once and for all.

Then, behind him through the rock, he heard a crackling sound and instinctively threw himself away just as Vilas's blazing blade sliced completely through the meteoroid, leaving each chunk of tumbling rock with a flat edge that was so smooth it looked like a molten mirror.

If he hadn't moved at the last instant, the lightsaber would have bisected Zekk just as it had the meteoroid!

He turned in the air to see Vilas hurtling toward him, slashing again. Zekk raised his blade to meet the other lightsaber, and their edges crossed in a shower of sparks. They pushed against each other, but found nothing for traction in weightlessness. They drifted aimlessly, blades locked, jaws clenched, glaring defiantly into each other's eyes.

When Vilas's eyes were drawn for a moment to a point just behind Zekk's shoulder, Zekk barely had time to wonder what his opponent was doing before a drifting metal rod crashed into the small of his back, sending an avalanche of pain along his spine. He gasped, then released his held breath in a rush. His lightsaber, still blazing, tumbled out of his hand.

The crowd roared as Zekk flailed in the air, trying to move away from his opponent. With an evil grin, Vilas charged toward him. Zekk could not reach his lightsaber in time: it spun like a fiery glowrod toward one of the balconies, where spectators scrambled to get out of the way.

With no weapon at hand, Zekk reached beside him to grasp the still-drifting metal rod. He grabbed the pole and swung it through the air with such speed that it made a sighing sound. But, in zero gravity, he was on the other end of the pivot point, and he began to spin around like a baton.

Vilas slashed at the oncoming metal pipe, slicing off half a meter of it. Zekk continued to spin, and Vilas swung again. The blow went wide. Zekk jabbed with the superheated end of the severed pipe, and the hot tip burned through Vilas's armor, searing his ribs.

Vilas yowled in pain and grabbed the pipe himself, flinging it sideways and using the momentum to toss Zekk free. Zekk sailed across space, rebounded off one of the floating meteoroids, and reached out with his mind to call his lightsaber back to him. The weapon stopped its spiraling plunge toward the wall, reversed itself, and zipped into his grasp.

When Zekk turned and looked for Vilas again, he found that his opponent had vanished. The brooding young man from Dathomir was hiding, just as Zekk had. Zekk narrowed his eyes and opened his mind to the Force, listening, trying to sense Vilas among the obstacles.

The noise of the crowd gave him no hints . . . but somehow he was able to hear a faint *tink-tink-tink*, coming from behind two joined cargo containers. Zekk struck out for that point. He didn't know what Vilas was doing, but he wouldn't give the other young man time to complete his plan.

Zekk used the Force to direct himself toward the noise, but when he grabbed the edge of the cargo container and pulled himself around it, his lightsaber at the ready, he found only a small chunk of rock invisibly tapping itself against the metal wall. Vilas had managed to distract him, creating a diversion with the Force, while he hid elsewhere and prepared to strike—

With a sudden powerful premonition, Zekk whirled. Vilas

had to be coming for him. Using his instinct, his sense with the Force, Zekk acted without thinking.

Before he could see, before he could consider what he was about to do, he pulled back to strike with his lightsaber, putting everything he had behind one powerful stroke.

In that instant, through the blaze of light smearing across his eyes, he saw Vilas launch himself out of the cargo container, wearing a predatory grin. He had hidden in ambush, hoping to kill the unsuspecting Zekk.

But Zekk had outsmarted him.

Zekk's slashing blade encountered resistance as Vilas flew across his path. Then, with a flash of smoke and a terrible stench, the bright energy blade cleaved through flesh and bone, cauterizing as it went. Vilas made a choking, gurgling sound and continued his tumbling flight through the air—but now his body moved in two separate, smoking pieces.

Vilas's death rattle was swallowed up in the triumphant roar of the crowd.

Zekk stared down at his pulsating scarlet lightsaber, too horrified at what he had done even to look at the body of Vilas. The spectators still cheered. This had been no simulation, he realized. *This was real.*

Zekk knew he had taken one giant step farther down the road to the dark side. He raised his head, speechless, as the voice of Brakiss echoed through the zero-gravity chamber, drowning out the praise of the onlookers.

"Excellent, Zekk! I knew you could do it."

Tamith Kai's somewhat petulant voice came next. "My congratulations, young Lord Zekk."

Then, to his absolute amazement, overwhelming even his shock at the violence he had committed, the air in the center of the arena shimmered until an ominous image engulfed the drifting obstacles. The huge hooded head of the Emperor himself offered its grim congratulations directly to Zekk.

"You have won this battle, Zekk," the Emperor said in a voice so filled with cold power it could freeze blood. Zekk drew in a quick gasp. All of the other trainees watched, absorbing their Great Leader's words.

"You are my Darkest Knight, Zekk. I have chosen you to personally lead my Jedi into battle against Skywalker's Jedi academy."

19

THE MUFFLED THUMP of an explosion in the middle of the night was already fading by the time Tenel Ka reacted and sat up, suddenly wide awake.

She strained her ears, but heard nothing more. She had slept fitfully a few times since coming to the thick-walled Reef Fortress—but she had never woken up without cause. Had she really heard the sound of a blast? She couldn't be sure. Perhaps it had merely been a part of her uneasy dream. . . .

Around her, the room was dark and shadowy, lit only by the metallic silver glow of moonlight spilling in from the window. The deep darkness was quiet. Too quiet. With a fluid motion Tenel Ka slid off her bed, stood, paused to listen, then crept forward to the fortress window.

Her skin prickled, but not from cold. She recognized the reaction of her Jedi senses transmitting messages of danger—an indefinable uneasiness that was rapidly growing closer to full-fledged alarm. Something was definitely not right.

Tenel Ka looked out the stone-framed window down to the glossy midnight ocean that stretched into inky blackness. The breakers, capped with moonlight, crashed against the dark reefs. She heard the rushing, hissing ocean—and realized that the sound should not have been so clear.

Where was the background hum of the night perimeter shields?

Leaning forward, Tenel Ka narrowed her eyes to study the

air. A telltale shimmer should have been visible to demonstrate that a protective field surrounded the fortress—but she saw nothing. Then her attention turned to a glimmer of light and a smudge of smoke rising into the air near the generator station.

The shield generator had been destroyed! That meant Reef Fortress now stood unprotected.

Tenel Ka drew back, intending to whirl around and sound the alarm—when a faint motion far below caught her eye. Her heart pounding, all Jedi senses alert, she glanced down to where the steep stone walls blended into the uneven lumps of the reef. A strange camouflaged ship, long and angular, floated just above the waves on repulsorfields.

"Ah. Aha," she said. "Assault craft of some sort." Then she sucked in a sharp breath as she saw figures moving—more than a dozen.

Black, many-legged creatures like large insects swarmed up the base of the fortress—*and scaled the sheer walls effortlessly.* Tenel Ka instantly recognized the tactics, the black body armor, the skittering, segmented movements. Her stomach tied itself into an icy knot, and adrenaline shot through her veins. The Bartokks, deadly humanoid insects, were legendary for their relentless and resourceful assassin squads.

Tenel Ka raced over to the comm unit mounted on a stone wall near her door and slapped the alarm button to sound a general call to arms—but nothing happened. She pushed the alarm firmly once again with her hand, and found that the entire warning system was dead.

"Lights," she called, but her room remained dark. All power, including backup generators, had been cut off to Reef Fortress.

They were in deep trouble.

Bending over and using the stump of her arm to hold the buckle in place, she took a moment to fasten her utility belt over the supple reptilian armor in which she slept. Tenel Ka pulled her hair back with a thong, letting the long red-gold braids drape like a crown around her head. It was time for action. She would have to rouse everyone.

Tenel Ka rushed down the corridor and pounded on the door to Jacen's room. Lowbacca bellowed from his own chamber and flung the door open. Jaina hurried out of the gadget room.

"What's going on?" Jacen asked, dragging unsteady fingers through his sleep-tousled hair.

"Something . . . dangerous," Jaina said, already sensing the situation. "A serious threat."

Lowbacca roared, his wildly disheveled fur standing out in every direction as he attempted to strap on the glossy white belt made of syren-plant fiber. "Emergency?" Em Teedee said. "Perhaps we are all simply overreacting."

"No. We are not," Tenel Ka answered. "The power to the fortress has been cut off, and our defensive force field no longer functions. The generating station has been destroyed. We are currently under attack by a Bartokk assassin squad."

Jacen shuddered. "Hey, I've heard of them. Insects, right? And they all work together as a hive, to assassinate their assigned target."

Tenel Ka nodded. "They are fearsome mercenaries, fighting as one organism. Once given a target, they continue to fight until the very last member of their hive has been killed—or until their victim lies dead."

"I'm sure that's terribly efficient," Em Teedee observed, "but they certainly don't sound very friendly."

Jaina frowned, looking determined. "Well then, what are we waiting for?" She retrieved her lightsaber from her quarters while Jacen ran back into the aquarium room to fetch his weapon, too.

Lowbacca, his lightsaber already at his waist, roared in challenge. "Now, Master Lowbacca, getting delusions of grandeur can be hazardous to your health," Em Teedee said. Lowie just snarled, the black streak across the top of his head bristling with anger.

Tenel Ka stepped into the Wookiee's room, marched to the

far wall, and yanked free the jagged ceremonial spear mounted there as ornamentation. Holding the spear one-handed, she said, "We must fight them."

Suddenly they heard a crash and a shout, then brief weapons fire from the far end of the corridor that led to the isolated tower containing the matriarch's quarters.

"My grandmother!" Tenel Ka said. "She must be their primary target."

Still holding the spear, she raced down the cold flagstones of the dim hall. All glowpanels had gone out, and only the moonlight streaming through the corridor windows lit her way—but Tenel Ka had known these twists and turns since childhood.

Growling, Lowbacca sprinted after her while the twins ran at top speed to keep up. Jacen and Jaina ignited their lightsabers, and the brilliant energy glow splashed ahead, shedding enough light for them to see. Tenel Ka heard more shouts, a loud scuffle, and her grandmother's voice calling for help.

"We must hurry," Tenel Ka said, putting on an extra burst of speed. Someone had to have contracted the assassin squad to remove the former queen, she reasoned. Was it Ambassador Yfra? Once Ta'a Chume was dead—and with Tenel Ka's parents gone—the ambassador probably would not consider a one-armed girl in lizard hide much of a threat to her power. She could easily take over the rulership of the Hapes Cluster.

While the idea enraged her, Tenel Ka could not afford to think about it at the moment.

Just ahead, a couple of black, clattering insects emerged from side corridors. The Bartokks, as tall as Tenel Ka, stood on two powerful legs and had a central pair of arms at their waists for grasping and manipulating objects, while their upper set of arms ended in long, hooked claws like scythes used to harvest grain. The serrated edges of the scythe claws swept from side to side, with razor edges that could clip an enemy to pieces.

The Bartokks chittered upon seeing these new and unexpected opponents, but Tenel Ka raced ahead with full momentum. Using all the muscles in her single arm, she jabbed with her spear, plunging it through the body core of the left assassin. Its upper four arms flailed in reflex, trying to bat the weapon out of Tenel Ka's grip—but she twisted the long blade, ripping it sideways. The insect's hard exoskeleton cracked and split open, spilling thick greenish-blue goop onto the stone floor. She yanked the spear free as the Bartokk clattered to the flagstones, its legs still flailing.

Beside her, Lowbacca met the second assassin with a sideways sweep of his lightsaber that sliced the Bartokk into smoking halves that fell twitching to the floor.

The twins rushed up. "Good one," Jacen said, panting. "That's two down."

Tenel Ka spoke over her shoulder as she continued running. "We cannot be certain those two are dead," she said. "And do not forget, the Bartokks have a hive mind. Now all of the assassins—there are usually fifteen in the hive— know we're coming to help my grandmother."

As they skidded around the corner near the armored door to the matriarch's chambers, five more of the insects moved to block their way. Ta'a Chume's two personal guards fought fiercely at the threshold to her chambers, but the remaining Bartokks had nearly succeeded in breaking in.

As the young Jedi Knights ran forward, Bartokk assassins captured both loyal guards outside the matriarch's door and dragged them away. The guards struggled, cried out, then ceased all movement.

Although this capture was intended to free the opening for a fresh assault on the matriarch's chambers, it also created a diversion for Tenel Ka and her friends to plow forward. With their lightsabers ignited, Jacen and Jaina slashed in, chopping the two frontmost Bartokks into quivering bug pieces. Lowbacca barreled into a third assassin, knocking it against the stone wall with such force that its black carapace split open.

"Inside," Tenel Ka shouted. She could hear the matriarch

calling for more guards, but there were none. Instead, four young Jedi Knights charged into her chamber.

"Lowie, help me get this closed," Jaina cried. The lanky Wookiee shoved his shoulder against the armored door as he and Jaina swung it shut against the powerful press of Bartokk arms and snapping claws. Startled, most of the insects jerked back, but then began to push and claw at the entrance again almost immediately. In that instant of surprise, however, the door groaned shut.

"Lock it," Jaina gasped, and Tenel Ka snapped a bolt into place.

Outside, Bartokk assassins pounded, scraping with their razor-edged claws against the doorjamb. The metal door rattled in its frame, and Tenel Ka knew their defenses couldn't last long against the onslaught.

But that was the least of her worries at the moment.

Three Bartokk assassins had been trapped *inside* the chamber with them, and now the ruthless black-shelled insects moved forward, focusing on their main target.

The old matriarch had barricaded herself in a corner and was doing her best to knock the creatures away with a broken piece of furniture. The young Jedi Knights rushed to defend the former queen, but one of the assassins lashed out with its razor claws at them.

Tenel Ka charged forward as the insect killer moved to meet her. She plunged her ornamental spear into it until the tip of her weapon bored all the way through the glossy shell and wedged into a crack between the wall blocks. She left the Bartokk pinned to the wall like a bug in a child's collection. Even so, the creature still writhed and snapped, thrashing to get at them.

Jacen ran forward and with a hissing sweep of his lightsaber, sliced off the multi-eyed head of another assassin as it leapt toward the matriarch.

With a roar, Lowbacca left his post at the rattling door and grasped the remaining Bartokk, lifting it bodily off the floor. Its many sharp arms thrashed as Lowie pushed forward to the high open window and heaved the creature over the ledge. The assassin tumbled nearly thirty meters to splatter on the jagged reef far below.

"Hey!" Jacen said, as the Bartokk he had beheaded, instead of collapsing into twitching death, continued to fight its way toward the alarmed matriarch. "Aren't you supposed to die?"

He slashed again with the lightsaber, this time cutting the legs out from under the headless Bartokk. The insect torso crashed to the floor, but with its remaining limbs it still hauled itself toward Tenel Ka's grandmother. The severed head lay on the flagstones near the wall, staring at its target through faceted eyes, somehow continuing to direct the body.

"These hive-mind assassins," Tenel Ka explained, "their brains are distributed through major nerve networks inside their bodies. Simply cutting off a head won't stop them. The pieces will still attempt to continue their mission."

With another blow from his lightsaber, Jacen chopped the remaining torso in half. "This is getting ridiculous," he said.

Lowbacca marched over to where the severed insect head lay near the wall. Then with great pleasure he stomped down, squashing it as one might step on an annoying beetle.

The wiry old matriarch tossed aside the broken piece of furniture she had been using as a weapon. "I thank you for your efforts to save me, my granddaughter," she said, "but it would seem that this plot is rather extensive. Our entire fortress is overrun, and I see no means of escape."

Across the floor the ichor-dripping pieces of the chopped-up assassin continued to squirm toward the former queen, blindly groping, yet still deadly. The skewered Bartokk hanging from the wall thrashed and flailed, trying to break free from Tenel Ka's spear.

Outside, in the corridors, the rest of the assassin hive hammered without pause against the armored plates of the door. From where Tenel Ka stood, she could see the rivets popping out and blocks crumbling to powder at the edges of the sealed door. The metal began to bend inward. . . .

It certainly wouldn't last much longer.

20

JAINA LOOKED AROUND the dim room where they had barricaded themselves, desperate to find some means of escape. With the hammering of assassins outside the door growing louder and louder, she found it hard to think. Pale moonlight streamed through the window from a deceptively calm sky, bleaching all colors in the room to black and white and gray.

"We have to get out of here somehow," Jaina said.

Tenel Ka nodded grimly. "This is a fact."

Jacen turned to the matriarch. "Hey, if you know of any secret passages that lead out of here, now might be the time to tell us."

"There are none," Ta'a Chume said. "This tower room was designed as a protected chamber, with no secret ways for an assassin to gain entrance. Reef Fortress itself was built to be impregnable."

Jaina snorted. "Maybe you'd better fire your architect."

Tenel Ka felt at her utility belt and removed her grappling hook and the strong fibercord. "I see no better way. We must escape by the same route those creatures used to break into the fortress. Not only must we flee the fortress, we must flee the reef island itself."

"Where can we go, Tenel Ka?" Jacen said. "We're stranded."

"I get it!" Jaina cried, seeing what her friend intended. "We take one of the fast wavespeeders and zoom out across the ocean. It's our best chance."

The stern matriarch went to the window and gazed at the sheer drop. "You mean *climb* down?"

"Yes, Grandmother," Tenel Ka said, setting the grappling hook firmly against the stone of the windowsill. "Unless you'd prefer using your diplomatic skills to negotiate a settlement with the Bartokks."

The matriarch's sharp eyes flashed with determination. "I've never allowed anyone but myself to control my fate—so I suppose falling to my death while escaping would be preferable to waiting around to be killed by giant insects in my own bedchamber. It's agreed, then. We'll try the climb, as you suggest."

Tenel Ka shook her head. "No, we shall *do* the climb. There is no try."

Jaina tugged on the cord. The grappling hook did not budge. "All right, let's get out of here."

Lowbacca blatted a comment and Em Teedee said, "Oh, dear—must I?" At the Wookiee's growled response, the little droid heaved an electronic sigh. "Master Lowbacca believes he would be the most sensible choice to go first—and unfortunately I'm forced to admit that he is correct. Firstly, because he is an experienced climber, and secondly because he is strong and will be able to hold the rope steady for the rest of you once he reaches the bottom."

"Can't argue with your logic," Jaina agreed. "Go ahead."

While Em Teedee twittered about the impending danger, Lowie swung himself over the sill and supported his full weight on the glistening fiber-cord. Then, using his long arms, he lowered himself hand-over-hand down the vertical stone wall. Em Teedee's pitiful moans grew more and more faint until finally Lowie touched down on the rocks below, stood away from the wall, and gave the rope a yank.

"Good," Tenel Ka said.

Persistence finally paid off for the Bartokks, who had continued their relentless battering at the armored door. One of the hinges groaned and popped out of the wall. With a loud creak, a corner of the door bent inward. Cluttering insect assassins thrust their sharp scythe claws through the gap.

"No more time," Tenel Ka said to the twins. "You two go now. The rope will hold both of you."

"We'd better be careful," Jacen said. The door rattled in its frame and the metal screeched, caving in further.

"Guess we can't afford that luxury," Jaina said in a terse voice. "What are we waiting for?" She slipped over the sill, grabbing the fibercord and began rappelling down the slick dark stones.

Jacen came after her. The rope was thin, and the descent treacherous, but they used their Jedi skills to keep their balance and make themselves lighter. At the bottom Lowbacca stood with his feet planted far apart on the rocky reef, holding the rope.

"Excellent climbing, Master Jacen, Mistress Jaina," Em Teedee encouraged. "You're almost here—you can make it!"

Even before they reached bottom, Jaina looked up to see Tenel Ka and her grandmother easing over the sill. The matriarch, unable to grasp the slender cord tightly enough in her old hands, steadied herself with an arm around Tenel Ka's waist. The young warrior girl had looped the rope once around her arm to allow herself more friction to control their descent.

With a firm hold on the fibercord, she slowly leaned backward, letting the strand slip through her fingers as her feet pressed against the outer wall of the fortress. The dangerous climb may have been more difficult and awkward with her handicap, but Tenel Ka did not seem the least bit hesitant. Despite her usual reluctance to use the Force, she took advantage of it this time without reservation.

"Come on, Tenel Ka!" Jacen called.

Before the girl and her grandmother had gotten more than halfway down the rope, though, a loud crash sounded from above. Suddenly swarms of multilegged figures surged to the open window, squealing their triumph.

Jaina heard Tenel Ka shout, "Hold on!" as she doubled her

speed, sliding down the cord so quickly that Jaina was sure she would get a rope burn on her hand and arm.

The Bartokks grabbed the fibercord and sawed at it with their serrated scythe arms.

Tenel Ka slipped down faster, faster.

Suddenly the strand parted. The insectoid assassins above gave a triumphant chitter.

Lowbacca roared and with lightning-fast reflexes dropped the end of the severed rope, held out his arms, and caught the old matriarch as she plunged. Using the Force to control her own fall, Tenel Ka landed heavily on her feet, but without injury.

"Good one, Tenel Ka," Jacen cried. "We made it!"

"Not quite yet," Jaina said, pointing upward. The remaining black Bartokk assassins started to boil through the upper window, crawling headfirst down the vertical stone block.

"We must hurry," Tenel Ka said, pointing toward the grotto. "To the wavespeeders."

At the far edge of the reef, Jaina saw the sharp-edged assault boat from the Bartokk hive near the smoldering wreck of the shield-generator station. For a moment she contemplated taking that craft instead—but when she noticed the knobby alien controls designed for simultaneous use by four claws, she couldn't be sure she or Lowie could pilot such a ship. Their best chance would be to grab one of the smaller wavespeeders.

Ducking under the moss-edged rock of the entrance, they ran into the sea cave: A wavespeeder, tied to the dock closest the entrance, bobbed gently on the water of the grotto.

"Everybody in," Jaina said. "Lowie and I can handle this. Let's just hope its top speed is better than what that assassin craft can manage."

"And that Ambassador Yfra hasn't sabotaged it!" Jacen muttered.

Lowbacca bellowed his agreement. Still dazed after her fall, the grim matriarch shook herself and climbed aboard as Jacen and Jaina hopped over the rail, followed by Tenel Ka.

With a roar, the repulsorlift engines raised the wave-speeder up off the calm waters inside the sheltered cave. Before Tenel Ka had managed to seat herself, Jaina pulled the boat away from the dock, whipped it around, and accelerated through the cave entrance, churning the water into froth beneath them. The wavespeeder shot away from the darkened, overrun Reef Fortress.

Lowbacca, sitting in the navigator's chair, turned his shaggy head to gaze back at the tall citadel with his dark-adapted Wookiee eyes. He growled, stretching out a hairy arm. Jaina risked a glance and saw the insectoid murderers swarming down the tower wall toward their assault craft.

"Better get our head start while we can," Jaina said grimly. She pushed hard against the accelerators, although they were already traveling at maximum speed. The small boat sped out to where the sea grew choppier.

Moments later an ear-splitting mechanical roar erupted behind them. Jacen shouted, and Jaina glanced back to see the Bartokk assault craft pull away from the reef, infested with black insect assassins.

The assault craft's engine thundered like a Star Destroyer in pursuit. "They must have come in using stealth silencers on their engines," Jaina said. "They're at full power now, though—no need to keep quiet." She watched the tactical panel in front of her and swallowed a lump in her throat.

Lowie growled. "Master Lowbacca estimates that they will overtake us within minutes," Em Teedee wailed. "What *are* we to do?"

The ocean was lit only by the twin moons high overhead in the midnight sky. Jaina saw froth ahead as the water surged around a rocky obstacle jutting from the sea—the Dragon's Teeth. "We'll go there," she said, "and try to cause some trouble as they dodge around the rocks. We're smaller, more maneuverable."

"I doubt they'll give up because of a navigation hazard," Jacen said.

"No," Jaina replied, "but we can hope they crash."

The pointed rocks thrust out of the water like jagged spires. Waves crashed against their faces, running like saliva drooling from a krayt dragon's mouth, and rippled around the submerged reefs at the base of the Teeth. The Bartokk assault craft screamed after them.

"Watch the waves—and count," Tenel Ka said, pointing as a plume of white water jetted up between the two sharp rocks. Five seconds later another plume spurted up just as high. "Timing could be our advantage."

Jaina nodded. "I see what you mean. Lowie, I'll need your help on the controls." They slowed just enough to let the assault craft approach them as they headed toward the narrow gap between the treacherous rock spires.

"It's going to be close, Jaina," Jacen said.

"Don't I know it," she agreed. "Okay, punch it, Lowie."

The Wookiee hit the accelerators full force just as the Bartokk assault craft nearly rammed them from behind. The insect assassins waved their clacking arms. One fired a deck-mounted cannon, and the blaster bolt struck the waves, creating a geyser of steam just beside their wavespeeder.

"Whoa," Jaina said as Lowie yowled. "Didn't expect that."

Unconsciously ducking her head as they streaked between the black rocks, she canted the wavespeeder to fit through the narrow gap. The hiss of their passage boomed and echoed, and a fine cold spray splashed them all.

The assault craft charged in behind them. Jaina didn't think the assassins could possibly fit through the narrow opening, but the ship slid into the gap with only a few centimeters of play on either side.

The ocean roiled just as the assault craft spat from the narrow cleft between the rocks. A jet of water rocketed through the gap, shooting out a high-powered plume that catapulted the Bartokk assault craft into the air and spun it end-over-end.

Three assassins toppled overboard and vanished into the churning seas before the assault craft righted itself and crashed back onto the water. The Bartokk pilot wrestled with the controls as Jaina streaked onward at top speed, stretching the gap between them.

Before long, though, the assault craft was hot on their tail again.

Sitting in back, Ta'a Chume recovered enough to reach inside her plush robes and withdraw a tiny holdout blaster. "For what it's worth," the matriarch said, "I'll use this—but it's designed for only two shots."

"What good is a blaster that only has two shots?" Jacen asked.

"The first shot is for an attacker," Tenel Ka's grandmother answered. "The second shot . . . well, sometimes it is preferable not to be taken alive."

Jaina gulped and continued to guide the wavespeeder away from the reef. Waves crashed against the front of their craft, but she couldn't gain any more height from their repulsorlifts. Fortunately, the Bartokk assault craft had sustained some damage in its passage through the Dragon's Teeth, and now the pilot of the impaired vessel had no choice but to hang back.

Pushing the wavespeeder to its redlines, Jaina maintained their lead—but just barely. Another hour went by as they sped over the dark wavetops under the pale light of the moons. The assault craft edged closer and closer.

"Is there any way to get back to civilization, get some help?" Jacen asked.

"Our fortress is extremely isolated—theoretically for our protection—and this wavespeeder travels much too slowly," the old matriarch said. "It would take us many hours to get back. I fear the Bartokks will have taken care of us before then."

"Not if I can help it," Jaina said, gritting her teeth as she diverted them toward a pale patch of water ahead, a wasteland covered with a rough, flattened texture and exuding a spoiled fishy smell. She realized full well where they were going. The coordinates had been familiar, and now she hoped to use her knowledge to their advantage.

Lowbacca, guessing her intention, let out a questioning whine.

"I know what I'm doing, Lowie," Jaina said.

Jacen must have smelled the same thing. He leaned toward his sister in alarm. "You're not actually going into that seaweed field, are you?"

Jaina shrugged. "They'd be crazy to follow us, wouldn't they?"

"The Bartokk assassin hive will follow us to the ends of the planet," Tenel Ka said. "They have no concern for their own danger."

"Good," Jaina said, "then maybe they'll get sloppy."

Suddenly the sound of the engines grew muted as they streaked over the writhing forest of carnivorous seaweed. Just below the hull of their wavespeeder, the weed thrashed in agitation. Clusters of red eye-flowers rose up, keeping a vigilant watch for new prey even in deepest night. The seaweed flickered and snapped, as if it remembered its near miss with the group of young Jedi only days before.

"I sure hope this thing is still hungry," Jacen said. "How about we give it some plant food?"

"As long as it's not us," Jaina responded.

The Bartokk assassins paid no heed to how the sea had changed, intent only on closing the gap between them and their prey.

The matriarch stood at the rear of the wavespeeder, holding her small blaster. "Two shots," she said, pointing her weapon at the approaching boat.

"Target their repulsorpods," Jaina shouted. "That's the only weak spot on a big assault craft like that."

The wavespeeder jostled, but the matriarch took careful aim and fired a high-powered blaster bolt. The streak of energy skimmed the bottom of the pursuing assault craft, leaving the repulsorpod undamaged. The shot reflected off the Bartokks' metal hull and sizzled into the churning seaweed creature.

"No damage," the matriarch said. "One chance left."

"Your shot was not wasted," Tenel Ka said. "Observe the plant."

The seaweed now seemed fully awake and *angry*. Its spined tentacles thrashed in the air and slapped at the craft roaring over its fronds.

The Bartokk assassins approached the wavespeeder, apparently unconcerned that one of their intended victims had just used a blaster. The Bartokk craft fired a return shot with one of its laser cannons, but Jaina, sensing the impending bolt through the Force, rocked the wavespeeder to the left. The blast struck the seaweed again, eliciting a hissing, low-frequency roar from the plant monster.

Ta'a Chume stood again, raised her tiny blaster, and aimed a second and last time.

"May the Force be with you," Tenel Ka murmured.

The matriarch took her final shot. This time the energy bolt struck one of the Bartokk repulsorpods squarely. Though the tiny weapon was not powerful enough to cause great damage, it was enough to throw the pursuing assault craft into a spin.

The stern of the assassins' boat rose up and, as the Bartokk insects scrambled for control, the bow plunged, grazing the ravenous seaweed. Before the pilot could regain stability, a dozen spiked tentacles whipped up to wrap themselves around the rails, snatching at the hull, the repulsorpods, the laser-cannon emplacements. The insect assassins chittered, more in anger than fear, because the hive mind couldn't comprehend its impending death.

Within moments, however, Bartokk assassin legs were flailing as spiked weed tentacles plucked the insects from their stations at the side of the boat and dragged them thrashing beneath the foaming waves. Soon the seaweed had engulfed the entire sharp-edged craft, dragging it under the roiling water.

Pincer-ended tentacles clamped down on hard chitinous shells, and Jaina heard muffled crunching sounds as the seaweed monster snapped exoskeletons apart to reach the tender parts inside. She stared at the water in horrified fascination.

"I think maybe this is our cue to leave," Jacen pointed out, giving his sister a nudge. Lowie roared his agreement.

Bloodred eye-flowers blinked hungrily up at them.

"Okay, what are we waiting for?"

Lowie revved the engines and then accelerated as Jaina guided the wavespeeder back out of the deadly tangle of seaweed.

Ta'a Chume made her way to the front of the wavespeeder. "I can pilot us to safety from here," she said. Jaina gladly relinquished the controls as the former queen headed the craft toward the mainland.

"An excellent shot, Grandmother," Tenel Ka said.

The matriarch nodded and looked with renewed admiration at her granddaughter. "So much for diplomacy."

Some five hours later, the entire bedraggled crew finally hauled themselves into the Fountain Palace.

Ta'a Chume was outraged to find that Ambassador Yfra had already assumed control. Declaring martial law, the ambassador had announced that there would be several hours of mourning over the untimely death of the dear, departed matriarch.

Tenel Ka marched beside her grandmother into the central throne room amidst gasps of horror, delight, and surprise from the guards. The most appalled expression, however, showed on the hardened face of Ambassador Yfra herself.

"Ta'a Chume!" she cried, standing up and trying unsuccessfully to hide the brief storm of anger that clouded her eyes. "You're—you're alive. But how—?"

"Your plot failed, Yfra. Guards, arrest this traitor!"

"On what charge?" Ambassador Yfra said in a reasonable tone, her confidence not yet shaken.

"Plotting to kill the entire royal household. I am only happy that Tenel Ka's parents were absent, for I'm sure they would have been at risk as well."

"Why, Ta'a Chume—I've never shown anything but loyalty to you." Yfra's voice was full of sweetness and offended innocence, though Tenel Ka could sense that she was lying. "How can you make such an accusation?"

"Because you took control. How could you possibly have known we were in danger if you hadn't set up the plot yourself?"

"Well, I—" Yfra blinked. "I simply responded to the distress call sent out from Reef Fortress, of course."

"Ah." The matriarch pointed her long knobby finger and a smile curved her thin wrinkled lips. "Aha! But no distress signal was sent. Your Bartokk assassins blew up our power-generating station. We escaped. This is the first word that has gotten out—but *you* knew." The matriarch nodded confidently. "Yes, you knew."

Before Yfra could sputter another excuse, the guards came forward and took her into custody.

"Oh, she'll be given a fair trial," the matriarch said, "but I think we have more than enough proof—don't you, Tenel Ka?" She raised her eyebrows.

"This is a fact," the young warrior woman replied. "And I believe I have more than enough proof for something else, as well." She stood straight, looking proudly into her grandmother's eyes.

"This adventure has shown me that I am fully recovered from my injuries. I wish to return to Yavin 4."

21

TENEL KA SAT up and looked around with brief disorientation before she remembered where she was. Letting her gray gaze skim across the ancient stone walls, arched doorway, and modest sleeping pallet, she experienced a sense of warmth and safety—and excitement.

It felt right to be back on Yavin 4, in her own student quarters in the Great Temple. She sat back on her pallet and began practicing her new skill—braiding her hair with one hand and her teeth.

Over the past weeks, the wrongness in her life had slowly dissolved, beginning with her parents' safe return to Hapes. Having foiled an attempt on their own lives by Ambassador Yfra's henchwomen, Teneniel Djo and Isolder had hurried back to find their daughter and her grandmother unharmed. They immediately sought out and purged the remaining conspirators from the royal court, while Ambassador Yfra awaited trial.

To Tenel Ka's great surprise, neither of her parents had tried to talk her into wearing a synthetic arm or discontinuing her studies at the Jedi academy. In fact, when she had expressed her desire to continue her training, her mother and father had readily agreed, asking only that she stay to visit with them for a few weeks before returning to Yavin 4.

"I believe you may become a stronger warrior than ever you imagined," Teneniel Djo said. "You have powerful legs, fast reflexes, and you still have your better fighting arm. From what your grandmother tells us, your wits have not been dulled, either."

"And I think you may teach many a future opponent that one cannot judge a warrior's worth by her outward appearance," her father added, hugging her. "Never be ashamed of what you are—or *who* you are."

When Luke Skywalker had returned in the *Shadow Chaser* to take Tenel Ka and the other young Jedi Knights back to Yavin 4, there had been no mistaking her parents' pride. Her mother's final whispered words still echoed through her mind: "May the Force be with you."

Now, after a good night's rest in familiar quarters, Tenel Ka felt ready to take her next step to recovery. She stood and stretched, delighting in the well-controlled response of her muscles.

She spent the next few minutes ransacking her belongings until she had collected the objects she needed. She found her remaining rancor-tooth trophy wrapped in its supple leather covering. She tucked it under the stump of her severed arm—not a completely useless limb after all, she noted with some satisfaction—while she searched for another item. When at last she located the jewel-encrusted tiara from Hapes, which her grandmother had insisted she take, she placed the two articles side by side on a tiny worktable in the corner and studied them.

Both objects were symbols of who she was, of her upbringing. The rancor's tooth came from Dathomir, a planet that was wild, untamed, fierce, and proud. The tiara symbolized her Hapan inheritance: regal bearing, refinement, power, wealth, and political shrewdness.

Tenel Ka had long believed that honoring one part of her heritage implied that she must *dis*honor the other. Just as she had believed that trusting in the Force implied a lack of trust in herself. Wincing at the thought, she was compelled to acknowledge that she had actually gained wisdom from the loss of her arm. She knew now that she had to use every ability she possessed—including her talent with the Force—to become the best possible Jedi.

But what of her heritage? she thought, picking up the rancor's tooth and turning it over in her palm. Hapes and Dathomir. Could she combine the best of both? She was, after all, only one person.

Coming to a decision, she grasped the rancor tooth tightly, lifted it over her head, and brought it smashing down on the glittering, jewel-studded tiara. The delicate crown broke into pieces.

Tenel Ka hammered again and again until bits of precious metal and gems lay strewn across the tiny table.

Yes, she decided. She was a product of two worlds, and she would learn to blend the best of her mother's *and* her father's. She laid down the rancor's tooth and reached for the other items she had assembled.

Then, selecting the finest jewels from her Hapan tiara, she began to build her new lightsaber.

*   *   *

Brilliant morning sunlight played across the top of the Great Temple and filtered through Tenel Ka's partially braided hair to form a red-gold nimbus around her. Jacen stood about a meter away, facing her, a gentle breeze ruffling his unruly brown curls. His face was filled with apprehension.

"You sure you want to do this?" he asked.

"Yes," she said simply, though she felt an uncertain fluttering in the pit of her stomach.

"Well, I'm not sure *I* can go through with it," he said in a low voice.

"You? But why—"

"Blaster bolts! The last time we did this, I ended up . . ." Jacen's voice trailed off and he looked significantly at what remained of her arm.

"Ah," Tenel Ka said. "Aha."

"So I'm asking you if you're sure," Jacen said, "because I'm not."

Gray eyes searched brandy-brown while Tenel Ka considered this. Her throat was tight with unaccustomed emotion when she finally spoke. "Jacen, my friend, I know of no better way to show that I trust you . . . that I do not blame you for what happened."

Jacen's face was solemn as he nodded his acceptance. "Thank you." He let his eyes fall half shut and took a deep breath.

Tenel Ka did the same, feeling the Force flow into her, through her. Her muscles tautened—not with fear, but with a delicious anticipatory tension. Reaching for the rancor's tooth clipped to her belt, Tenel Ka held it steady in front of her and pressed the power stud.

A blade of sizzling energy sprang from the ivory hilt, glowing a rich turquoise, produced by the rainbow gems she had installed from her tiara. A heartbeat later, Jacen's emerald lightsaber hummed to life.

As if in slow motion, the two friends raised their blades until they hovered at eye level, just centimeters apart. With a crackle of discharged energy, their lightsabers touched once. Then again.

Hesitantly at first, Tenel Ka thrust with her turquoise blade, and Jacen parried with a barely perceptible nod.

The Force flowed between them, around them, and soon they were moving in ancient patterns and rhythms, as in a well-rehearsed exercise routine, an intricate dance. Somehow both of them knew that neither would come to any harm.

Their eyes locked, while the silent music that accompanied their movements built to a crescendo, then began to fade. But their confidence in each other did not wane as their movements slowed.

They stood still at last, lightsabers barely touching, a look of amazement on both of their faces. Jacen opened his mouth as if to speak, but no sound came out.

A moment later, an ear-shattering roar split the air as Lowbacca and Jaina ran across the rooftop to greet them.

Jaina laughed. "I agree with Lowie: it's good to see you holding a lightsaber again, Tenel Ka. For a while I was worried that you thought you were too different from us, that you couldn't be our friend anymore."

"Perhaps for a while I did," Tenel Ka said. "But I have learned that differences can be positive, that they can be blended together to form a stronger whole."

"We *are* pretty different," Jacen pointed out.

Jaina switched on her amethyst energy blade with a snap-hiss. "But we're all going to be Jedi Knights."

Lowbacca ignited his lightsaber as well. Its shaft glowed a molten bronze.

"Stronger together," Tenel Ka said, raising her turquoise lightsaber high over her head.

Lowbacca lifted his lightsaber to touch hers.

"Yes, stronger together," Jacen and Jaina said in unison, crossing their glowing blades with the other two.

The four lightsabers blazed into the morning light.

Darkest Knight

To Skip Shayotovich,
whose enthusiasm knows no bounds

acknowledgments

The usual round of thanks to Lillie E. Mitchell and her fast fingers for transcribing our dictation; Lucy Autrey Wilson, Sue Rostoni, and Allan Kausch at Lucasfilm for their helpful suggestions; Ginjer Buchanan at Berkley for her whole-hearted support and encouragement; and Jonathan MacGregor Cowan for being our test reader and brainstormer.

1

THE MASSASSI TREES that towered over Yavin 4's jungles were smaller than the enormous wroshyr trees on the Wookiee homeworld, but Lowbacca considered them to be the next best thing. Especially when he needed to be alone, in a place where he could sort out his thoughts.

As twilight descended on the jungle moon with a blanket of colors deepening in hue, Lowie ascended one of the thickest, tallest trees in the vicinity of the Great Temple, the site of Luke Skywalker's Jedi academy. With his retractable Wookiee claws and muscular arms, he grabbed on to branches and hauled his lanky body up one level after another, increasing the distance between himself and the ground. It seemed that if he kept climbing, he might almost be able to reach the stars . . . and be closer to home.

Stopping to rest momentarily, Lowie reached out to grasp a hairy green vine, tugged to make sure it would hold his weight, then used it to climb even higher. He had to reach the top. The top was the best place.

The best place to think.

It had been a long time since he had been back to the Wookiee world of Kashyyyk. He hadn't seen his immediate family since departing for Yavin 4 to begin training as a Jedi Knight. Although Lowie loved tinkering with computers—as did his sister and his parents—he wanted more than anything to make use of his special, undefinable talent, a potential for using the Force that few Wookiees in his family line had ever exhibited.

When Lowie first arrived at the Jedi academy, uncertain and alone, his uncle Chewbacca had given him a T-23 sky-hopper as a gift, so he could cruise far out into the jungle. Sometimes he brought his friends Jacen and Jaina and Tenel Ka. At other times, though, he just needed to be by himself, far from everyone. And this was one of those times.

He missed his family very much, especially his younger sister Sirrakuk. A very dangerous time in her life was fast approaching. . . .

With a great heave, Lowie used one long arm to draw his body up to a leafy nest of branches, where he disturbed a shrieking horde of the voracious tree rodents called stintarils. Stintarils normally ate anything in sight, anything that moved—but when Lowie treated them to his best Wookiee roar, the chittering rodents scampered away through the trees, kicking up clouds of broken twigs and leaves.

At last, surrounded by the dimming colors of dusk, Lowie parted the final blanket of leaves overhead. He braced his broad, flat feet on a sturdy branch, pushed his head above the treetops, and stood there, drinking in the distance. He looked across the sprawling jungle that spread all around him like an ocean of greenery, occasionally broken by the protruding ruins of temples. He smelled the damp scents of approaching evening: night-blooming flowers from vines that curled through the leaves, the rich moistness of the Massassi trees themselves, a fine mist rising above the canopy as if the forest itself were exhaling in its sleep.

The looming coppery gas-giant of Yavin shimmered low in the sky like a dying ember, a huge sphere of swirling gases. Not far from the orangish planet, though invisible to Lowie's eye, orbited GemDiver Station, Lando Calrissian's mining operation that retrieved valuable Corusca gems from the gas-giant's core.

Lowie looked away from the planet setting on the horizon, though, as deeper night seeped into the sky. Specks of starlight dusted the midnight blue canopy.

Finding a comfortable spot to lean against the outspread

crown of the Massassi tree, he remained still, breathing deeply, drawing comfort from the sight of the endless trees . . . and thinking of Kashyyyk.

He should be calm, but he was very worried about his sister. He could do nothing to help her, and she had to make her own choices—and face the consequences of those choices. Even so, Lowie understood the dangers she intended to face deep in the underlevels of the rain forest on the Wookiee planet.

He ran his long, strong fingers over the pearly strands of his fiber belt, woven from threads harvested from the deadly jaws of the carnivorous syren plant. It had been quite an ordeal for him to obtain those strands, but he had succeeded. Alone.

Lowie sat still as the air cooled and the noises of the jungle grew louder. Evening insects and predators stirred and went about their business.

At his side the miniaturized translating droid, Em Teedee, remained silent—switched off, so that Lowie could ponder his concerns without being interrupted by synthesized chatter. He sat back, and time passed. He would be late for evening meal back at the Jedi academy, but he didn't mind.

He had more important things to worry about.

By the time Jaina Solo finished her meal inside the Great Temple, most of the other Jedi trainees had left the eating area. Preoccupied, she slurped the last morsels of roasted crab nuts and salted boffa fruit, dabbing up the juice with a chunk of fresh bread.

Beside her at the table, her twin brother Jacen had only half finished his meal; a droplet of greenish syrup ran unnoticed down his chin. Jacen spoke excitedly, his brandy-brown eyes blinking as he ran a hand through his tousled brown hair.

"And I did manage to catch that stinger lizard down in the hangar bay. It's taken me weeks to coax him out of hiding. He's all by himself now in that new cage you built for me, but

I'm not sure what he eats." He paused briefly to stuff some food into his mouth.

Jaina nodded, only half listening. She was concerned that Lowbacca hadn't shown up to eat. Their Wookiee friend had been reserved lately, keeping to himself, speaking little even to his closest friends.

"Not to mention that several of the cocoons for my beetle moths are about to hatch!" Jacen continued. "I think I'm going to let most of them go, but I want to keep two as specimens, to see if they'll lay eggs in captivity. And you should see the fascinating blue fungus I found in a crack between some stones down by the river."

He gulped more juice, then suddenly held up a finger as he remembered something. "Oh yes, I've been meaning to ask—could you check the cage for my crystal snake? I think he's up to some mischief, maybe even trying to break out again—and you *know* what trouble that would cause."

Jaina couldn't help indulging in a quick giggle, remembering the pandemonium the nearly invisible snake had caused the last time it had gotten loose: the serpent had bitten the uppity student Raynar, sending the boy instantly to sleep. Not all of Jacen's pets caused trouble, though. Another crystal snake had helped to divert the lost TIE pilot Qorl from his attack on the Jedi academy, shortly after the twins had found Qorl living in self-imposed exile deep in the jungles of Yavin 4.

Jaina had hoped the old TIE pilot might have a soft spot for them after their efforts to help him, but Qorl had chosen not to become their ally. Instead, the Imperial brainwashing he had undergone resurfaced and became even more deeply entrenched. The pilot had returned to the remnants of the Empire, where he had fallen in with the Shadow Academy.

Jaina nodded to her brother, shaking herself from her reverie. "Okay, I'll take a look at the crystal snake cage."

She whirled as she heard the tinny mechanical voice of Em Teedee saying, "Master Lowbacca, I must urge you to ingest a wider variety of nourishment than that. According to your species' nutritional requirements, those foods are insufficient for a growing Wookiee to maintain a healthy level of energy . . . though I must admit you *have* been sulking lately instead of engaging in physical activities. Your diet should consist primarily of large quantities of fresh meat, which is substantially higher in protein than those fresh fruits and vegetables you're presently consuming."

Lowbacca answered with only a halfhearted growl as he carried his food into the eating area. Without even looking for his friends among the other Jedi trainees, he sat by himself at a small table against the stone wall.

"Lowie!" Jaina got up and hurried over to the ginger-furred Wookiee. "We were worried about you. You didn't come join us for the meal."

Lowie grunted something too brief for Em Teedee to translate.

Jaina pulled up a wooden chair across from their Wookiee friend and straddled it. Tucking a long strand of straight brown hair behind her right ear, she looked with concern at Lowie's shaggy head. The Wookiee turned his golden eyes down and studied the fruits and greens on his platter.

"Lowie, will you please tell us what's wrong?" Jaina said. "You can talk to us. We're *friends*, remember? Friends help each other."

Em Teedee spoke before Lowbacca could respond. "He won't answer you, Mistress Jaina. Even *I* can't get a response out of him. I'm afraid I'll never understand Wookiee behavior. Do all biological creatures have these unpredictable moods?"

Jacen sat down beside his sister. "Hey, maybe Lowie just wants to be left alone."

The young Wookiee groaned and nodded dejectedly. Jaina sighed, gradually realizing that perhaps the best thing she could do for her friend would be to respect Lowie's wishes and let him solve his problems on his own. He knew he could talk to Jaina or Jacen anytime he wanted—but right now he didn't want to.

"All right," Jaina said, maintaining her deeply troubled expression, "but remember we're here for you, whenever you need us."

Lowie nodded, then stretched out one hairy arm to clasp Jaina's hand in his. The Wookiee's large grip engulfed her entire hand. During the brief touch, she reached out with the Force, hoping to find a clue to Lowie's strange behavior, but all she sensed was warmth and friendship.

Jaina stood up and gestured to her brother. "Come on, Jacen. Let's have a look at that crystal snake cage."

Lightsabers flared into the night, reflecting off the ancient stone walls of the Great Temple. Tenel Ka gripped the carved rancor-tooth handle of her new weapon as its brilliant turquoise beam pulsed through the activating crystal, a precious rainbow gem of Gallinore she had taken from her own royal tiara.

The warrior girl stood in the flagstoned courtyard at the side of the ziggurat temple, a newly refurbished training area the students had reclaimed from the ever-encroaching jungle. The hardworking Jedi candidates had cleaned and polished the carefully set stones for exercises just such as this.

Tenel Ka gazed across at the alien mother-of-pearl eyes, elven features, and long quicksilver hair of her opponent— Tionne, the Jedi trainer and historian who often assisted Master Skywalker. The Jedi woman used her lightsaber with precision, matching Tenel Ka's moves stroke for stroke.

During an earlier training accident, Tenel Ka's poorly constructed lightsaber had exploded, and her friend Jacen's lightsaber blade had severed her left arm. Now Tenel Ka lived and fought with only one hand. But she wielded her glowing energy blade with strength and confidence.

Although skilled biotechnicians had offered her the best prosthetic arm replacement in the Hapes Cluster, Tenel Ka had turned them down. She prided herself in *being* herself— relying on her own abilities, her own strength and prowess. She did not want the artificial assistance of a biomechanical limb. Instead, she chose to alter her means of achieving her goal. She was determined to be as strong and as capable as ever before.

And when Tenel Ka determined to do something, she usually accomplished it.

Bright lights on the cleared landing grid in front of the temple illuminated the jungle, attracting thousands of nocturnal insects and the flying predators that fed on them. In the flagstoned courtyard, though, only the flares and flashes of intersecting lightsaber blades disturbed the night, bathing the area in a dazzling multicolored glow.

Tionne countered the warrior girl's stroke. "Very good, Tenel Ka," the teacher said. "You are learning to focus on precision rather than brute strength, to anticipate my moves and your own reactions using the Force."

Tenel Ka nodded, and her heavy red-gold braids danced around her head. The beads she had woven into the braids jingled and clacked together. She fought harder, sensing the control and skill of this older Jedi, who had been training for more than ten years now.

Several other students had come out to watch the exercises. All of Master Skywalker's Jedi candidates had intensified their training efforts, now that the New Republic was sure of the growing threat posed by the Shadow Academy and the Second Imperium. For more than a thousand generations, Jedi Knights had been the forces of light throughout the galaxy, and Luke Skywalker intended to continue the tradition.

Tionne swung her weapon with a calm, smooth gesture so unexpected that Tenel Ka barely reacted in time. She had sensed no intention of a counterattack from the silver-haired scholar, and so Tionne had surprised her. Their blades locked and sizzled—and then Tionne pulled her lightsaber back.

"Halt," she said, and switched off her weapon, leaving the warrior girl to stand with her own lightsaber blazing in her hand.

Tionne gestured up into the night sky of Yavin 4. The other students around the flagstoned courtyard stood up to watch.

Just then, the twins Jacen and Jaina emerged from a low stone arch in the side of the Great Temple, hoping to observe Tenel Ka at her exercises. Instead, they all saw a glowing light streaking toward them like a tiny meteor.

"Hey, it's a ship!" Jacen said.

"Not just any ship," Jaina added. "I'd recognize it anywhere!"

Jacen blinked. "Hey, Dad never told us he was coming!"

Within a few moments the ship swooped down with a roar of its sublight engines and powered-up repulsorlifts. The flat, pronged disk of the *Millennium Falcon* settled with a loud hiss onto the landing pad.

Talking excitedly with each other, Jacen and Jaina rushed from the courtyard out onto the close-cropped weeds of the landing field to greet their father. The modified light freighter's boarding ramp extended, and Han Solo strode down it. A lopsided grin appeared as his children greeted him with wild enthusiasm.

When Chewbacca bounded down the ramp, Tenel Ka heard a bellow of greeting from behind her. She turned to see Lowbacca on one of the pyramid's stone ledges above the training area. He swung himself over the ledge and scrambled down the sloping temple blocks to reach the ground. Chewbacca roared a response to his nephew.

Lowbacca had been very troubled recently, and Tenel Ka could sense many deep thoughts working through his brain. She had decided to honor her Wookiee friend by letting him fight his own battles . . . unless he asked for help. But when she saw the expressions on Chewbacca's and Lowie's faces, Tenel Ka grasped a strange and interesting fact.

Although the twins had been surprised by the unexpected appearance of the *Millennium Falcon*, Lowbacca had known full well that the ship was coming.

JAINA REALIZED SHE was grinning like an idiot as she hugged her father. "What are you doing here? We didn't even know you were coining."

Beside her, Jacen gaped at Han Solo's unfamiliar costume of tattered cloth and furs. His hair had been cut raggedly, and he looked much tougher. "Blaster bolts, Dad! Why are you dressed like that?"

Before Han Solo had a chance to reply, Jaina glanced behind him. Even in the dimness she could see that some of the *Millennium Falcon*'s plating had been replaced with dark anodized hunks of metal, new storage pods had been mounted on the bow, and a second transmitting dish was attached to the rear. Her jaw dropped. "And what did you do to the *Falcon*? It looks so . . . different!"

"One question at a time, kids," Han said, laughing and holding his hands palm out at chest level, as if to ward off an oncoming charge. "There've been a few problems in the Outer Rim recently; so in her official capacity, the New Republic's Chief of State—"

"You mean Mom," Jaina said.

"Right." Han's grin was boyish. "Anyway, she's been after me and Luke to do some scouting for her. Says I need to keep busy or I'll get old too fast. And ever since he started this Jedi academy, your uncle's made it a practice to spend some time away from Yavin 4, just to make sure his skills stay at their peak performance. Still, we figured it might be a good idea to keep a low profile, though, so—"

"You disguised yourself and the *Millennium Falcon*," Jacen finished for him. Jaina continued to stare at all the lumpy, patchwork modifications to the light freighter.

"And Luke, too." Han Solo nodded behind them to where their uncle, clad in a rumpled brown flight suit, emerged from the base of the temple. "Hey, Han, did you bring the last components for those new shield generators?" Luke called. He brushed a greasy hand down the front of his stained outfit. He looked very much like a down-and-out pilot who had deserted his post.

"You bet, Luke," Han said. "Leia's worried about your Jedi academy with the Second Imperium on the loose, so we've got to install those new shield generators and get them running with enough power to stop an attack."

"I still think my Jedi Knights would do a good enough job defending themselves if it came to that," Luke said, smiling at the trainees standing around the temple. "The Shadow Academy would be foolish to underestimate us."

Han shrugged. "Doesn't matter what you say, Luke—indulge me, or Leia will never sleep a wink."

Laughing, Luke called for Jedi students to unload the heavy components from the *Falcon*'s storage bay. "I'll have some of my students install the systems while you and I are away."

The disguised Jedi Master strode over to the pair of Wookiees, who stood in earnest conversation. He seemed to be bidding Chewbacca farewell. Jaina thought she heard Luke say something about the time being near, but before she could ask about it, her brother spoke up.

"But what about Chewie?" Jacen asked. "Isn't he going to be your copilot this time?"

Their father looked a bit uncomfortable. "I'll manage without him somehow. Back home on Kashyyyk, he and Lowie have kind of a family emergency, you might say."

"Emergency?" Jaina said. "Is anyone hurt?"

"Naw, nothing that simple. You've never met Lowie's sister Sirra, have you?" Han lifted his chin to point in the direction of his Wookiee copilot, who was deep in conversation with Lowbacca. "Anyway, give the two of 'em a chance to talk first. Afterwards I have a feeling Lowie'll tell you all about it. Meanwhile, I've brought messages from your mom and Anakin—and I've got a couple of surprises for you on the *Falcon*."

"Uh-oh," Jaina said. "*More* surprises on the *Falcon*?"

Han chuckled and put an arm around each of the twins' shoulders. "Yeah, presents for you two."

"Hey, that reminds me," Jacen said, "I've got a new joke. Wanna hear it?" Before either of them could talk him out of it, he forged ahead. "What do Jawas have that no other creature in the galaxy has? Give up?" He raised his eyebrows. *"Baby Jawas!"*

Even their father had difficulty feigning amusement. Jaina studied her brother in silence for a moment, then turned to Han, getting back to the subject at hand. "So, what were you saying about those gifts you brought us?"

"Well, I brought a mate for Jacen's stump lizard, along with some of those starflower blossoms they like to eat so much, and a refurbished micromotivator that still needs some tinkering. 'Course, you two'll have to fight over who gets which gift," he added, ruffling the twins' hair as they walked up the boarding ramp together.

Jaina snorted indelicately. "That shouldn't take long."

In her quarters, Tenel Ka sat fascinated by the tiny holographic image of dark-haired Anakin Skywalker holding a cluster of brightly colored twine. She couldn't figure out why the twins' little brother would have sent *her* a message. She had only met the boy once, on Coruscant not long ago.

"I know how independent you are, Tenel Ka, so I hope you don't mind my doing this," Anakin's recorded voice said. "But when Jacen and Jaina told me how hard it is for you to braid your hair since the accident, I took it as a problem to solve. You may have figured out a bunch of this stuff for yourself already"—Anakin's holographic face smiled faintly—"but even if you have, it was still a challenging puzzle, and I enjoyed it."

The Solo twins, who had delivered the holographic message to Tenel Ka after a long visit with their father, sat nearby on the floor of her chambers. Jaina rolled her eyes and chuckled. "That's my little brother."

"This is a fact," Tenel Ka said, shifting her concentration back to the glowing hologram.

The boy's image held the multicolored twine in one hand and threaded the fingers of the other hand through it, neatly separating the colors into individual clumps. Tenel Ka unconsciously lifted her hand to her head and threaded her fingers through some unbraided strands of her red-gold hair.

Moving with deliberate precision, Anakin slid his hands down the brightly colored strands, twining them together with the fingers of one hand as he went. "See, it can be done, if you approach the task from a different perspective." The sequence cycled through again in slow motion while Anakin said, "I tried adding decorations several ways, but it worked best for me if I put the bead or feather in my mouth first. That way I didn't have to let go of the braid to pick it up."

"Ah." Tenel Ka nodded her approval of the logic. "Aha." Experimentally, her fingers began to twine a few strands of hair, following the single-handed technique Anakin had concocted.

The hologram shifted to a different scene, Anakin standing beside a fall of long glossy brown hair, caught up in a dozen Dathomiran warrior braids decorated with feathers and beads. The view pulled back, and Anakin gestured to his handiwork, looking both pleased and a bit embarrassed. "As you can see, Mom let me practice on her." The tiny holographic image of Chief of State Leia Organa Solo turned with a warm smile and then spun in a graceful pirouette to give a better view of the braids.

As the holorecording ended, Tenel Ka nodded seriously, considering the new technique. With practice, she thought she could manage it herself.

A loud questioning growl sounded from the doorway of Tenel Ka's quarters. She looked up to see Lowbacca standing at the arched entrance.

"Enter, friend," Tenel Ka said, indicating a spot on the floor beside her. "Sit with us if you wish."

"Lowie, is everything all right?" Jaina asked with a look of concern.

The lanky ginger-furred Wookiee ambled over and sat between Tenel Ka and Jaina on the floor. For a long time none of the companions spoke. Then Lowbacca reached toward his belt and flicked a small switch on Em Teedee's back. "Ah, thank you, Master Lowbacca," Em Teedee said. "That was indeed a refreshing shutdown cycle, although considerably longer than I had anticipated. Oh, look—we have company."

Lowbacca interrupted the little droid with a rumble and a short bark. "Why, most assuredly, Master Lowbacca. I'd be delighted to provide a translation. That *is* my primary function, you know. I am fluent in over six forms of communication."

Preoccupied, Lowbacca didn't even scold the translating droid. Slowly, haltingly at first, the Wookiee began to speak, and Em Teedee translated. "Master Lowbacca knows that his recent . . . *distress* has been apparent to all of you, causing you no small measure of concern—a concern shared by myself, I might add."

Jaina put a hand on Lowbacca's shoulder. "Well, you did have us worried. We wanted you to be able to talk to us."

"We're your friends," Jacen added.

Tenel Ka merely nodded and waited for Lowbacca to continue.

He squared his shoulders and went on with his explanation. "In recent months a family matter has arisen that has caused Master Lowbacca no end of worry over his sister Sirrakuk's safety.

"As you may recall, young Wookiees occasionally take it upon themselves to perform a feat of great danger and difficulty, either alone or accompanied by friends. This gains them much respect, especially at a time when they are choosing their life path.

"Master Lowbacca decided to prove himself with such an act of bravery, since he knew that it would be difficult for many Wookiees to accept his decision to train at the Jedi academy rather than follow a more traditional calling. He was so proud of his intellectual skills that he chose to rely only on his wits; he descended to the deep forest levels on Kashyyyk without telling a single friend. Alone, he harvested these fibers from the dangerous syren plant. Though Master Lowbacca emerged unharmed with the trophy he had sought, he now admits that his solo expedition was foolhardy and ill-advised. And he fears that Sirrakuk is considerably more impulsive, more impetuous than he."

Here Lowbacca paused to finger the glossy fiber of his webbed belt. Its intricate braiding reminded Tenel Ka of Anakin's message to her, his technique of one-handed braiding.

Jaina gave Lowie a measuring look. "Ah, so now you're afraid that your sister might try to go it alone just because you did?"

Lowbacca looked down at the floor and gave a series of low rumbles and growls. Resting both elbows on his furry knees, he held his head in his hands as he spoke.

"I'm afraid the situation is rather more serious than that, and Lowbacca believes that the responsibility is largely his," Em Teedee said. "You see, since childhood Sirra's best friend was Raabakyysh—or Raaba, as Master Lowbacca's family referred to her—intelligent, strong-willed, beautiful, and adventurous. In fact, Master Lowbacca had always felt that . . . Well, go on," the little droid prompted. "You thought that *what*? You can't simply stop in the middle of a sentence."

Lowie gave a low groan and began to speak again. The dark streak of fur over his eyebrow fluffed up, showing his agitation.

"Approximately one month ago, Raaba prepared to show her own skills in the face of danger, since she wanted to join a difficult and exclusive pilots' school, hoping one day to become the captain of her own ship. Sirra and Raaba had agreed to accompany one another—but the night before they had planned to go, Raaba impulsively decided to go alone.

"In secret, she descended to the lower jungles at night,

leaving behind nothing but a brief message to explain to Sirra what she had done and why. According to her note, Raaba had hoped that by duplicating Lowbacca's feat of bravery she might impress him enough that he would someday consider her a worthy mate for a Jedi—when they were old enough. However . . ."

Lowbacca paused and heaved a deep sigh before continuing. "However—oh dear!—I'm afraid Raaba never returned from her ordeal," Em Teedee continued. "When her family searched for her they found only her bloodstained toolpack. Nothing more. Raaba was gone."

"Oh, Lowie." Jaina leaned her head against the Wookiee's shoulder.

Tenel Ka looked at her friend, sensing his pain. "Ah. This is why you feel responsible."

Lowie spoke again, this time in strangled tones. "Since Raaba's . . . loss, Sirra has become increasingly reckless, as if she hardly cares whether she lives or dies. Sirra has refused all offers from other friends to accompany her on her rite of passage, insisting that Raaba was the only one she trusted enough to take along. A while ago, in desperation, Master Lowbacca sent Sirra a message asking if she would accept *him* as a suitable substitute. Chewbacca has just brought word of her answer." Em Teedee paused for a moment. "Oh, thank goodness—she's accepted!"

"Hey, that's great," Jacen said in a relieved voice.

"Oh, indeed," Em Teedee chirped.

Lowbacca didn't respond immediately. He seemed to be intently studying a chip in the flagstoned floor.

"Something's still bothering you, Lowie," Jaina said.

Tenel Ka glanced down at the stump of her severed left arm, then gave Lowie an understanding look. "You fear to face your loss. The loss of Raaba."

"That's it, isn't it?" Jaina said. "It's going to hurt to go back to Kashyyyk, because your friend Raaba won't be there. And you feel responsible that she died trying to copy something you did."

After Lowie's response, Em Teedee said, "Master Lowbacca is also concerned that his grief over the loss of Raabakyysh will render him less capable of supporting his sister at this critical time. He realizes that it may not be feasible, but he was hoping to impose on one of you to accompany him to his homeworld."

Tenel Ka answered immediately "You came when I needed you, after my accident. I can do no less, my friend." She reached out her hand to touch Lowbacca's.

"Hey, I'll come too," Jacen said, placing his hand over both of theirs. "We're stronger together. All of us."

Jaina placed her hand over the others. "I guess we all go then," she said. "Stronger together."

Lowbacca hung back, standing near the disguised *Millennium Falcon* while the Solo twins said good-bye to their father.

Han Solo gave his kids a lopsided grin. "Yeah, I kinda had a hunch that all of you were gonna volunteer to go with Lowbacca," he said. "As soon as Chewie told me the situation, I cleared it with your mom. Should be a good opportunity for you kids to brush up on Wookiee language comprehension, too."

Just then Luke Skywalker, wearing his tattered jumpsuit, emerged from the hangar bay with Chewbacca. Lowie could smell the grease stains and solvents on the old fabric. "Everything ready?" Master Skywalker asked.

"Ready as it'll ever be," Han Solo replied with another grin. "You and Chewie finished prepping the *Shadow Chaser*?"

Luke turned to Chewbacca, who had come up beside him, and said, "The *Chaser*'s a good ship; don't let anything happen to her." The big Wookiee shrugged and gave a bark of agreement.

Han Solo thumped Chewie on the back. "Take care of yourself. I'm trusting you with my kids, you know. Keep 'em all in one piece, okay? We'll see you in a couple of weeks."

With that, Han gave the twins one last hug and went aboard the *Millennium Falcon*.

Before walking up the ramp, Master Skywalker looked around at the young Jedi Knights with calm confidence. "Don't forget that you're stronger together," he said. "May the Force be with you."

When the departing *Falcon* was just a speck in the distance, its bank of sublight engines glowing white, Lowbacca heaved a sigh and growled questioningly at Jaina.

She chuckled. "Right. What are we waiting for?"

3

THE SLEEK *SHADOW Chaser*, with its Imperial design and oily-looking quantum armor, glistened in the early-morning sun as Chewbacca piloted it slowly out of the sheltered hangar bay beneath the Great Temple.

Jacen stood next to his sister and Tenel Ka, watching the vessel move under silent power. Considering Lowie's recent distress, Jacen was glad his uncle Luke had let them take the *Shadow Chaser*—just the kind of fast, stealthy ship needed for an urgent mission. He was proud that Lowie wanted them along, that he and his sister and Tenel Ka could be of some help to their Wookiee friend.

Lowie stood at the far end of the clearing, motioning with his shaggy arms to direct Chewbacca's piloting. When the *Shadow Chaser* came to a halt, its entry ramp extended. Chewbacca stood at the top, gesturing with his cinnamon-furred arms and bellowing.

"Master Chewbacca cordially requests that we all come aboard," Em Teedee translated, speaking in a wobbly voice as he bounced with each running step Lowie took.

Jacen slung his satchel of belongings over one shoulder. He turned to see if he could offer any assistance to Tenel Ka, but when he saw the determined look in the warrior girl's gray eyes, he decided he'd be better off if he didn't ask.

They climbed aboard the *Shadow Chaser* and waved a brief good-bye to the other students and Tionne, who held up a hand in farewell. Even before the ship was completely sealed and ready to take off, Tionne had ushered the trainees back to their studies. With the threat of the Second Imperium loose in the galaxy, the new Jedi Knights had no time to relax.

With a smooth surge of acceleration, so powerful yet gentle it seemed almost to glide against gravity, the *Shadow Chaser* aimed its nose upward and arrowed straight into the mist-shrouded skies of the jungle moon.

En route to Kashyyyk, Jacen watched Lowie and Chewbacca in the two front seats of the narrow cockpit as the *Shadow Chaser* lurched into hyperspace. When the pair spoke rapidly in the Wookiee language, they sounded like two ferocious beasts challenging each other—but Jacen knew it was just a conversation, though he could make out only a few words. Teedee had been instructed not to bother translating, so that Lowie and Chewie could have some uninterrupted words in relative privacy.

While his sister tinkered with her multi-tool, disassembling a tiny mechanical gadget she had brought from her workshop on Yavin 4, Jacen took the opportunity to amuse Tenel Ka. He decided that, rather than telling jokes this time, he would explain to the gruff girl *why* certain things were funny, why she should be laughing at his punch lines—well, some of them, anyway. Jacen had begun to wonder if perhaps the girl simply didn't understand, and that was why she didn't laugh.

After all, it couldn't be that *every one* of his jokes was bad.

He explained how ridiculous answers to straightforward-sounding questions were supposed to be funny. He showed her how doing unexpected things with food or simple items of clothing might be considered amusing.

Tenel Ka watched him gravely, with full and unwavering attention. But she never cracked a smile.

With a sigh, Jacen told a few of his best jokes, then gave her some of his worst, trying to explain the difference by way of example. Tenel Ka didn't laugh at either.

In desperation, he considered going to the food-prep unit, ordering a pan of chilled Deneelian fizz-pudding, and then comically tripping so that the entire mess splatted in his face—but by this time, Jacen figured that even such a spectacular pratfall would have no effect on the young warrior woman.

Shaking his head in surrender, Jacen decided to leave Tenel Ka alone. He would occupy himself with something less discouraging for the time being. His spirits instantly perked up as he reached out with Jedi senses and detected something interesting in the back of the *Shadow Chaser* . . . the faint glow of a life-form, some creature out of place by the engine compartments. Jacen decided to go snoop. Nobody else was likely to be interested, anyway.

In the shielded rear compartment beyond the sleeping bunks and the food-prep area, Jacen heard the pulsing, pounding thump of engines as the *Shadow Chaser* sped along through hyperspace. He looked at the intricate control panels and access grids, the weapons batteries charged with spin-sealed Tibanna gas, and the shield generators that projected a canopy of protection around the sleek ship. But through all the din and the vibrating power of the engines, Jacen could still detect the faint emanations of some small creature, lost and frightened.

"Don't be scared," Jacen said, speaking with his voice and at the same time thinking the words through the Force. "I'm your friend. I can help you. Let me see you. It's okay."

He lowered his voice to a whisper as he bent down, looking in crannies between the control grids. He followed his senses. "I won't hurt you. I just want to see you. I know you're afraid. You can trust me." He touched his fingers lightly to one of the cool metal access panels, gently brushing the ion shield generators with his mind.

He sensed the creature hiding back there, trembling, guarding something. A little nest?

"It's just me," Jacen said. "Relax. I'll take care of you."

He popped the metal covering off the access panel to the ion shield generator. Inside, in a comfortable little pocket of colorful debris, cowered a furry eight-legged rodent, a mouse-like creature with puffy frost-gray fur. It looked up at him with tiny black eyes that glittered in the dim light. It wiggled its damp nose. Judging by the pair of long teeth that protruded from the center of its snout, this rodent was a gnawer, not a flesh eater.

"Come here," Jacen said. "That's not a safe place for you to be." He reached in and calmly drew the rodent out. Its eight legs trembled and tickled against his palm like a plump furry spider, but a friendly and gentle one.

Jacen stroked its back, then bent to peer at the nest again. The rodent had chewed tiny strips of insulation from the power cables, yanked threads and wires and fabrics and plastics from the shield generator to create a soft pocket in which squirmed four smooth cylindrical grubs, the creature's young.

"Oh, what a nice nest you have," Jacen said soothingly. "But I don't think you were supposed to use those components. We need this ion shield generator, you know. It protects the whole ship."

He continued stroking the rodent and retrieved the nest carefully so as not to disturb the young. He held the nest in his hand and placed the mother back on top, snuggled against her little ones. "I'll keep you safe," Jacen said, "but we'll have to tell Jaina and Lowie about this, so they can make repairs."

Preoccupied with calming his new pet, Jacen returned to the forward compartments. He went to his sister who was still tinkering with an incomprehensible mechanical gadget. "Hey, Jaina? I've got some bad news."

She turned, holding up a small hydrospanner. "What?"

Before he could answer, though, the *Shadow Chaser* gave

a sudden lurch and rocked as if it had slammed into something invisible. The deck tilted sideways, throwing Jacen to his knees. He struggled to protect his new pet.

The colors of hyperspace swirled like a psychedelic flood in all directions out the windowports. When the *Shadow Chaser* gave another violent lurch, Jacen tumbled backward to the deck; it took all his concentration to guard the precious nest.

"Uh, never mind," he said. "It can wait."

Jaina gripped the armrests of her seat while the ship rocked back and forth. Her tools and the electronic di-scanner remote she had just repaired flew like projectiles to the bulkheads, then smashed onto the deck-plates, ruined.

When the ship momentarily stabilized, her brother crawled to his feet, cradling something in one arm, his hair even more tousled than usual. He checked to make sure Tenel Ka was okay. The warrior girl stood up, planting her booted feet wide apart, seeking balance as the *Shadow Chaser* shuddered and bucked its way through the disturbance.

"What is happening?" Tenel Ka said.

Ahead in the cockpit, Lowie and Chewbacca roared to each other, fighting the controls.

"An ion storm?" Em Teedee chimed in with an electronic wail. "Are you absolutely certain? We're doomed!"

Jaina's lips pressed into a tight, grim line. "It's an ion storm, all right. Just bad luck. Couldn't predict this. We plotted the shortest path to Kashyyyk using the navicomputer. The on-line catalogs only display stable astronomical hazards—star clusters, black holes, and high-energy nebulas—but ion storms come and go. They don't have any set position, but they sure ripple up hyperspace when you pass through 'em."

"Is it serious?" Jacen asked. Droplets of sweat broke out on his brow. "I've got a bad feeling about this."

"Just have to wait and see," Jaina said.

Tenel Ka stood with her hand to her utility belt, ready to

fight some tangible foe with a throwing knife, her lightsaber, even her fibercord. But none of those would do any good against an ion storm.

Chewbacca and Lowie grappled with the controls, hairy fingers flying over panels, yanking levers. The *Shadow Chaser* winked out of hyperspace and lurched back into the fringes of the furious ion storm.

"Uh-oh," Jacen said. "I forgot to tell you that we might have some damage to our ion shield generator." He held up the nested bundle of wires and insulation.

Jaina whirled, more worried than ever. "Oh, no! That could—"

As the *Shadow Chaser* plummeted into the space storm, they were immediately surrounded by a spiderweb of high-energy lightning bolts, powerful discharges that arched across the seething knot of hot gas that formed the unexpected interstellar hurricane. The ship thrashed like a mad bantha, throwing its passengers about.

Jacen braced his shoulder against a control bar, and Tenel Ka fell into him. He held the warrior girl upright, pinning both of them against the wall, still cradling his newfound pet in one hand. Jaina, trying to struggle toward the cockpit, fell flat on her face.

The *Shadow Chaser*'s rear engines kicked in, and the sublight drive heaved them away from the rippling ion cloud. In the pilot seat Chewbacca groaned, gripping the controls and wrestling to keep them on a straight course, the shortest path out of danger.

Lowie cried out as fingernails of icy blue electricity skittered across the control panels, burning out subsystem after subsystem.

Behind the back bulkheads, the straining ion shield generators squealed loudly in surrender. Then, with a loud bang, they fell silent.

The rippling colors dwindled outside the cockpit window, and the *Shadow Chaser* careened onward, spiraling out into open space, safe at last from the storm. Still, Jaina shuddered to think of how much damage the stray ion bursts must have caused.

Jacen brushed himself off and forced a lopsided grin. "Now, uh, as I was saying about that damage to the ion shields . . ." He held out the eight-legged rodent, which cowered in her nest, as if she comprehended the trouble she had caused. "I found this critter's nest in the machinery. I took her out, but I needed one of you to fix the damage."

"It would appear that we now have plenty of time to fix it," Tenel Ka said. "We are *capable* of fixing it, are we not?"

From the cockpit Lowie and Chewie consulted in growling voices.

"Oh, excellent!" Em Teedee said. "Master Lowbacca says we have been quite lucky. Our propulsion and life-support systems are largely intact and can be repaired quite easily. My, that *is* wonderful news."

Em Teedee fell silent as the Wookiees continued, and then the little droid piped up. "Excuse me—what did you say, Master Lowbacca? Oh dear! It seems, however, that our navicomputer has been completely disabled. We have lost all coordinates for getting from here to anywhere else. Oh my. We're . . . we're lost in space."

Chewbacca and Lowie both roared in outrage at the translating droid, and Em Teedee quickly fell silent. "Well, I suppose I *should* find it comforting that you both have such confidence in your navigational abilities," Em Teedee muttered after a moment.

The two Wookiees busily consulted with each other and began punching and programming numerical values into the navigational control panel, double-checking each other's calculations. Before long, after everyone had helped with temporary repairs, the *Shadow Chaser* was on its way again.

At first Jaina was surprised that they were back on course—then she realized that she shouldn't have been. After all, Kashyyyk was the only Wookiee planet, and both Lowie and Chewbacca greatly revered the place.

Why should she find it unusual that they had both memorized the coordinates for their homeworld?

4

IN A SECLUDED meeting chamber at the Shadow Academy, Zekk stood proudly, struggling to hide any sign of nervousness. He raised his chin and waited to receive his long-anticipated reward. It had come to this, at last.

The air smelled cold and metallic, exhilarating. Brilliant light stabbed down from the metal ceiling, making him squint his emerald eyes; the irises were ringed with a darker corona, like the shadowy outline around his personality. Zekk tossed back his shaggy dark hair, one shade lighter than black, and looked up, blinking, as Lord Brakiss approached him in the harsh light.

The master of the Shadow Academy was wrapped in rippling silvery robes of a fabric that looked as if it might have been spun by deadly spiders. Against one wall, wearing her spined and glittering black cloak, stood Tamith Kai, the fierce commander of the new Nightsisters. Her violet eyes burned beneath a generous mane of ebony hair.

Beside Tamith Kai waited two other prominent Nightsisters—attractive and petite Garowyn and muscular Vonnda Ra, both from the planet Dathomir. In their black-spined capes and lizard-hide armor, the three Nightsisters reminded Zekk of hungry birds of prey.

Next to them, the grizzled TIE pilot, Qorl, stood at attention, surrounded by a stormtrooper escort of his most promising Imperial trainees. Beneath the white armor, one of the burliest of these was the gangleader Norys, who had led the Lost Ones on Coruscant not long ago. While the other stormtroopers stood rigidly at attention, weapons shouldered, Norys fidgeted and seemed angry and uncomfortable with the ceremony. His senses finely tuned by his own anxiety, Zekk could pick up the harsh muttering words from behind the bully's white helmet. "Trash collector . . . gets all the breaks."

Moving quietly and unobtrusively, Qorl rested his powerful droid replacement hand on the stormtrooper's shoulder armor in a gesture that was firm and clearly meant to quiet the bully. Zekk knew Qorl's droid arm was powerful enough to crack the white armor like an eggshell. Norys fell silent, though he obviously remained upset.

Zekk didn't mind. This was his moment of glory, and he smiled faintly at the thought of how much had changed in only a few months—and how now he had arrived at the peak of his triumph.

For this presentation and initiation, Zekk had worn his new leather uniform; heavy round studs decorated the reinforced pads on his shoulders, creating a kind of armored hide. His hands were encased in thick black gloves that made a warm, satisfying creak as he clenched and unclenched his fists.

Brakiss's porcelain-perfect face smiled with pride. He held out a gift, a flowing black cape lined with deep, vibrant crimson, like fresh dark blood.

"Young Zekk, I present this to you as a symbol of your importance to the Shadow Academy," Brakiss said. "You have proven to be an avid pupil, a true asset to the Second Imperium. Our efforts would be greatly disadvantaged had you not joined us in our struggle. In your duel to the death with Vilas, our other powerful candidate, you proved yourself to be our champion, our new hope—our Darkest Knight."

Zekk blinked back stinging tears of pride and accomplishment as Brakiss draped the heavy fabric over his padded shoulders, then fastened the cape at his throat with a clasp shaped like a ferocious silver scarab.

Zekk watched Tamith Kai, who stood coiled with deadly energy, like a rogue assassin droid. He saw the tall Nightsister flinch at the mention of the slain Vilas, who had been her student, her candidate for the Shadow Academy's champion. But Zekk had defeated the surly, overconfident young man, and now *he* wore the black cape . . . while Vilas was little more than space dust ejected from the garbage port.

Brakiss stepped back and folded his hands in front of him; silvery sleeves flowed down his wrists, swallowing up his manicured hands. "The time has come for you to embark on your first important mission for us, Zekk. You will be given command of troops to prove your skills."

Zekk's heart leaped. He didn't think he could stand any more exhilaration in one day. "What," he stammered, "what do you wish me to do?"

"As a final stage in preparing for our attack on Rebel fortifications, we must launch another raid to obtain vital supplies. You will lead an assault team to the Wookiee world of Kashyyyk. There, in one of their technological tree cities, is the fabrication facility for the most sophisticated computer equipment used by our enemy's ships.

"If your raid is successful in obtaining guidance and tactical systems, we will have an enormous advantage in our overall conflict. We will then be able to throw the Rebel fleet into confusion and use their own computers against them to transmit conflicting signals. We can also use these systems to mimic their secret ship ID patterns, so that Second Imperium fighters can travel freely in enemy territory by identifying themselves as Rebel ships.

"Because of the importance of this mission, you will be assigned a powerful team. I am giving you use of the new holographic disguises we have developed for just such an infiltration effort. Everything depends on you, Zekk. Do you feel up to the task?"

Zekk nodded enthusiastically. "Yes! Yes, I can do that for you."

Tamith Kai strode forward into the pool of bright light that poured down on Zekk. He turned to look at the tall, ominous woman. Her wine-dark lips curved down in a serious expression. As if pronouncing his doom, she said, "There is one other part of the plan. Through an intercepted transmission, we have learned that those troublesome young Jedi brats are even now on their way to Kashyyyk. They sent a message to say good-bye to their mother—luckily Qorl has been monitoring all comm traffic from the vicinity of Yavin 4 back to the capital world." She stared at her claw-like fingernails, as if she found something interesting there.

"We had originally planned to wait a few more weeks before conducting this raid, but now . . . the timing couldn't be more perfect." Her violet eyes flashed with pleasure. "Your second assignment is to make sure that Jacen and Jaina and their difficult friends are . . . removed, so that we can proceed with our galactic conquest without worrying about their meddling."

Zekk swallowed hard when he heard the new orders, but did not reply. Jacen, and especially his sister Jaina, had been good friends for much of his youth. They had parted ways, though, when the twins went off to the Jedi academy, abandoning Zekk to his squalid life in the underworld of Coruscant. He had had no hope for a bright future until the Shadow Academy found him.

"All right," Zekk said in a voice low and hoarse. He tried to speak louder, not willing to let self-doubt show through. He had made his own choices, and now he had to follow through on them despite the difficulties his conscience might encounter. "All right," he repeated. "When do we leave?"

"As soon as possible," Tamith Kai answered.

In the outer docking bay of the Shadow Academy, Tamith Kai and the other two Nightsisters loaded the ship for its assault mission. The vessel, marked with neutral insignia, was a small cargo freighter stolen from a lost trader who had ventured too close to the Core Systems. Tamith Kai wondered idly if the trader still languished deep in an Imperial prison . . . or if the guards had gotten around to executing him yet, since the Second Imperium could never afford to let the man loose with his knowledge of the Core Systems and the commandeered freighter.

In the observation bubble above the docking bay, Qorl

stood by the cloaking shield controls, monitoring preparations for the launch of the mission. The old pilot would not accompany them himself, but he had chosen a handful of the Second Imperium's newly constructed TIE fighters and bombers to be loaded into the freighter's cargo bay.

"We'll see if Brakiss was wrong to place confidence in his young pet," Tamith Kai murmured in her low, rich voice. "I still don't trust him. What is it Norys calls the boy—trash collector? I sense that Zekk hasn't yet given himself entirely over to the dark side."

Vonnda Ra frowned, her squarish face puzzled. "But after all the work he's done—look at his training. How can you question Zekk's abilities?"

"It is his *motives* I question, not his abilities. I had no such doubts about the loyalty of my Vilas."

Garowyn interrupted. "Perhaps, Tamith Kai. But Vilas is dead. Zekk proved to be a better fighter. Perhaps you're simply being a sore loser."

Tamith Kai's eyes flared like twin violet stars about to explode. "I am *not* a sore loser," she snarled.

"Obviously not," Garowyn said, turning away with an ironic smile.

Tamith Kai clenched her fists in rage. "I think Zekk still has feelings for those obnoxious Jedi twins. His friendship is not so easily given up." She calmed herself. Her lips, dark as overripe fruit, twisted into a smile. "That's why I made sure this mission would be more than just a simple raid. Let us watch how Zekk takes care of his other assignment."

Vonnda Ra stored a crate of weapons inside the cargo shuttle and went to fetch the heavy belts that carried their holographic-disguise generators. "I thought the computer guidance and tactical systems were our most important objective."

"For you, perhaps, and for the Second Imperium," Tamith Kai said, nodding distractedly, "but not for me."

Garowyn crossed her wiry arms over her small chest. "You may be my nominal superior, Tamith Kai, but I can set my own priorities as well. I'll assist you in this raid, but the main reason *I'm* going along is to retrieve our . . . stolen property."

"What stolen property?" Vonnda Ra asked, the belts and holographic control packs still dangling from her outstretched arms.

"Our greatest ship, our most ambitious design, with quantum armor and powerful weapons—the *Shadow Chaser*. It is the peak of the Second Imperium's engineering success, my one joy. But Skywalker and that traitorous girl from Dathomir tricked me into an escape pod and stole my own ship out from under me! The Jedi acedemy has been using it ever since. I had all but given up hope of ever regaining what was rightfully mine, but now I've learned that the Wookiee and the Jedi brats have taken my ship to Kashyyyk. Now is our perfect chance to retrieve what is ours."

"Well, if you do get the *Shadow Chaser*, there will be more room for us when we return in the assault shuttle, then," Vonnda Ra said.

Tamith Kai directed a cool stare at the short, bronze-haired Nightsister. At last she smiled, with just a trace of warmth. "So. I see we each have our own agendas," she said. "Let us hope we all succeed."

5

"WHY, CERTAINLY, MASTER Lowbacca. I'd be happy to be of service in such a manner," Em Teedee said as they approached Kashyyyk. "Calculation of that trajectory is really quite simple."

Lowie accepted the finding from the little droid and input it manually on the *Shadow Chaser*'s control panel. Beside him, his uncle drew in a deep, happy breath when the rich brown-green planet appeared in the viewport, as if anticipating the tastes and smells and sounds of home. Despite the heavy heart with which he was returning, Lowie also felt a rush of excitement and pleasure. He would soon be in the safe, peaceful treetops of Kashyyyk.

"Well done, Masters Lowbacca and Chewbacca!" Em Teedee caroled. Lowie grunted an absentminded acknowledgment, still captivated by the sight of his planet. It looked much the same as it had on the day he left with his uncle and Han Solo in the *Millennium Falcon* to become a Jedi student. How long ago was it now?

Too long. Lowie's yearning to see his family again became almost overwhelming. The two Wookiees worked at the piloting controls with an urgency that came from happy anticipation. As the *Shadow Chaser* approached the thick canopy below, Chewbacca pointed with a certain wistfulness toward the treetop city in which he and Lowie's mother had grown up. With all of Chewie's travels across the galaxy, Lowbacca wondered if his uncle ever felt as homesick as he himself occasionally did on Yavin 4. He knew Chewbacca would somehow find the time to visit his own city and the rest of his family in the next day or so.

Behind him, the twins and Tenel Ka uttered exclamations of admiration at the beauty of Kashyyyk and the size of the trees. "Even though I've been here before, I always forget how big they are," Jaina murmured, pressing her fingers against the windowport.

"Impressive," Tenel Ka agreed. "But where are the cities?" Chewbacca let the sleek ship dip a bit lower, and Lowie pointed to where clusters of high trees extended their crowns above the lower canopies. Nestled in the masses of thick branches, gleaming towers and platforms were visible, signs of habitation that folded into the natural formation of the trees. "Ah," she said, sounding somewhat surprised. "Aha."

"Neat, huh?" Jacen said, leaning closer to the warrior girl. "They like to make nature and technology work together."

Lowie growled his agreement. "Master Lowbacca points out that technology and nature need not be mutually exclusive," Em Teedee translated. "Blending the two can be more pleasant than separating them."

When he finally caught sight of his home city, Lowie felt a renewed impatience. It was all he could do to keep himself from unbuckling his crash webbing while Chewbacca guided their damaged ship toward the nearest landing platform.

The moment the *Shadow Chaser* touched down, Lowbacca sprang from the copilot's seat and rushed to the exit hatch. Through the cockpit window, he could see his family waiting for him on the platform—his father, Mahraccor; his mother, Kallabow; and his younger sister, Sirrakuk.

Lowie opened the hatch and stood in the sunlight for a split second, taking in every detail, sniffing the air, letting his eyes be bombarded by the rich greens and browns of the treetops. Then he and his family all roared greetings. His parents looked well and happy if a little tired. His mother's kind blue eyes, surrounded by auburn whorls of fur, shone with pride. The dark streak in his father's fur showed no signs of graying with age.

Only his sister looked different—taller, sleeker, and prettier than he had remembered her, but with a heavy sadness about her face. Sirra had trimmed her fur in unusual patterns, had shaved decorative designs around her head and arms. But her fangs were white and sharp, the fur around her nose and mouth well-groomed and long. She was definitely growing up.

His father raised both arms over his head and bellowed another greeting. Lowie roared back and ran toward them.

Jacen looked around the dining table in consternation, wishing for the tenth time that he understood the Wookiee language better. Ensconced between Lowie and Sirra, he looked across the table to where Jaina and Tenel Ka sat on either side of Chewbacca; he wondered if they felt as confused and overwhelmed as he did in the middle of the loud and incomprehensible dinner conversation.

Transparent mesh cages filled with swarms of tiny, luminescent bugs hung from the ceiling branches, providing a fuzzy, warm light. Exotic spices and incense wafted around the room and out the open window notches into the humid night. The air was thick with mouthwatering smells of the welcome meal Lowie's parents had prepared.

The table was a huge slab of wood, a slice from a broad-boled tree: its hypnotic concentric rings indicated how long the tree had lived. All the chairs and furniture in Lowie's home seemed overlarge, built for bodies much taller than the average human. Jacen shifted uncomfortably on the high bench at the table.

Something finally clicked in his head. "Hey, where's Em Teedee?" he asked. "We could really use his translating skills here."

Jaina flushed, her mouth forming a small "oh" of surprise. "I, um, guess that's my fault," she stammered. "I kind of borrowed him and hooked him up to the *Shadow Chaser*'s diagnostics so he could give us a readout of the parts we need to repair the ship." She bit her lower lip. "I suppose it would have been more polite to wait until *after* we had had a chance to chat with Lowie's family a while."

Jacen shrugged and squeezed his eyes shut. He tried to concentrate in the new environment, to pick out individual words. But with five Wookiees barking, bellowing, growling, and roaring, it was difficult to make sense of their speech. He took a slow breath and tried to relax, planning to reach out with the Force to see if he could sense some meaning in the conversation.

Outside, Jacen could hear a warm afternoon rain running gentle fingers through the leaves of the stately wroshyr trees. Inside, the battle of tones continued, strange voices mixing with familiar ones. In the undertones, he felt joy and apprehension, hope and sorrow. He felt . . .

He felt the touch of a furry hand on his arm. Jacen looked up in embarrassment to find Lowie's sister Sirra holding out a platter laden with roasted meats and vegetables. Sirra uttered a polite but curious woof.

"Blaster bolts! I'm sorry, is that plate for me?"

Lowie chuffed a laugh and then swept a hand around the table to indicate that everyone else had already been served. Each of the Wookiees' plates was filled with coarsely chopped fresh meat and mounds of raw vegetables. Jaina had a platter of food similar to his own, while Tenel Ka's held a mixture of vegetables and meats, both cooked and raw. Jacen was amused to note that Tenel Ka's appetite reflected the conflicting preferences of her primitive and refined upbringings. Kallabow and Mahraccor had worked hard to accommodate the dietary preferences of their human guests. Jacen accepted the platter from Sirra and thanked her.

When the Wookiees all fell silent, expectant, and turned to Lowbacca, he held one furry hand over his plate of food as he crooned a few short phrases in a low voice. Jacen recognized the Wookiee ceremonial speech of thankfulness that he had heard from Chewbacca so often.

Lowie stood then, raised his arms high and spread his hands as if forming a protective leafy canopy over his family and friends, and repeated his brief speech. Lowie's mother crooned a sad, low note.

A moment later, both Wookiees and humans attacked their food as if none of them had had a decent meal for weeks.

The next day, Jaina murmured something noncommittal and looked dubiously at the list that Em Teedee had downloaded to her datapad. Jacen and Tenel Ka sat near her in Lowie's spacious room, which had been hollowed out from part of a massive wroshyr tree. Lowie disconnected the lead wires from the diagnostics panel, tucked them back into Em Teedee's casing, and closed it with a snap. While Jaina and Lowie worked together to catalog the *Shadow Chaser*'s ills, Chewbacca had taken the opportunity to go to the other side of the planet to visit the rest of his family whom he had not seen in some time.

A few leftover spatters of rain from another brief shower dripped outside the open window. Sirra sat with them, her patchy fur standing on end. She didn't want to be alone, apparently, but she didn't participate much in the conversation either.

"Take a look at this, Lowie," Jaina said, holding up the datapad.

The Wookiee studied the list of ruined components with a thoughtful growl. Jacen and Tenel Ka crowded in to get a look as well. Jacen flashed his sister a mischievous grin. "Hard to believe that an itty-bitty ion storm could cause so much damage, huh?"

Jaina sent him a withering look. "If that furry pet of yours hadn't chewed all the circuits—"

"Hey, that's not fair! I'd never even seen her before we left Yavin 4." Jacen removed the fluffy creature from the temporary cage he had made for her and her babies. The little eight-legged rodent seemed very pleased with her soft new nest. "She didn't mean to cause any trouble—did you, Ion?"

He held the fluffy ball close to his face and stroked her with one finger. The tiny creature made a faint cooing sound. Jacen would set the rodent free when they returned to Yavin 4, but for now he would take good care of her.

"The fault was not Jacen's," Tenel Ka said in a mild voice. "And blaming the creature serves no purpose."

Jaina shrugged one shoulder. "Yeah, I know. I'm sorry. Just don't let Chewie catch sight of that pesky little thing when he gets back tonight."

Lowie handed the datapad back to Jaina with a confident bark. "Master Lowbacca believes that we can obtain most of these parts at the local fabrication facility, or create reasonable substitutes," Em Teedee said.

Jaina felt hopeful. "You mean the factory where your parents work?"

"Blaster bolts," Jacen said. "Are you sure? There's a lot of stuff on that list. What do they make at the factory, anyway?"

Lowie gestured with his hands and growled an answer. Jaina could vaguely sense what he was saying. Em Teedee said, "The fabrication facility that employs Master Lowbacca's parents, as well as most of the other inhabitants of this tree city, produces a variety of sophisticated computer equipment for use in a wide range of transportation applications."

Jaina's interest sharpened at the idea of a factory filled with exotic and complex systems.

"Like what?" Jacen asked, placing Ion back in her cage. The little rodent inspected her grubs, rooting around in her fuzzy nest.

After more of Lowie's growling and gesticulating, Em Teedee said, "Among other things, the facility produces guidance control systems for planetary control towers, navigational subsystems and backups, tactical systems, communication encryption generators, multiphasic—"

"Hey I think we get the idea. Thanks, Em Teedee," Jacen broke in.

Jaina tried to suppress a chuckle. Her ever-curious brother had gotten more explanation than he had bargained for. "Lowie, is there any way we can move the *Shadow Chaser* closer to your home so we can work on it more easily? The hangar bay where we stored it is way on the other side of the city. Not very convenient, if you know what I mean."

Lowie shook his head, but growled a suggestion. "Master Lowbacca proposes—" Em Teedee began.

"Yeah, I think I got it," Jaina said, struggling to understand a few of the Wookiee words. "We can pull out the damaged subsystems one or two at a time, bring them here to Lowie's house, and work on 'em." She beamed. "That's a great idea. So what are we waiting for?"

6

THE MORNING BREEZE ruffled Lowie's ginger-colored fur as he stood with his friends outside on the treetop observation platform. The area was broad and smooth, empty of equipment or visitors—the perfect place for them to stretch their muscles and perform Jedi exercises in the fresh outdoors.

The air was enriched with the scent of spring blossoms, new leaves, and sun-warmed wood. Beside him on the wooden platform, Sirra crouched in pensive silence, watching the Jedi trainees as they worked through their individual exercise routines.

Lowie tried not to make it obvious that he was keeping an eye on Sirra. Too great a show of concern on his part, he figured, would probably only annoy his sister and make her more stubborn. They had left many issues unspoken between them, but he knew they would have to talk soon.

He flicked his golden eyes around the platform and watched as Jacen did push-ups and Jaina practiced gymnastic tumbles. Tenel Ka, limber as ever, stood on one leg, the other pulled up high behind her, pointing toward the sky.

Lowie bent over, placed both hands flat on the warm wood of the platform, kicked his feet into the air, and balanced there. When Jaina turned a cartwheel past him, he risked another look at Sirra. His brash younger sister had spoken very little since his arrival yesterday, though she had instinctively remained close to him. Lowie couldn't help wondering what she was thinking. Did Sirra in any way resent him because he had inherited Jedi potential, while she had not? Did she blame him for Raaba's death? Did she resent the friends he had brought home with him?

He and his sister were so different that Lowie wondered if there had ever been a time when they understood each other completely. Lowie was thoughtful, analytical, introspective, while Sirra was wild, confident, outspoken. He preferred not to draw attention to himself, while she enjoyed surprising people with her appearance—why else would she trim the fur at her ankles, knees, wrists, and elsewhere in such a strange patchwork style?

Sirra and Lowie had always trusted one another, though— but did she *still* trust him?

Tenel Ka whirled through Lowie's field of vision, performing aerial somersaults. He felt himself begin to lose his balance, but quickly regained it and began doing vertical push-ups.

"Hey, Lowie," Jacen yelled from behind him, "can you spare a little concentration from your exercises to teach us a few words in your Wookiee dialect?"

Lowie grunted his assent. "Master Lowbacca says he would not be averse to the possibility of instructing you," Em Teedee translated.

Jaina chuckled. "Gee, that's funny, Em Teedee—it sounded to me like all he said was 'yes.'"

"Well, I suppose that *is* an alternate translation," Em Teedee said, sounding somewhat miffed. "Though it's rather unimaginative."

Lowie gave a bark of laughter and looked over at Sirra to see if she had listened to the interchange. She returned his look for a moment, then deliberately turned and sat with her back to him at the edge of the platform, dangling her legs over the side, above the leafy canopy far below. She stared down toward the unseen depths . . . where Raaba had disappeared.

"Well then," Em Teedee said, sounding hurt now, "once you've taught the others your dialect, Master Lowbacca, I suppose you won't require my services anymore."

"Of course we'll still need you, Em Teedee," Jaina said. "We'll never be able to understand *every* word Lowie says."

Lowie absently grunted his agreement, still looking at Sirra's hunched shoulders. It occurred to him that although he had come home to support her in this difficult time, he had no idea *how* to do it. Clearly, his presence alone was not enough. He wanted to try talking with her, but what if she had problems he couldn't solve? What if *he* was part of the problem, having set a dangerous example that his sister felt obligated to follow, though it might mean her death?

Still balanced on his hands but deep in thought about Sirra, Lowie lost his concentration and his balance again, this time with embarrassing results. He teetered precariously for a moment, trying to regain his equilibrium. Em Teedee let out a squeal of surprise, then Lowie toppled over, landing on his rear end with a loud thump.

Jaina rushed over, adding to the Wookiee's embarrassment. "Are you all right?"

Lowie wished his friends had ignored the entire incident. To Jaina's credit, as soon as she had determined he was unhurt, she made a hasty retreat and became absorbed in her exercises again, studiously pretending not to notice while Lowie picked himself up off the platform's floorboards and dusted off his fur.

Still a bit self-conscious at his clumsiness, Lowie told Em Teedee to shut down for a rest cycle as he ambled over and seated himself by Sirra at the platform's edge, letting his legs swing free beside hers. He waited for a while, hoping his withdrawn sister would say something, since he had no idea where to begin. Watching her out of the corner of his eye, he pondered again what had caused them to turn out so different from each other, how two such opposites could spring from the same set of parents.

Lowie had a strong aptitude for the Force, whereas Sirra showed neither potential nor interest in the Jedi Knights. Lowie's quiet introspective nature had always been a sharp contrast to her confident outspokenness—until recently, that is, when she'd become so quiet. And, while Lowie could sit engrossed for hours in the intricacies of a computer system, Sirra became restless quickly and longed for excitement and adventure. In addition, Lowie had always prided himself in being obedient, finding it simpler to do what was expected of him than to expend effort on meaningless acts of rebellion against authority.

At that thought, Lowie's eyes were drawn to the bands of close-cropped fur on Sirra's body. It was not a style sported by any adults that Lowie knew, and very few youth. He finally decided to ask her about it, hoping to start a conversation somehow. Lowie blurted out the question, asking if the style kept her cooler during warm weather.

Sirra shrugged. That was not why she did it.

A symbol of mourning, then? For Raaba?

Sirra snorted at the suggestion.

Rebellion, then?

Sirra thought for a moment before sighing in confusion, obviously at a loss about how to explain. She thought of it as . . . a way of showing on the outside what did not show on the *inside*: that she was different.

Lowie considered this, rumbling deep in his throat. He had thought it was already clear enough that everyone was different.

Sirra shook her head and sprang to her feet on the platform. Lowie saw at once that she was irritated, that he had misunderstood her, for his sister walked all the way around the edge of the platform before motioning for him to join her. When he did, he practically had to run to keep pace with her.

At last Sirra spoke again, her agitation apparent in her voice. She pointed to her shaved wrists and elbows, explaining in more detail that she did this to show others that she was not like *them*.

Lowie cocked his head quizzically, trying to think of a response, but Sirra resumed her explanation. She said that since she didn't have Force potential as he did, their parents had always just assumed that she would work in the fabrication facility. But Sirra had no wish to work there like everyone else did. She didn't enjoy assembling computers, and was only a mediocre programmer. She raised a fist and barked loudly— she wanted something much more exciting!

Lowie shook his head sternly. Wookiees could excel in engineering, in science, in piloting—anything they wanted to. But such success did not come easily. He nodded toward his friends to indicate how hard they were training at the moment. Lowie and Sirra walked together for a while in silence.

Jacen, Jaina, and Tenel Ka finished their exercises and perched at the edge of the platform, looking down at the beautiful tree canopy. Jacen pointed. "Hey, Lowie—how do you say the name for those trees?"

Lowie barked the answer—wroshyr.

After he and Sirra had skirted the trio, Lowie asked his sister what she wanted to do with her life. Sirra groaned and shrugged uncertainly.

Lowie thought for a moment. Well, what did she *like* to do? he asked.

Sirra heaved a heavy sigh, spreading her hairy arms wide to encompass the forest and the sky. She loved to be out and around, to visit new places and learn new things. She enjoyed feeling free, the way Lowie himself did when he'd travel alone in his skyhopper. And Sirra liked making her own decisions, not being told what she had to do and when.

Lowie growled the names of distant cities of Kashyyyk, suggesting other factories, other jobs. Sirra waved a hand as if to brush the idea away. She wanted to do something important, something unusual. Her voice suddenly sounded resentful of Lowie and his Jedi friends. They had been given a tremendous opportunity, and she wanted one for herself.

The twins and Tenel Ka took turns reaching out with the Force to make temporary furrows in the leafy canopy below, as if a giant invisible bird of prey were skimming over the leaves in search of its quarry. Sirra grumbled in disgust and pointed to the Jedi trainees "racing" their Force furrows through the leaves, crisscrossing and intertwining them.

She would never squander talent like that, she insisted. Knowing that she soon intended to prove her strength and bravery against a syren plant, Sirra expressed her doubts that the young Jedi Knights would last even five minutes down in the forest underlevels. Their Force powers would not keep them safe, she asserted, if this was how they used them.

Lowie fixed his sister with a challenging look, trying to explain difficult concepts. His friends were merely "exercising" their abilities. Learning and practice were never wasted. He insisted that his friends were much stronger than they appeared.

Sirra shrugged away the comment and began pacing the flat, sun-drenched platform again. Exasperated, Lowie demanded to know how she expected him to help her solve her problem.

Surprise registered on Sirra's face. She hadn't *asked* him for a solution.

It was Lowie's turn to be perplexed. If he saw his sister confused or in pain, he asked, shouldn't he assume she wanted help?

Sirra's eyes narrowed. With a quick series of gruff words, she reminded him of when he had fallen down a few minutes earlier and bruised his . . . his *dignity*. Had he wanted anyone to solve his problem for him?

Lowie shook his head. Sirra raised her eyebrows, asking if now he understood.

Lowie saw what his sister was getting at, but that had not been the same thing. He *knew* she needed help.

Sirra sat down again at the platform's edge, looking out across the wroshyr trees. Lowie squatted beside his sister with earnest concern, and her expression softened. She didn't want him to solve her problem, she said, but that didn't mean he wasn't helping.

Lowie realized that it was helping her just to have someone who listened.

He clasped her shoulder, and Sirra sat closer to him. For now, that seemed to be enough.

7

FROM HER UNUSUAL perch, Jaina surveyed the high-tech tree city and realized how much Kashyyyk looked like an organic version of Coruscant.

Here at the canopy level, surrounded by industrial structures and Wookiee living quarters, Jaina saw tall exhaust ports and crystalline windows that reflected the hazy gray-white sky. The crowns of tall trees thrust above the main canopy like skyscraper towers covered with foliage. A huge clump of majestic growth in the distance sat like an island above the leafy waves of the unbroken treetops; from this distance, it reminded her of the pyramidal towers of the Imperial Palace.

Jaina thought with a twinge of homesickness that she missed her mother. The last time she and Jacen had returned to the capital world, though, they had lost their friend Zekk, who had been captured by the Shadow Academy. . . .

Clusters of Wookiee homes dotted the canopy, compact dwellings connected to the computer factory complex by natural roadways that extended like the spokes of a wheel across the treetops. Imported banthas trudged along the wide, wooden roads, brushing against encroaching leaves. They plodded along sturdy worn branches hundreds of meters above the untraveled and treacherous lower levels of the primeval forest.

The bantha Jaina and her friends rode from Lowie's home to the computer fabrication complex was large enough that all five companions could ride on the padded seats strapped to the beast's back. The bantha had a rich, spicy animal scent that tingled in her nostrils. A harness made of bright red ribbons jingled with burnished brass bells.

Her brother Jacen patted the wiry cinnamon-brown fur of the enormous beast of burden. Riding this bantha seemed to be the most enjoyable part of their trip for him so far. The driver, a mousy Sullustan with huge, dark eyes that glinted in the sunlight, hunched between the enormous ridged horns that curved around the bantha's head. The docile beast moved along the wooden walkway, paying no heed to the lush vegetation on all sides.

"Banthas were bred for desert travel," Jacen piped up, "but this guy seems to love it here."

Indeed, Jaina thought, the beast seemed fat and healthy, content to carry passengers from the residential districts to the main fabrication facility. They passed other Wookiees walking to work, eating up the distance with long-legged strides.

Beside her on the padded riding structure, Tenel Ka stared

ahead, her expression unreadable but alert, ready for anything. Lowie and Sirra sat on the back cushions, chatting comfortably in the Wookiee language.

Jaina looked forward to her tour of the computer factory. She couldn't wait to see the engineering marvels and industrial facilities the Wookiees had installed on their wilderness world. Lowie probably would have been eager as well, if he hadn't been so concerned about his sister.

The bantha stopped and let them off at an outer checkpoint that gave access to the technical complex. Using handholds on the padded seats, the companions climbed down the hairy back of the bantha and jumped to the interlocked wooden deck. Since the bantha transportation systems were designed for use by tall Wookiees, the drop was a meter longer than Jaina expected. She wondered how the diminutive Sullustan driver ever managed to climb his way onto the beast's head.

Lowie paid the driver a few credit chips, and the bantha trudged back down the cleared arboreal highway toward the residential islands in search of new passengers.

Jaina looked at the multiplatformed industrial facility, seeing decks mounted in tiers on the uppermost branches. Lowie growled in excitement and pointed to a level platform high above and behind them. From this angle, Jaina couldn't see anything on its surface, but then a small craft rose with a grating roar of supercharged sublight engines.

"That's an old Y-wing," she said, recognizing the outdated designs of the craft. The Y-wing had a triangular cockpit flanked by two long engine pods that together gave the fighter its characteristic shape like the letter for which it had been named. This starfighter had been refurbished and upgraded, and its engines were loud and powerful. The craft's afterburners kicked in behind the engine poda and the Y-wing streaked into the skies of Kashyyyk.

Another identical starfighter rose from the platform, hovered for a moment as the pilot adjusted the controls, then streaked off after its companion. A third and a fourth Y-wing also soared away.

"How many of them are there?" Jacen asked.

Jaina watched in admiration. "Probably an entire squadron," she suggested, then suddenly remembered something she had heard. "The New Republic needs all the military strength it can get if we're going to fight the Second Imperium. We don't have time to build all new ships, so I think they're refurbishing the old ones that have been mothballed since the fall of the Emperor."

"What do you mean, refurbishing?" Jacen asked.

"Well, there's nothing actually *wrong* with the old Y-wings," Jaina said with a shrug. "They were great fighters during the Rebellion, but with new technology we can modernize the engines, increase their hyperdrive multipliers. Since we're on Kashyyyk, I'll bet they're getting new navicomputers, guidance and tactical systems, and central processors installed."

Lowie and Sirra nodded their shaggy heads vigorously to show that Jaina was right. She looked into the sky and watched as, one after another, Y-wings shot upward in a spectacular aerial display.

Sirra said something else, and Em Teedee translated. "Mistress Sirra suggests we remain here to watch, since the upgraded ships often test their new systems. She assures us it is quite a breathtaking sight." Lowie bellowed in agreement. Jaina wanted nothing more than to witness the demonstration.

When twelve of the ships had been launched into the air, circling over the treetop industrial facility, they flew in tight formation, one behind the other, a chain of powerful spacecraft. Their engines boomed like distant thunder through the upper atmosphere. The pilots followed their leader, swooping down, cracking the whip in the sky.

The Y-wings formed convoluted figure eights, flying so close to each other that their hulls were almost kissing. But the new guidance systems and engines did not fail them. The refurbished Y-wings performed flawlessly, and Jaina felt a warm satisfaction inside. She held her breath, amazed.

If Qorl and the Second Imperium could see this demonstration, she mused, they might think twice before attempting to tackle the New Republic.

From one of the connecting structures that linked the perimeter platform to the central levels of the fabrication facility, a door dilated open. An excessively tall, spindly droid appeared, its legs like thin support pipes, its long arms coppery. The droid had a squarish head with rounded corners and optical sensors mounted on all sides. It strutted out, moving with spidery grace as it balanced round footpads on the deck.

"Greetings, honored guests," the tall droid said, weaving on its leg hinges as it walked. "I am the Tour Droid, happy to serve you this morning. I have received instructions to give you the complete tour of our facilities—in fact, the expanded VIP tour. I will speak Basic, unless you prefer to converse in Wookiee, Sullustan, Bothan, or another native language."

Jaina shook her head. "Basic will do fine, thanks."

The Tour Droid turned a pirouette on one long rodlike leg, and Jaina guessed that the droid had been constructed so tall in order to comfortably accommodate speaking with Wookiees.

The droid strode ahead with a mantislike gait. "You've already seen our air show for this morning," it said. "Now for the good stuff."

Since Jaina loved learning about the way things functioned, every workstation inside the fabrication facility intrigued her. Interesting smells of lubricants, cryogens, and electrical solder surrounded her. The air was filled with buzzing, humming sounds against a background of white noise from thousands of complicated manufacturing labs.

Jaina looked to the ceiling high above their heads and saw embedded glowpanels that suffused the corridors with a constant white light. At regular intervals, where hallways intersected, they passed trapdoor hatches that provided access to the underside of the factory and emergency evacuation routes down into the lower forest levels.

The Tour Droid led the group into a room full of transparent cylinders that stretched from floor to ceiling, pillars filled with a bubbling fluid and sparkling diamondlike matrices.

"Here you see our crystal-growing tanks," the droid said, raising the volume of its speaker patch to drown out the gurgling noises and whir of air-recirculation fans. "In these carefully modulated tanks we send electrical impulses in specific currents through the nutrient fluid to distribute crystalline molecules in solution. This encourages them to grow into a precise matrix with facet angles and electronic pathways mapped for our galaxy-renowned computer cores. A building is only as strong as its foundation, and these crystalline cores form the critical foundation of our computer architecture."

Jacen rubbed his fingers against a curved tank, tracing the paths of tiny bubbles as they rose toward the ceiling. "This is neat," he said.

"Please don't touch the cylinders," the Tour Droid said. "Faint electrostatic discharges from your body could disturb the crystallization processes inside."

Jacen pulled his hand away and looked sheepishly at his sister. She didn't bother to chide him for it, though, since she had wanted to do the same thing herself.

The next room was exceedingly cold, with puffs of white steam curling around the door frame. The air smelled of scoured metal and frost. Inside, robotic arms moved about, sloshing thin metallic wafers through baths of liquid oxygen, pools of ultracold fluid that halted any contaminants from spreading across the surface. "These wafers are delicate circuit boards," the Tour Droid said, "a perfectly pure substrate on which we pattern complex memory maps."

Jaina drew a long frigid breath, blinking her eyes. Even with their thick Wookiee fur, Lowie and Sirra shivered, though Tenel Ka in her scanty reptilian armor displayed no sign of discomfort. "Fascinating," she said.

The Tour Droid turned and, with long scarecrowish strides, led them through the cold room. The next chamber was large and bustling, filled with hardworking Wookiees, each wearing a mesh bodysuit made of fine wires that held their fur in place. White cloth masks covered the lower halves of their hairy faces.

The workers looked up and chuffed greetings to the visitors. Lowie waved, recognizing his mother at her workstation. Kallabow nodded, blinking her eyes in their whorls of dark fur, then bent back to her tasks, carefully concentrating on the circuits.

"For the past few months our workers have logged extra-long shifts and odd hours to meet the heavy quotas necessary to prepare our defense against the Second Imperium," the Tour Droid said. "Here the Wookiees are installing finished chips. The mesh suits you see them wearing are electrostatic screens to prevent even the faintest stray foreign particles from drifting into the air. Any contamination could be disastrous, since these components are so complex."

"I can believe it," Jaina said.

The Wookiee technicians bent over their workstations, using delicate forceps and tweezers to remove minuscule chips patterned and cut from the large glittering wafers they had just seen in the cryogenic lab.

"These basic designs are used for many different systems," the Tour Droid said. "While our specialties are in tactical systems, central guidance computers, and mainframe system controls, some of our chips are used in sophisticated droid models. Most droids are manufactured on robotic industrial worlds, however, such as Mechis III."

"Oh my, did he say *droids*?" Em Teedee chirped. "Do you suppose any of my components might have been manufactured here?"

Lowie rumbled a comment, and Jaina nodded. "Chewbacca helped put you together, Em Teedee. I suspect that lots of your components came from here."

"Oh dear, you don't think he used defective or rejected parts, do you?" Em Teedee asked. Lowie chuffed with laughter, and the little droid scolded him. "My question was entirely serious, Master Lowbacca."

After they walked through the chamber, Em Teedee continued to exhibit his curiosity. "Master Lowbacca, would you mind turning around so that I can see the entire room? If this is my birthplace, I'd like to give it a good look. . . . How fascinating!"

Lowie obliged, turning his waist so that the small translating droid's optical sensors could record every detail. "And I thought this trip was going to be dull," Em Teedee said. "This is ever so much more interesting than those dangerous adventures you insist on having."

For the end of their tour the long-legged droid took them to the highest platform in the entire facility, the transportation control and shipping tower, a computer-filled room with workstations so high off the floor they were at Jaina's eye level where she couldn't easily reach them. Several Wookiees stood around the stations, gazing up through the transparent dome overhead. The dome was reinforced with support girders that criss-crossed in triangular patterns against the hazy sunlight shining down.

"Because we are such a busy commercial facility," the Tour Droid said, "a constant stream of space traffic comes through this complex. Here we verify every incoming transport craft to make certain we receive no unwelcome visitors. We also have security monitoring satellites in orbit, ready to defend Kashyyyk, once they receive orders from the control tower."

The Wookiee traffic controllers worked as a team, communication headsets mounted to their shaggy heads and voice pickups clamped to their throats. They did not divert their attention even for a moment as the visitors entered.

Before the Tour Droid could continue, Chewbacca strode in, accompanied by Lowie and Sirra's father, Mahraccor. Mahraccor waved at his children; his dark streak of fur stood out much like Lowie's. Chewbacca bellowed a greeting and held out a large misshapen object, a blackened device that had once been a polished, precisely angled crystal.

"That's the *Shadow Chaser*'s computer core," Jaina said.

Chewbacca nodded vigorously and spoke low growling words.

"Chewbacca and Mahraccor here say they have been searching for you children," said the Tour Droid.

"Excuse me," Em Teedee chimed in, "but *I* serve as the translator droid here. Master Chewbacca, after returning from a pleasant visit with his family, has removed the *Shadow Chaser*'s damaged navicomputer central processor core. As you can see, he has spoken with Master Mahraccor, and they have successfully located the suitable replacement components to get the ship up and running again. Hooray!"

Chewie pointed to the burned pathways on the *Shadow Chaser*'s removed navicomputer core. Lowie's father also spoke up, and Em Teedee said, "Master Mahraccor asserts that this is an exciting new design, an Imperial configuration he has never seen before. Fortunately, however, he is confident that the facilities here on Kashyyyk can repair it quite nicely."

The Tour Droid bent over on its long, stretched-out body. "You are quite good at translating Wookiee speech, my colleague," it said, "but you lack the finesse for being a true Tour Droid. You seem not to have the ability to make interesting comparisons that customers can understand. For instance, you might have said, 'With our facilities here we can place this damaged core in one of our crystal baths, flush out the impurities and the carbon scoring, and use our own master computers to retrace the circuits and map the electronic pathways. In short, we will provide a bacta tank to heal the computer core.'"

Em Teedee wasn't impressed. "They certainly didn't *need* to hear all of that. Of course, I wouldn't presume to tell you *your* job," he said. "We have more important things to do."

The Tour Droid did not respond to the insult, since he had no doubt been given thorough programming in tactfulness.

"Thank you for the tour," Jaina said. "It was very interesting."

The Tour Droid stood up straighter, and the optical sensors

mounted on all sides of its boxy head brightened with pleasure. "That is the finest compliment you could have given me, Mistress Jaina Solo."

8

SURROUNDED BY DIMNESS in his private office, lit only by recorded starlight from distant parts of the galaxy, Brakiss contemplated the plans of the Second Imperium.

Time slipped away from him as he allowed himself to be swallowed up in thoughts. Possibilities for conquest engrossed him, and he ran them over and over in his head, contemplating the complete destruction of the Rebels and his former mentor, Luke Skywalker. Such imaginings soothed him. Resting his elbows on the polished black desk, Brakiss touched his fingertips together and smiled.

Suddenly, a startling signal destroyed his concentration like a thunderbolt. The potent alarm pulsed again, and he used his much-needed Jedi skills to calm himself. "This is Brakiss," he responded.

"Qorl here," a voice replied. An image appeared on the flatscreen communicator built into his desk. The old TIE pilot seemed rattled—and that surprised Brakiss even more than the alarm had. Qorl was one of the steadiest officers in the Second Imperium.

"We have a coded message coming into the Shadow Academy, sir. It carries the highest level of encryption. Every marking indicates that the transmission is of the utmost importance. You must receive the message yourself and respond personally."

Brakiss blinked. "Any indication of the sender's identity?" His thoughts whirled. Tamith Kai and Zekk had already departed on their mission to Kashyyyk, but even they were incapable of sending such a high-level message.

"No indication, sir," Qorl said, "but I would recommend that you respond without delay."

"I'm on my way," Brakiss said, and switched off, propelling himself out of his chair in one fluid motion.

He raced through the curved metallic corridors, taking an automated lift platform to the transmitting and receiving tower, which contained the machinery that cast a cloaking field around the spike-ringed station.

Several stormtroopers stood alert as Brakiss swept into the transmitting tower. Qorl worked at the receiving stations, scanning computerized readouts and recording the coded signal. Brakiss noted that the man used his biological right hand, letting his bulky robotic limb hang motionless at his side. Qorl blinked at the Shadow Academy leader. "They have begun transmitting again, Lord Brakiss," he said. "They seem to be quite impatient."

"All right, let's input the decryption routine." Standing beside Qorl, Brakiss had to think for a moment to summon the correct string of symbols and numbers, then keyed in his password so that the Shadow Academy computers could translate the high-level coded message.

Qorl handed Brakiss a dangling headset. "The message is for your ears only. Listen on this channel." Qorl helped Brakiss mount the earphones and microphone snugly against his head.

Brakiss listened to the crackle of static as the convoluted message ran through its code-deciphering algorithms and finally resolved itself into coherent words. The voice pounded against his eardrums, harsh, almost reptilian, dripping with evil.

Brakiss's eyes widened, and fear drove a spike through his mind. He cleared his throat twice before he could respond. "Yes, my lord," he finally answered. "Yes, at once." He drew a deep breath to continue, but the sender terminated the signal. Brakiss heard only static.

He stood rigid, using all of his Jedi strengths to keep himself from trembling. Qorl waited beside him, leathery face emotionless, his eyes unblinking. Only a slight furrow across the TIE pilot's forehead showed how concerned he was.

Brakiss spoke quietly, looking at Qorl but knowing that the stormtrooper guards were also listening intently "The Emperor," he said hoarsely, "the Emperor is coming here!"

An ominous transport shuttle dropped out of hyperspace in the vicinity of the Shadow Academy. The shuttle was an Imperial design, the Emperor's private escort ship, armored with tarnished hull plates. Its configuration was similar to a triangular *Lambda*-class transport, except that this craft bore very special weaponry, sensing devices, and ultrapowerful hyperdrive engines. Even such extreme modifications, though, were of little consequence when compared to the importance of the passenger it carried.

Brakiss stood within the hangar bay, struggling to drive back his anxiety. In all this time he had never met the Emperor face-to-face, despite his unwavering service to the Second Imperium.

The Great Leader of the Second Imperium, Emperor Palpatine, must somehow have escaped death years earlier—though Brakiss had been sure the Emperor had been destroyed . . . several times, in fact. He did not know what secret Palpatine had used, or how he had managed to restore himself to life, but Brakiss didn't care—all that mattered was that the Second Imperium was in the most capable hands imaginable.

The comm buzzed and Qorl's voice made an announcement. "Lord Brakiss, the Emperor's private transport has just come out of hyperspace. I await your orders."

Brakiss leaned closer to the wall speaker. "Very well, drop the Shadow Academy's cloaking field and transmit our greetings to Emperor Palpatine. We are honored by his visit."

"Yes, sir," Qorl said, signing off.

Brakiss could feel no difference, not even through the Force, as the invisibility shield dissolved around the station. He stood with an honor guard of stormtroopers inside the cleared docking bay. The transparent atmosphere containment field flickered.

Brakiss stared out into open space, watching the awesome craft approach. The stormtroopers stood more rigidly, their armor locking into place, boots clicking together.

The Emperor's transport followed Qorl's signal. The three-bladed shuttle glided through the atmosphere containment field, which flickered and sparked as it folded around the hull of the ship. The Imperial transport coasted to the center of the broad deck, then lowered itself to a stable position.

Brakiss swallowed a large lump in his throat. He transmitted to Qorl. "Reactivate the cloaking shield, please—we don't want to expose ourselves any longer than necessary."

"It is done, sir," Qorl said.

The stormtroopers shouldered their weapons and stood in perfect ranks. Brakiss stepped forward to offer greeting, but paused when nothing happened. The Emperor's transport remained silent except for a few hissing and ticking sounds as the ship settled. He saw no movement inside. The hatch remained stubbornly shut. Brakiss waited for any sign.

Finally, a voice boomed from loudspeakers mounted outside the Emperor's shuttle. "Attention, all Shadow Academy personnel! The Emperor has arrived. As a security precaution, we insist that everyone depart the docking bay immediately. The Emperor has a private escort of Imperial guards and wishes no further contact at this time."

The announcement took Brakiss completely by surprise. When he noticed that his mouth was hanging open in foolish astonishment, he closed it so quickly that his teeth clicked together. The Emperor had come to the Shadow Academy—and now Palpatine refused Brakiss's honor escort. The Great Leader wanted to be left *alone*?

Brakiss realized that he had hesitated in following Palpatine's instructions. Aghast and trying to make up for lost time, he turned and clapped his hands smartly. "You heard the orders! Everyone, about-face. Clear the docking bay. The Emperor wishes his privacy."

The stormtroopers turned and, with a booming clatter on the metal deck, marched out of the docking bay and into the curved corridors.

"Sir," one of the stormtroopers said, breaking ranks to stop in front of Brakiss, "I had requested to be part of the Emperor's personal escort squad. I'll stay here to greet him as he disembarks."

Brakiss blinked in shock, noting the stormtrooper's service number. He recognized Qorl's trainee, Norys. Qorl had said the burly young man was ambitious and ill-tempered, but Brakiss was nonetheless stunned at the impertinence.

"You will follow my orders, trooper," Brakiss snapped. "The Second Imperium has no room for those who don't understand discipline." He drew in a cold breath. "If I see any further instance of your failure to obey commands, you will be ejected from the airlock into space. Is that understood?"

As Norys clomped off without acknowledging Brakiss's rebuff, the master of the Shadow Academy turned to look back at the silent Imperial shuttle. He himself was unable to comprehend why the Emperor had come here if he had no intention of interacting with the Shadow Academy, or at least meeting with Brakiss personally.

However the Emperor was the ultimate master, and Brakiss would not dare question Palpatine's orders.

The last one to leave the docking bay, he turned with a swirl of his silvery robes and stepped outside before transmitting the signal that closed and sealed the doors to the docking bay.

As he stood in the outer corridor, though, Brakiss made a decision of his own. He was master of this station—and was required to know what happened aboard it, wasn't he? He had followed the Emperor's wishes to the letter, but now he needed to see what was going on. Brakiss went to a videomonitor designed for observation of docking and loading procedures.

With the docking bay emptied of stormtroopers and Shadow Academy representatives, the hatches finally opened on the Emperor's shuttle. On the monitor Brakiss was impressed to see four Imperial guards stride out, shrouded in scarlet robes. The intimidating red guards had been the most feared elite corps of Palpatine's forces, and now four of them had accompanied the Emperor here. Smooth red armor covered their heads and shoulders like cowls, reminding him of historical images he had seen of ancient Mandalorian uniforms.

The red Imperial guards moved away from the ship and took up defensive positions, their robes flowing like flames around them. A shudder ran down Brakiss's spine. He tried to feel the intense dark force crackling from the core of the Imperial transport ship. The Emperor, he knew, must be in there somewhere.

Through the voice pickup mounted in the docking bay, Brakiss heard a clanking, slamming sound. Two pairs of squat, powerful worker droids tromped down the wide extended ramp, carrying an enormously heavy isolation chamber. The worker droids, little more than the powerful arms and legs mounted on a stocky body core, hauled their burden without complaint.

The droids were gentle with their cargo, moving smoothly, carefully, despite the immense power in their hydraulic limbs. They carried the huge tank off the Imperial ship and into the docking bay. Side panels on the isolation chamber's black riveted walls blinked with multicolored lights; computer displays showed life monitors and external communications.

The four red guards surrounded the chamber, looking protective and menacing. Then they marched toward the broad doors—two in front of the chamber, two behind—into the main core of the Shadow Academy

Brakiss hurried to open the doors for them, but somehow the computer-locked seals were automatically broken before he could do so. The doors slammed open, as if controlled by the Emperor's dark side powers.

The red guards strode forward, still surrounding the worker droids. The huge isolation tank hissed and buzzed and bleeped as a thousand electronic systems monitored its supremely important occupant.

Brakiss stopped in front of the foremost pair of Imperial guards. "Greetings. I am Master Brakiss of the Shadow Academy."

The leader of the red guards turned his armored head, and Brakiss felt a cold scrutiny through the black eyeslit. "You will leave us alone. We have important work, and we require privacy. You may guide us to our chambers—and then leave."

Brakiss could barely contain his dismay. "But . . . I am the Master of the Shadow Academy."

The red guard said, "And the Emperor is the master of the galaxy. He wishes privacy for now. We suggest that you do not displease him."

Brakiss backed away, bowing quickly. "I have no wish to displease the Emperor. Forgive my impudence."

After Brakiss indicated the quarters to which the visitors had been assigned—the plushest and most spacious accommodations aboard the station—the red guards and worker droids marched into the chambers, leaving Brakiss alone out in the corridor.

He felt belittled, insignificant, stepped on, as if all of his accomplishments and work meant nothing to the Emperor. It baffled him. What could be the purpose of it? He frowned as thoughts whirled inside his head.

The Emperor had originally died in the destruction of the second Death Star, but six years after his defeat, Palpatine had been resurrected in a series of clones, which had also—presumably—been destroyed.

Now, after observing the isolation tank, the secrecy, the inexplicable behavior of the four Imperial guards, Brakiss felt a new and deeper fear coil through his body. He wondered if something could be wrong, if the Emperor could perhaps be in failing health again. . . .

If that was the case, the Second Imperium was indeed in great trouble.

AS A FORMER TIE pilot, Qorl had been trained in the Imperial way, with loyalties and duties and responses drilled into him. No questions, only orders. His mind had been programmed to turn him into a perfect fighting machine for the Empire.

The cornerstone of that training had been *discipline*. And one thing Qorl knew: the young man who stood before him was not disciplined.

He wondered if perhaps Brakiss and Tamith Kai had been too hasty in accepting Norys and his band of young ruffians from Coruscant to be trained as stormtroopers and pilots. True, the battles ahead to recapture lost glory, to reclaim stolen territory, would require every set of capable hands for the Second Imperium. But even if Qorl did manage to turn the rest of the Lost Ones gang into serviceable troopers and pilots, this one was *trouble*.

At the control pad of the simulation chamber, Qorl programmed in a new set of targets while Norys recharged his blaster rifle. He vowed to train this one, and *keep* training him, until he saw some genuine progress in the ambitious fighter.

"I still say I should have been sent on the raid with Tamith Kai," Norys grumbled, waving his weapon as if it made him feel more secure. "I could have taken out a few enemies, evened the score a little bit for our side. Set a few of those big Wookiee trees on fire."

Qorl set the simulated targets in rapid motion: black, orange, and blue for Rebels, and white for stormtroopers. "It's a small raid," Qorl said. "Zekk is directing the troops. There was no need for a second leader."

Norys took aim at a blue target and missed. He liked target practice better when the targets were slow simulations like mynocks. It was fun to kill them. "Then they should have sent me alone, old man. I'm a better leader now than that trash collector will ever be."

Trouble, Qorl thought, *definitely trouble*. "Why do you say that?"

"Because," Norys said, taking aim at an orange target, but only nicking the edge of it, "my followers are so afraid of me they'd never *dare* disobey my orders." He missed once more. "Is the aim-point on this blaster offset again?"

"You aren't concentrating on your target," Qorl said, then addressed the candidate's comment in a neutral tone. "Your example is indeed one method of leadership. But you have much to learn."

Norys bristled and missed another shot. He rounded on the former TIE pilot with a menacing growl. "Like what, old man?"

Qorl didn't flinch or back down. He had faced tougher adversaries than this young bully—though perhaps none with such pure mean-spiritedness. "You could learn to concentrate on your weapon and shut out distractions. You could also learn how to aim and hit your intended target each time, rather than just talking about it," Qorl pointed out. "The way you are shooting today, you would have become a casualty in only a few seconds in a real firefight."

"Really, old man?" Norys's lips pulled back in something between a snarl and a grin. He turned back toward the targets and, moving his blaster rifle in a slow semicircle, flooded the area with blaster bolts, never removing his finger from the firing stud. When he was finished, every target had registered a hit. A complete slaughter. Norys turned back toward Qorl with a satisfied smirk. "How much more target practice do I need, old man?"

"Enough practice so you don't destroy our own troops during a raid," Qorl replied.

Norys shrugged. "We all make a few sacrifices to meet our goals." He glanced back at the targets. "Seems like a fair trade-off to me." He tossed the spent blaster rifle at Qorl, who caught it with his good arm.

Trouble, Qorl thought, *definitely trouble*.

STARS BURNED IN the midnight sky like a billion white-hot embers on a slab of black marble. Jacen, Jaina, and Tenel Ka had long since retired to their beds—but Lowie couldn't sleep. Perched comfortably on the wide railing of the upper verandah, with the simmering night sounds of the forest all around him, he kept a watchful eye on his sister's window.

Sirra still insisted she wanted to imitate Lowie's feat with the syren plant, and he could not talk her out of it. Now he feared she would leave him behind at the last moment, go alone on her dangerous quest—as Raaba had done. So far, though, he had seen no sign that his sister was planning anything so foolish.

Because of increased production quotas for the New Republic's military requirements, their parents had both volunteered to work the night shift at the computer fabrication facility. Kallabow and Mahraccor had spent their lives at their jobs, contented if somewhat unchallenged, and seemed baffled that neither of their children wanted to follow in their footsteps.

But Sirra demanded constant challenges, and went out of her way to create some when life didn't provide her with enough of them.

The light in Sirra's room shimmered like a warm fire behind the window's leafy shade. Small glowing mesh cages rested outside her window and on various platforms throughout the Wookiee residential district—containers filled with a sweet-smelling substance that proved an irresistible attractant to a species of tiny glowing gnats called phosfleas. When the cages were placed outside, clusters of the harmless phosphorescent insects swarmed around them to provide a natural, pollution-free light source.

Sitting alone outside under the starlight, Lowie had watched Sirra's shadowy figure moving about in her room, pacing as if agitated, but he had seen no sign of her for some time now. Perhaps his sister was trying to sleep, he thought.

But though vague foreboding crackled like static through his mind, he liked being alone in the restful darkness, high above the ground, where he could think. It felt good to be home on Kashyyyk. He drew in a lungful of the wood-scented air and practiced a Jedi relaxation technique, slowly willing his tense muscles to unknot—

—only to jump a meter into the air as a set of cold claws pricked his back. Lowie stumbled to his feet and spun toward the railing, his defensive Wookiee instincts coming into play.

Sirra, shaking with silent laughter, hauled herself up over the railing onto the verandah and resheathed her claws, complimenting him on his reflexes. At least, she said, he had convinced her that he might be of some help during her quest. Lowie groaned, trying to quell the surge of adrenaline. He asked her if the surprise had been designed strictly to test him.

Sirra's voice grew more serious, and she lowered her head. She had wanted to demonstrate that she could slip off alone, if she wanted, and Lowie wouldn't have been able to stop her. Sirra turned her head up so that the starlight gleamed on the pattern-shaved tufts of her fur. Then she looked at her brother and promised that she wouldn't go without him.

Lowie reseated himself on the railing and gazed up at the stars. He grumbled about the unexpected ways she made her points.

Sirra purred, thanking him for the odd compliment, making herself comfortable beside him.

Lowie grunted, not sure he had intended his remark as praise, but the fact that Sirra was pleased by the comment spoke volumes. She enjoyed being different, just as her friend Raaba had. . . .

As if sensing the direction of his thoughts, Sirra began talking about Raaba, how the sleek, dark Wookiee had loved the stars. Even when they were small, the two young females used to sneak out at night and watch the skies for hours.

Lowie's shoulders slumped. Raaba should not have died. She had taken a foolish risk, going alone.

Sirra growled, pointing out that Lowie had taken exactly the same risk.

Lowie barked in agreement—yes indeed, he had been a fool.

His sister's voice was harsh. If he had it to do again, would he do anything different? Would he take a friend?

Lowie nodded a quick affirmative. Sirra said nothing, but even in the darkness Lowie could see her fur bristling in disbelief. After a long silence he finally sighed, then shook his head.

After another long pause Sirra told her brother how much Raaba admired him, how much she had wanted to be like Lowie.

Lowie looked up at the sky again, at the stars that Raaba had loved. He gave a questioning growl. When he had left for the Jedi academy, Lowie and Raaba had been too young to speak of making a life-bond. He still had his Jedi training ahead of him . . . and Raaba had plans too. With Sirra.

Here Sirra's voice broke. She crooned a low mournful note and then another. After a time, Lowie added his voice to hers, and together beneath the stars, they poured out their grief for a lost friend.

Hours later, Lowie felt more refreshed than he would have thought possible, even had he slept the entire night. It had been better to spend the time growing closer to his sister.

Sirra's husky voice broke into his thoughts, asking about his Jedi friends. Would they grieve for him, if he were gone? Like she and Lowie had done for Raaba?

He nodded emphatically, and she told him he was fortunate to have found them.

Encouraged, he asked her more about the plans she and Raaba had made.

Sirra did not speak for so long he was afraid he had offended her or reopened an old wound. Finally she described how they were going to be pilots, galactic adventurers. They had planned to work on freighters until they earned enough credits to buy their own ship and explore the stars. They could have been rich traders. She chuffed with bitter laughter. Raaba even had some fur-brained notion that they could make their names by charting out new hyperspace routes.

Lowie's fur bristled, and he commented that such a career was a dangerous business.

Sirra's tone was wry, pointing out that danger had never deterred their friend Raaba. Sirra spread her hands, confessing that she didn't want to do that anymore. Not without Raaba. She didn't know what she wanted to do now—but she definitely didn't want to stay on Kashyyyk.

Sirra paused again and stared upward. Lowie followed his sister's gaze, wondering if she imagined Raaba out there among the stars, exploring and having the adventures the two of them had always dreamed of.

Sirra sighed. It was difficult to lose a friend, she said.

Lowie realized how easy it was to take friends—and family—for granted. He found it hard to imagine how lonely his sister must be.

Sirra hesitantly asked him if he would spend the day with her while Chewbacca and Jaina continued to tinker with the *Shadow Chaser*.

Remembering his earlier feeling of foreboding, Lowie gladly agreed.

11

AS MIDMORNING SUNSHINE drove off the last shreds of mist that clung to the wroshyr treetops, four muscular Wookiees marched to the transportation control tower of the computer fabrication complex.

The four looked just like any other Wookiees dressed appropriately for work in the high-tech factory. They were tall and powerful and carried no visible weapons. The newcomers punched in the correct access codes and passed into the high-security tower that rose high above the other tree platforms. Their timing was perfect for the morning shift change.

When they crossed the checkpoint station into the control tower, the four passed an electrostatic air-filtration grid. The images of the four Wookiees flickered in the unseen discharge, just for an instant, before their appearance restored itself.

No one noticed.

The real Wookiees who had been assigned to the next shift lay stunned inside a small supply chamber in an outer storage platform. The Wookiees on duty, weary from hours of monitoring the ships that came and went from the computer facility, were happy to finish their shift and return home. They signed off their stations and handed over the equipment to the new crew, who gruffly acknowledged them in synthesized Wookiee grunts and growls.

The earlier crew departed, leaving the facility's control points, the lockout systems, and Kashyyyk's satellite defense functions in the hands of the newcomers.

One of the new Wookiees sealed the control tower door, pulled out a concealed blaster, then melted the alarm systems and intruder detection devices. Sparks flew. Metal and plasteel dripped, smoldering black. All four Wookiees then touched their waists, switching off the hidden holographic generators belted there. Their images shimmered, dissolving away, to reveal a commando team from the Shadow Academy.

"The holo-disguises worked perfectly," Zekk said, brushing at his leather armor and straightening his crimson-lined cape, happy to be himself again.

The stormtrooper stationed at the door said, "Alarm systems disengaged. No problems here."

The other two infiltrators, the Nightsisters Tamith Kai and Vorinda Ra, stood before the complex computer systems. The

Wookiee-level panels forced them to reach up to use the controls. Vonnda Ra craned her neck to examine the readouts and identify systems.

Tamith Kai brooded, mulling over various details. She clasped her long-nailed hands together. "This plan must proceed according to schedule," she said. "If it does, it looks as if success will be ours."

"We'll succeed," Zekk said confidently. "I won't disappoint Master Brakiss."

Vonnda Ra worked at two of the control panels, studying keyboards and diagnostics. Satisfied, the Nightsister slipped an insulated vibroblade from her belt sheath and flicked on the humming knife. She bent down under the panels and slashed sideways to sever the power cords. Bright sparks spat out, followed by curling white electrical smoke.

She backed away, covering her nose against the acrid smell, then stood up straight again, looking satisfied. "Kashyyyk's orbital defense systems have been permanently disabled."

Zekk nodded at the destroyed control panel, his green eyes flashing. "Sure looks permanent to me."

"You're in command of this mission, Zekk," Tamith Kai said, plugging a hand-held translator into the communications console. "Don't you think it's time you transmitted your signal to lure those Jedi brats here, where we can take care of them?" The Nightsister looked insufferably pleased with herself.

Zekk swallowed, his mind whirling. He had known this moment would come, and he had to face it.

"Do I sense hesitation?" Tamith Kai snapped.

"No," he answered, "just working out the proper wording for the message. They must be intrigued and concerned . . . and convinced."

Zekk hovered over the communications console, pondering his words, then punched them into the translator that would convert them to the appropriate Wookiee dialect and send a text message with the highest priority to where Jacen and Jaina were staying with their friends.

If he worded it correctly, he knew the twins would come.

Back in the Wookiee home high in the trees, Jacen did his best to keep up with his friends in the fast-paced computer skill game. But the other players—Lowie, Sirra, and Tenel Ka—far outmatched his reflexes. Jaina, meanwhile, had gone with Chewbacca to work on their damaged ship.

The friends sat at the four sides of a rectangular control grid, each with one hand on the small, flexible motion sensors that guided tiny laserprojected simulations of space fighters. They fought a miniature reenactment of the original Death Star battle.

Lowie and Sirra flew fast X-wing fighters, while Jacen and Tenel Ka were stuck with flanking defensive ships, sluggish old Y-wings. The computer did its best to pursue them all, its simulated TIE fighters firing repeatedly, while enormous turbolaser cannons emplaced in the Death Star trench criss-crossed space with deadly fire-lines.

Jacen was good at target shooting; he and Jaina had often used the *Millennium Falcon*'s quad laser cannons to blast chunks of space debris out of Coruscant orbit. But Lowie and his sister were more intimately familiar with complex computer games, and Tenel Ka had the finely honed reflexes of a warrior from Dathomir.

Jacen's fingers flew across his motion sensor, banking his Y-wing—but a TIE fighter clung close to his rear engine pods. Jacen spun about. "Hey, get off my back," he cried. By sheer luck, the TIE fighter crossed into one of the turbolaser blasts from the trench guns, conveniently saving Jacen.

Anxious to divert attention from his so-so performance in the game, Jacen tried to distract the other players in the most obvious way. Between spins and banks and firing, he told a joke.

"Hey, guys, do you know what sound Whiphids make when they kiss?"

"I have neither seen nor heard Whiphids kiss," Tenel Ka said.

"Master Lowbacca says he's certain he would never wish to," Em Teedee said.

"Come on," Jacen interrupted. "It's a joke. What sound do Whiphids make when they kiss?" He paused a second, cocking an eyebrow. "*Ouch!*"

Tenel Ka looked perplexed, and Lowie groaned, but Sirra endeared herself forever to Jacen by chuffing uproariously at the joke. Then, after only a moment, Sirra sent her holographic fighter ahead of his with redoubled effort.

Little green lances of laser fire shot toward him, but he managed to roll his Y-wing and avoided getting himself blasted. Another Imperial ship clung to his tail, scoring hits and causing increasing damage as it came inexorably closer. Suddenly the pesky TIE fighter erupted in a tiny puff of an explosion with spangles of computer-imaged debris as Tenel Ka brought her Y-wing fighter to the rescue.

"It appeared that you needed some help, Jacen," she said.

"I did—thanks." He and Tenel Ka flew side by side as they followed close behind the streaking X-wings piloted by Lowie and Sirra. Their target approached, a small thermal exhaust port just waiting for them to drop a proton torpedo inside so they could blow up the horrendous superweapon Grand Moff Tarkin had built and—

The comm system chimed with a high-priority signal. Sirra reached out to pause the game, freezing the fightercraft images in position over the grid. Lowie hurried to receive the message, already blinking his golden eyes at the sudden emergency announcement that appeared on his screen.

Jacen and Tenel Ka went to look as Lowie bellowed in alarm. "Master Lowbacca, what is it? Let me see," Em Teedee said. "How can you expect me to translate if you won't let me read the text?"

Lowie punched a button so that Jacen and Tenel Ka could see the message. The comm system translated the words on the screen back into Basic.

"Just a fragment," Jacen said, his blood growing cold. "Something interrupted the transmission."

"It appears serious," Tenel Ka said.

Jacen read, "Emergency . . . injured at computer fabrication facility . . . need your help . . . please come right away. We—" He frowned, feeling his heart start to pound. "But who sent it? Who could it be from?"

"It was sent specifically here, to this house," Tenel Ka said. "Someone must have wished to contact us directly."

"But only Jaina and Chewie know we're here," he said, "and they went off to one of the repair docks to work on the *Shadow Chaser*, not to the computer fabrication facility."

"Perhaps they changed their plans," Tenel Ka said.

Sirra yowled, and Lowie added his own roar. "Oh my," Em Teedee said, "Master Lowbacca and Mistress Sirra's parents are at the facility."

"We cannot ignore this problem," Tenel Ka said. "We must go now and confront it. This is a fact."

"You're right about that," Jacen said.

Lowie punched some buttons on the comm system controls a few times, then pounded the apparatus in frustration. "Master Lowbacca says he is unable to reply to the message," the translating droid said. "Something appears to be wrong with communications at the facility itself. They've been completely cut off from outside transmissions."

Lowie roared for his sister to summon the fastest bantha mount in the area, while he, Jacen, and Tenel Ka fastened lightsabers to their belts, ready for the worst. The four of them rushed out the door of the tree dwelling.

A shaggy bantha lumbered to their platform in response to Sirra's frantic call. The Sullustan crouching on the beast's wide neck appeared deeply weary, ready to go off shift—but when the two young Wookiees bared their teeth and roared that this was an emergency, the mousy alien perked up instantly. Jacen clambered aboard and reached down, offering his hand to help Tenel Ka up; she took the aid without complaint. Sirra and Lowie leaped onto the beast of burden's back, and the bantha plodded off.

"This thing can go faster," Jacen cried. "I saw them stampeding once on Tatooine."

Lowie barked an order and the Sullustan urged the creature to greater speed until its pounding feet vibrated the entire wooden walkway.

High in orbit over Kashyyyk, defensive satellites bristled with weapons, designed to target on invading enemy forces. But the satellites remained silent and motionless as a disguised shuttle, drifting in place, opened its hangar bay doors so that a squadron of TIE fighters could drop out.

Weapons powered up, the Imperial fighters ignited their twin ion engines with a loud roar and streaked toward the thick forest below, flying in tight formation. The general battle plan had already been input into their computers. The Imperials intended to strike swiftly, surgically, causing the greatest damage possible in as little time as necessary. They needed to grab their prize, then vanish into space.

Kashyyyk's defensive satellites picked up the enemy on their sensors and transmitted an urgent report, a call for action, to the control tower in the computer fabrication facility. The sensors continued to track the enemy's flight path, but they received no arming instructions or attack confirmation from the control tower. The planet remained silent. The satellites did not fire.

Although the satellites' weapons were inactive, the sensors continued to file data from the impending attack for future reference . . . if anyone on Kashyyyk survived the Imperial assault.

When the weary bantha finally arrived at the fabrication facility, Lowie, Sirra, Tenel Ka, and Jacen leaped off its back and rushed to the entrance.

The tall, spindly Tour Droid stood waiting. Seeing new visitors, it unplugged itself from a recharge port and assumed its security posture, since no guests were expected at the moment. "Halt!" it said.

"Where's the emergency? We've got to get inside," Jacen shouted.

"We are responding to the distress call," Tenel Ka said.

Lowie and Sirra both roared an explanation, believing that the Tour Droid might respond better to Wookiee than to Basic.

"No emergency has been reported," the Tour Droid said, its arms dangling from its shoulders like metal rods.

"There *must* be," Jacen said. "We received a high-priority transmission telling us to come immediately."

"Accessing," the Tour Droid said as it plugged one of its dowel-shaped fingers into a computer port. It paused a moment as a blur of characters streamed across the screen. "Are you certain you have the right coordinates? Could I offer you some promotional brochures?"

"Ah. Aha." Tenel Ka looked gravely toward Jacen. "Perhaps we have been tricked."

"Blaster bolts!" Jacen said. Hearing a roaring sound from high above, he pointed frantically to the sky. "It looks like there's *about* to be an emergency!"

Lowie tilted his head back and exposed his long fangs, howling in rage.

A wave of Imperial TIE fighters dropped out of the clouds, arrowing straight for the computer fabrication facility. Their weapons began blazing even before they arrived.

12

IT WAS COMFORTING to work with someone who loved machinery as much as she did, Jaina thought. Apparently she and Chewbacca were the only ones around today.

Cool breezes crept in through the open bay doors. The fresh air and the view out over the ocean of leaves made her glad they kept the hangar open. Constructed in a crown of trees rising above the overall canopy level in an outlying area beyond the Wookiee residential district and the computer fabrication facility, this hangar bay was used for major vehicle repairs.

Aside from Jaina's and Chewie's clanking and thunking noises as they tinkered, the cavernous, wooden-walled bay remained relatively quiet and deserted. That was fine with Jaina. She loved nothing more than relaxing with a fine piece of equipment, making the pieces fit together properly, fiddling with the components.

And the *Shadow Chaser* was still state-of-the-art.

When Chewbacca bellowed a request up the boarding ramp, Jaina crawled out from under the cockpit control panel she was working on and hollered back. "Didn't get what you said, Chewie. *Which* tool are you looking for?"

A large hairy head appeared in the entryway and Chewbacca pointed to the tools he needed.

"Just about done here," Jaina said, hoisting the case up to where the Wookiee could reach. "I can finish up with my pocket multitool, so go ahead and take the rest of 'em." Chewie growled his thanks as Jaina crawled back under the console.

She completed her task, reattached the access panel, and trotted down the ramp, where she found Chewbacca cleaning lubricant off the lower armored hull. He rumbled a question.

"Did you ask me if I was hungry?" Jaina asked, struggling with the Wookiee language. She grinned. "Sure. Working on modevariance inhibitors always gives me an appetite."

With another growl, Chewie spread his arms and shrugged.

"What are we waiting for?" Jaina interpreted with a chuckle. "Couldn't have said it better myself." Hearing a faint roar, like the sound of distant thunder, Jaina chuckled again. "Is that your stomach? You must really be hungry."

Chewbacca suddenly went still and cocked his head, as if listening. He squinted his blue eyes. The sound came again, this time punctuated by sharp thuds like blaster bolts hitting their targets, underscored by a low-pitched buzzing Jaina couldn't quite identify. "That's coming from outside," she said. "What could it possibly—"

Chewbacca held up his hand for silence. The Wookiee woofed and loped toward the hangar bay door, with Jaina hot on his heels. Outside, the treetops spread in a green and brown carpet well below the sheer edge of the hangar bay. Uprising branches held the hangar platform high above the remainder of the forest.

Peering out into the hazy sky, Jaina had no trouble identifying the overlapping sounds: explosions, blaster bolts, and a distinctive engine howl.

"TIE fighters! What would TIE fighters be doing here? And what are they firing at?" She looked at Chewbacca in alarm.

The Wookiee pointed in the direction the sounds had come from and barked an explanation: the computer fabrication facility.

Jaina groaned. "It has to be the Second Imperium! We never thought they'd strike here." Chewbacca roared in anger, and she needed no translation. "I know. We've got to get over there. Let's call for help—where's the closest comm unit?"

The Wookiee bounded to the communications panel next to the open bay door, slapped the switch, and bellowed an alarm. Jaina whirled as a stuttering whine erupted behind them. "Now what?"

The sound came from the *Shadow Chaser* itself. Chewbacca and Jaina exchanged glances and sprinted toward the sleek ship they had been repairing. Through the viewport, inside the cockpit, Jaina could see a petite woman with wavy bronze hair clad in polished lizard hide—a Nightsister.

"How did she get in there?" Jaina cried. "Hey, she's trying to steal the ship!"

The *Shadow Chaser*'s engines filled the hangar bay with a sound like millions of swarming insects. The whine stopped, started, then stopped again with a cough. The engines wouldn't fire. In the cockpit, the face of the Nightsister twisted into a scowl. Her creamy brown skin mottled with rage.

Jaina looked up with equal anger. "We've got to stop her."

Chewbacca dove under the belly of the ship, barking reassurance.

"You're sure it won't start?" Jaina said. "How do you know?"

His head inside the still-open engine access hatch, Chewbacca grunted and nudged a piece of equipment on the floor with his foot. Jaina recognized the primary initiator module that the Wookiee had pulled for repairs.

The *Shadow Chaser* would never start—much less fly—without it.

The annoying whine came from the engines again, and Chewbacca yelped. There was a sharp thunk, and the noise stopped as a shower of sparks sprayed from the engine hatch. The Wookiee ducked back out.

Then Jaina heard the low hum of an extending entry ramp. But before they could rush aboard to apprehend the would-be thief, the Nightsister herself sprang out onto the hangar bay floor and faced them. Jaina thought there was something familiar about the set of the woman's face, the icy beauty and cold anger.

Chewbacca bellowed a challenge, but the petite warrior rounded on the Wookiee, eyes blazing. "I came to reclaim my rightful property. You would be a fool to stand in my way. The *Shadow Chaser* is mine."

"Then you're that Nightsister—Garowyn," Jaina said. "Tenel Ka and Uncle Luke told me about you."

Garowyn shifted her glance to Jaina, her anger turning sour. "Why aren't you at the factory with the rest of your friends, Jedi brat?"

"Factory?" Jaina said in confusion. Why would her friends go there?

"No matter—it is too late to save them," Garowyn snarled, raising her arms overhead as if to hurl something, though her hands were empty. "It will all end here now—with me." She laughed. "You never had a chance."

Chewbacca bared his fangs and coiled his body, ready to lunge.

Suddenly, the meaning of Garowyn's words sank in, and Jaina cried, "We've got to help the others, Chewie! Forget about her." She ducked, hoping to make a run for the hangar bay door and the lift mechanism that would take them down to the main levels of the tree city.

"You're going nowhere!" Garowyn shouted.

One of several large wooden crates of engine components sailed through the air and knocked Chewbacca to his knees. He went down with a *woof* of pain and surprise.

Garowyn stood by the *Shadow Chaser*'s ramp, her hands on her scale-armored hips. With dark fire flickering behind her eyes, she used the Force to snatch other heavy objects from where they rested.

Jaina cried out as a similar crate flew directly at her head. She instinctively deflected it with a shove from the Force. Eerily, it reminded Jaina of the training sessions she had undergone while a prisoner at the Shadow Academy. Fear gripped her as the Nightsister tossed barrels, heavy bolts, mallets, metal sheeting, hydrospanners, and anything else she could fling, quickly and without moving a muscle, at her two captives.

Chewbacca tried to scramble for shelter behind a half-dismantled skyhopper, but Garowyn sent more sharp and hard objects flying after him.

While doing her best to deflect the flying objects from herself and Chewbacca, Jaina huddled behind one of the fallen crates and concentrated. Even in the midst of her own danger, she felt an urgency about reaching Jacen, Tenel Ka, Lowie, and Sirra.

Unfiltered lubricant oozed out of a broken container, making an acrid-smelling puddle on the floor. Jaina was frustrated that she only had time to react. She was too busy defending herself to formulate any plan.

Though Chewbacca had no Jedi defenses, he also had no intention of remaining a stationary target. Jaina saw him slip away from the skyhopper's fuselage and lift a crate with his strong, hairy arms. With a powerful heave, he sent the crate smashing into an incoming pail of lubricant tossed by the Nightsister. As iridescent liquid sprayed into the air and splashed to the floor plates all around Jaina and Garowyn, Chewie scooped up his discarded toolkit and, with a mighty bound, leaped onto the hull of the *Shadow Chaser*.

"Tell me what you've done to my ship," Garowyn shrieked, now directing the barrage of objects at Jaina. "How can I fix it?"

The crate Jaina was crouched behind finally splintered under the attack, spilling hundreds of rattling, loose cyber-fuses in every direction. Jaina scrambled to find other cover.

Panting, she dodged some of the thrown objects and deflected others with her skills. Perspiration streamed from her forehead and into her eyes, making it difficult to concentrate. "Damaged in an ion storm," she gasped, wiping an arm across her eyes. "You'll never be able to fly it."

"In that case, you're worthless to me," Garowyn sneered. "I'll take care of you immediately." Even as the Nightsister stretched out her hands, her fingers crackling with blue fire, Jaina cast about for a way to distract her.

From out of nowhere an impedance tester sailed toward Garowyn, followed by a hydrospanner and a barrage of rivets and heavy clamp-bolts. Chewbacca did not need the Force to hurl heavy objects.

Now it was the Nightsister's turn to dodge and deflect. Garowyn directed her attention to the Wookiee, and with a muttered oath sent a bolt of blue fire sizzling up at him. Chewbacca yowled and ducked, tumbling back over the opposite side of the sleek ship.

The distraction was brief, but it was long enough for Jaina. Reaching out with the Force, closing her eyes in concentration, Jaina gave the Nightsister's body a powerful shove.

Caught completely off guard, Garowyn slipped in the lubricant that coated the floor around her. With another forceful shove, Jaina sent her sliding toward the yawning hangar bay entrance.

"Give it up, Garowyn," Jaina said, her voice harsh with exertion. "You'll never get the *Shadow Chaser*."

"You haven't seen the last of me yet," the Nightsister yelled.

Then, to Jaina's amazement, instead of trying to stop the momentum of her slide toward the gaping outer door, Garowyn gave herself an invisible shove in the same direction. Chewbacca scrambled after the woman, but the floor was too slippery for him to overtake her.

As she reached the entrance, Garowyn flung out one arm to grasp a vertical railing that ran along the edge of the doorway. Without slowing, she used her momentum to swing herself out and around in a tight half circle to land on the verandah that ran along the side of the hangar.

Wind whistled around the open door. Inside, the sounds of loose equipment clattered and clanked, and small components rattled out of broken crates. Jaina scrambled across the slippery floor plates, trying to reach the doorway through which Garowyn had escaped. Before she could reach the outside, Jaina heard a puttering, buzzing sound.

"Quick, Chewie," she cried, "she's got a speeder bike."

Jaina stumbled toward the entrance, slipping as she went. She grabbed on to a wall rail to prevent herself from pitching forward in a long drop to the canopy below.

Her heart sank when she saw the fleeing Nightsister on a speeder bike zip across the hanger bay opening, heading toward the computer fabrication facility, which Jaina knew was under attack from Imperial forces.

Moving with amazing speed, Chewbacca launched himself forward. To Jaina's horror, the Wookiee gave a ferocious howl and leaped straight out the door toward Garowyn's buzzing vehicle, with nothing beneath him but thin air—

—and grasped a pipe on the speeder bike with one strong, furry hand.

Still slipping, Jaina held the wall rail and watched Wookiee, Nightsister, and speeder bike spiral down toward the leafy sea. Jaina clung to the rail and reached out with one hand, but she was too far away to help Chewbacca.

As the speeder bike crashed on the treetops, Chewie quickly regained his balance. The Nightsister, still covered with slimy lubricant, dismounted and scrambled for purchase on one of the narrow branches. Chewie swung himself to the thicker branch beneath her and shook the limb on which she stood, growling a challenge.

A harsh laugh escaped Garowyn's lips, and a triumphant look lit her face. Jaina could hear her voice even at this distance. "So you wish to die?" The Nightsister stretched out a hand that crackled with discharges of blue electricity. "You deserve it for what you've done to my ship."

Chewbacca, though defenseless in the face of her discharge of dark power, snarled at her.

In desperation Jaina tried the only trick that sprang to mind. Letting her eyes fall half closed, Jaina sent a rippling furrow through the leaves behind Garowyn. This time the invisible plow made a loud, rustling sound, like a stampede.

The Nightsister whirled to defend against the supposed attack on her from behind. Flinging up an arm to ward off her unseen enemy, Garowyn lost her footing on the narrow branch. She fell backward.

Jaina gasped as she heard Garowyn's head strike a lower tree branch with a solid *thud*. Without another sound, the Nightsister's compact body tumbled like a shooting star, through sharp and clinging branches into the of the jungle far, far below.

13

THE SCREAMING SOUNDS of TIE fighters ripping through the atmosphere sent a chill of primal terror down Jacen's spine. He knew the howl was only exhaust from the powerful engines, but he felt certain the Imperial ship designers must have delighted in the hellish noise.

In the bustling fabrication facility, a cacophony of alarms rang out from platform loudspeakers. Growling, barking announcements hammered through the air. Wookiee workers ran in all directions, activating security systems or evacuating the area.

TIE bombers streaked low over the treetops, dropping proton explosives that set the dense network of branches aflame. Dark gray smoke billowed from burning leaves.

"We must help defend against this threat," Tenel Ka said, looking for some weapon substantial enough to use against the invading fighters. Her face wore an expression of stony determination.

Sirra and Lowie howled in rage at seeing the destruction of the tree dwellings. The spindly Tour Droid spun its boxy head around, despite its numerous optical sensors. "Do not panic. Have no fear," it said in its tinny voice. "This must be a drill. No attack has been scheduled for today."

At Lowie's waist, Em Teedee piped up in a scornful tone. "Why, you silly Tour Droid, switch on your optical sensors! Can't you see this is a crisis situation? Hmmmf!" The miniaturized droid muttered a deprecating comment about the questionable intelligence of public-relations models.

The Tour Droid continued to issue calming messages, though its thoughts were obviously scrambled. "Kashyyyk has numerous satellite defenses. No enemy ships can approach this facility. We have sophisticated defense mechanisms, including powerful perimeter guns. They should begin firing any moment now."

"Perimeter guns?" Tenel Ka said, her cool gray eyes flashing. "Where? Perhaps we can use them against these enemies."

Sirra roared, gesturing with her long hairy arm to show that she knew the way.

"A splendid idea," Em Teedee said. "I do hope we won't be blown to bits before we can implement Mistress Tenel Ka's plan. Oh my!"

"As my sister would say," Jacen said, "what are we waiting for?" He, Tenel Ka, and the two young Wookiees barged past the Tour Droid into the complex.

Sirra led them down an open-air corridor amid the din of explosions and laser blasts. They reached a network of pulley-driven vines, ropelike lifts that yanked them to a higher level. Sirra grabbed one vine, tucked her foot into a loop, and the rope sprang upward, drawing her toward the higher platforms. Lowie did the same. Jacen followed suit, looking down to watch Tenel Ka, who wrapped her arm around the vine and stepped into a loop with no problem whatsoever. Within seconds, they were all whisked to an upper platform at the outer perimeter of the complex.

Because of their quick reaction, the companions reached the defensive guns before most of the Wookiee defenders. Jacen saw unattended ion cannons with spherical power sources and needlelike barrels aimed toward the sky—but his eyes lit upon a pair of old-model quad-laser cannons, exactly like those in the *Millennium Falcon*'s gun wells.

"Hey, we can use those!" Jacen said. He raced over to the nearest emplacement, checking the status panels. "They're powered up and ready to go." Tenel Ka gruffly agreed and stationed herself behind one of the other weapons.

The two Wookiees chattered to each other. Em Teedee called, "Master Jacen! Master Lowbacca and Mistress Sirrakuk have decided to use the computers to determine where the breakdown in the facility's defensive systems occurred. Perhaps they can prevent further Imperial fighters from getting through. Oh, I do hope they're successful."

"They'll do their best," Jacen said, grabbing the quad-laser's targeting controls. He sank down into the voluminous seat in front of the cannon, feeling the energy thrum through the firing sticks in his fingers. Since the widely spread controls had been designed for large Wookiee bodies, he adjusted the targeting circle.

Imperial fighters continued to howl overhead, launching strikes against the Wookiee residential districts, but leaving the central computer facilities relatively untouched . . . though thrown into complete chaos.

A glance to Jacen's left told him that Tenel Ka was in position. Gripping the firing stick with her right hand, she seemed already familiarized with the weapon's control systems. In seconds her eyes began to track the enemy fighters overhead.

Three tall Wookiees charged onto the defensive platform and took up positions at the ion cannons, glancing curiously at the two humans, confused by this unexpected assistance. But they didn't waste time asking for explanations. Instead, they fired powerful blasts from the ion cannons.

One of the crackling yellow-white shots caught a TIE fighter that soared through the edge of the blast. The Imperial control systems flickered out and the TIE fighter spun dead in the air, its engine silenced. Unable to regain control, the pilot crashed into the distant forest canopy with a dull, booming explosion.

Jacen used his targeting circles to lock onto a sluggish, fully loaded TIE bomber that arrowed toward the clustered residential structures. The bomber came in, picking up speed while preparing to drop its deadly explosives.

Jacen grasped the firing controls and gritted his teeth. "Come on . . . come on," he said. Finally, the target lock blinked as the TIE bomber settled directly in the crosshairs.

He squeezed both controls, launching searing blazes of laser energy from all four cannons. The beams targeted on the bomber just before it could drop its proton explosives. Instead of destroying the homes of hundreds of Wookiees, the bomber became a brilliant ball of fire and smoke. The belch of detonations grew louder as the TIE fighter's own proton bombs fed into the eruption.

"Got one!" Jacen crowed.

Tenel Ka fired repeatedly until another pair of TIE fighters exploded in the air. "Two more," she said.

By now, additional Wookiee defenders had arrived to assume positions at the remaining guns. Jacen fired again and again, rotating his chair to aim at the rapidly moving targets. He blasted another TIE fighter out of the sky.

"Just like our practice runs in the *Millennium Falcon*," he said. "Only this time, hitting the targets is a lot more important than winning a contest with my sister."

"This is a fact," Tenel Ka said.

Another wing of TIE fighters swooped down, and Jacen shot wildly. So many Imperial targets, he thought, all of them bristling with lethal weaponry. . . . His quad-laser cannon spat beams of energy, but they all missed as the fighters spun evasive loops in the air.

"Oh, blaster bolts!" Jacen said.

Wookiees kept appearing, leaping off the vine pulley-lifts and rushing to their positions, although now there were more defenders than guns. Lowie and Sirra hurried over to Jacen and Tenel Ka, speaking loudly. Their grunts and growls overlapped, so that Em Teedee had difficulty translating both.

"One at a time, please!" the little droid said. "All right, I believe I understand the basics of what you're saying. Master Lowbacca and Mistress Sirrakuk have determined that a single-point defensive failure occurred in the traffic control tower for this facility. Somehow, all of the central command systems have been compromised. It appears that the attack is being guided from there."

Lowie roared a suggestion. "Oh dear," Em Teedee said. "Master Lowbacca suggests we would be well advised to go to the heart of the problem and leave these well-trained Wookiee gunners to continue the fight here. While I agree that it might be safer to move inside—I am skeptical about the wisdom of rushing into greater danger."

"Good idea, Lowie," Jacen said, ignoring Em Teedee's warnings. He fired the quad-laser one more time, almost offhandedly, and was astonished to see his quick shot destroy the side panel of another TIE fighter, which spun out of control and crashed to the treetops. "Hey, got another one," he said.

Barricaded in the traffic control tower, Zekk listened to outraged Wookiees pounding against the sealed door. A sizzling, melting sound worked its way into the background din as the Wookiees used high-intensity laser torches to slice through the armored metal. Their own well-constructed defenses worked against them, since they had intended Kashyyyk's command center to be impregnable. Slowly but surely, though, the Wookiees made headway, slicing through the door one centimeter at a time.

Using the security monitors, Zekk watched the hairy creatures out in the hall. With bestial rage one of them picked up a metal pipe and hammered at the door—to no effect, of course, because of the thick plating, but the Wookiee seemed satisfied just to be able to vent his fury.

Tamith Kai crossed her arms over her reptile-armored chest. "The noise level out there is most annoying," she said, then glared at the stormtrooper standing guard. Her violet eyes flashed with a twisted idea. "Why don't we trigger the locking mechanism and let the Wookiees stumble inside. We can easily take care of the whole lot before they recover from their surprise."

Vonnda Ra chuckled. "That would be amusing to watch."

Before Zekk could voice an indignant protest that *he* was in command of this mission, the stormtrooper activated the door controls. The panel suddenly slid aside, shocking the Wookiee engineers who had been working to gain access. They howled.

The stormtrooper used his blaster rifle to mow them down

in a few seconds, every one of them. Even encased in white armor, the stormtrooper's body language showed his pleasure. He keyed in the sequence to slam the heavy door shut again, leaving the fallen Wookiees out in the corridor.

"At last, peace and quiet," Tamith Kai said.

Overhead, TIE fighters and bombers continued to attack, dodging bursts of weapon fire from the tree facility's perimeter defenses. The reinforced dome overhead showed the battle in the skies. Several contingents of stormtrooper reinforcements had already landed.

Vonnda Ra worked at one of the computer stations, scanning security images. A minute later, she gave a gasp of surprised triumph. "Ah, I believe I've found them," she said. "The vermin were firing the perimeter guns, but now they're in the corridors. They seem to be making their way . . . ah! They're making their way here. Delusions of grandeur. That could prove quite convenient."

"Who?" Zekk said.

Vonnda Ra raised her eyebrows. "Why, those Jedi brats, of course. Had you forgotten your other goal for this mission?"

Zekk thought of Jacen and Jaina and their friends. "No, I didn't forget," he said. But he didn't want to confront the twins here, not in front of the evil Tamith Kai. This should have been his own private battle, the consequences of the choices *he* had made. "We'll meet them on the way. Ambush them. Lock down their location."

"Simple enough," Vonnda Ra said.

Reinforcing his position of command, Zekk turned sharply and issued brisk orders. "Tamith Kai, you will remain here and continue organizing the mission. Our primary goal is to get those computer systems for the Second Imperium. You—" he nodded toward the stormtrooper "—will stay here as guard. Vonnda Ra and I will take care of the young Jedi Knights."

Tamith Kai scowled at being ordered about, but Zekk rounded on her, his cape swirling. "Is that assignment beyond your capabilities, Tamith Kai?"

"Indeed not," she said. "Is yours? Just be certain you eliminate those brats."

When the stormtrooper unsealed the armored door again, Vonnda Ra followed Zekk, and they strode out into the corridor, stepping around motionless Wookiee engineers sprawled on the floor, heading toward a confrontation with Zekk's former friends.

Jacen rushed along, shoulder to shoulder with Lowie and Sirra. The interior corridors were full of smoke, debris, and noise. Glowpanels in the ceilings flickered off and on with energy fluctuations from the attack.

Jacen and Lowie drew their shimmering lightsabers and held them ready. Tenel Ka picked up a loose metal rod, a piece of destroyed pipe that had fallen from an overhead assembly, and loped along behind them, guarding the rear. She held the rod like a spear, as if hoping to find some enemy target.

Lowie and Sirra turned the corner in the corridor, and Jacen thought he recognized the route they had taken to the monolithic control tower during their visit with the Tour Droid. Suddenly, Lowie gave a surprised roar; Sirra bellowed in alarm. Tenel Ka brandished her long metal rod.

"Hey, it's Zekk!" Jacen shouted, skidding to a stop.

There in the corridor, as if waiting for them, stood the dark-haired scamp who for years had been a friend to Jacen and Jaina . . . who had taken them on excursions through Coruscant's abandoned building levels and dim alleys. Now the once-scruffy boy wore expensive leather armor and a crimson-lined black cape—and bore a scarlet-bladed lightsaber. He looked ominous.

Tenel Ka saw Zekk, too, and held her metal staff at the ready. In a flash of memory, Jacen thought of the warrior girl's initial meeting with Zekk, back on Coruscant: when the young man had dropped down from above to surprise them, Tenel Ka had whipped out her fibercord with blurring speed and lassoed him before he could jump out of the way.

Now, though, Tenel Ka had only one hand, and she did not choose to drop her long steel rod to grab for her rope, or her lightsaber.

For a moment Zekk's face seemed to open. His eyes grew round and uncertain. "Jacen," he said, "I—"

Tenel Ka glared at the Nightsister and spoke in a low, threatening voice, "I have your name, Vonnda Ra. I saw you try to lure others from the Singing Mountain Clan on Dathomir. In your encampment at the Great Canyon you chose me as a trainee for the Shadow Academy, but instead we rescued my friends—and defeated you utterly. We'll defeat you again."

The muscular Nightsister held up her claw-like hands. "Not this time, Jedi brats!" she said. "I shall enjoy destroying you."

Jacen felt her dark power crackle through the air, and he held his lightsaber high in defense. Fire-blue lightning bolts danced at Vonnda Ra's fingertips, burning through her body and sizzling behind her eyes.

She flicked her wrists to hurl her dark lightning at them— but Zekk shouldered the Nightsister to one side. The bolts of evil force flared past them like shadowy flames and scorched the wall plates.

Vonnda Ra glared at Zekk, but he snapped, "They are mine to deal with! *I* am in command here."

With a thundering sound of booted feet, a contingent of Imperial fighters charged down the corridor. Jacen looked up in alarm. Reinforcements had arrived—far more than he could hope to fight with his lightsaber, even with the help of Lowbacca, Sirra, and Tenel Ka.

Stormtroopers must have landed on the upper platforms, Jacen surmised. The Second Imperium apparently wanted something here at the fabrication facility. Judging from the alarms and explosions, the Imperials had already overrun most of the platforms.

Zekk stood waiting to battle the Jedi trainees, as if gathering up his courage and his anger, while the rebuffed Nightsister seethed with dark fury. The stormtroopers drew their weapons.

Jacen knew with sudden certainty that they could never win a face-to-face fight here. Tenel Ka pushed herself one step forward, brandishing her metal rod. "We must turn back," she said, darting a look at him over her shoulder.

"Good idea," Jacen said, casting a glance behind him.

"You, girl, are a traitor to Dathomir!" Vonnda Ra spat, just as Tenel Ka hurled the long pipe in her direction. The rod struck the Nightsister, knocking her sideways. Stormtroopers clattered toward them as Lowie and Sirra turned to charge back down the corridor.

"After them!" Zekk called, gesturing with one black-gloved hand.

The stormtroopers thundered in pursuit. Vonnda Ra cast the pipe aside. Patches of it were bent and red-hot where fire from within her fingers had super-heated the metal.

Sirra yelled something to her brother as they sprinted down the corridor, with Jacen and Tenel Ka right behind them. "Access hatch?" Em Teedee translated. "Escape? Yes, that sounds like an excellent idea. By all means, let us escape."

At an intersection of corridors, Sirra stopped beside a clearly marked floor panel. Reaching her long fingers down, she hooked the tiny ring-handles. With her powerful muscles, she hauled upward, pulling the heavy hatch free to reveal a trapdoor. She growled and gestured.

Without hesitation Lowie leaped into the hole, catching a strong vine that hung underneath. The tinny voice of the translating droid wailed, "But this leads to the underlevels of the forest! Master Lowbacca, we *can't* go down here. It's far too dangerous!"

Lowie merely grumbled and continued his descent. Tenel Ka followed next, hopping lightly over the edge, wrapping her muscular legs around a vine. Grasping it with her hand, she lowered herself into the darkness.

Jacen turned around just in time to see Zekk and Vonnda

Ra rushing toward them, flanked by stormtroopers. "Down into the underworld, huh?" Jacen said, glancing at Sirrakuk. "Looks like you'll get an early chance to complete that risky adventure of yours."

Sirra growled her agreement. With that, both of them plunged over the lip of the trapdoor and descended into the murky, leafy depths below.

Scrambling downward into the tangled foliage, Jacen looked up through the dense branches to see the silhouetted figures of Zekk and Vonnda Ra conferring at the edge of the glowing patch of light. Jacen could hear their voices faintly as he fled deeper into the thick forest.

"We'll have to follow them," Zekk said.

"You should have allowed me to destroy them when I had the chance," the Nightsister snapped. "Now they will cause difficulties."

Zekk answered sharply. "*I* am in charge here. We'll do things my way." He turned and shouted to the stormtroopers. "Down into the forests. All of you."

Zekk, Vonnda Ra, and the stormtroopers plunged after their prey into the underworld of Kashyyyk.

14

BRAKISS PACED THE corridors of the Shadow Academy, like an inspector general ensuring that his troops were prepared for imminent combat. He glided along with silent footsteps. His robes whispered around him.

The Master of the Shadow Academy looked too clean, too handsome to be an ominous threat. And although command of the new Dark Jedi rested firmly in his hands, his mind was instead focused on resolving his own doubts.

Brakiss allowed a flicker of anger—*anger*, the heart of dark side power—to flash through him. His right fist clenched . . .

then he dismissed the emotion. He must not lose control, he told himself, for therein lay a greater weakness. Now he must be strong.

Through his own work, he had created the armored space station as a Dark Jedi training center. He had done it all for the glory of his Great Leader, to help bring about the Second Imperium and restore the galaxy to order and firm paternal control. He had done so much work, risked so many things. . . .

And now the Emperor had snubbed him.

Since the secret Imperial transport had arrived at the Shadow Academy and the four scarlet-cloaked Imperial guards had taken Palpatine's sealed isolation chamber off to a restricted section, Brakiss had neither seen nor spoken to the Emperor, despite his many requests for an audience. He had been so honored to learn that the Great Leader would visit. . . .

But now Palpatine's presence threw all of his thoughts and plans into turmoil.

Brakiss glided along the curved corridors. The lights had been dimmed for the sleep cycle; most of the Dark Jedi students had sealed themselves inside their quarters for the evening. A small shift of stormtroopers continued their patrol duties.

Qorl had been successful in training new military recruits from the Lost Ones gang on Coruscant. The TIE pilot had paid particular attention to the burly Norys, who had a knack for Imperial enforcement techniques—though the insolence Norys showed gave Brakiss cause for concern. Still, only rarely did stormtrooper trainees show such . . . enthusiasm.

As Brakiss drifted along the quiet corridors, he fleetingly wished he were wearing stormtrooper armor himself, so that his footsteps could make resounding, forceful clangs. But unfortunately, such a demonstration of pique would have been deemed unworthy of a Jedi superior.

Brakiss was a powerful man—or so he had thought, until the Emperor's entourage arrived. The red guards seemed to consider him the lowliest of servants. This was an unfair dismissal of all he had accomplished, he told himself. Perhaps the Emperor truly was ill; perhaps the Second Imperium was in greater danger than Brakiss had feared. He decided it would be best to speak directly to Palpatine, to see for himself.

He had been patient. He had been helpful. He had accommodated every whim passed along by the faceless Imperial guards—but now Brakiss needed answers.

Brakiss took a deep breath to center himself, to focus his thoughts to a razor edge of calm resolve. Propelled by his growing confidence, he turned about and made his way toward the isolated chambers of the Emperor and his followers.

Brakiss would not be turned away this time.

The section reserved for the Emperor's group seemed even dimmer than the rest of the Shadow Academy. The light had been polarized somehow, so that it contained a reddish tinge that made it difficult to see. The ambient temperature felt colder.

Two red guards stood posted at the intersection of the corridor. They towered over Brakiss as he approached, the folds of their scarlet robes gleaming in the reddish light as if they had been oiled. The guards carried force pikes, ominous-looking weapons that might simply be ornamental . . . but Brakiss did not want to test that theory.

"No intruders are allowed," one of the red guards said.

Brakiss stopped short. "I believe you are ill-informed. I am Brakiss, Master of the Shadow Academy."

"We are aware of your identity. No intruders beyond this point."

"I am not an intruder. This is my own station," he said, taking another bold step forward and trying to impart power to his words.

One of the guards shifted his force pike. "This station belongs to the *Emperor*. He holds the right to claim ownership of everything he considers valuable to his Second Imperium."

Following that thread of argument would do him no good, Brakiss decided. "I must speak with the Emperor," he said.

"That is impossible," the guard answered.

"Nothing is impossible," Brakiss countered.

"The Emperor sees no one."

"Then let me speak to him over the comm. I'm certain he will wish to see me once he and I have had a brief discussion."

"The Emperor has no desire for 'a brief discussion'—with you or anyone else."

Brakiss placed his hands on his hips. "And when did the Emperor delegate the authority to speak for him"—he spoke the words scornfully—"to his mere *guards*? By what right did you become his mouthpiece? I do not recognize your authority, *guard*. How do I know you're not holding him hostage? How do I know that he isn't ill or drugged?"

He crossed his arms over his robed chest. "I accept orders only from the Emperor. Now let me speak to him immediately, or I shall call forth all of my troops on this station and arrest you for mutiny against the Second Imperium."

The two red guards stood motionless. "It is unwise to threaten us," they said in unison.

Brakiss didn't back down. "It is unwise to ignore me," he replied.

"Very well," one guard said, and turned to a comm station on the wall. He pushed a button and, though Brakiss heard no words from beneath the armored helmet, the Emperor's voice instantly slid through the speakers, like sounds made of snakes.

"Brakiss, this is your Emperor. Your insolence annoys me."

"I merely wish to speak with you, my lord," he said, forcing his voice to remain steady. "You have not addressed the Shadow Academy or me since your arrival here. I am concerned for your personal well-being."

"Brakiss, you forget your place. You can do nothing to protect me that I cannot do myself—with ten times the power."

Brakiss felt his anger dwindling, but he clutched his pride for one last moment. "I have not forgotten my place, my lord. My place is as the Master of the Shadow Academy, to create an army of Dark Jedi for you and your Second Imperium. My place is *at your side*—not cast out and ignored like an insignificant bureaucrat."

Palpatine seemed to pause before snapping a reply through the speaker. "Do not forget, Brakiss, that when this station was constructed I saw to it that explosives were planted throughout the superstructure to ensure your obedience. I can destroy this Academy on a whim. Don't tempt me."

"I wouldn't dream of it, my lord," Brakiss said, feeling his anxiety grow. "But if I am to be part of your plans of conquest, I must be consulted. I must be permitted to give my input, because I alone can provide the valuable fighters you require to defeat the Rebels and their upstart new Jedi Knights."

The Emperor snapped, "You will learn of my plans when I wish you to learn of them! I require no advice from you or from any other. Perhaps you need to be reminded that you are merely an expendable servant. Do not demand to see me again. I will emerge from my quarters when it suits me."

With a click like the sound of a breaking bone, the comm unit switched off. Brakiss felt worse than ever. More insignificant, more confused.

The red Imperial guards stood firmly in their positions, holding their force pikes upright. "You will depart now," one of them said.

Without replying, Brakiss spun on his heel and marched in silence down the hollow, echoing corridors of his Shadow Academy.

15

TOO STUNNED AT first to move, Jaina hung on to the edge of the hangar bay doors on the platform high above the rest of the treetops. She stared down in unwilling fascination at the spot where Garowyn had fallen through the branches. Replaying the scene in her mind, still not quite able to believe what had happened, she saw the Nightsister falling . . . *falling.*

By the time Jaina managed to tear her gaze away, Chewbacca had retrieved the speeder bike and buzzed back up toward her. With an urgent sound in his voice, he pointed to the explosions and flickers of laser cannon fire in the distant fabrication facility. TIE fighters shot overhead, pummeling the residential areas with bright energy bolts.

Chewbacca gestured with a long hairy arm, pointing to the seat behind him on the speeder bike. Jaina gulped. Surely he didn't intend for *both* of them to ride that thing? The tiny vehicle was already wheezing and chugging under the Wookiee's considerable weight.

On the other hand, the two of them had walked to the hangar bay this morning, and they had no other vehicle to take them to the besieged fabrication facility—and they had to help. There was no time to call for a bantha. She hoped her brother and her friends were all right.

Chewbacca brought the speeder bike to an unsteady hover in front of the repair bay and motioned for her to get on. Jaina squelched her reservations and climbed on behind him. She found little room to sit, and her legs were still slick from spilled lubricant, so she threw her arms around Chewie's broad chest as far as they would go, threading her fingers through his thick fur to keep herself from sliding off.

With Jaina's added weight, the speeder bike sank. Chewbacca revved its engine, and they took off. Though their forward progress was faster than Jaina had expected, the vehicle continued to lose altitude until it barely skimmed over the bushy treetops. The engine sputtered. Jaina could feel the toes of her boots brushing against taller branches and sprigs of leaves. The wind in her hair blew the strands wildly in every direction.

Jaina yanked her foot up to avoid an upthrust bough, and nearly capsized the little speeder. But Chewbacca felt the change in balance and managed to compensate by shifting his weight in the other direction. Jaina clung to his fur and gratefully maneuvered herself back upright.

"Can't we go any faster?" she shouted into his fur-covered ear. Her heart pounded, and the sweat of fear evaporated in the cold breeze of their wild flight. The Wookiee roared back at her; clearly understanding the danger their friends might be facing.

When they reached the fabrication facility, Jaina could hardly believe her eyes. Grayish white smoke curled up from half a dozen different windows and skylights in the factory. Splintered and charred wroshyr branches lay scattered about like the broken playthings of a spoiled giant. Imperial fighters still flew in formation in the skies, but they dwindled in the distance, heading back to orbit.

"Is the attack over already?" Jaina asked in disbelief. Chewbacca echoed her surprise.

The Wookiee had a hard time controlling the laboring speeder bike as they landed, and both he and Jaina tumbled off. Not bothering to check their bruises, they picked themselves up and rushed to the closest entryway, calling for Jacen, Lowie, Tenel Ka, and Sirra.

The scene inside the factory was utter chaos. Frantic Wookiees rushed about bellowing orders, extinguishing small fires, righting toppled machinery, and helping injured or trapped friends. The smell of charred wood and singed fur stabbed at Jaina's nostrils. Pale chemical smoke stung her eyes, but most of the fires were already contained, and a fresh breeze blew in through the open windows to clear the fumes.

Chewbacca roared in recognition as he rushed to his sister

Kallabow—Lowie and Sirra's mother. She was bent over another injured worker, tending his wounds. With nimble hands Kallabow had shaved the fur from around a bleeding cut and covered it with a coagulant bandage.

Lowie's mother looked up, blinking dazed eyes set within whorls of auburn fur; and she and Chewbacca engaged in a rapid, barking interchange. Jaina caught only parts of the conversation, but learned enough to know that the devastating raid was indeed over. The Imperials had struck with lightning speed, causing enormous damage to the outlying facilities—but their main objective had apparently been to raid the equipment stockpiles and steal computer components and encryption devices.

Jaina was reminded of Qorl's previous raid on the New Republic supply cruiser *Adamant*, when he had commandeered an entire shipment of hyperdrive cores and turbolaser batteries. The Second Imperium was definitely making plans for an all-out war—and soon.

Jaina bent down next to Kallabow. "Have you seen Lowie and Sirra? My brother Jacen, or maybe Tenel Ka?"

Lowie's mother rattled off a series of woofs, growls, and barks in a worried tone. She spread her arms to indicate the surrounding pandemonium, then gripped Jaina's shoulder, asking her to track down her children. Another Wookiee wailed in pain farther down the corridor; still dazed, Kallabow blinked wearily and moved past Jaina to help the victim to his feet.

"We've got to find them," Jaina said, and Chewbacca nodded vigorously.

Chewie made his way deeper into the damaged facility, assisting wherever he could and barking out phrases that were incomprehensible to Jaina. Never one to stand around wringing her hands in an emergency, Jaina helped to bind up minor wounds and put out small fires. Occasionally, she used the Force to help muscular Wookiees heave aside smashed equipment. Every time she asked about her brother and her friends, however, she received only confused answers.

Moment by moment, the cacophony around Jaina increased with a confusing mix of Wookiee yowls, barks, and growls. Oh, how she wished that Em Teedee were here to interpret all the nuances. Her head spun with confusion and disorientation, and she was relieved to see Chewbacca motion her over to help him tend a wounded engineer. Chewie greeted her with animated gestures and an excited bark.

"What did you find?" Jaina asked, biting her lower lip.

The injured engineer spoke, her voice just above a wheezing purr. Still unable to understand, Jaina turned to Chewbacca for an interpretation. The irony of the situation might have struck her as funny had the circumstances not been so serious.

Chewie explained slowly enough that Jaina could follow. The engineer had seen the two young Wookiees and two human visitors run down the corridor behind her. Not long afterward, she had noted some of the Imperial attackers in the same corridor—stormtroopers and humans in dark capes.

"Any way out in that direction?" Jaina asked hopefully. "Is it possible they escaped?"

The engineer shook her head. No exits, only maintenance trapdoors that opened to the dense and dangerous forests below.

Trapdoors.

Chewie finished binding the engineer's wounds, thanked her, and hurried off down the corridor she had indicated. Jaina skidded to a stop at the edge of a gaping hole blasted in the floor, where an access hatch had been ripped from its hinges. Chewbacca had to pull Jaina back physically to keep her from toppling over the brink. He growled, sniffing around the burned metal edges.

Jaina nodded. "Yeah, looks like the work of stormtroopers. They must've thought the trapdoors needed to be wider and did a little remodeling." She blew out a long, slow breath, trying to calm herself. "Lowie told us how dangerous it is down there. But I guess it didn't stop *them*."

Chewie opened an emergency locker on the wall. He

yanked out two knapsacks filled with supplies and tossed one to Jaina. Then, with a barely audible growl, he pointed down at the hole in the floor.

"You're right, of course," Jaina said. "What are we waiting for?" She peered down into the inky darkness below.

"Your jungle," she said at last. "I guess you'd better lead."

16

DEEP INSIDE HIS hairy chest, Lowbacca felt his heart contract with primal fear. He had known since childhood the dangers of descending into the perilous, untamed forests of Kashyyyk. The darkened depths often proved deadly even to those who entered fully armed and trained.

Nobody went to the underlevels willingly . . . but now, with Zekk and Vonnda Ra and the stormtroopers pursuing them, Lowie knew the primeval forest was their only chance.

The last time he had ventured beneath the secure treetop cities had been to search out glossy fibers from the syren plant, from which he wove his prized belt. He had thought himself so brave to accomplish the task alone.

Sirra's friend Raaba had also gone by herself—because Lowie had. Despite her skills and courage, though, the dark-furred Wookiee female had never returned. But Lowie was not alone this time. He and his friends could fight together against whatever dangers the forest held.

Above and behind him, he heard the crashing of boots and the snapping of twigs as armored Imperials followed them, shining brilliant glowbeams into the dank, forever-night levels, startling exotic creatures that had never seen the light of day. A few random shots rang out as stormtroopers blasted forest animals. Burned leaves smoldered, then went out in a gasp of thick smoke.

Lowie and Sirra did their best to lead Jacen and Tenel Ka,

using their darkness-adapted Wookiee vision to find broad, sturdy branches along the trunks of the wroshyr trees. Panting with the desperate effort, Lowie wheezed encouragement. The friends pressed on blindly, with no specific destination, knowing only that they had to keep going if they were to lose their pursuers in the maze of the forest underworld.

Em Teedee's round, yellow optical sensors shed a bright glow into the murk, the most illumination they could risk. "Do be careful of those branches, Master Lowbacca," the droid said as a twig scratched his outer casing. "I wouldn't want to break loose and fall. That happened to me once already, if you'll recall, and it was a frightfully unpleasant experience."

Lowie groaned, remembering the misadventure on Yavin 4. Losing the translating droid had caused other problems as well, since no one at the Jedi academy had understood Lowie's warnings that Jacen and Jaina had been captured by the TIE pilot Qorl.

Behind them, lightning shot through the darkness and branches crackled as the stormtroopers opened fire again. Lowie instinctively ducked, and Sirra dropped to a lower branch without bothering to test it for sturdiness. Streaks blazed across the thickets, erupting in fire and choking smoke.

"Hey, look out!" Jacen cried.

Tenel Ka grabbed on to a branch with her hand and swung down to Sirra's level. "This way!" she said. "It is safe."

Lowie leaped after her, one arm around Jacen's waist, then sprinted across the moss-covered boughs. Farther from the warm sunlight, each forest level had a different ecosystem made up of matted platforms of interlaced vines, branches that grew together, accumulations of mulch in which other plants—fungi, lichens, squirming flowers—flourished. Thousands of insects, reptiles, birds, and rodents fled at the sound of the intruders.

Lowie chuffed for the others to follow him. Racing along on his flat feet, he wrinkled his black nose and sniffed the odor-congested air. His nostrils tingled with a tantalizing, ter-rifying scent—a scent he had smelled before. Something that had nearly cost him his life.

In the lambent glow from Em Teedee's optical sensors, Lowie saw the wide-open maw of a syren plant, its glossy-yellow petals atop the blood-red stalk looked like a gaping mouth waiting for a meal. The plant had somehow taken root in a crook between two intergrown branches, and fed upon denizens of this forest level. The sparkling fibers that formed a plume at the carnivorous flower's center shone temptingly bright, while a delicious scent lured unsuspecting victims.

Beside him, Sirra also sniffed the air and spotted the deadly plant. She growled in anticipation, her patchwork-shaved fur standing on end. But Lowie put a hand on her arm, shook his head, then gripped her arm firmly. He could tell his sister wanted to secure the precious syren fibers and prove her bravery as soon as possible.

Sirra groaned in disappointment, but she clearly under-stood their priorities. Behind them, several levels up, the pur-suing stormtroopers fired again, this time at some large creature crashing through the tree levels.

Far too dangerous. The Imperials were too close.

With a growl Sirra took the lead, and Lowie guided his friends behind her.

As she raced through the morass of branches, ducking her head to keep her red-gold braids from snagging on thorns or low-hanging limbs, Tenel Ka reveled in the calisthenics that pushed her body to its limits. But she would have preferred to do it without the threat of sudden death from the blaster of a stormtrooper.

Her reptilian armor covered only her torso, leaving her limbs unprotected from scratches and insect bites—but she did not allow such minor inconveniences to bother her.

As the companions ran deeper into the forest, Tenel Ka took care to maintain her balance and watched out for her friend Jacen. Though he was highly skilled in sensing strange life-forms, Jacen was not as physically capable as she was. This was the chase. The hunt. Here *she* was in her element.

But at the moment Tenel Ka was not the stalker, but the prey.

Her reflexes were sharpened by her inability to see through the forest shadows. Her lightsaber could have lit the way, but she didn't dare ignite it for fear of drawing attention to their position. At the moment her focus had to be on simply running.

All around, she detected looming dangers that grew worse, more foreboding, as they leapt from one level to the next, descending into thicker and thicker primeval wilderness. Tenel Ka sensed that the two Wookiees felt the increasing threat; Lowie and Sirra moved more cautiously, supporting each other as they used their night vision to choose a path.

At a broad, open intersection of wide branches, the Wookiees paused, panting for breath. Jacen slumped beside Tenel Ka, utterly exhausted. They knew they couldn't stop for long.

During the brief rest, Tenel Ka remained standing. She turned in a slow circle, granite-gray eyes narrowed, sharply attentive for movement, for predators lurking in the surrounding trees. Her Jedi senses detected no dangerous animals, only a tingling underlying threat that grew more and more powerful.

Just then, a leathery plant tentacle wrapped quickly around Tenel Ka's waist and drew itself snug. Thin thorns dug into her flesh through her reptilian armor. She cried out—and suddenly the air around them came alive with whipping, writhing vines from above.

Both Wookiees howled and thrashed. Jacen yelped. The thorny vines yanked him into the air, legs kicking, hands flailing. In an instant Tenel Ka snatched out her lightsaber and—ignoring the threat of revealing their position to the stormtroopers—ignited the glowing turquoise blade. Her arm swept sideways, severing the vines that grasped her waist.

Jacen yelled again and managed to get his lightsaber out, too. Swinging it above his head, he slashed through the vicious plant stems with a sizzling, wet sound. The spicy smell of burned sap cascaded into the air.

Lowbacca roared and ignited his Jedi weapon, striking left and right with the molten bronze blade. Hungry tentacles snaked toward him, eager to pull the Wookiee upward to where the knotted cluster of vines came together in a cavernous opening that emitted a sound like rocks grinding together, a slavering gullet ready to smash them into digestible pieces.

Two of the vines caught Sirrakuk and wrapped themselves tightly around her arms. She bared her Wookiee fangs and, bunching her powerful muscles, ripped the vines free of the central stem with brute force. The plant seemed not to notice; it went on thrashing its tentacles, and its open gullet continued to mash and grind.

Within moments, three flashing lightsabers sliced away the clinging tentacles and left only twitching stumps at the end of the voracious vine creature.

"We've escaped!" Em Teedee said. "Oh, how wonderful!"

"This is a fact," Tenel Ka agreed. She examined the red welts and oozing scratches she had received during the battle, then looked up toward the next level of branches. "But our lightsabers have attracted the enemy."

The others turned to follow her gaze. On the branches above them, completely surrounding the group, stood a contingent of fully armed stormtroopers, their blasters pointed down at the young Jedi Knights.

Jacen shut off the emerald beam of his lightsaber and squatted on the branch, breathing hard as he surveyed the encircling stormtroopers. In other circumstances, he would have found the underworld of Kashyyyk fascinating, filled as it was with insects and trees, ferns, vines, flowers, lizards—a million new pets for him to inspect, then set free. He found many of the life-forms to be incomprehensible, unlike anything he had ever experienced. Even now, with stormtroopers like pale statues above, blasters at the ready and aimed at him, Jacen could sense the hidden creatures around them.

Near one of the stormtroopers who stood on a decaying branch, Jacen noticed that a broad patch of bark lay wet and damp, like a mottled tongue wrapped around the tree. It was slick, glistening, moving on a cellular level.

Two more dark figures joined the gathered stormtroopers. The ominous Nightsister Vonnda Ra, with her hard muscles, broad shoulders, and glittering black body armor, stood next to Zekk, his dark hair neatly tied back with a thong at the nape of his neck, his swirling scarlet-lined cape undamaged by leaves or twigs. The stormtroopers shone glowrods down on the scene.

"You are trapped, Jedi brats," Vonnda Ra said. "It could be amusing to watch you grovel for your lives—but I can assure you it would do you no good."

"We do not intend to grovel," Tenel Ka said, and the Nightsister glared at the young warrior girl from Dathomir.

Jacen focused his concentration on the wide, mysterious slick patch wrapped around the branch. It seemed like a river of damp leather; and as he concentrated, he felt a dim awareness, a rudimentary brain that was more a cluster of reflexes. But reflexes were all Jacen needed right now.

"I'm sorry it has come to this," Zekk said, "but I owe my allegiance to the Second Imperium now, and you are my sworn enemies. I can no longer deny it. That was my choice." Despite his words, the expression on Zekk's high-cheekboned face and the disturbed look in his green eyes showed Jacen how troubled he truly was.

One of the stormtroopers moved sideways to get a clearer shot at them.

Jacen watched. *Just a little more, just a little more . . .*

Perhaps he sent out the thought with the Force, because the stormtrooper did indeed take one more step. His heavy, booted foot planted itself squarely on the wide wet patch.

Without warning, the creature reacted.

A slithering flap of wet, slimy meat in the form of a monstrous sluglike beast raised itself from its sleeping position. The motion knocked the stormtrooper completely off the branch, and he tumbled screaming into the depths of the forest.

With a thick slurping sound the enormous slug creature reared up and up and *up*, thrashing from side to side, knocking two other stormtroopers from their positions. The Imperial soldiers were thrown into pandemonium, shouting and shooting.

Jacen did his best to send a thought to the thing, identifying the white-armored guards as the enemy and planting the idea that Jacen, the two Wookiees, and Tenel Ka were the slow-witted creature's friends.

Stormtroopers opened fire on the monster, but the blasters did little more than annoy it. Branches crashed and snapped. Energy bolts ricocheted around in the forest as the slug creature continued its reflexive attack.

Jacen stood transfixed, fascinated with the battle and the havoc the beast had already caused. Zekk and Vonnda Ra shouted conflicting orders.

The next thing Jacen knew, Tenel Ka slammed him aside. A blaster bolt sizzled past him as she wrapped a vine around her arm, grasped his waist, and dove to a lower branch. The two Wookiees were already ahead of them in their headlong flight.

Making quick use of the diversion, the young Jedi Knights continued down, *down*—dropping all the way to the bottom levels of the forest.

17

THE FOREST DARKNESS was so thick Jaina could practically taste it. She followed the agile Chewbacca more by sound than by any other sense, finding herself relying more and more on the Force to guide her hands and feet. The air was cooler here below the canopy. Jaina shivered, though she doubted it was entirely because of the drop in temperature.

With his sharp Wookiee vision, Chewie led the way without hesitation. He barked an occasional warning about a patch of slippery moss or a weak branch. Neither made any great attempt to keep quiet: their one concern was to catch up with their friends before it was too late.

Gradually Jaina's eyesight adjusted enough that she could make out the shadowy forms of tree trunks, black against deep gray. It wasn't much to go by, but it helped. Chewbacca made a snuffling sound and gave a low woof of triumph.

"They came this direction?" she asked.

He yipped an affirmative. Their smells were here. He detected four . . . no, *five* of them, as well as a faint smell of metal. Jaina decided he must be picking up on Em Teedee. Chewie growled low in his throat, muttering about other smells too: plasteel, burned branches, the thunderstorm-smell of ozone from blaster discharges.

Jaina's heart skipped a beat. "Definitely sounds like the Nightsisters brought stormtroopers down here with them."

Chewbacca increased his speed, following the fresh trail. Once Jaina misjudged the spacing and almost fell between a pair of tree branches that were farther apart than she'd thought. "Chewie, I can barely see," she said.

With a chuff of understanding, the Wookiee stopped briefly, rummaged through the emergency pack he had taken from the fabrication facility, and pulled out a small mesh jar. Jaina recognized a phosflea lure. He broke the seal.

Moments later, as if the glowing specks had materialized directly from the air, the lure's surface was covered with tiny phosphorescent insects. Chewbacca fastened the lure to a strap around Jaina's waist. The "light" now shed a pinkish glow directly in front of her that swirled like a comet's tail as she moved along.

Chewbacca pointed below Jaina to a freshly broken branch

and the burned scoring from weapon fire. The others had come this way.

"You're right," Jaina said. "I can feel them, not too far ahead."

The Wookiee helped her across the broad gap and they resumed their descent. Jaina climbed after him, watching handholds and footholds more carefully now as the glowing phosfleas lit her way. A feeling of dread mounted more strongly within her as they descended to each deeper level. She could feel the weight of the overlying forest pressing down on them.

Unseen predators bounded across leafy limbs, pursuing their quarries; the shriek of victims fallen in the endless hunt echoed through the thick labyrinth of branches. Smaller creatures chirped, buzzed, and chittered. None of them sounded friendly to her.

Jaina knew that her friends were good fighters, but she knew, too, that even Lowie, the strongest of all of them, feared the jungles of Kashyyyk. That alone was cause for worry, but the young Jedi Knights and Sirra had more to fear than the deadly plants and animals that populated the lowest levels of the forest.

Jaina could feel that something was about to happen. "No time to lose!" she urged. She picked up her pace. Chewbacca, sensing her urgency, did the same, barely taking time to rest his foot on one limb before bounding down to a lower branch.

In the distance Jaina heard a shout, a human voice that sounded loud and chilling, mixed with the wild noises. When she stopped to look in that direction, she saw flickers of and heard the sizzle of blaster fire.

Just then, the rotting branch beneath her feet creaked and threatened to give way. In her haste, she had not bothered to check the branch before stepping on it. Chewbacca spun and reached out to pull her to safety on a thicker branch closer to the trunk. She scrambled for purchase.

But the whole side of the wroshyr tree must have been weakened by rot or disease, for at that moment the bough on which the large Wookiee stood gave way as well. Snapping and popping, the gnarled wood dropped out from beneath him.

Jaina watched, her mouth open in a silent scream, as Chewbacca plummeted, crashing into the darkness below.

18

EXHAUSTED, ZEKK STOOD with the lightsaber still gripped in his sweaty hand. He found it hard to breathe the thick, cloying air of the underworld.

The smoking carcass of the dead slug beast, now sliced in pieces, lay draped across the overspreading branches. Burned slime bubbled with a noxious stench. Small fires crackled from stray blaster bolts that had ignited portions of the dense foliage. The surviving stormtroopers shouted to each other over helmet comlinks, completing their damage assessment.

Vonnda Ra stood trembling, jaw set, face drawn, as if the fury she had unleashed to fight the monster had drained her somehow. The new Nightsisters were supposedly proof against the physically damaging effects of the evil powers they invoked, but the tremendous battle Vonnda Ra and Zekk and the stormtroopers had waged against the mindless slug had left her looking shriveled.

Zekk slumped against an upright tree trunk, feeling the soft squish of blue moss mixed with ichor from the slug creature.

Only four stormtroopers remained with their party. The slug beast had crushed the others or flung them into the unseen depths below. Chunks of the dead thing sloughed off the main branches, oozing down to where rodents and scavengers rustled through the darkness in a feeding frenzy.

Zekk heard a crash and a crackle of snapping twigs far behind them. Suddenly, with a tingle through his own Force senses, he knew that two others followed, attempting to catch them—and he identified one of the pursuers. In astonishment, he blinked his green eyes into the forest shadows, reaching out with the focused power of his senses.

"It's Jaina Solo," he said to Vonnda Ra. "Behind us. She's coming this way." He planted his black boots firmly on the branch. He had to choose, but he could not. With all of Brakiss's promises, he had never thought it would be so difficult.

Ahead Jacen, Lowbacca, Sirra, and Tenel Ka had succeeded in eluding Imperial pursuit so far—but Jaina, completely unaware, was heading straight toward them. He would have to confront her himself.

"We must split up," Zekk said. "I will go back alone and stop Jaina. The rest of you, continue after these others."

"Yes." Peering ahead into the forest maze, Vonnda Ra seethed. "I'll make them pay for what they've done to us!"

With a gesture of her clawed hand, the Nightsister and the remaining stormtroopers set off after the young Jedi Knights.

Though Jacen fought to stay within sight of his companions, this deep level of the forest had become so dark he felt as if he were swimming through a pool of ink. Finally, surprisingly, the depths began to shimmer with wonder. He noticed the cold illumination of phosphorescent organisms, glowing insects, pulsing fungi and lichens that threw heatless chemical light into the smothering darkness.

All around him in the branches and leaves he could see spangles like starlight, as if—instead of being deep within a dense forest—he stood on a sprawling plain under a clear night sky. Jacen found it breathtaking, and nudged Tenel Ka's warm arm to get her attention. The immensity of it overwhelmed him. He had never thought he'd experience something so wonderful down here.

As he and Tenel Ka stared upward, wordlessly sharing the experience, an unexpected volley of blaster shots streaked across the jungle like fireworks. A sparking white-hot globe of fire blazed toward them like a meteor—the stormtroopers had shot a dazzling flareball that spewed light in all directions.

The flareball crashed into the crook of a nearby tree and lodged there like a tiny sun, sputtering as it burned hot and bright. The flare sharpened the shadows and washed the humid air with garish light, stripping away the cloaking darkness.

Jacen saw to his dismay that four stormtroopers were standing on a single wide branch and aiming their weapons at the exhausted Jedi trainees, though the brilliant flareball had dazzled their eyes as well.

Tenel Ka shoved Jacen away from her. "Hide!" she said, and dashed off into the thick branches. Jacen ducked just as a blaster bolt sheared off a steaming chunk of wood above his head.

A rustling noise through the branches told him that Lowie and Sirra had also fled. He heard somebody else, but he could see only the four stormtroopers. He wondered if it could be Zekk . . . and he wondered if his dark-haired former friend would show them any mercy.

"Oh, blaster bolts," he said as another shot tore through the air too close to him. "Hah—no kidding," he muttered to himself.

In the strobing light he could discern only brilliant colors dancing before his aching eyes. Then he glimpsed the flickering movement of a slender figure suddenly sprouting a bright turquoise blade—Tenel Ka with her lightsaber . . . and she was just beneath the four stormtroopers!

The Imperial troopers saw her, too. They shouted excitedly and took aim—but too late.

With a single stroke, Tenel Ka slashed through the bough that supported the stormtroopers. Her rancor-tooth lightsaber flared, and sparks spat off in all directions as her blade severed the centuries-old tree branch.

Tenel Ka dove out of the way. Wood cracked, vines snapped, and leaves were torn asunder under the enormous weight of the surprised Imperial soldiers. They fired randomly, shouting in panicked bursts through their comlink helmets as the branch fell away, spilling them into the forest floor below. The four stormtroopers toppled to their deaths, blaster rifles still firing.

Looking fiercely satisfied, Tenel Ka deactivated her lightsaber and clipped it to her belt. Jacen, standing within her view, gave the warrior girl a round of silent applause.

Farther down, in the shelter of a curved and stunted tree, Lowbacca crouched close to his sister Sirra as the thick branch bearing the four hapless stormtroopers plummeted past them through the darkness. With his dark-adapted Wookiee eyes, he could see Sirra sniffing the air, waiting.

Sirra seemed preoccupied with testing the air and studying her surroundings. Then Lowie caught a twinge of scent—the frightening, tingling aroma of a syren plant, a large one, farther below.

With a quiet groan, he searched the area with his golden eyes until he saw the monstrous carnivorous flower in the thick underbrush of the ground level, its glossy yellow petals spread wide, its blood-red central stalk giving off a tempting scent. Sirra maneuvered herself until she was above the dangerous plant, then sought a safe way to get down to it.

Suddenly, Vonnda Ra leaped out of nowhere and slammed into Lowie, her hands crackling with evil lightning force. Jolts of searing electricity coursed through Lowie, and his fur began to smoke even as he staggered backward with a bellowing roar, stunned and disoriented.

In a blur of claws and teeth, Sirra leaped into the fray, flashing her ferocious Wookiee fangs. Her strong arms pushed Vonnda Ra away from her brother. The Nightsister turned on Sirra and released a bolt of her sizzling evil power.

Sirra cried out in pain and stumbled, then regathered her strength, launching off with powerful leg muscles into a fullbody tackle of Vonnda Ra. Together, they went over the edge of the slippery, moss-covered branch and out into open air, tumbling and slashing.

Lowie shook himself and leaped into motion, rushing toward his sister. He reached out and caught the falling Nightsister's black cape, but the tough, slick fabric slipped through his fingers.

Sirra and Vonnda Ra fell.

Lowie howled in despair as the two combatants careened directly toward the waiting jaws of the syren plant.

Struggling as they dropped, Sirra managed to get on top. With an impact heavy enough to knock the wind out of a gundark, they crashed onto the broad, deadly petals. Vonnda Ra's back struck the soft sensitive tissues inside the syren plant's open maw first. Sirra instantly pushed herself up to her feet, but the huge petals squeezed together in a reflexive, hungry action.

Roaring, Lowie leaped off the high branch, frantic to do something. His attention fixed on the glossy petals as they contracted, folding around its two new victims. High above, Jacen and Tenel Ka yelled down to him.

Vonnda Ra squirmed as the plant's trap squeezed tighter. Lowie saw his sister's head disappear as the thick muscular petals swallowed her up. Only one arm with pattern-shaved fur extended from between the deadly flower's jaws.

Lowie reached the syren plant, then grasped the leathery petals with his clawed hands, pulling, straining. The roots of the plant squirmed, digging deeper into the forest loam.

Lowie didn't dare take out his lightsaber and slash the flower to pieces, because he knew that would kill his sister as surely as the plant would. He tugged, groaning, and the sealed petals peeled slightly apart. The syren plant made a gurgling, gasping sound. Sirra's hand still protruded from the opening, flexing and struggling, as if she were in great pain.

While Jacen grasped a vine and began to climb down, Tenel Ka dropped beside Lowie, one of her throwing knives in her hand. She stabbed at the leathery wall of the plant, but her knife could not penetrate the tough skin.

Then a burst of black lightning and static from within caused the plant to convulse. Its petals flapped open again, as if in a gasp of agony. Inside, Vonnda Ra struggled to her knees, teeth gritted together and eyes blazing with the Dark Force concentrated in her. Lowie took the opportunity to reach in and get a firm grasp on Sirra. He pulled.

Laboring for breath, the young Wookiee moved as rapidly as she could across the slippery, shifting petals. Tenel Ka grabbed for Sirra's outstretched arm, and pulled. The syren plant began to contract. Jacen gripped the edge of one waxy petal to slow its closing and murmured low, soothing words to the plant. Lowie braced himself and leaned back, dragging his sister away with all his strength. Her feet slipped free of the petals just as the syren plant clamped shut again—with Vonnda Ra still inside.

Its deceptively beautiful, fleshy yellow petals squeezed with viselike muscles, squashing its remaining prey. A few flashes of black lightning flickered from within the plant and Vonnda Ra gave one last, muffled cry. The lumpy form caught in the folds of the flower struggled once, twice, then subsided into stillness.

Lowie held Sirra, knowing she might be injured and might need help to get back up to the higher levels. He noted with anguish the burned patches on his sister's fur where Vonnda Ra's power had singed her—yet to his amazement Sirra seemed happy, even delighted. She let out a roar of greeting.

Her eyes sparkled as she lifted her other arm up so he could see what she was clasping as if it were the greatest treasure she had ever held. During her ordeal inside the syren plant, before it had opened long enough for her to escape, Sirrakuk had managed to grasp a handful of the gossamer fibers with her trapped hand and yank them free.

She held up the silken strands in triumph, and Lowie barked with proud laughter. He embraced his sister and pounded her goodnaturedly on the back with enough force to crack stormtrooper armor.

19

MOVING TO A stronger branch and gripping the tree trunk to ensure her balance, Jaina leaned over, anxiously peering into the forest depths where Chewbacca had tumbled. "Chewie!" she shouted.

She heard a Wookiee howl of pain rise toward her from the murky shadows below. He was still alive—and conscious—though she knew he must be injured.

Adjusting her grip on the vine-draped trunk of the wroshyr tree, Jaina bent over and cast the pale, pink light of the swirling phosfleas into the leaves below. As she had suspected, the light did not penetrate far enough for her to locate her friend. "Chewie, I'm here," Jaina yelled, using the Force to amplify her call. "Can you move? Can you climb back up here?"

She heard a far-off rustling and crackling of branches, then a loud yelp. Chewbacca groaned in dismay and then roared something about a fractured leg.

His words doused Jaina's sense of relief like an icy torrent of rain on a candle flame. A wave of weakness spun behind her eyes. Jaina clung to the tree, pressing her face against its rough bark.

Kashyyyk's jungle was dangerous enough for a healthy human with a full-grown Wookiee guide, but Jaina had no idea how to get *herself* out of the jungle—much less herself and an injured friend whom she'd undoubtedly have to carry. And then how could she help her brother and the others?

Meanwhile, she realized, Chewbacca's injury might even draw predators hoping for an easy kill. . . .

The thought snapped Jaina out of her momentary weakness. She had to think; she had to help Chewie. She was in training to be a *Jedi Knight*—and this problem certainly couldn't be impossible to solve, she told herself. First things first. She had to get down to Chewbacca right away. She felt ashamed that she had wasted precious seconds with her panic.

"Chewie," she yelled again, "keep calling to me until I find you."

She would have to move quickly. She felt around for a sturdy vine, yanking one after another until she found a rough strand that would hold her weight. Pressing the toes of her boots against the tree trunk, Jaina lowered herself hand over hand, maneuvering around the splintered stumps of branches broken by the Wookiee's fall. "I'm coming," she said, as much to reassure herself as to comfort Chewie.

By the time she located the injured Wookiee, her feet ached, her palms burned, and every muscle in her body shook with weariness. She unstrapped the phosflea lamp from her waist and held it close to Chewbacca's body to get a better look at him. The fuzzy light swirled as she moved.

A quick examination of his injuries told Jaina that the news was grim. The minor scrapes, bruises, and cuts could be dealt with easily enough, but one leg was broken. Chewbacca would never be able to walk out of here.

Jaina knew she was not equal to the task of transporting a wounded Wookiee hundreds of meters up to the forest canopy, even if she used the Force. She had barely made it this far herself.

Besides that, her brother and the others still needed her help. Jaina didn't know what she could do for them.

She thought the problem over while she used a few of the meager emergency supplies their packs to clean Chewie's wounds. He groaned and did his best to help her.

Clearly, Jaina had no choice but to abandon her search for the others. Jacen, Tenel Ka, and the two young Wookiees were still fleeing from the Imperials. Jaina was no tracker, and she had little chance of finding them down here.

But she and her twin brother had always shared an uncommonly close mental bond, just like the one their mother Leia shared with her twin Luke. Perhaps if she sent out a cry for help, Jacen might be able to find *her*.

Concentrating all of her mental effort, Jaina sent out a cry—*"Help me!"*—that rang through her mind like a mallet striking a cymbal.

Opening her eyes, Jaina checked the fracture in Chewbacca's leg again. The bone fragments had not torn through the skin, but the injury was still serious. Jaina raised her phosflea light high and looked about for any sturdy material she could use as a splint.

The pinkish glow fell on a pair of black boots. A familiar voice said, "Did you call for help?"

Jaina started and nearly fell off the branch. Growling, Chewbacca bared his fangs, though he could make no move to attack.

"Zekk—what are you doing here?" Trying to check her astonishment, Jaina stood and held the glowing light higher, but the leather-clad figure took a step backward, keeping his face partly in shadow.

"I had business here on Kashyyyk."

"*Imperial* business?" Jaina asked, and bit her lip as soon as she had said it. Her heart contracted painfully. "What's happened to you, Zekk? How could you stay with the Shadow Academy? I thought we were friends."

He ignored the question, and asked two of his own. "Why are *you* here, Jaina? Why couldn't you have stayed away? I don't want to hurt you."

Chewbacca voiced a snarl of warning at these words, though at the same time he hissed in pain from his injury.

"Then don't hurt me, Zekk," Jaina said reasonably. She took a step along the branch toward her former friend. "I'm no threat to you. I'm your friend. I *care* for you."

"Step back and stay out of my way," Zekk snapped. "It's already too late for the others."

Jaina flinched and shut her eyes, feeling the blood drain from her face. Could it be true? Had Zekk already killed Jacen, Lowie, Tenel Ka . . . even an innocent stranger like Sirra?

No, she decided at last, it couldn't be. She would have felt it. Her brother and her friends were still alive. They had to be. She couldn't believe that Zekk's heart had become so scorched and black that he could murder someone he had once called a friend.

In an effort to distract him, as she had done with Garowyn, Jaina tried her trick again. She used the Force to riffle the leaves in the branches surrounding him, as if a chill wind were blowing through the claustrophobic cage of the forest underlevels.

Zekk looked up, his green eyes bright even in the shadows. It took him only a moment to realize what she was doing. His pale lips curled in a smile, then he gestured with one hand. The wind picked up, the branches clacked together, and a storm of dislodged leaves and twigs whipped through the air with the force of a small tornado.

Jaina shut her eyes, shielding them and shrinking back from the whirlwind. Chewbacca yowled, but Zekk paid no attention to the Wookiee. "I'm not impressed with your tricks, Jaina," he said. "Don't play games with me."

Then, with a *whoosh*, a sizzling brightness stabbed her eyes to see Zekk holding the weapon of a Jedi, his face lit by its pulsating scarlet glow. "Don't go for your lightsaber, Jaina," he warned.

She shook her head. "I won't raise a weapon against you, Zekk. And I don't believe you'd kill me either."

Zekk's face distorted with warring emotions. "Then stay away from the Jedi academy. If you ever get out of here, don't go back. The Second Imperium will soon target Yavin 4—and I will fight as a loyal warrior for my Emperor."

"Emperor? Zekk, you don't know what you're saying," Jaina pleaded.

"Stop treating me like I'm an ignorant street kid!" he snarled back. "You've always underestimated my abilities, denied me opportunities. But Lord Brakiss doesn't. He has shown me what I'm capable of." He tilted his head to look up into the dark nest of branches overhead, as if he could see the daylight far above.

"I've already sent a signal for a fast ship to pick me up. I believe our raid has been quite successful. Time for me to return to the Shadow Academy."

Zekk twitched his lightsaber from side to side as if shaking a finger in warning. "For the friendship we once had, I'll spare you this time, Jaina. But don't ever test my loyalties again."

With a harsh laugh, Zekk swept his lightsaber upward, releasing a storm of leaves and twigs that showered down on Chewie and Jaina, knocking the phosflea light from her hand. Jaina ducked and covered her head. She couldn't see.

A moment later Zekk was gone, his hollow laughter ringing behind him as he left them in darkness.

20

LEFT ALONE AGAIN, Jaina shouted once more through the Force as the deep forest sounds grew thicker, more threatening around her. Predators, hidden in the leafy branches, cautiously approached, attracted by Chewbacca's muffled sounds of pain. They sensed helpless victims, easy prey.

"We need help!" she called. Her words quickly died to silence in the jungle gloom.

Then a blaze of rainbow light shattered the shadows: a flash of turquoise, a streak of emerald green, a slash of molten bronze. Lightsabers, like hot machetes, chopped the underbrush aside. Jacen, Lowie, and Tenel Ka pushed their way forward, with Sirrakuk following close behind, grinning so widely her fangs flashed in the vibrant light.

Chewbacca bellowed a greeting, and Lowie and Sirra clambered up to help their uncle.

"Hey, Jaina!" Jacen called. "Are you all right?"

She wiped grimy tear streaks from her cheeks, still shaken from the confrontation with her former friend. "I'll survive," she said, then drew a deep breath. "Zekk was here. He said the Second Imperium is going to wipe out the Jedi academy, and that he was going to fight along with them."

Lowie growled, looking up from tending Chewbacca. Tenel Ka stood rigidly, holding her rancor-tooth lightsaber high. "Not if we can help it," she said.

Jaina indicated the injured Wookiee. "We have to get Chewie up and out of here. I think his leg is broken—nothing a medical droid and a few hours in a bacta tank can't fix. But if we don't get back up to the treetops, we're all going to be somebody's lunch."

Sirra growled in defiance. Now that she had succeeded in her dangerous quest against the syren plant, Lowie's sister looked as if she could take on the whole jungle by herself.

As the two strong Wookiees carefully eased their uncle to a standing position, Jacen and Tenel Ka did what they could to help, using the Force and their hands. Jaina took the lead along with Sirra, blazing a trail with her lightsaber.

Together, the companions made their way back up to the light.

21

THE CAMOUFLAGED ASSAULT shuttle hovered in the void of space, waiting for confirmation, until the Shadow Academy shut down its cloaking shields. The ominous spined ring of the Imperial training station shimmered into view just long enough for Zekk to give the order to dock. He was tense as the shuttle approached, unsure of the reception Brakiss would give him.

Beside him, in the command cockpit, Tamith Kai seethed silently, her wine-dark lips pressed together in a cold line, but she said nothing. Zekk had lost not only the team of stormtroopers directly under his command in the treetop city, but also two of her greatest Nightsister allies. Both Vonnda Ra and Garowyn were presumed dead in the depths of Kashyyyk's jungles.

Though Zekk had not been with either Nightsister when they had died or disappeared, Tamith Kai blamed him for the debacle, as she blamed him for the death of her prime student Vilas. Tamith Tai resented his presence—though presumably she and Zekk both worked toward the ultimate victory of the Second Imperium. All other losses, he felt, should simply be considered the price of their ultimate triumph.

But Tamith Kai was not pleased with how the young man had handled himself on Kashyyyk. And so, during their return from the fateful mission, Zekk kept to himself, avoiding direct contact with the Nightsister.

He brought the assault ship in, sitting in the command chair while other Imperial pilots handled the controls, guiding the craft into the Shadow Academy's open docking bay. As they entered, he saw another armored shuttle—an impressive Imperial transport surrounded by deadly force fields—and wondered what had happened during his absence.

The battered assault craft, with its precious cargo of stolen computer components, settled into place with what sounded like a mechanical sigh of relief. "We have landed, Lord Zekk," the pilot said.

The tactical officer studied the controls. "The Shadow Academy's cloaking device has been reactivated. The station is once again undetectable by Rebel sensors."

The hatches opened, and the crew began filing out. Stormtroopers marched up from the Shadow Academy's interior to surround the battered shuttle, ready to unload the stolen cargo as soon as Zekk released it.

Tamith Kai stood beside him in the cockpit; with a flick of her shoulder, she tossed her spined black cape back. Her long-nailed fingers balled into fists as she struggled to contain the fury within her. The electric fire in her violet eyes boiled like lava.

Zekk closed his dark-ringed emerald eyes and drew a deep

breath to focus his thoughts, center his concentration. He let her anger wash over his mind and drain away. His greatest concern was Master Brakiss and how he would face him. His teacher had such high hopes for him, and he might be even more displeased than Tamith Kai. Contemplating the probable disappointment of his mentor hurt Zekk more than any display of rage by the continually bothersome Nightsister from Dathomir.

Squaring his shoulders, he straightened his padded leather armor and adjusted his crimson-lined black cape. He tossed his long dark hair behind him and turned toward the assault craft's hatch, making himself an imposing figure, ominous and menacing. He had learned such posturing from observing Tamith Kai herself, and it amused him to think he could use her own techniques of intimidation against her.

With the tall Nightsister following him, Zekk strode down the ramp like a conquering hero. Inside his heart, though, dread grew.

The sculpture-handsome teacher stood at the edge of the airlock bay, watching the proceedings. As Zekk emerged, Brakiss glided forward with smooth, even footsteps. His silvery robes clung around him like whispers.

Zekk held his chin high, looking into the open, clear gaze of Brakiss. The master of the Shadow Academy folded his hands in front of him. "Young Zekk, my Darkest Knight, you have returned from your first mission. Report. Were you successful?"

Zekk swallowed hard and gave his straightforward account. "Unfortunately, Master Brakiss, our mission did not come off as smoothly as we had planned. During our battles at the fortified Wookiee facilities, we lost fourteen TIE fighters and bombers, as well as eleven ground assault troops.

"It is also my duty to report that we lost two of our Nightsister companions: Vonnda Ra in the lower levels of the forest, and Garowyn, who was apparently murdered when she tried to reclaim our *Shadow Chaser*."

Brakiss showed no reaction and waited. Finally he said,

"But the computer components—the guidance and tactical systems? Did you succeed in obtaining the vital resources the Second Imperium requires?"

Zekk flinched. "Yes, Master Brakiss. All of the computer equipment is stored inside this assault transport, ready for distribution to the Second Imperium."

Brakiss clapped his hands together. "Excellent! Then your mission was a success, with acceptable losses of personnel. Those other . . . *inconveniences* are insignificant in our overall conflict. You have achieved our most important goal."

Tamith Kai's eyes widened with anger, and her normally pale face flushed a blotchy red. "Master Brakiss!" she hissed. "Zekk also claims to have removed those Jedi brats. But although Vonnda Ra accompanied him to this confrontation, Zekk returned alone . . . claiming victory."

Zekk stood rigid. "The young Jedi Knights are no longer a problem," he said. "This I swear."

Tamith Kai obviously didn't believe him. But Brakiss did, and that was all that counted.

Zekk didn't know how long he could keep up the charade. He had fallen to the dark side—and he had also protected his friends. The two seemed incompatible. Sooner or later, Brakiss would learn what he had done—and then Zekk would face an impossible choice. But, as always, no one else would make Zekk's choices for him . . . and no one else would face the consequences.

"The Second Imperium applauds your efforts, Zekk. The history of the galaxy will remember you as an instrumental fighter in our grand cause."

Zekk knew he should have felt better, prouder . . . but he could summon no emotion other than dread. And disappointment in himself. He was no longer sure of where his past decisions would lead him.

One of the stormtroopers standing in ranks within the hangar bay shifted uneasily. Zekk focused his attention on the burly trooper—instinctively identifying Norys. Qorl stood beside the bully, frowning in disapproval at his white-armored trainee. The leader of the Lost Ones still bore a chip on his shoulder, resulting in a perpetually surly attitude.

Suddenly, the air in the huge docking bay shimmered. Zekk looked up as the other stormtroopers backed away. Beside him, Brakiss grew tense, almost fearful, but stood his ground against the projection.

An image formed in the air, a giant cowled head with yellow eyes and an age-ravaged face that emanated dark power. The visage of Emperor Palpatine was incredibly clear and focused, as if the transmission came from very close. Very close indeed.

"My subjects at the Shadow Academy," the Emperor's shuddering voice said, "my fellow fighters in the cause of the Second Imperium, I am pleased to learn of this successful mission! Through our various raids and by gathering the scattered remnants of my lost Imperial glory, we now have the might to move on to the next phase in our plan of conquest. The new hyperdrive cores and turbolaser batteries have already been installed in our secret battle fleet. I have commanded that the new computer components be incorporated immediately. We must strike again while the Rebels are still reeling."

Under the leather padding, Zekk felt a cold, damp shiver work its way down his back.

"It is our mission to remove the only real line of defense the Rebels have against us. Brakiss, you promised me an invincible fighting force of Dark Jedi Knights. The time has come to make use of them.

"Together, as our primary campaign, we shall attack and destroy Luke Skywalker's Jedi academy. Those light side Jedi will be crushed to dust beneath our feet.

"I command you all to move out. Set the Shadow Academy forces in motion. We must transport our station to the jungle moon of Yavin 4 without delay. Once we have eliminated the new Jedi Knights, the galaxy will be ours for the taking."

Zekk stood stunned. Brakiss stared at the fading image of

the Emperor in amazement. Then, as if a power switch had
been flicked on, all of the stormtroopers sprang into motion.

The Shadow Academy rushed to prepare for its greatest
battle.

22

IN THE AFTERMATH of the devastating attack on the
Wookiee computer fabrication facility, Jaina knew they could
not afford to wait. Too much was at risk—and right now.

While the New Republic forces sent a few nearby ships
filled with a complement of engineers and soldiers to help in
reparation activities, Jaina and Lowie worked tirelessly with
Chewbacca to complete repairs to the *Shadow Chaser*. The
tall Wookiee still limped on his sore leg, but his injuries had
mostly healed, and he didn't let a little stiffness slow him
down.

Inside the crowded power-supply bulkhead of the *Shadow
Chaser*, Jaina, the smallest of the workers, crammed herself
deep into the tightest spaces, hooking up power leads and dis-
connecting diagnostics. All the replacement parts had been
ready even before the Imperial attack on Kashyyyk, but now
the sleek vessel needed to be reassembled.

"Power it up before I crawl back out of here," Jaina said.
"All the circuits are grounded and shielded, but I want to
make sure everything checks out before I fight my way into
open air again."

Lowie grunted and flicked a power switch. He and Chewbacca simultaneously roared an affirmative.

Jaina heaved a sigh of relief. "Well, I'm glad the ship's
functioning again," she said. "We have to get out of here and
back to Yavin 4 before the attack comes. We need to be ready
for the Shadow Academy." She swallowed. "We've all been
training a long time for this."

Lowie roared in agreement, though he and Chewbacca and Sirra seemed somewhat saddened. Sirra growled a series of notes, and Em Teedee said, "Mistress Sirrakuk says that she will stay to help her people clean up and make repairs, but she understands that her brother Lowbacca must return to fight with the other Jedi. There are many Wookiees who can assist here on Kashyyyk, but there aren't many other Jedi Knights . . . and she is exceedingly proud that her brother is one of them."

Lowie rumbled his appreciation.

Em Teedee added, as an aside, "I do believe she's quite pleased with him."

Sirra patted her big brother on his hairy shoulder, then proudly ran one hand over her glossy new belt, woven from the strands of fiber she had harvested from the syren plant. Jaina knew that Sirra's personal opportunities were now wide open, possibilities for her life that had always been there . . . but that she would now be better able to take advantage of.

Jacen rushed aboard the *Shadow Chaser* carrying the small cage with his pet Ion and her babies. He cooed reassurances to the furry rodents.

Tenel Ka accompanied him, looking confident in her freshly polished reptilian armor. She had reworked all of her braids meticulously, brushing her hair out and plaiting it using the new one-handed technique Anakin Solo had developed for her. "We are prepared to depart," she said. "And we are ready to fight as true Jedi Knights."

Lowie roared with enthusiasm. Sirra embraced her big brother, and then each of the young Jedi Knights.

Chewbacca limped up the ramp and strapped himself into the *Shadow Chaser*'s pilot seat. Lowie slid into the seat behind his uncle, flipping on the controls and powering up the various subsystems. The two Wookiees barked a preflight checklist back and forth.

Sirrakuk slipped back out of the sleek ship and stood watching as the craft prepared to depart. Within moments the

Shadow Chaser rose up on its repulsorlifts, bearing its message of warning to Luke Skywalker and his Jedi academy.

"We've just sent the alert to Yavin 4, but now we have to go," Jaina told her brother. "Uncle Luke is back from his scouting mission with Dad—but the Jedi academy is still in danger."

"I've got a bad feeling about this," Jacen agreed.

He held the small cage in his lap, still whispering soothing words. Tenel Ka sat beside Jacen, eager to go. She brushed her fingers over the weapons at her belt, anticipating the fight to come.

Chewbacca yowled a brief order to prepare for acceleration, then the *Shadow Chaser* leaped skyward. A few minutes later, they catapulted into hyperspace and left Kashyyyk behind.

They raced back to Yavin 4 at full speed, knowing they had to prepare for the greatest challenge of their lives.

The Shadow Academy was coming.

Jedi Under Siege

To Letha L. Burchard,
a supporter, fan, and friend
who "knew us when" . . .

and is still speaking to us

ackNowledGMeNts

The usual round of thanks to Lillie E. Mitchell, whose flying fingers transcribe our dictation and whose dedication to our characters and stories keeps our interest focused; Lucy Wilson, Sue Rostoni, and Allan Kausch at Lucasfilm for their above-and-beyond-the-call helpful suggestions and open minds; Ginjer Buchanan and the folks at Berkley/Boulevard for their wholehearted support and encouragement over the course of this entire series; and Jonathan MacGregor Cowan for being our most avid test reader and brainstormer.

1

IN THE UNCERTAIN predawn light, Jaina watched her uncle, Luke Skywalker, maneuver the *Shadow Chaser* into the Jedi academy's hangar bay at the base of the Great Temple. Her father, Han Solo, and Chewbacca had not even stayed long enough to perform that chore after the young Jedi Knights returned from the Wookiee homeworld of Kashyyyk.

With the Shadow Academy on the move, they had no time to lose.

Jaina found it hard to believe that barely two days earlier Kashyyyk had been under attack by Imperial forces led by none other than her friend Zekk, now a Dark Jedi in the service of the Second Imperium. When she'd confronted the dark-haired young man in the forest underlevels, he had warned her not to return to Yavin 4 because the Shadow Academy would soon attack.

Jaina had to believe the warning was a sign that Zekk still cared about her and her twin brother Jacen.

She and her friends had been back on Yavin 4 for only a few minutes. None of them had gotten much sleep on the swift hyperspace flight back, but they all ran on adrenaline. Jaina felt as if she would explode if she couldn't *do* something right away. So many preparations to make, so much to plan.

Standing beside her near the entrance to the hangar bay, Jacen gave her a nudge. When she glanced at him, his brandy-brown eyes looked straight into hers. "Hey, it'll be *okay*," he said. "Uncle Luke will know what to do. He's been through plenty of Imperial attacks."

"Sure, that makes me feel a lot better," she answered, not believing it for a minute.

As usual, Jacen resorted to one of his favorite weapons to get her mind off the battle that was sure to come. "Hey, want to hear a joke?"

"Yes, Jacen," said Tenel Ka, striding up to join them. "I believe humor could be of some use now." The warrior girl from Dathomir glistened with perspiration from having spent the last ten minutes running "to stretch her muscles" in an effort to work off her own tension.

"Okay, Jacen. Fire away," Jaina said, pretending to brace herself for the worst.

Tenel Ka pushed back her long, reddish-gold braids with one arm. Her left arm had been severed in a terrible accident during lightsaber training, and she refused to accept a synthetic replacement. She nodded to Jacen. "You may proceed with the joke."

"Okay, what time is it when an Imperial walker steps on your wrist chronometer?" Jacen raised his eyebrows, waiting. "Time to get a new chronometer!"

After a heartbeat of dead silence, Tenel Ka nodded and said in a serious voice, "'Thank you, Jacen. Your humor was quite . . . adequate."

The warrior girl never cracked a smile, but Jaina thought she detected a twinkle in her friend's cool gray eyes. Jaina was still groaning in mock agony when Luke and the young Wookiee Lowbacca climbed out of the *Shadow Chaser*.

Deciding there wasn't a moment to lose, Jaina hurried over to them. Apparently Uncle Luke must have felt the same way—when Jacen and Tenel Ka trotted up behind Jaina, the Jedi Master began to speak without preamble.

"It'll take the Second Imperium some time to install the new computer components they stole for their fleet," Luke said. "We may have a few days yet, but I don't want to take any chances. Lowie—Tionne and Raynar went out to the temple on the lake for a training exercise. I'd like you to take your T-23 and go bring them back here. We all need to work together."

Lowie roared an acknowledgment and sprinted for the small skyhopper his uncle Chewbacca had given him. From the clip at Lowie's waist the miniaturized translating droid Em Teedee said, "Why certainly, sir. It would be Master Low-bacca's great pleasure to be of service. Consider it done." Reprimanding the little droid for its embellishments with an absent growl, the young Wookiee climbed into the small T-23 and closed the canopy.

Luke turned to the warrior girl from Dathomir. "Tenel Ka, gather as many students as you can and give them a crash course in ground combat against terrorist attacks. I'm not sure what strategies the Shadow Academy will use, but I can't think of anyone better to teach them about commando tactics than you."

"Yeah, she was great against those Bartokk assassins on Hapes," Jacen said.

Tenel Ka surprised Jaina by blushing pink before she gave a curt nod and sped off on her assignment.

"What about Jacen and me, Uncle Luke?" Jaina asked, bursting with impatience. "What should we do? We want to help."

"Now that the *Millennium Falcon* is gone, we need to get the new shield generators back up and running to protect us from an aerial attack. Come with me."

The primary equipment for the Jedi academy's new defensive shield generators was located in the jungle across the river, but the shields were controlled from the Comm Center. Han Solo had recently brought the components from Coruscant as a stopgap measure while the New Republic scrambled to assemble a major defense against the impending Imperial attack.

"Hey, should I send a message to Mom?" Jacen asked, sitting down at one of the consoles.

"Not until we know more," Luke answered. "Your dad and

Chewie were going to contact her and explain everything once they were under way. Leia has her hands full mustering troops to station here as permanent protectors for the Jedi academy. At the moment, *we've* got to do everything we can to guard it ourselves.

"Meanwhile, Jacen, monitor all the communications bands. See if you can pick up any signals, especially ones that might be Imperial codes. Jaina, let's get those shield generators powered up and running."

"Already on it, Uncle Luke." Jaina grinned at him from the control station. "Shields are up and at full strength. Guess I should run a complete readiness check, though, just to make sure there are no gaps in our defenses."

Jacen put on a headset and began scanning through the various comm frequencies. No sooner had he begun than a loud crackle erupted from the earpiece, followed by a familiar voice.

". . . requesting permission for landing and all that usual stuff. Here I come. *Lightning Rod* out."

"Hey, wait!" Jacen said into the voice pickup, on the verge of panic. "You can't do that—I mean, we have to drop our shields first. Give me a minute, Peckhum."

"Shields? What shields?" the old spacer's voice came back. "Me and the *Lightning Rod* been doin' the supply run to Yavin 4 for years now. Never had to worry about shields before."

"We'll meet you down at the landing pad and explain everything," Jacen said. "Hang on a minute."

"Am I going to need a code to get in?" Peckhum asked. "No one gave me any codes before I left Coruscant. Nobody told me about any shields."

Jacen looked up at Luke. "It's old Peckhum in the *Lightning Rod*," he said. "Does he need a code to get in?"

Luke shook his head and motioned for Jaina to drop the shields. Jaina bent over the control console, her lower lip caught between her teeth. After a minute she said, "There, that ought to do it. Shields lowered again."

For some reason, now that the shields were down Jacen felt a cold tingle of vulnerability run up the back of his neck. "Okay, Peckhum," he said, "you're clear to land. But make it quick, so we can power up again."

When the old spacer stepped out of his battered supply shuttle, he looked the same as every other time Jacen had seen him: pale skin, long lanky hair, grizzled cheeks, and rumpled flight suit.

"Come on, Peckhum," Jacen said. "I'll help you get the supplies inside. We need to hurry, before the Imperials get here."

"Imperials?" The spacer scratched his head. "Is that why you've got energy shields up? Are we under attack?"

"It's okay," Jacen said, impatient to get the *Lightning Rod* unloaded. "The shields are back up. You just can't see them."

The old spacer craned his neck to stare up into the misty white sky of the jungle moon. "And the attack?"

"Well, we heard a rumor—a pretty solid one." He hesitated. "From Zekk. He's the one who led the raid on the computer fabrication facility on Kashyyyk—and he warned Jaina that the Shadow Academy is on its way. We'd better get inside."

Old Peckhum looked at Jacen in alarm. The teenager Zekk had been like a son to him; they had lived together in the lower city levels on Coruscant . . . until Zekk had been kidnapped by the Shadow Academy.

As a familiar cold tingle crept up the back of Jacen's neck, Peckhum whispered, "Too late." He pointed into the sky. "They're already here."

FROM THE HIGHEST observation turret on the Shadow Academy, Brakiss—Master of all the new Dark Jedi—looked down at the insignificant green speck of the jungle moon. The devastating assault was about to begin, and before long Yavin 4 and its Jedi academy would be crushed under the might of the Second Imperium.

As it should be.

Through the winding metal corridors of the station, stormtroopers manned their battle stations, newly trained TIE pilots conducted preflight checks on their ships, and the eager Dark Jedi students prepared for their first major victory.

The ultimate battle would be a two-pronged assault led jointly by the most powerful of the new Nightsisters, Tamith Kai, and Brakiss's own protégé, dark-haired Zekk, whose enthusiasm to make something significant of his life had left him an easy target for conversion to the dark side.

Brakiss closed his eyes and drew a deep breath of the recycled air that rushed through the ventilation shafts. His silvery robes swirled around him.

Though he stood isolated here, he could sense the accelerating preparations affecting everyone in the spiked station; tensions mounted, as did hunger for battle. In the undercurrent of swirling thoughts, he clearly felt the troops' dedication to the Second Imperium's great leader, Emperor Palpatine. He also detected an undertone of anxiety over the coming attack, but this only made his lips curl upward. Fear would give an added edge to their fighting abilities, enough to make them cautious . . . but not enough to paralyze them.

Brakiss longed to see Luke Skywalker defeated. Years ago, he had infiltrated the Jedi academy as a student to absorb the methods the New Republic taught, then bring them back to the remnants of the Empire. But Brakiss hadn't been able to fool the Jedi Master. Instead, Skywalker had tried to turn him away from his devotion, undermine his dedication to the Second Imperium. Skywallker had tried to "save" him—he thought with a sneer—and Brakiss had fled.

But because of his willingness to dabble in the dark side, Brakiss had by then learned enough to form his own Dark Jedi training center.

Now it would be a marvelous showdown.

Beside him, the air shimmered. Brakiss opened his calm, beatific eyes and sensed an ominous static surrounding the projection of the Emperor. The mysterious great leader of the Second Imperium hovered in front of him in holographic form, a cowled head as tall as Brakiss's entire body, a towering image with glittering yellow eyes and a wrinkled face pinched by shadows.

"I grow eager for my domination again, Brakiss," the Emperor said.

"And I am eager to give it to you, my master," Brakiss answered, bowing his head.

Accompanied by four of his powerful red Imperial guards, the Emperor himself had recently taken up residence on the Shadow Academy, arriving in a special armored shuttle. While the fearsome, scarlet-clad guards kept all prying eyes away, the Emperor remained sealed in an opaque isolation chamber. Palpatine had never spoken directly to his loyal Shadow Academy subjects, nor had he even conversed face-to-face with Brakiss. The Emperor had appeared only in holographic transmissions.

"We are ready to launch our strike, my Emperor," Brakiss said. He glanced up at the forbidding image. "My Dark Jedi guarantee you victory."

"Good—because I have no wish to wait further," the Emperor's image said. "The remainder of my newly constructed fleet has not yet arrived, though they shall be here within hours. My Imperial warships are presently being refitted with the computer systems stolen from Kashyyyk. My guards report that many vessels are ready to fight, and the rest will be finished shortly."

Brakiss bowed again, clasping his hands in front of him. "I understand, my lord. But let us withhold the military strike force for our next major assault on the more heavily guarded worlds of the Rebel Alliance. On Yavin 4, we have only a few weakling do-gooder Jedi to deal with. They should cause no problem for my Force-trained soldiers."

Inside his shadowy cowl, the Emperor looked skeptical. "Do not let your overconfidence betray you."

Brakiss continued speaking with greater passion. He let his feelings come to the fore, hoping to convince his great leader. "With this important strike on the Jedi academy, the Second Imperium becomes more than just an undisciplined band of pirates raiding equipment. We mean to retake the *galaxy*, my lord. This battle must be a battle of philosophies, of willpower. This is the *Imperial* way against the *Rebel* way—and so it should be my trainees against Skywalker's, Jedi versus Jedi. A shadow play, if you will, of darkness against light. We still intend to harass them with TIE fighter strikes from the air, but the main conflict will be direct and personal—as it must be! We can crush their very hearts, not merely breach their defenses."

Brakiss smiled, looking up to meet the glowing yellow eyes of the Emperor. "And when we defeat them utterly with the powers of the dark side, the remainder of the Rebels will scatter and hide, trembling at their own nightmares, as we recapture what is rightfully ours."

The Emperor's holographic face did something frighteningly unusual. The withered, puckered lips curled in a satisfied *smile*.

"Very well. It shall be as you request, Brakiss—Jedi against Jedi. You may begin your assault when ready."

THE SHADOW ACADEMY dropped its cloaking device, dissolving its shield of invisibility. As the spiked station appeared over Yavin 4, two specially equipped TIE fighters dropped out of its launching bay. Silently moving in tandem, they plunged into the misty atmosphere.

The fighters had been coated with a stealth hull plating to blur their sensor signatures, and the output from their high-powered twin ion engines had been damped. Their mission was to strike in secret, not to provide a show of force.

Commander Orvak swooped into the lead, while the second TIE fighter, flown by his subordinate Dareb, flanked him. Together, they shot around the small moon and skimmed lower into the atmosphere, spiraling entirely around the equator back to the coordinates of the ancient temple ruins where Skywalker had established his Jedi academy.

Orvak flew with the controls gripped in his black-gloved hands. He felt the quiet thrumming of the Imperial fighter's engines as if he were riding an untamed beast of burden. He piloted with careful concentration, dancing on the air currents, buffeted by thermal updrafts from the jungle below.

"Keep steady," he muttered to himself. This commando run would require the utmost precision and piloting skill. Along with a new batch of TIE fighter trainees chosen from the ranks of young stormtroopers, Orvak had completed the simulations over and over again en route to the Yavin system.

But this was the real thing. Now the Emperor was depending on him.

Massassi trees formed a chaotic carpet of green below. Gnarled branches thrust above the thick canopy like monster claws. Orvak glided in low, watching the wake of his passage disturb treetop creatures who fled from the blast of his hot exhaust.

His companion Dareb spoke over a tight line-of-sight

beamed channel. The other pilot's words were encrypted and
descrambled by a special coding system in Orvak's cockpit.
"Long-range sensors are picking up the protective energy
field," Dareb said. "The shield generators are right where our
covert information said they would be."

"Target verified," Orvak acknowledged, speaking into the
microphone built into his helmet. "Lord Brakiss, who endured
some time here, knows much of the layout of the Jedi academy itself—if the Rebels haven't moved things around."

"Why would they?" Dareb said. "They're far too compla-
cent, and we are about to show them their folly."

"Just don't show me *your* folly," Orvak said. "Enough
chatter. Head for the target."

The invisible shields hovered like a protective umbrella
over a section of jungle where a river sliced through the trees
and an ancient-looking stone pyramid rose majestically.
Orvak hoped that by the end of this day Skywalker's Great
Temple would no longer be standing.

But before the Shadow Academy could begin the primary
assault, Orvak and Dareb had to complete their preliminary
mission: to knock out that shield generator and open the doors
wide for a devastating attack.

Orvak checked his sensors. In the infrared and other portions of the electromagnetic spectrum, he could see the deadly
ripples of the hovering force field dome that protected the
Jedi academy. Yet, because of the tall Massassi trees, the
shield did not reach all the way to the ground, halting instead
five meters above the treetops. Five meters—a shallow gap
between foliage and sizzling energy, but wide enough for a
crack pilot to negotiate. Here and there, a few upthrust
branches were singed and blackened where they had intruded
into the crackling energy dome.

"It'll be a tight squeeze," Orvak said. "Ready for it?"

"I feel like I could take on the whole Rebel Alliance by
myself," Dareb said.

Orvak didn't acknowledge this display of overconfidence.
"Closing in," he said.

He brought the stealth TIE fighter lower, just skimming the treetops. Leaves whispered beneath him, chattering and scratching against the wings of his ship. The air seemed to ripple in front of the fighter, a faint indication of the energy shield, and he hoped the sensors were correct.

"Stay on target," he said. "Once we get under the shields, our real work starts."

Just as they passed underneath the invisible boundary Dareb swerved to one side to avoid an unexpected moss-covered branch that elbowed up only a meter above the canopy. The young pilot overcompensated and struck a corner of his square wing panel another branch, which sent him tumbling.

"I can't hold it!" he shouted into the comm system. "I'm out of control!"

Dareb's TIE fighter pinwheeled up into the deadly force field and exploded as it hit the disintegrating wall. Intent on his mission, Orvak streaked onward, looking into the rear viewers to see the flaming debris of his partner tumbling out of the sky.

He clenched his teeth and drew a deep breath through the oxygen mask in his helmet. "We're all expendable," Orvak said, as if trying to convince himself. "Expendable. The mission is all-important. Dareb was my backup. So now it's up to me. Alone." He swallowed hard, knowing that now the Rebels must be aware of his covert mission.

Without pause, Orvak honed in on the isolated shield-generating station. The machinery looked like a set of tall disks half buried in the jungle underbrush, surrounded by a cleared maintenance area that provided just enough space for him to land his small Imperial fighter. Visible in the distance rose the great pyramid that housed Skywalker's Jedi academy.

He shut down the muffled twin ion engines and opened the cockpit door, heaving himself out. Reaching into the stowage compartment behind his pilot's seat, he retrieved the pack of supplies that contained all the explosives he would need for a full day's work. . . .

Orvak stepped on the squishing, plant-covered ground. The jungle brooded around him, chaotic and threatening. Overhead, he could hear the crackling hum of the energy shield that had destroyed his partner.

Compared with the clean, sterile Shadow Academy, Yavin 4 felt disgustingly *alive*. It swarmed with vermin, plants growing everywhere, little rodents, insects, strange biting creatures that moved in every direction and hid in every cranny.

He longed for the precise and spotless corridors of the Shadow Academy, where his boots could ring loud and clear on the cold, hard metal plates, where he could smell the recycled air flowing through the ventilators, where everything was regimented and in its rightful place . . . just as the Empire would be again after its victory over the Rebels. Orvak took comfort in his solid leather gloves and the helmet that protected him from infestation by the parasitic creatures of this uncivilized world.

Taking the pack that contained his demolition equipment, he sprinted away from his TIE fighter toward the humming shield generator station. It hulked over him, powerful and unguarded. Doomed.

Although the shield generators were obviously new, vines, creepers, and ferns grew in tangled profusion close to the warm machinery. Orvak could see hacked ends and broken branches where someone had chopped away the foliage in an attempt to keep the access clear. The irresistible jungle, though, kept pressing its advantage. Orvak shook his head at the folly of these Rebels.

When he reached the pulsing station, Orvak hunched over and glanced from side to side, expecting Rebel defenders at any moment. Opening his pack, he withdrew two of his six high-powered thermal detonators, shaped charges he would place against the generator's power cells. These two explosives would be sufficient to take down the Jedi academy's shields.

He would save the rest of the explosives for the second part of his mission.

Orvak synchronized the timers. Then, removing his recalibrated compass and glancing at the coordinates he had programmed in, he ducked and fought his way through the underbrush toward his next target, which was some distance through the jungle and across a river.

The Great Temple.

He paused for only a moment, opaquing his blast goggles as the timers ran down to zero—and the explosive charges detonated.

The boom was deafening, and a pillar of fire rose to the sky, singeing the surrounding Massassi trees. Satisfied, Orvak congratulated himself on an excellent explosion. Most spectacular.

But the next one would be better yet.

4

WITH RAYNAR AND Tionne crowded in the back, Lowie piloted the T-23 skyhopper back toward the Jedi academy at full speed. As they skimmed along the treetops, Lowie explained the situation as best he could, with Em Teedee translating.

". . . and that is why Master Skywalker requested that Master Lowbacca retrieve you with such haste," the little droid finished.

"Well, well, well," Raynar said in a sour voice. "I suppose you think this is going to make you heroes for coming back to save the Jedi academy. I'm sure *I* could have managed quite nicely without your help. While you were off playing, I was here training with Tionne."

Lowie could tell by the blond-haired boy's tone of voice that he was none too pleased to be stuffed unceremoniously into the cramped rear seat, with his brightly colored robes tangled about him. Raynar's parents had once been minor royalty on Alderaan, before that planet was destroyed by the Death Star, and now they had made themselves into wealthy merchants. He was not accustomed to taking a backseat to anyone.

"No, Raynar," Tionne chided. The silvery-haired Jedi teacher blinked her alien mother-of-pearl eyes. "No one does as well alone against an enemy, and we must all work together to prepare. Without preparation, a battle is all but lost."

Raynar snorted, trying to straighten his robes. "Battle? We don't even know there's going to *be* a battle. Why should we believe the word of some traitor boy who's gone over to the dark side? He could just be lying to get us all worked up. He's probably laughing at us right now."

Lowie's growls rumbled louder than the engine of the T-23. "Master Lowbacca wishes to point out," Em Teedee said, "that for many years Zekk was a close friend to Master Jacen and Mistress Jaina."

Raynar pouted. "Then Jacen and Jaina Solo need to be more careful about the friends they choose."

"Sometimes," Tionne said in a firm voice, "the gap between friend and enemy is not as wide as you may think. Help often comes from unexpected sources."

Lowie wasn't sure why, but senses in the back of his mind urged him to go faster still. The small skyhopper shuddered and dipped as he pushed its engines to their limits, and then beyond. He flew in among the trees, below the deadly dome of the energy shield that protected the Jedi academy against an attack from the skies.

"Hey, watch out for that big branch!" Raynar yelped as Lowie swerved to one side. "Save the heroics for when the Shadow Academy shows up—*if* they come, that is." Lowie was pleased to sense, though, that Tionne not only remained calm, but actually approved of the way he piloted the little T-23.

Lowie looked up into the sky and understood why he had

felt the sudden need to accelerate. He gave a sharp bark, pointing up at the ominous spiked ring shape barely visible as a silhouette through the film of the atmosphere. "Master Low-bacca says—oh dear!—it seems that the Shadow Academy has arrived!"

Raynar fell silent, finding nothing more to criticize about Lowie's piloting. Before long, a blade of piercing sound sliced through the silence, followed by several explosions. According to Lowie's sensors, the flickering energy shield above had failed. He growled out the news.

Without waiting for a translation, Tionne said, "We can still return to the Jedi academy, but we should leave the T-23 at the edge of the jungle. I have a feeling it's not safe to approach the temple landing field or the hangar bay. It's bound to be under attack." She sat up straight between the two young Jedi trainees. "It has already begun."

The Great Temple of the Massassi had stood nearly unchanged for thousands of years. The stone blocks in the walls and floors were as solid as they had been the day they were assembled. Even so, Jaina felt a vibration in the floor of the Jedi academy's control center. Warning lights flashed across the shield generator console.

"Something's wrong, Uncle Luke," Jaina said. "There's been an explosion out in the jungle . . . oh no! Our defensive shields are down!"

Luke stood behind the chair where Jacen sat at the communications controls. He nodded grimly to Jaina. "Can you get the shields back on line from here?"

She frantically flicked switches and checked connections, trying to bring the shields back up. She scanned the display screens and diagnostics, continually pushing buttons. "Don't think so," she replied. "Power's out. The entire generator might be gone."

Her brother Jacen blew out his breath and pushed back from the comm console. "I've got a bad feeling about this," he said, running fingers through his tousled brown curls. "I'll bet it's sabotage."

Luke caught Jaina's eyes, then Jacen's, and came to a decision. "I'm calling an all-hands meeting in five minutes. We may need to clear out the Great Temple, go into hiding in the jungles where we can deflect the assault. Send a message to your mother that we're under attack *now* and need those reinforcements right away. Then meet me in the grand audience chamber."

Jacen looked at his sister in a state of near panic. "My animals . . ." he said. "I *can't* leave them in their cages if the Jedi academy's under attack. They'll stand a better chance of surviving if they're free. And if Uncle Luke's going to evacuate all of the students—"

"Go ahead," Jaina said, waving him away. "Take care of your pets. I'll get a message to Mom."

Already running for the door, Jacen tossed a "thank you" over his shoulder.

Jaina plopped down at the comm station, selected a transmission frequency, and tried to make a connection to Coruscant. She received no response, only dead static. With a sigh of disgust over the erratic behavior of the old equipment, Jaina tried a new frequency.

Still nothing.

Odd, she thought. Maybe the main comm screen wasn't working. She donned the headset and selected yet another frequency.

Static. She switched again. Stronger static, as if something had swallowed up her desperate signal. Soon the crackling hiss built to a crescendo squeal loud enough to set her teeth on edge. Jaina snatched the headset off her ears and tossed it down with a shudder.

"We're being jammed!"

Jaina checked the readouts on the communications console just to be sure. Their long-range transmissions were being blocked by the Shadow Academy.

She had to let Luke know right away.

*   *   *

In his chambers inside the ancient temple, Jacen lifted the latches and slid aside the doors to each cage that held his menagerie of unusual pets. He could see that Tionne had kept them well fed while he was gone on Kashyyyk. The near-invisible crystal snake with its iridescent scales glittered with languid satisfaction, but the family of purple jumping spiders in the adjoining cage bounced up and down in agitation.

"It's all right," Jacen sent the message with his mind. "Be calm. You'll be safe if you get to the jungle. Just get into the jungle."

One cage rattled with two clamoring stintarils, tree-dwelling rodents with protruding eyes and long jaws filled with sharp teeth. In another damp enclosure tiny swimming crabs peeked out of their mud nests. Pinkish mucous salamanders slid out of their water bowl, gradually taking a distinct form. Iridescent blue piranha-beetles swarmed against the tough wires of their cage, chewing and eager to be free.

He turned them loose one by one, carrying them to the window as carefully as he could, moving with a controlled urgency. Jacen had just set the last of his creatures free—his favorite, a stump lizard—when he heard a loud Wookiee roar, followed by the voice of Em Teedee.

"Oh, thank goodness, we're not alone in the temple after all."

Jacen turned to find Lowie, Em Teedee, Tionne, and Raynar standing in his doorway.

"Did the others leave without us?" Raynar asked with a look of forlorn worry on his face.

"Everyone's up in the grand audience chamber," Jacen said. "We need to get there as quickly as possible. Master Skywalker's giving his final instructions before the battle begins."

When the group stepped out of the turbolift into the grand audience chamber, Jaina was already there talking in a low voice with Luke and Tenel Ka while the other students sat in frightened silence.

A look of relief washed over Luke's face when he saw that Lowie had returned successfully from his mission. Tionne stretched out her hand toward Luke, and he gave it a brief squeeze.

"I'm glad you're safe," Luke said.

"What did Mom say?" Jacen asked his sister.

Jaina bit her lower lip, and Tenel Ka answered for her. "The Shadow Academy is jamming our transmissions. We were unable to send our distress signal."

Jacen felt the blood drain out of his face. How long would it be, then, until reinforcements arrived, if they couldn't even send a distress call?

Luke spoke in a loud voice, addressing the gathered Jedi students. "We can't rely on outside help to save us. We must fight this battle ourselves. I believe the Great Temple will be the initial target of attack. Tenel Ka has already briefed you on ground tactics, so we're going to move this battle to the jungle—where the territory will be new for the Shadow Academy's troops, but familiar to us. We'll fight them one-on-one.

"But we must evacuate the Jedi academy immediately."

5

FROM THE SHADOW Academy's crowded hangar bay, Zekk watched the final preparations for the attack. The frenzy of bustling troops, mixed with their brooding anger and lust for destruction, galvanized him. He felt as if the lines of Force around him had been set on fire.

The hub of the activity was an immense hovering battle platform that dominated the hangar bay. Constructed specifically for this most important assault on the Rebel Alliance, the movable tactical platform bristled with weaponry. Stormtroopers crawled over its armored surface, preparing to launch. Guided by the ominous Nightsister Tamith Kai, the platform would be the staging point for the ground combat, Jedi versus Jedi.

At the battle platform's helm she stood, eager for vengeance. Her long black cape slithered around her with a hissing sound, like snakes coming out to strike. Spines, taken from the carapace of a murderous giant insect, protruded from her shoulders. Her black hair curled around her head like ebony wires, writhing and crackling with dark powers, each strand seemingly alive and malevolent.

Tamith Kai's violet eyes burned as she ordered the stormtroopers to board the battle platform, gathering her inner power. Her onyx-scaled armor clung to her muscular, well-formed body. Her demeanor spoke of power and confidence—and a yearning for destruction.

Zekk tended to his own duties. He himself had been a target of Tamith Kai's suspicious thoughts. The Nightsister didn't trust him. She felt that his commitment to the dark side wasn't strong enough, that he was blinded by his former friendship with the Jedi twins, Jacen and Jaina Solo.

Zekk had been trained as the prize student of Lord Brakiss, and had defeated the Nightsister's own protégé Vilas in a duel to the death. By winning the duel, Zekk had gained the title of Darkest Knight. And Tamith Kai—perhaps because she was simply a sore loser, or perhaps because she sensed his flickering doubts—rarely let him out of her sight.

But Brakiss had given *him* command of the Shadow Academy's new Force-wielders who would be the vanguard of the battle to reclaim the galaxy. He himself would lead the Dark Jedi strike force, dropping like death from the skies to obliterate Master Skywalker's trainees.

Zekk drew a deep breath, smelled the metallic tang in the cold air. He heard coolants pumping, engines powering up, the clatter of stormtrooper armor, preparatory signals as systems were locked down. They were ready to launch.

Zekk turned to his group of Force-talented warriors. He wore his crimson-lined black cape and his leather armor; his lightsaber hung clipped at his side, waiting to be used. He had secured his long dark hair in a neat ponytail, and his emerald-green eyes flashed at those gathered around him.

"Feel the Force move through you," he said to the other trainees. They stood with their jaws set, their eyes alert, eager for battle. They had been trained for this.

He gestured to the waiting platform, and the Dark Jedi moved with a fluid motion as they entered the armored vessel. "We must strike the Jedi academy now, before we lose our element of surprise."

The TIE pilot's helmet fit perfectly on his gray-haired head. Along with the breathing mask, goggles, black flight suit, padded gloves, and heavy boots, the uniform seemed to transport Qorl back to a different time, a time when he had been much younger . . . a pilot for the first Empire.

Years ago, he had flown with his wing of TIE fighters from the original Death Star to attack the desperate fleet of Rebel X-wings. He had been shot down in combat, spiralling down to crash-land in the wilds of Yavin 4. When he had looked behind him, to his absolute horror and disbelief Qorl had watched the invincible Death Star blow up, leaving him stranded on the miserable little moon.

After recovering from his injuries, Qorl had lived like a hermit for over twenty years until four young Jedi trainees had stumbled upon him . . . setting in motion the events that had returned him to the Second Imperium.

And now, Qorl found himself boarding another TIE fighter, launching from another battle station—once more ready to defeat the Rebels. This time, though, he was sure it would end differently. This time the Empire would make no mistakes.

Qorl stood in front of his wing of twelve TIE fighters. Crowded into the side of the launching bay, the small fighters would take off as soon as the battle platform descended. He turned to his troops, all of them unproven fighters, taken from the ranks of the most ambitious new stormtrooper trainees. The new pilots had never seen combat. They had only practiced, performing simulation after simulation—but he knew they were itching for a real fight. The pilots stood beside their ships, clothed in identical black flight suits and helmets.

One new pilot fidgeted with obvious eagerness, glancing toward his TIE fighter, studying the laser cannon turrets, anxious to be off. He finally stepped forward. The fighter removed his helmet and held it against his chest. Even before seeing the young man's wide face, though, Qorl knew it was the broad-shouldered Norys, former leader of the Lost Ones gang.

"Excuse me, sir—I have a suggestion," Norys said. "In light of my superior performance during the simulations, since I scored better than any of these others, I think I should be the one to lead this wing."

Qorl quelled his anger. "I . . . understand your reasons, Norys. You have done excellent work in your cross-training as a TIE pilot and stormtrooper. You are eager to learn and, presumably, to *serve* the Second Imperium. But I must turn down your request this time."

"On what basis?"

Sensing the challenge in the young man's voice, Qorl kept his answer firm and direct. "On the basis that Brakiss chose me to command this mission. If you prefer not to follow orders, however . . ." He shrugged, leaving the implication hanging in the air between them.

The boy was rude and so often insubordinate that if he hadn't shown such a true aptitude for weaponry and fighting skills, Qorl would certainly have left him behind. Too much was at stake in this mission to allow an overeager young man to botch things up.

Norys flushed. "I think *you* are afraid, Qorl. You're old and haven't flown a mission in years. You're leading the wing so you can hold us back to cover your own failures."

"That will be all," Qorl said in a voice that, although quiet, was so commanding that the air cracked with tension. "I give you the choice: say the word and I'll ground you from this mission, or hold your tongue and fight for your Emperor." At the moment Qorl didn't care what the surly young man chose. He would gladly take a smaller fighting wing if it was the only way to ensure that all his pilots were well disciplined.

Fuming, Norys struggled to keep silent and rammed the black helmet back onto his head.

Qorl spoke, more to divert attention from the outburst than for any other reason. "We have successfully jammed all signals from the Jedi academy. They are unable to call for reinforcements. Since no battleships are in orbit, the foolish Jedi Knights must have assumed that their own powers and their puny energy shield would be enough to thwart us.

"According to our monitoring systems, our first Imperial commando raid has already succeeded in removing their shields. The Jedi academy lies open and vulnerable to our attack.

"When Tamith Kai launches her battle platform to guide the military strike, Lord Zekk will take his Dark Jedi trainees and combat the Jedi Knights directly. Our wing will fly harassment strikes from the air. Although we are meant to cause considerable damage, our mission is to *support*, not to serve as the front line of attack. Is that understood?"

The pilots murmured their understanding. Qorl couldn't tell if Norys's voice had joined them.

"Very well. To your ships," he said.

His pilots scrambled into their cockpits, and Qorl settled in behind the pilot's controls of the lead TIE fighter. He drew a deep breath through the filtering mask, smelling the delicious and familiar chemical taint of the air from his tanks.

He smiled. It felt so good to be able to fly once again.

From the helm of the tactical battle platform Tamith Kai shouted, "Let us be off. We shall return victorious before this day is done!"

The great hangar bay doors opened, revealing the blackness of space shared with the emerald moon, behind which loomed the boiling orange cauldron of the gas giant Yavin. The moon looked insignificant against the panorama of the universe—but it was the Shadow Academy's target, destined to become the site of a furious battle and an Imperial victory.

Tamith Kai commanded the battle platform to rise up on its repulsorlifts and head out of the Shadow Academy. The military vessel appeared to be a large, flattened sailbarge with rounded corners, two levels high, with an upper command deck that would open to the air once they reached the atmosphere. Armed stormtroopers and ground assault forces filled the first level, while Zekk and his Dark Jedi took their positions in the bottom bay near the drop doors.

The battle platform descended through space toward the thin fingernail of atmosphere around the green moon. As the minutes passed, Zekk paced back and forth. He looked out the viewports and saw the ring station high overhead, dwindling as the battle platform increased speed toward Yavin 4.

"Packs ready?" he asked, adjusting the equipment strapped across his chest and back. His black cape hung over it, its scarlet inner lining flashing as he moved. His squad of Dark Jedi checked their weapons, scores of identical lightsabers manufactured aboard the Shadow Academy. The team members adjusted their repulsorpacks on their shoulders. One by one they declared their readiness.

The blackness of space was streaked with white haze as the battle platform plunged headfirst into the atmosphere. Zekk felt a buffeting vibration as the winds clawed the armored plates.

The hull heated up, and Zekk could sense the ionized scream of the shockwave through the air, but Tarnith Kai piloted the battle platform expertly, without hesitation, directly toward their target.

The Nightsister's deep, hard voice came over the comm. "We're approaching target altitude. Zekk, prepare your Dark Jedi for departure. The air-drop doors will open in one standard minute."

Zekk clapped his gloved hands, ordering the Dark Jedi to stand in ranks. "The repulsorpacks will carry you," he said, "but use your Force abilities to guide your descent. We must strike directly. These are our sworn enemies, Luke Sky-walker's Jedi Knights. The future of the galaxy hinges on our victory today."

Zekk fixed his penetrating gaze on each one of the trainees, trying to impart a fraction of his determination to them. They were valiant warriors, vowing to succeed in their quest.

But Zekk had not yet dealt with his own inner turmoil. He knew in his heart that Tamith Kai's doubts about his loyalty had a legitimate foundation—he *did* feel a longing friendship toward his dear friend Jaina Solo and her brother Jacen.

Deep in the forests of Kashyyyk he had warned Jaina to stay away from the Jedi academy. He did not want her to be part of this battle today. He did not want her to become a victim.

But he knew with equal certainty that the Jaina Solo he knew and cared for would never stay away to save herself and leave her friends to die. He dreaded the thought that she might be down there ready to fight against him.

Zekk was grateful to have his thoughts interrupted as the floor thumped and the drop-bay doors creaked open. A line of brighter air like a thin, toothless smile appeared at their feet and then yawned wide. The jungle treetops were visible below, punctuated by the protruding stone towers of ancient Massassi temples.

"All right, my Dark Jedi," Zekk shouted into the howling wind. "The hour is ours. Depart!" Leading the charge, he dove into the sky, switched on his repulsorpack, and tumbled toward the unprotected Jedi academy.

Behind him the other Dark Jedi dropped from the battle platform one by one, falling like deadly birds of prey.

In flight Zekk ignited his lightsaber, holding it out like a glowing beacon. He glanced up to see the other assault troops similarly extending their blazing weapons, capes fluttering behind them.

Dark Jedi rained down from the sky.

THE SHRIEK OF twin ion engines ripped apart the relative quiet of the grand audience chamber. Tenel Ka's reflexes took over even before she recognized the source of the sound, and she found herself running in a crouch toward the closest window slit, with Jaina, Jacen, and Lowbacca right beside her. Through the slit in the stone wall, Tenel Ka saw TIE fighters on a strafing run—coming straight toward the Jedi academy!

"Master Skywalker, we are under attack," Tenel Ka shouted.

Luke Skywalker raised his voice to be heard throughout the chamber. "Everyone, stay in the jungles until the battle is over. Fight with all your skills and abilities. Remember your training . . . and may the Force be with you."

A series of hollow-sounding explosions punctuated his command. A loud *crack!* echoed through the chamber as a proton bomb struck the lowermost levels and dug a crater in the jungle soil outside the pyramid.

From where she stood, Tenel Ka observed the other Jedi trainees and judged that their reactions to Master Skywalker's orders were commendable. Several students gasped in surprise, and Tenel Ka could sense conflicting emotions—nervous anticipation, homesickness, trust in the Force, dread at the possibility of having to kill. But she caught no hint of confusion, panic, or denial.

Without waiting for further instructions, Jedi students streamed out of the grand audience chamber. Luke Skywalker dashed to the window where Tenel Ka's group stood and motioned for Peckhum to join them. The old spacer ducked as stone powder fell from the ceiling, shaken loose by the pounding from above.

The Jedi Master began issuing instructions immediately, and Tenel Ka marveled at how calm he seemed in the midst of the turmoil. "Jacen, take the *Shadow Chaser* into orbit. See if you can break through the jamming signal and send a message to your mother that we're under attack. Artoo-Detoo's down in the hangar bay already waiting with the ship. He's all the copilot you'll need."

Jaina, who loved to fly, was about to protest when Luke turned to her. "I need you to go across the river and check out the shield generator equipment. See if there's any chance of getting our defensive shields back up. Lowie, I want you and Tenel Ka—" The comlink clipped to Luke's belt interrupted him, signaling an urgent message.

Another explosion vibrated through the Great Temple, this one closer than the others. As soon as Luke switched on his comlink, Artoo-Detoo's alarmed bleeps and whistles issued from it.

"What's that, Artoo? Calm down," Luke said.

"If you would allow me, Master Skywalker," Em Teedee said, "I was able to parse your astromech droid's message and could provide a translation for you. I am fluent in over six forms of communic—"

"Thank you, Em Teedee," Luke Skywalker cut off the little droid's chatter, "that would be very helpful."

"Artoo-Detoo reports that—oh dear!—the front of the hangar bay has been hit. Rubble has completely sealed off the entrance. No ships can get in or out. The *Shadow Chaser* is trapped inside."

"Hey," Jacen said after a moment of thought, "Peckhum, what about the *Lightning Rod*? It's not sealed in."

Tenel Ka felt a frown crease her forehead at the thought of Jacen facing an Imperial attack in the rickety old cargo shuttle.

"The *Lightning Rod* doesn't have the *Shadow Chaser*'s quantum armor," Luke pointed out.

"Too dangerous," Jaina said.

"Hey, we're *all* in danger here," Jacen said in a low, firm voice. "And we have to get a message out."

"Sure, we could do it," old Peckhum said. "I've learned

some pretty good evasive maneuvers in my day—enough to make it to orbit without gettin' blown up, I'd guess."

Just then Lowbacca gave a warning yelp and pointed toward the window slit. Hovering over the jungle in the distance was an ominous-looking construction, a giant weapon-studded tactical platform, like a deadly raft carrying enemy troops.

Tenel Ka felt a stab of recognition. "Tamith Kai is there; I can feel her," she said.

"It looks like she's directing the ground battle from up there," Luke said.

"Then we must disable that battle platform," Tenel Ka replied without a pause. "I volunteer. The Nightsister is mine."

Lowbacca barked a comment. "Master Lowbacca wishes to point out that his T-23 is still out near the landing pad. Using the skyhopper, he and Mistress Tenel Ka could easily reach that platform within minutes."

Luke nodded. "We each have our missions. I'll do one last sweep of the pyramid to make sure no one was left behind. I'll see you all out at the rendezvous point in the jungle."

As the young Jedi Knights raced down the stairs inside the temple, Tenel Ka's mind already began moving ahead to the coming confrontation. Adrenaline pumped through her veins, and her mind was alert. She had been bred and trained for battle.

Although fighting with only one arm would present her with new challenges, she felt neither afraid nor overconfident. She was simply *ready*. A Jedi must always be ready, she knew. Master Skywalker and Tionne had trained them all well. Tenel Ka had her lightsaber and her Force skills. Together, she was certain, that was enough for her to defeat any enemy.

By the time they all reached the landing pad, Jaina had already split off from the group, plunging toward the river and the shield generator station. Tenel Ka was surprised to note that the old pilot Peckhum had kept up with them as he and Jacen sprinted toward the battered supply shuttle.

Dodging energy bolts from the TIE fighters that swooped overhead, Tenel Ka and Lowbacca scrambled into the T-23 skyhopper while Peckhum and Jacen boarded the *Lightning Rod*.

Watching Jacen run up the ramp into the *Lightning Rod*, Tenel Ka felt a tug at her emotions she could not explain, even to herself. Almost at the same moment, Jacen reappeared and stared at Tenel Ka with a serious expression. His face broke into a grin. "I'll tell you a joke when we get back—a good one this time." Then he was gone again.

As Lowie fired up the T-23's repulsorjets, Tenel Ka answered, though she knew he couldn't hear her, "Yes, my friend Jacen, I would like to hear your joke. When we all get back."

7

THE *LIGHTNING ROD*'S engines whined as the ship strained against gravity. Just after liftoff, the battered vessel gave a sharp jolt. Alarm bells went off inside Jacen's head. "We're hit!" he cried, not even bothering to check the read-outs.

"Naw," old Peckhum answered. "*Lightning Rod*'s been doin' that ever since I switched out the power coupling to the rear repulsorjets. I guess I'll have to take a look at that again one of these days."

The knot of panic in Jacen's stomach eased a little—but only a little. "Maybe Jaina can help you with it later," he said.

An energy bolt streaked by as a TIE fighter sang past them on its descent toward the Jedi academy. "Hey, that was a close one!" Jacen said.

"Too close," Peckhum agreed. "Hang on, young Solo—I'm gonna try some evasive maneuvers."

Lowie focused his full concentration on getting the T-23 to cover. With his peripheral vision he could see other Jedi students dodging fire from TIE fighters as they sprinted for the safety of the trees. When they reached the edge of the forest, the young Wookiee pulled his skyhopper into a sharp climb.

The dense network of leafy branches had always signified protection to Lowie, and he longed for a few peaceful moments in the treetops. But no peace awaited Lowie and Tenel Ka up there. Not this time.

Lowie clenched the steering controls tightly and zigzagged the flight path across the treetops, trying to throw off any pursuers who might be on their track. Today trouble rained down on them from above, and he could flee to no safe height. His best bet lay in remaining among the trees.

An energy bolt spat past the T-23 and sent up a plume of dirt and singed turf behind them. "Let the Force guide you, Lowbacca, my friend," Tenel Ka said from the passenger seat in back.

Lowie rumbled an acknowledgment and took a deep calming breath. He flew onward, letting the Force control his weaving and dodging. They headed toward the wide, greenish-brown river over which Tenel Ka and Lowbacca had seen the Nightsister's sinister battle platform. Even from half a kilometer away, they could see lances of laser fire shoot out from the armored vessel, incinerating trees along the banks.

Suddenly, Tenel Ka gave a shout of surprise. "Look. There!"

From the sky above a group of figures descended like swooping birds of prey—human forms. Dark Jedi dropped from the clouds in a dispersed attack pattern, lightsabers flashing as they controlled their direction with repulsorpacks.

A proximity alarm sounded the moment Lowbacca diverted his attention, and a laser cannon blast from a passing TIE fighter struck them. A jet of smoke and sparks spewed from the T-23's rear engines. The tiny skyhopper shimmied and bucked in the air. With a shriek of shearing metal, one of the attitude-control fins gave way.

"Oh my," Em Teedee wailed. "I can't bear to watch."

Lowie, reacting with the instinct of his Jedi training, wrestled with the controls. Directed by the Force, one of his sharp-clawed hands flew across the control panel, while his free hand guided their descent. Smoke poured into the cockpit, and the skyhopper sputtered and rocked. Without knowing quite how he did it, Lowie cut the rear engines and bled off their momentum into a steep upward climb. Then, letting the little ship fall back toward the treetops, he used one final burst from the repulsorjets to slow their descent—enough, he hoped.

The T-23 crashed onto the jungle canopy.

With every breath, Tenel Ka drew fire into her aching lungs. Nearby a Wookiee groaned, but she could not make sense of the growled words. She could see nothing.

"Mistress Tenel Ka!" A strident electronic voice broke into her foggy consciousness. "Master Lowbacca urgently requests your assistance removing the T-23's canopy."

Tenel Ka tried to look around. She saw only roiling, changing shapes of light and dark. The shifting patterns stung her eyes, and she squeezed them tightly shut.

A voice loud enough to wake a Jedi Master from a healing trance wailed in Tenel Ka's ears. "Oh, curse my sluggish processor, I'm too late. She's dead!"

Lowbacca bellowed a loud denial. At the same time, something reached out and gave her a sharp nudge.

"No," Tenel Ka managed to croak. "I'm alive."

Lowbacca gave a few crisp barks, and Tenel Ka found herself responding to his instructions even before Em Teedee could clarify, "Master Lowbacca asks you to push against the canopy with all your might whilst throwing your weight toward the port side—to the left, you know."

Tenel Ka knew. She pushed and rocked. Despite the choking clouds of smoke from the burning engines, she grew calm enough to let the Force flow through her.

Even through her closed eyelids, Tenel Ka could tell when Em Teedee switched on the bright yellow beams of his optical sensors to cut through the smoke. "It would seem," the little droid went on, "that the T-23's canopy is wedged against a tree branch. Oh, we're doomed!"

Then, just as the little droid finished his lament, the skyhopper's canopy popped free, and fresh air flooded the cockpit. Both Tenel Ka and Lowbacca stripped out of their crash webbing and scrambled free of the wreckage. As they moved away from the smoldering craft, panting for breath and waiting for their vision to clear, Tenel Ka's hand went automatically to her lightsaber to be sure it was still clipped firmly at her waist. It was.

"Oh dear," Em Teedee exclaimed in a tiny voice. "Now we'll most likely become lost in the jungle and captured by woolamanders. Do be careful, Master Lowbacca. I should hate to repeat that dreadful experience."

Balancing on a tree limb beside Tenel Ka, Lowbacca turned to gaze at the crashed T-23 and uttered a low, mournful note. Tenel Ka could see that his distress came not from the thought of jungle creatures, but from the loss of his beloved vehicle. The warrior girl understood loss. She reached out her single hand to touch Lowbacca's arm briefly and let the strength of the Force comfort him. Then, as one, they turned to seek out their destination: the giant battle platform—and the evil Nightsister.

To Tenel Ka's relief and surprise, Lowbacca had managed to crash-land barely two hundred meters from where the battle platform hovered above the crowns of the Massassi trees. Before she could speak, though, her Wookiee friend gave a low woof of warning and pointed downward toward cover.

Tenel Ka understood immediately and scrambled down into the leaves and branches until she was hidden. If they could see the giant battle platform, then they themselves could be seen. They would need to make their way to the battle platform *beneath* the rippling green leaves, like swimmers below the surface of an ocean.

With only one arm to help her balance and pull herself along, Tenel Ka had to trust the Force to place her feet securely at each step. She even welcomed Lowbacca's help when he offered it in crossing weak branches or broad gaps.

Tenel Ka wasn't sure why she felt compelled to speak. Perhaps it was the air of sadness that hung about her Wookiee friend. "We will spend many enjoyable days repairing your T-23, Lowbacca my friend—you, Jacen, Jaina, and I. After this battle is over."

The Wookiee stopped, looked at her quizzically for a moment, then chuffed with laughter. After a series of woofs, Em Teedee said, "Master Lowbacca adds that Master Jacen will most likely be delighted to have a captive audience to entertain with his jokes."

Tenel Ka felt her own spirits brighten at that thought, and they moved forward at a more rapid pace. Her mind focused on the goal of defeating the Second Imperium once and for all.

Suddenly, she felt a tingle run up her spine. "Halt!" she said. A TIE fighter swooped low across the leaves, rippling the canopy around them with its hot exhaust as it circled to inspect the crashed skyhopper. Lowbacca growled, and Tenel Ka held his arm to restrain him from any rash action. The Imperial ship circled again over the wreckage, as if looking for survivors. Tenel Ka hoped the pilot wouldn't blast the already-downed craft into a smoldering lump of slag and debris. After a tense moment, the enemy ship roared away in search of new prey.

She and Lowbacca pressed on through the trees toward where the battle platform waited.

It seemed like no time at all before Em Teedee said, "Unless my senses have become completely uncalibrated by the crash, we should be directly below the leading edge of the battle platform right now."

Lowbacca held out a hand, motioning for Tenel Ka to wait,

and scrambled up a few branches to check their location. At his low bark of triumph, she climbed after him and pushed her head above the leafy canopy. There, hovering ten meters over the treetops, was the underside of the giant battle platform, massive and threatening, armored for assault, bristling with weapons.

"It should be a simple enough task to destroy it," Tenel Ka said.

The sounds of shouted orders and clomping booted feet carried down to them. Lowbacca pointed upward and then shrugged as if to say, What next? The platform was too high above the trees to make a jump, and they had no repulsor-packs of their own. Tenel Ka reached for the grappling hook and fibercord she kept at her belt.

"We'll have to climb for it," she said.

The platform hovered higher than Tenel Ka was accustomed to aiming, but the grappling hook caught firmly on the armored edge on her second throw. Tenel Ka tested her weight on the fibercord. The grappling hook did not budge. Then, wrapping her arm and her legs around the cord, she began to climb, using the Force to help levitate her when her single arm couldn't provide enough support.

Above on the platform waited Imperial stormtroopers, heavy armaments, and a Nightsister from Dathomir.

Tenel Ka swallowed hard. She knew that although the Force was with them, the *odds* definitely were not.

8

THE GREEN-BROWN RIVER that flowed sluggishly through the primeval forest was broad and powerful, yet outwardly calm. The current showed not the least bit of disturbance from the titanic struggle of good and evil taking place on Yavin 4.

The river hosted numerous life-forms: invisible plankton

and carnivorous protozoans, water plants, trees that dangled sharp roots into the flow, and camouflaged predators that disguised themselves as innocuous parts of the landscape.

But as blaster shots rang out and the buzz of lightsabers droned through the jungle, other creatures moved in the thick branches over the river and in the water itself . . . creatures trained in using the Force.

Rounded reptilian snouts broke the surface of the murky river. Breathing slits rose up, nostrils flaring to draw in welcome oxygen. The three scaly creatures moved slowly enough that only slight ripples whispered across the water. Settling into position deep in the mud, they sniffed and lay in wait near the path at the river's edge.

Their enemies would come soon.

Moving stealthily yet radiating a supremely confident power, three of the Dark Jedi trainees from the Shadow Academy strode through the underbrush, hacking away the dense vines and branches with their lightsaber blades. They reached the riverbank and paused to consult with each other, still searching for their opponents.

"Skywalker's Jedi trainees are cowards," one said. "Why don't they come out and fight? They all hide in the jungle like terrified rodents."

"How can they not be afraid of us?" another one said. "They know the power of the dark side."

Consulting silently, with only a faint stream of bubble for communication, three of Luke Skywalker's reptilian Cha'a trainees lunged out of the river, spewing a stream of water at their enemies. They used the Force to summon a hammering flow of the river, a column of drenching wetness that reared up like a snake, then splashed down. The Dark Jedi lightsaber blades sizzled and steamed. The three Cha'a hissed and chattered with laughter as they summoned up more and more water.

The waterlogged Dark Jedi sputtered and thrashed from side to side as they attempted to summon up dark-side powers with which to strike back at their reptilian opponents.

Just then, from the dense shelter of the trees above, a trio of feathered avians left their perches and plunged down. They let out a high, fluting whistle of a battle cry.

The Dark Jedi were distracted for a moment, torn between two enemies. Then the avians landed on top of them, driving them to the ground and knocking them unconscious. The avians chirped and screeched in victory as the Cha'a hauled themselves dripping out of the river mud and slogged toward the three new captives.

Working together, Skywalker's alien Jedi trainees removed whiplike vines from the underbrush and lashed the arms and legs of their prisoners together. One of the Cha'a picked up the discarded Shadow Academy lightsabers, studied the poor construction and unimaginative workmanship. One by one, he tossed the tainted weapons into the river. They splashed, and sank without a trace.

Meanwhile, the avians crouched over the unconscious captives and used their Jedi powers to probe the minds of Brakiss's students. They added strong Force suggestions to make sure their enemies would continue to sleep for a long time. . . .

Tionne tossed her long silvery-white hair behind her to get it out of the way. She would need her vision unobstructed, with no distractions.

She looked at the other Jedi students with her gleaming mother-of-pearl eyes. Master Skywalker frequently entrusted her with training these students, and now Tionne would do battle. The Yavin 4 academy had often been a target of the forces of evil—but the true Jedi Knights had won before, and she had no doubt they would win again.

She and her students stood around the flat marble slab and broken columns of what had once been an open-air Massassi temple before it was swallowed up by the jungle. This was the place at which they had chosen to make their stand.

"Are you all ready?" Tionne said. "Remember what you

have been taught. *There is no try.* We must succeed in defeating the warriors of the dark side."

Her students shouted their agreement, looking at her with eyes full of confidence in their abilities and her plan. One of the young women nodded to Tionne, took a deep breath, then ran off into the forest in search of the invading Dark Jedi. Within only moments the young woman cried out, shouting, challenging the trainees of the Shadow Academy.

Tionne heard a lightsaber sizzle. Branches fell . . . and then came the sound of footsteps crashing through the forest as her student hurried back toward the trap they had set. Tionne gestured silently for the others to prepare themselves.

"Come back here, Jedi vermin!" one of the enemy called, hidden by the thickets.

Four Dark Jedi came plunging through the jungles, bursting into the temple clearing where the panting student stood on the other side of a flat marble slab hanging above their heads. Tionne's student looked defeated.

The invaders stepped forward. "We will crush your mind with the dark side!" one said.

"Now!" Tionne shouted. From their shadowy hiding places, four of her special students reached out with the Force: in an unexpected, irresistible move, they snatched the four lightsabers from enemy hands. The Dark Jedi cried out in alarm and surprise at losing their weapons. Then Tionne and her students emerged from the underbrush and surrounded them.

"We don't need our lightsabers to defeat you. We can still flatten you with our power!" said the first overconfident opponent. "The power of the dark side!" All four of the enemy Jedi stood in a tight cluster, back to back, raising their hands.

"I wouldn't do that if I were you," Tionne said calmly, letting her pale lips show a brief smile. "You wouldn't want to distract us—a brief fluctuation in our concentration might become a *crushing* defeat for you."

She glanced upward. Her four students remained motionless with their eyes closed, focused on their task.

The Dark Jedi looked up and saw that the marble slab they had thought to be the ceiling of a crumbling temple was completely unsupported, a hovering rectangle of rock weighing many tons, balanced over their heads. It floated, held up by nothing but the power of the Force. Tionne's students maintained their concentration.

The Dark Jedi swallowed hard.

"You can try to escape if you like," Tionne said. "Maybe you have enough power to subdue all of us with enough left over to catch that block of stone before it falls down on your heads. Maybe." She shrugged. "It's your choice, of course. But I wouldn't risk it."

The four Dark Jedi exchanged glances, unable to find words. Finally, one by one, they lowered their clenched hands and surrendered.

Tionne heaved a quiet but heartfelt sigh of relief.

Another tree stood in the forest, short and stunted, with a thick trunk. Branches extended out in such a way that, if looked at in a certain light, it had an almost humanoid appearance: one of Master Skywalker's Jedi, a slow-moving, long-lived plantlike creature.

She often went out to spend days in the sunlight, using photosynthesis to drink in nourishment, absorbing minerals from the soil, water from the river, and carbon dioxide from the air.

She would spend all day, many days at a time, simply contemplating the Force and her place in the universe. Trees remained alive for a long time and did not rush into ill-considered action; yet at times such as this, she could manage to move fast enough. She understood the importance of protecting the Jedi academy.

She had entered into her training to understand the Force, vowing to defend the side of light—and here she found herself in a clear-cut battle against the Shadow Academy. Dark Jedi enemies coursed through the jungle, searching for victims, but Master Skywalker had taught all the trainees well. The light-side students would put up a good fight.

The treelike Jedi stood motionless, watching, sensing the jungle . . . and she knew her enemies would come to her. She had only to wait. Her roots dug deeper into the soil, drawing on it for greater energy. She felt the sap pulsing through her, boiling in her veins, allowing her to gain the speed for the unwavering action that she would require just this once . . . she hoped.

She had chosen her spot well, next to an ailing Massassi tree, tall with outspreading branches. Its trunk was nested with vines and dripping with parasitic shelf mushrooms that had tapped into its heartwood and begun devouring the great tree from within.

The Jedi could tell that this great-grandfather of a tree had lived for centuries and centuries. . . . It was the way of things, the cycle of the forest. As plants grew, they went to seed to bear their young, and then slowly decayed to warm organic matter and fertilized the forest for subsequent generations. She saw how the old Massassi tree leaned, observed the surrounding jungle . . . waited.

She reached out with the Force subtly, gently, so that even the adepts of the Dark Side would not know they were being manipulated. "*Come here*," she thought, broadcasting it over and over again. At least one of them would catch the hint. They would think they had detected one of their lightside enemies—but it would be all the plant Jedi's doing.

After an indeterminate period—she did not measure time in small increments—she sensed a clumsy disturbance: two attackers from the Shadow Academy storming through the forest, as if the delicate ecosystem was no more than a nuisance that they would eradicate completely, given the chance.

The Jedi waited. She had to concentrate. She had to act at the right moment and not waste time thinking, or else her opportunity would pass.

Curled within one of her gnarled branches—a handlike appendage—was a knobby lightsaber built to accommodate her wooden grip.

The two Dark Jedi came into the clearing and stopped. "I see nothing here," said one. "Lord Brakiss would be ashamed of you. Lord Zekk would take away your lightsaber. The powers of the dark side are wasted on you."

"I tell you, I sensed it," said the other. He stepped forward, looking from side to side, studying the quiet jungle. His companion stood next to him, scowling.

At that moment the Jedi used all her stored reserves—and acted. She ignited the lightsaber and slashed sideways with her branch arm, like a bent sapling suddenly released to snap straight again.

"I am sorry, Grandfather Tree," she said—and her lightsaber blade cleaved through the trunk of the tottering old Massassi tree, severing it from the stump and letting the arms of gravity embrace it. Its wide-branched top leaned over and the tree crashed onto the two Dark Jedi intruders. They had time only to look up with a muffled outcry of surprise as a meteor of branches and vines smashed down upon them.

The Jedi deactivated her lightsaber, then felt a trembling through her entire wooden body. In one act, she had drained months and months of her energy reserves. She stretched her branches up toward the sunlight, dug her roots deeper.

It would take her a long time to recover from this day.

9

AFTER CROSSING THE river, Jaina fought her way through the jungle, seeking a suitable path through the thickest underbrush while keeping herself hidden from other attackers. Right now, the tangled forest was her ally, and she could use the cover to her advantage. She wasn't afraid to combat the

Dark Jedi threatening the academy—but she had a vital mission in mind . . . something more to her tastes.

As long as the defensive energy shields remained down and the generator damaged, the entire area was vulnerable to repeated attacks from the skies. Luke Skywalker's trainees were defending themselves . . . but if Jaina could somehow repair the shield generator and get the protective force field up again, the new Jedi Knights could take care of these audacious enemies one at a time.

Jaina finally made her way to the clearing where her father and Chewbacca had recently installed the new energy shield generator. With only a glance she saw that the machinery was irreparable, despite her usual knack for fixing things.

Normally, she could make temporary repairs to get systems up and running again, at least for a while. But not in this case. An Imperial saboteur had used thermal detonators to wipe out the entire generating station. It was hopelessly ruined, a pile of shrapnel; no simple fix-up would do.

Jaina's attention remained on the generator for only a moment, however. She caught her breath.

There in the clearing sat an Imperial TIE fighter in perfect condition.

Ever since Chewbacca had given Lowie the T-23 skyhopper, Jaina had longed for a vehicle of her own. That, in fact, had been the impetus behind her desire to repair the crashed TIE fighter the young Jedi Knights had found in the jungles— Qorl's TIE fighter.

She stopped and stared, frozen with excitement and apprehension. But other than the muffled noises of battle in the jungles and the distant shouts and blaster fire near the Great Temple, she heard no sound.

Jaina withdrew her lightsaber and pressed the power stud. The beam sprang outward, glowing an electric violet. Then she crept forward stealthily, ready to fight if the TIE pilot emerged with his blaster drawn. But she sensed no one else around, heard no noise from the craft.

"Hello?" Jaina called. "You'd better surrender if you're an Imperial!" She waited. "Uh, is anyone here?"

Only the simmering jungle noises answered her.

Moving forward, letting her eagerness take over, she ran to the abandoned TIE fighter. It was a sinister-looking ship: a rounded cockpit suspended between two flat hexagonal power arrays, twin ion engines that would propel the small fighter across space, a bank of deadly laser cannons.

Ideas and possibilities thundered through her mind. If she could pilot this ship into the enemy's midst, Jaina would be in disguise. She could slip in among them, and they wouldn't *know* she was actually an enemy . . . until it was too late.

Switching off her lightsaber again, Jaina opened the cockpit hatch and crawled inside. She had studied how TIE fighters worked when she and her friends had replaced the components of Qorl's crashed ship. She knew the buttons on the control panels, knew how the systems activated. Though the exiled old pilot had flown off in his ship before Jaina had had a chance to take it on a flight, she was confident she could handle the craft.

She settled into the pilot's seat, noting the oily scent of stale lubricants and the sour odors the Empire did not bother to remove. A rebreather mask hung next to a small life-support console. The cockpit walls closed around her like a protective shell, giving her little room to move, but all the controls were at her fingertips. Through the ship's front ports, she could see outside.

Jaina found the power switch and toggled it on, felt the engines' thrumming, systems gearing up, batteries charging. Control panel lights winked on in a brilliant flurry around her. She drew a deep breath, strapped herself in, and clutched the controls.

"All systems ready for takeoff," she whispered to herself. She glanced at the sky, looking for the black specks of other Imperial ships. "Okay, TIE fighters, prepare for some company!"

The Imperial craft raised up as Jaina worked the controls.

Clearing the jungle treetops, she felt the exhilaration of actually flying. The ship seemed unbelievably quiet inside, until she realized that its noisier primary engines had been disengaged. This TIE fighter flew so quietly because it used only the lesser-powered engines. So *that* was how the enemy pilot had gotten under their shield unnoticed! No doubt the original systems remained intact, but the enemy commando had slipped in without the familiar howl of TIE engines.

All right then, Jaina thought—she could be silent and deadly as well. Finally skimming the treetops, she scanned around, acquiring targets. She shot forward, reveling in the thrill of flight, the landscape passing beneath her in a mottled green blur.

Up ahead she saw six TIE fighters flying in formation, firing down at the treetops, pounding the temple ruins, even structures that had never been used for training Jedi. The Palace of the Woolamander, an ancient ruin already nearly collapsed, was pummeled with brilliant streaks from laser cannons, though Jaina didn't believe any Jedi Knights had gone there.

She kept the Imperial comm channels on so she could hear the terse, gruff chatter as the TIE pilots discussed their overall plan, choosing targets, firing at moving figures sheltered by the thick Massassi trees.

Jaina kept her microphone off, though, as she joined the formation of TIE fighters, slipping in at the rear. Over the comm system she heard them acknowledge her arrival; rather than making them suspicious by speaking with a young woman's voice, she just clicked an okay over the microphone.

Then she powered up her laser cannons.

One of the TIE fighters broadcast, "Plenty of targets here for everybody. Let's cause some damage."

Jaina bit her lower lip and nodded. "Yes," she muttered to herself, "let's cause some damage."

She let her eyes fall partially closed and concentrated, feeling the Force. Despite the sensors and systems available in the TIE fighter, nothing could match heightened Jedi perceptions for enhancing her movements. She needed to target and fire and target again with lightning speed. She would have only one chance.

Jaina gripped the control stick of her weapons and focused on the aiming mechanisms, flying smoothly behind the un-suspecting Imperials. She had to disable them with one shot each. She couldn't risk repeated fire on a single target, be-cause once she started shooting, they would be rather upset with her.

Jaina sought out the most vulnerable points: their engines and the joints that held the planar power arrays to their sides. If the TIE fighters turned side-on to her, she would blast the power arrays themselves—large targets, impossible to miss.

Giving herself a silent countdown, Jaina pointed her lasers at the closest ship. What am I waiting for? she asked herself.

Gritting her teeth, she fired a single shot, then swiveled the laser cannons, moving with hyperspeed, to target a second TIE fighter. Even before her second bolt struck the narrow joint next to the cockpit and sliced off the planar array, the first TIE fighter careened into a spin.

Jaina blasted again at the rear engine pods of the second ship. The TIE fighter exploded in front of her, momentarily blinding her, but she quickly averted her eyes. As she brought the laser cannons to bear on a third target, Jaina heard the TIE pilots shouting in outrage and panic. The formation began to split apart.

She didn't have much time.

The third TIE fighter turned toward her, and Jaina strafed across its surface, severing one of the planar arrays and strik-ing the viewports in the cockpit. The third ship went down—but by now the remaining three Imperials had spun around and were headed straight toward her.

Jaina blinked as fiery bolts from their laser cannons shot past her. She put her TIE fighter into a spin. Now using the Force to anticipate the incoming weapons fire just as her uncle Luke had used his lightsaber to deflect blaster bolts, she spun and turned and banked, then began to fly away at her fighter's top speed.

But the other three Imperial ships came howling after her, releasing a constant volley of laser fire, ignoring targets below now that they had acquired a single target . . . a traitor in their midst.

Jaina ducked and dodged, no longer enjoying the thrill of flight. She had a bad feeling about her impulsive attack. She streaked over the jungle, the three TIE fighters hot on her tail.

10

THE DIM FOREST floor near the Great Temple was familiar ground for Luke Skywalker and most of his Jedi trainees. Even with a battle of light and dark raging around him—or perhaps *because* of the battle—he found it soothing to be out in the wilds. The jungle itself was rich with life, and therefore rich in the Force that bound all life together.

Reaching down to confirm that his lightsaber was securely attached to his belt next to his comlink, Luke drew on the Force. He let it flow through him, let it show him the skirmishes all around him.

Alert to the emotions of his students, Luke reached out to bolster flagging confidence in one trainee, to warn another against an unexpected attack, to send encouragement to yet another who was growing tired.

An energy bolt from a TIE fighter sliced through the trees close by and set fire to the underbrush, forcing Luke to retreat behind a thicket to avoid choking fumes from the burning vegetation.

With his mind he searched for the center of the battle, the place where he could do the most good. Decades ago, when the Death Star had loomed over the jungle moon, his mission had been clear. The battle station's superlaser could turn an entire planet to rubble. Luke had had no doubt in his mind that the Empire's most powerful weapon must be destroyed. And with the Force to guide him, he had succeeded.

But today's battle was different—it had no focus. This time he had no superweapon to disable. The Jedi academy's long-range transmissions had been jammed, the defensive shields sabotaged. With Artoo-Detoo and the *Shadow Chaser* trapped in the Great Temple's hangar bay, Luke had no way of reaching orbit to fight the Shadow Academy directly.

The ground assault itself was directed from the giant battle platform that hovered over the treetops a few kilometers away, but Luke sensed that the military component of the attack was mere harassment.

TIE fighters had made direct attacks on the Great Temple—and yet *ground* forces and Dark Jedi had been sent to fight on a nearly even footing against Luke's students. With a different strategy, the Shadow Academy's victory would have been far easier—it almost seemed as if Brakiss *wanted* to do it the hard way.

Luke knew that must be the answer.

A loud incoming message signal on his comlink startled him. Students at the Yavin academy rarely earned comlinks, but the Jedi Master kept one at his side during times of turmoil so that he could be reached more easily. Even though the Shadow Academy had jammed long-range transmissions, local signals from Artoo could still get through.

Luke switched on the comlink. "Sit tight, Artoo. We'll be able to get you when the fighting's over." Before he could say more, a man's voice blared from the tiny speaker.

"—essage for Luke Skywalker. Repeat: this is a message for Luke Skywalker. If anyone can hear me, respond immediately."

Luke stared at the small device before replying, "Who is this?" But before he heard the answer, his Jedi senses told him the man's identity.

"You can call me *Master* Brakiss," the voice said. "Tell

your teacher that I'm transmitting on all channels. He will want to speak to me."

"This is Luke Skywalker," he said. "If you have a message, Brakiss, you can give it directly to me." Luke's heart knocked painfully against his rib cage, though from surprise rather than fear.

A cultured laugh came over the comlink. "Well, my old teacher . . . the man I once called Master. This *is* a pleasure."

"What do you want, Brakiss?" Luke asked.

"A meeting," the smooth voice replied. "Just the two of us. On neutral ground. As equals. We didn't have a chance to finish our . . . conversation when you came to my Shadow Academy to rescue your Jedi brats."

Luke paused to consider. A meeting with Brakiss? Maybe this was the answer to the problem he had been trying to solve. After all, who was more central to this battle than the leader of the Shadow Academy himself? If Luke could reason with Brakiss, turn him away from the dark side, this battle could be won before too many lives were lost.

"Where, Brakiss? What neutral territory do you propose?"

"I think both your academy and mine are out of the question right now."

"Agreed."

"Away from the fighting, then. Across the river in the Temple of the Blue Leaf Cluster. But you must come alone."

"Will *you*?" Luke asked.

Brakiss gave a rich chuckle. "Of course. I have no need for reinforcements—and I know you are true to your word."

Luke paused to reassure himself that the Force was indeed guiding his actions. Both he and Brakiss were strong enough in the Force to sense any betrayal by the other.

"Very well, Brakiss. I'll meet you there. Alone. We can settle this once and for all."

"HEY, THAT WASN'T so hard," Jacen said, leaning forward in the copilot's chair of the *Lightning Rod*. The chair creaked, its padding bulging out through countless small rips and tears in the cushion. The engines rumbled and coughed and whined as the cargo shuttle finally broke free of the atmosphere.

"You had to say that, didn't you, boy?" Peckhum said as sensor alarms squealed on his control panel. Incoming enemy ships. Again. "We got TIE fighters coming, four of 'em. Looks like they were launched directly from the Shadow Academy."

Jacen swallowed, studying the pattern, and shook his head. "Oh, blaster bolts! We'd better transmit our distress message now before they get us. Otherwise help for the Jedi academy will come too late."

Peckhum looked over at him, his eyes red-rimmed, his haggard face serious. "You'll have to take care of that message yourself, Jacen. I'm gonna be mighty busy doing some fancy flying here—if she'll hold together." He patted the cockpit controls. "Sorry to do this to you, girl, but I didn't name you the *Lightning Rod* for nothing. Let's show these Imperials our stuff."

Jacen fumbled with the unfamiliar comm system, tuning frequencies and feeling completely inadequate. He wished his sister were here—*she* was the expert on these systems. She would know how to cut through the double-talk, the chatter, the Imperial transmission block.

He sent a subspace message blaring on all frequencies at the maximum levels of volume and power the *Lightning Rod* could spare and still keep her shields up.

"This is Jacen Solo," he said, then cleared his throat. He had no idea what to say, but he supposed the details didn't exactly matter. "Attention, New Republic. We have an emergency! This is Jacen Solo on Yavin 4, requesting immediate assistance. We are under attack by the Shadow Academy!

"Repeat. Imperial fighters attacking the Jedi academy—request assistance immediately. Our shields are down. We've got ground battles taking place and air strikes from TIE fighters. We desperately need immediate assistance." He switched off the microphone, then looked over at Peckhum. "Hey, how'd I do?"

"Just fine, kid," Peckhum said, and lurched the ship to one side, going into a clockwise spin as the four TIE fighters roared past, belching fire from laser cannons. One shot struck the *Lightning Rod*'s lower shield, but the other bolts streamed harmlessly into space, intersecting the empty void where the cargo ship had been only a moment before.

"I used to be a pretty good flier in my day," Peckhum said. "And I still am . . . I think."

One TIE fighter broke away from the other three and spun in a tighter circle, firing repeatedly without taking the trouble to aim, spraying space with its deadly fire.

Peckhum dove down, skimming the atmosphere, so that the lower hull of the *Lightning Rod* grew hot. Then he bounced back into space again, turning about in a tight backward loop and heading up over the determined TIE fighter, which shot again and again. Sparks flew from the battered supply ship's control panels. Lights winked red on their system diagnostics.

"Uh, Peckhum? What do all those alarms mean?" Jacen said.

"It means our shields are failing."

"Don't you have any *weapons* on this ship?" Jacen scanned the panels, looking for any sort of targeting system, some firing controls.

Peckhum coughed and put the ship into a sharp dive toward Yavin 4. "This is a cargo ship, boy, and she's seen better days. I wasn't expecting to take her into battle, you know. Heck, I'm lucky the food-prep units still work."

The rest of the Imperial squadron zoomed away to continue the attack on the Jedi academy, but the one persistent TIE fighter came in again single-mindedly. This time he had them locked on target, so that most of his laser cannon blasts struck the *Lightning Rod*.

"This guy really wants to take us out," Jacen said.

Peckhum pushed his accelerators well beyond maximum safety levels. The *Lightning Rod* groaned and creaked as it rattled down through the atmosphere, buffeted by air turbulence.

Jacen was thrown from side to side. He grabbed the comm system again. "This is Jacen Solo with a personal distress this time. We are in deep trouble. Someone is on our tail. Request assistance. Please—can anyone out there help us?"

Peckhum looked over at him. "Nobody's going to get here in time."

Jacen remembered stories of how Luke Skywalker had been in a similar situation on the run down the Death Star trench, trying to send his proton torpedo through a small thermal exhaust port. His X-wing had been in Darth Vader's sights, unable to shake the TIE fighters and interceptors on his tail. Things had looked hopeless—and then Jacen's father, Han Solo, had appeared out of nowhere, saving the day.

But Jacen didn't think his father was anywhere close by now, and he couldn't imagine anyone else who might pop unexpectedly out of the skies to take care of the enemy. That was too much luck to hope for.

With a crackle of static over the comm system, a gruff and gloating voice spoke—but it wasn't any rescuer. "Well . . . Jacen Solo! You're one of those feisty Jedi brats we ran into down in the lower levels of Coruscant. Remember me— Norys? I was the leader of the Lost Ones gang. You stole that hawk-bat egg from us . . . and now I think we're about to even all the old scores. Hah!"

Jacen felt a shiver go down his spine as he remembered the broad-shouldered bully who had such an appetite for destruction. Norys continued.

"The little trash collector, Zekk, joined us in the Second

Imperium, but *you* have made the wrong choice, boy. I just wanted you to know who was to going to blast you to slag." The TIE pilot signed off and continued the conversation with a volley of laser bolts.

"Well, I'm glad he picked such a fine time to contact us," Peckhum said, fighting with the controls, unable to fly an evasive pattern anymore. He worked with all his talent just to keep the *Lightning Rod* from falling apart in the sky. "I don't think we'll last much longer, and I'm sure that Norys kid would have hated to blow us up before he got a chance to say his little goodbye."

The engines of the *Lightning Rod* began to smoke. More alarms blared from the control panels. Behind them Norys's TIE fighter continued to fire mercilessly, pounding their hull, trying to crack open the battered cargo ship.

Jacen stared at the comm unit, but didn't think it would do any good to send out another distress signal.

The jungle treetops rushed by beneath them. Jacen looked wildly from side to side. "I don't suppose it would be a good time to tell a joke," he said.

Peckhum shook his head. "Don't feel much like laughing right now."

12

THE THICK BRANCHES of the damp and shadowy jungle closed around him, pressing in. It reminded Zekk of the murky lower levels of Coruscant. It felt almost like home.

He and his troops of Dark Jedi had fallen from the skies, buoyed by repulsorpacks. After coming to rest in the upper branches, they'd worked their way down to ground level and spread out to surround the fleeing Jedi trainees Master Skywalker had brainwashed into supporting Rebel philosophies.

Zekk knew little about politics. He understood only who

his friends and supporters were—and who had betrayed him. Like Jacen and Jaina . . . especially Jaina. He had thought she was his friend, a close companion. Only later, after Brakiss had explained it, did Zekk understand what Jaina really thought of him, how easily she dismissed his Jedi potential and the possibility that he might be an equal to her and her high-born twin brother. But Zekk *did* have the potential, and he had proved it.

In spite of this, he hoped Jacen and Jaina would not fight him, because then he would have to demonstrate his power— and his loyalty to the Second Imperium. He remembered his first test against Tamith Kai's prize student Vilas, and Vilas had paid with his life.

In the upper branches of a tree overhead, one Dark Jedi fighter had become tangled. Zekk watched as the bright arc of a lightsaber blade slashed boughs out of the way, clearing a path for the fighter to descend to the lower levels.

Overhead a wing of TIE fighters roared across the skies, firing into the forest. The Dark Jedi spread out, looking for potential victims on their own. Zekk gathered three of the nearest fighters to his side and they marched along, crashing through the underbrush.

They reached the edge of the wide river, whose brown-green currents lapped quietly through the jungle, stirring overhanging fronds. Farther downstream, closer to the tall Massassi temple ruins, he saw Tamith Kai's hovering battle platform.

Zekk stood beside his Dark Jedi companion's on the river-bank. The other fighters exchanged glances and pointed sky-ward. Zekk nodded, knowing what they wished to do. "Yes," he said. "Let us conjure a storm, a great wind to knock the jungle flat and send these Jedi cowards scurrying."

He looked up into the clear blue skies and reached deep within his heart, finding a shadow of anger, the pain he had felt in his life. He knew how to use anger as a tool, a weapon. Zekk gathered the winds. Beside him, he felt the other dark-side warriors doing the same, drawing thunderheads until lumpy black clouds rolled in from the horizon.

The wind picked up and grew colder, charged with static electricity Zekk's scarlet-lined cape rippled around him. Stray strands of his dark hair whipped around his face as the wind snatched them free of his ponytail. Flashing bolts of lightning skittered from one thunderhead to another. The rumble of noise drowned out even the sound of TIE fighters crisscrossing overhead.

Zekk smiled. Yes, a storm was coming, a victorious storm.

But as the clouds continued to swell, releasing a powerful weather energy, he heard sounds of repeated laser cannon fire and glanced to the sky, where another battle was taking place: a one-sided dogfight. A smoking ship careened overhead, pursued by a lone TIE fighter that shot its energy bolts again and again, mercilessly pummeling its prey.

Astonished, Zekk recognized the clunky patchwork form of the *Lightning Rod*, the cargo ship of his old friend Peckhum, the man with whom he had lived for many years.

Peckhum! They had been close companions, good friends despite how little they had in common. Too late, he remembered that the old spacer earned extra credits by making occasional supply runs to Skywalker's Jedi academy. Could it be that his old friend had been here on the jungle moon when this morning's attack began?

His heart sank, and a wrenching dismay filled his stomach. His concentration on the storm faltered.

In the backlash, winds whipped the trees closer to him, blowing back branches as the other Dark Jedi struggled to retain control of the gusting squall.

"No, Peckhum," Zekk said, looking up as he watched the TIE fighter blasting the hapless *Lightning Rod*. A small explosion flared on its hull, and Zekk knew that the battered supply ship had just lost its shields.

The *Lightning Rod* was going down—and there was nothing he could do about it.

He heard shouts of surprise next to him as the Dark Jedi

Knights completely lost control of the gathering storm. The winds continued to snap branches and uproot saplings, then gradually dissipated as the dark-side warriors stopped manipulating the weather.

Their attention had been drawn to a young Jedi trainee they discovered in the underbrush—someone who had either been creeping up on them or simply hiding from Zekk's advance.

The boy scrambled out of the weeds, spiky pale hair blowing around his flushed face. His clothes and robes were so ridiculously garish—bright purples and golds and greens and reds—that they hurt Zekk's eyes. How could this young man have thought to hide while dressed like that?

The boy appeared frightened, but determined. He thrust his lower lip out and stood with his hands on his hips, his rainbow-colored robes rippling around him in the last vestiges of the angry wind.

"Very well, you give me no choice," the boy said, then cleared his throat. "I am Raynar, Jedi Knight . . . uh, in training. You will either surrender now—or force me to attack you."

Two of Zekk's companions laughed in wholehearted amusement, ignited their lightsabers, and stalked toward the trapped young man. Raynar stepped backward until he bumped against the rough trunk of a tree. He squeezed his eyes shut, struggling to concentrate. He held his breath until his face turned bright red, then purplish.

Zekk felt a slight invisible push as the boy attempted to use the Force to drive them back. The two lightsaber-bearing Dark Jedi seemed not even to notice.

Zekk found, though, that he had no stomach for outright slaughter. This boy seemed proud and brash, but there was something about him—an innocence . . .

Thinking quickly, before his two companions could drive in and make short work of Raynar, Zekk reached out with the Force, grabbed the boy by his bright robes, and yanked him off his feet. With a flick of his mind, he hurled Raynar over the heads of his companions, tossing him out into the river.

Raynar yowled as he flew, then plunged belly-first into the thin, muddy waters.

The two Dark Jedi whirled, looking angrily at Zekk. Out in the water, Raynar splashed to the shallows, completely soaked in mud, his robes covered with river slime.

"It is a greater victory to utterly humiliate your enemy than simply to kill him," Zekk said. "And we have humiliated this Jedi in a way he will never forget."

The dark warriors next to him chuckled at the observation, and Zekk knew he had defused their anger . . . for the moment, at least.

Then he looked longingly into the sky, hoping to spot any trace of the *Lightning Rod*, but he saw only a dissipating cloud of smoke overhead. He wished he could find some way to help his friend; would he be forced to count the loss of Peckhum as part of the cost of victory?

The wounded ship had passed out of sight to where the battle would reach its foregone conclusion. He was certain he would never see the *Lightning Rod* or Peckhum again.

13

QORL'S TIE FIGHTER flew low over the jungle, mapping out targets for the assault squadron. The rest of his fighter wing had their own orders, and they flew in their own attack patterns.

He doubted, though, that his student Norys would bother to follow orders once the battles actually started and laser shots began to fly. The bully would blunder from target to target like a mad gundark, likely to cause as much damage to the Imperial plans as he did to the Rebels.

Qorl felt cold inside, liquid dismay hardening to ice. He had expected to be exhilarated by flying and fighting again, piloting his own TIE fighter in battle for the Second Imperium.

Instead, he had only reservations and second thoughts. He dreaded the possibility that he had made a bad decision and that the Second Imperium might have to pay the price.

Norys continued to be a great disappointment. When Qorl had selected the tough young man, he knew the bully's personality had hardened during years of harsh living, though he had lorded over the Lost Ones on Coruscant. The broad-shouldered boy had been dedicated, vowing to become an Imperial soldier because it gave him a feeling of power and confidence—exactly what the Second Imperium needed.

However, a loyal soldier was also required to obey orders. A servant of the Empire couldn't be a loose cannon, following his own wishes rather than the commands of his superiors. As he'd grown accustomed to his situation, Norys had become increasingly disrespectful, even insubordinate.

The bully was truly bloodthirsty, wanting simply to dominate, to cause pain, to achieve utter victory. He did not fight for the glory of the Second Imperium, or for bringing back the New Order—or for any sort of political goal. He fought simply to *fight*. And that was a deadly attitude, no matter which side he fought for.

Qorl circled, zeroing in on a raging forest fire that had been started by one of the TIE bombers, then streaked along the river to where Tamith Kai's battle platform hovered over the trees. Over his cockpit communication channel, Qorl heard a loud, desperate transmission on all bands—and recognized the voice.

"Attention, New Republic. We have an emergency! This is Jacen Solo on Yavin 4, requesting immediate assistance. We are under attack by the Shadow Academy!"

Qorl sat up, adjusted his black helmet, and flew steadily. He remembered the young twins who had helped fix his TIE fighter, the brother and sister who had been his prisoners around the campfire in the depths of the jungle. They had offered him friendship . . . and tried to turn him from his loyalty to the Second Imperium. But he had been indoctrinated too well.

Surrender is betrayal.

So Qorl had escaped and made his way to the Shadow Academy, where he had watched as the twins were brought in to be trained under the murderous tutelage of Tamith Kai and Brakiss. Qorl had been deeply disturbed by the violence of their instruction, the disregard for the lives of the fresh students.

No one had ever found out that Qorl had discreetly assisted the young friends in their escape as they fled the Shadow Academy. After that Qorl had privately done everything he could to atone for the indiscretion, making his raid on the Rebel convoy to steal hyperdrive cores and turbolaser batteries, then working hard to train Norys and the other new stormtroopers.

A smoking ship streaked overhead: a blaster-scarred and battered cargo transport. Qorl recognized the model of the ship, an unarmed carrier vessel of old design. Its engines were sluggish, its shields not designed or reinforced for combat.

And now he saw that it was being pursued by a relentless TIE fighter.

Qorl was ashamed to see the TIE pilot waste shot after shot, although sheer luck allowed some of the laser bolts to strike the hull. It would be only a matter of time before the cargo ship exploded in midair.

Qorl tuned his cockpit comm systems to a direct channel with the other TIE fighter. "TIE pilot, identify yourself."

The gruff voice that responded came as no surprise to Qorl. "This is Norys, old man. Don't bother me—I've got a target in my sights."

He swallowed, but his throat remained dry. "Norys, you have already crippled the target. That cargo ship is not our main objective. Your orders are to disable the Jedi academy. That ship won't be causing any more trouble for the Second Imperium."

"Leave off, old man," Norys said. "This is *my* kill, and I'm gonna score it."

Qorl tried to keep his anger in check. "We don't keep score, Norys. This assault is for the Second Imperium—not for your personal glory."

"Go stick your head up an exhaust tube," Norys said. "I'm not letting an old coward tell me what to do." Then the bully switched off his comm system and plunged after the burning cargo ship, firing with absolute abandon.

Qorl's disappointment turned to outrage. This young man's attitude flew in the face of everything admirable about the Empire. Qorl remembered his earlier TIE fighter training, how he and his fellow pilots had all worked together like a machine: precise, well mannered, respectful, listening to orders—promoting the orderly lifestyle the Emperor had brought to the galaxy. *That* was worth fighting for.

But Norys did not represent such a philosophy. He didn't care.

The broadband comm signal came across his speakers again. "This is Jacen Solo with a personal distress this time. We are in deep trouble. Someone is on our tail. Request assistance. Please—can anyone out there help us?"

Qorl flew beneath the aerial dogfight just above the treetops, anguished inside. Jacen Solo was an honorable opponent. The boy had a strong heart, though he had fallen in with the Rebel band instead of the Second Imperium. But could the boy be blamed? After all, his mother was the Chief of State of the Rebel government.

Norys, however, *did* have a choice. The broad-shouldered boy knew what he had been trained for. He had adopted his Imperial uniform and his ship willingly . . . yet now he refused to play by the rules. Norys was no better than a ruthless, murderous bully.

The pursuing TIE fighter continued to fly in the slipstream of the crippled cargo vessel. Black smoke curled up from her engine pods, and Qorl observed the precise moment at which the shields failed.

Norys fired again, staining the hull with a slash of black blisters.

Qorl flicked on his own laser cannons and activated the targeting systems. The *Lightning Rod* would explode in a matter of seconds under Norys's continued assault. If it did, Qorl wouldn't be surprised if the bully continued to shoot the burning wreckage to make sure there were no survivors.

Disgust welled up within him. Switching off his comm system, he muttered, "Do I lose any honor by destroying someone who has no honor of his own?"

Qorl had studied every subsystem on the Imperial TIE fighters. He knew their weak points. Qorl knew how to destroy them.

He targeted Norys's reactor exhausts.

Ignoring his teacher entirely, Norys fired again. His lasers had fallen into a slower repeating rhythm now, as if he savored these last few moments.

The *Lightning Rod* lurched, in one last helpless attempt to dodge the laser fire.

Qorl closed in on Norys's ship.

And fired.

Norys's TIE fighter exploded in the air, annihilated so quickly and completely that the young bully didn't even have time to cry out in surprise.

Ashamed that his act had been a betrayal of the Second Imperium, Qorl made no attempt to contact the *Lightning Rod*. He simply changed course and swerved back toward the main battlefield, while the faltering *Lightning Rod* struggled to remain aloft . . . or at least to land without crashing too badly.

14

WHILE BATTLES RAGED above the Jedi academy and in the jungle around it, Imperial commando Orvak crept forward, intent on his mission.

He had left his TIE fighter behind in the wake of the explosions at the shield generator facility, but he would come back to it once he had finished here. For hours now, he had made his way secretly through the thick forest.

Several trees burned in the jungle nearby, sending up coils of putrid smoke from the wet vegetation. He heard blaster fire and shouts, the distant hum of lightsabers. He kept low and quiet, not willing to risk giving away his position.

Skywalker's Jedi had abandoned their Great Temple to engage in scattered skirmishes in the forests . . . leaving it open and unprotected for him to do his work.

Approaching the ancient edifice, still hidden by the jungle, Orvak saw black streaks on the thick stone—blaster scoring and scars from proton explosives dropped by TIE bombers. The ubiquitous vines that clung to the pyramid's sides had withered under the fire and fallen away in heaps. One close explosion had wrecked the temple's hangar bay door, preventing Skywalker's fleet of guardian ships from launching.

So, Orvak thought, after all these millennia, this ancient structure had finally been damaged. But it wasn't damaged enough. He would take care of the rest.

Moving carefully, ducking his helmeted head, he crept through the foliage, ripping up vines and uprooting ferns to clear the way until he finally emerged from the underbrush and stood behind the tall temple.

Above, TIE fighters streaked like birds of prey across the sky. Orvak looked up, silently urging them on.

To one side of the pyramid he saw a newly laid flagstone courtyard. Across it, at the base of the stone structure, a darkened entrance stood open. Imagining what sort of fearful sorcerous exercises the Jedi students performed there, he stepped cautiously into the courtyard.

Already weeds had begun to push up between the flagstones. The jungle would no doubt reclaim its own within a matter of months after he destroyed the temple—and it would be good riddance to this place, he thought. By then he hoped either to be back on the Shadow Academy or perhaps promoted to officer rank on a Star Destroyer . . . if his mission today turned out well enough.

When the fighting became particularly loud, and proton bombs exploded in the jungle not far away, Orvak made his move. He rushed across the heavy flagstones to the dim doorway that led into the Rebels' secret temple.

He paused at the threshold for a moment, glad for his helmet in case poisonous vapors might seep out from the interior. Who knew what booby traps the Jedi sorcerers might have laid?

He used the sensors in his helmet to check for traps, but found none . . . which wasn't surprising, since the Shadow Academy's attack had been completely unexpected; the Jedi Knights had not had time to prepare.

Orvak entered the Massassi temple, shouldering his pack. He raced down the corridors, unfamiliar with the layout of the pyramid. He saw living quarters, large dining halls . . . nothing of significance that he could destroy.

He made his way down to the rubble-sealed hangar bay, where he thought he could plant his detonators to best effect and blow up all the Rebel starfighters. But when he emerged from the turbolift, he squinted in the dim lighting, unable to believe what he saw. Orvak found only a single, sleeklooking ship, all curves and angles. Nothing more. No fleet of spacecraft, no major defenses. He snorted in disbelief.

Suddenly, alarms squealed out from the hangar bay. Flashing red lights stabbed at his eyes. A small barrel-shaped droid hurtled toward him, whistling and screeching. Blue electric bolts sparked from a welding arm that protruded from its cylindrical torso.

Orvak slammed himself back into the turbolift, punching the controls to seal the doors. Could the Jedi have installed a force of assassin droids? Lethal, weapon-wielding machines that would never, *ever* miss?

But as the doors sealed shut and the turbolift whisked him upward, his last glimpse showed him that the attacker was simply a lone astromech droid trundling across the floor, sounding the standard alarms installed in its base. Apparently, however, no one remained in the temple to hear them.

He chuckled nervously. One astromech droid! It annoyed him when mere machines held too great a sense of their own importance. He no longer feared a trap.

Orvak had to find a different place for his purposes anyway. Someplace more special.

He finally located it on the highest level of the great pyramid.

Taking the turbolift to the top, and holding his blaster ready to shoot anyone who came out of the shadows, the Imperial commando stepped into the grand audience chamber.

Here, the walls were polished and inlaid with multicolored stones. At one end rose a great stage, from which Orvak could imagine the Rebels gave lectures to their students, handed medals to each other after victories in the war against the rightful rulers of the galaxy, perhaps even performed their disgusting rituals.

Yes, he thought. *Perfect.*

Moving quickly, heart pounding with the thrill of accomplishing the mission that had already cost the life of his companion Dareb, Orvak unslung his pack. He pulled off his black helmet to see better in the light that filtered through the temple skylights.

Smoke blackened the sky outside, like burnt paint brushed across the air. Distant sounds of the continuing attack echoed like ricochets inside the audience chamber. But he heard no one else nearby, no movement. The temple was empty, and he had the time to work.

Orvak strode up to the stage, his boots thumping on the

stone floor. Yes, that would be the best place, a central location where the incredible blast could reflect from all sides. He yanked off his heavy gloves so that he could tinker with the fine electronic components.

Working cautiously, he removed his seven remaining high-powered detonators and linked them together. Then, he plugged all of the explosives into a central countdown timer and spread them out like the spokes of a wheel in the grand audience chamber.

Yes, it would be a fine explosion.

Ideally, when all the detonators went off simultaneously, the explosion would rip off the top of the temple like a volcano erupting. The shock wave would punch through the floor to the levels below and blast the walls outward. The entire pyramid would come tumbling down, no more than a pile of ancient rubble—as it deserved to be.

Orvak returned to the central unit and fiddled with the controls, kneeling on the polished surface of the stage. He thought with smug satisfaction that no more Rebels would ever lecture here. No future Jedi Knights would learn Rebel ways. This room would hold no more victory celebrations.

Soon it would all be gone.

Kneeling on the ground, Orvak keyed in the initiating code. All around the chamber, detonator lights winked green, ready to go, waiting for him to send the final command. Surveying his handiwork, he smiled and pressed the ACTIVATE button. The timer began to count down. Not much time left for the Jedi academy.

As he moved, resting his hand on the floor, Orvak caught a glimmer of motion out of the corner of his eye . . . something glittering and translucent, almost transparent; it had caught a reflection of the light somehow.

He pulled out his blaster, remaining in a protective crouch. "Who's there?" he called.

Then he saw it again, an iridescent sinuous shape slithering toward him across the stage. He lost sight of it once more.

Orvak fired his blaster, gouging holes in the floor around

him. Streaks of energy bolts ricocheted around him. He flattened himself on the stage, afraid of return fire. He couldn't see the shimmering invisible thing anymore, and wondered what it could have been. Some sorcerer's trick, no doubt. He shouldn't have dropped his guard, but the Jedi would never get him.

Just then, Orvak felt needles of pain sting his hand. He looked down to see tiny droplets of blood welling from two punctures in his palm—and the triangle head of some kind of viper, a glassy crystalline snake!

"Hey!" he shouted.

Before he could lash out at it, the crystal snake dropped away from him and slithered toward a narrow crack in the wall. Orvak saw a last spangle of light, and then the serpent disappeared. . . .

But by now he was beyond caring, because a warm fog of sleepiness had begun to steal over him. The pain from the snakebite in his hand dulled to a throb, and Orvak thought drowsily that a long sleep could only make it better.

He collapsed into a deep slumber right beside the countdown timer.

The numbers ticked inexorably downward.

15

TENEL KA STOOD at the edge of the Imperial battle platform, her muscles tense, her body and reflexes ready to react.

She coiled her fibercord before returning it and the grappling hook to her belt. Then, with her single muscular arm, she held up her rancor-tooth lightsaber and ignited it. Beside her towered Lowbacca, ginger fur standing on end, dark lips peeled back to reveal fangs. The Wookiee used both hands to grip his clublike lightsaber with its molten bronze blade.

Surprised to see unexpected enemies, stormtroopers on the

battle platform marched forward with blasters drawn, confident of their victory.

Em Teedee wailed. "Oh dear, Master Lowbacca—perhaps we should have planned this attack a bit more thoroughly."

Lowie snarled, but Tenel Ka stood tall, her confidence unshaken. "The Force is with us," she said. "This is a fact."

A single TIE bomber swooped overhead, dropping proton torpedoes into the forests. The sounds of blaster fire ricocheted around them.

On the raised command deck of the battle platform, the Nightsister Tamith Kai stood in her black cloak like a preening bird of prey. She turned, her midnight hair writhing around her head with static electricity, her wine-dark lips curled in a sneer. Tenel Ka and Lowie took three brave steps toward the waiting stormtroopers.

One of the white-armored soldiers, apparently nervous at seeing the two young Jedi Knights, fired his blaster—and Tenel Ka whipped her energy blade across to intersect the incoming energy bolt, deflecting it into the sky.

Then, by unspoken agreement, she and Lowie charged forward, yelling. They slashed with their lightsabers so furiously that though the stormtroopers sent out a volley of blaster fire, they were thrown into chaos. Lowie and Tenel Ka forced their way through them like a whirlwind.

On the command deck above, Tamith Kai strode forward to gaze down at the skirmish. "The girl is mine. I'll crush her heart myself," she said.

Tenel Ka slashed once more with her lightsaber taking out another charging stormtrooper. She turned. Her heart thudded, but her breath came slow and even. Her muscles sang. She was prepared for this fight, sure of her physical abilities. This would be her best battle ever.

"That leaves all the other stormtroopers for you, Lowie," she said, springing up onto the command deck to meet her nemesis.

The young Wookiee roared his readiness, though Em Teedee did not sound quite as courageous. "Please be cautious, Master Lowbacca. It wouldn't be wise to get delusions of grandeur."

The stormtroopers pressed forward, fifteen against one gangly young Wookiee. Lowbacca didn't seem to think the odds were too bad.

Tenel Ka stood before the Nightsister, holding herself tall and proud, her turquoise lightsaber in front of her. She remembered the first time she had taken the evil woman by surprise and nearly crippled her. "So, how is your knee, Tamith Kai?"

The Nightsister's violet eyes flashed, and she shook her head mockingly. "Why not surrender now, weakling girl?" she said. "This is hardly a worthwhile test of my abilities. Ha! A one-armed child who dares to think she can be a threat to me."

"You talk too much," Tenel Ka said. "Or do you intend to use your foul breath as a weapon against me?"

"You have been around those twin Jedi brats too long," Tamith Kai said. "You've learned disrespect for your superiors." The Nightsister jabbed the air with her fingers and sent a bolt of blue-black lightning toward the warrior girl from Dathomir.

"I see no one here who is my superior," Tenel Ka said, intercepting the lightning bolts with her lightsaber blade. Then she used the Force to build her own positive thoughts and feelings, which she pulled around her like a shield. The Nightsister retreated a step, taken aback.

Down one level, Lowbacca slashed with his bronze lightsaber in one hand while picking up a white-armored figure with his other. He tossed the stormtrooper into three other attackers, knocking them all down. The Imperial soldiers were crowded too closely together to use their blasters. They seemed intent on taking down the angry Wookiee through the sheer force of their own numbers.

It was a big mistake.

Up on the command deck the Nightsister circled, eyeing her young quarry with amusement. Tenel Ka held her lightsaber steady, locking her granite-gray eyes on the violet irises of her opponent.

Overhead, TIE bombers swooped down, though the pilots seemed more interested in the duel on the battle platform than in their bombing runs.

The Nightsister curled her hands, and a ball of blue lightning crackled in each palm, gathering strength. Tenel Ka knew she had to use the Nightsister's moment of concentration for a quick surprise.

Tamith Kai stood near the edge of the upper command deck as Lowie and the stormtroopers continued to battle one level below her. The Nightsister raised her hands. Evil fire crackled at her fingertips, waiting to be released.

Tenel Ka feinted with her lightsaber and then, completely without warning, used the Force to reach forward like an outstretched hand. She nudged the Nightsister, pushing her just enough that she stumbled over the edge. With a wild shriek, Tamith Kai toppled backward. Bolts of blue lightning sprayed harmlessly into the sky and barely missed a heavily armored TIE bomber that swooped overhead.

The Nightsister crashed among the stormtroopers and Lowbacca, who snarled at her. Stormtroopers rushed the Wookiee, trying to drag him down, but Tamith Kai blindly released her anger, blasting them all away from her.

From the command deck Tenel Ka looked up toward the loud sound of an approaching engine—and saw a TIE bomber cruising in low, targeting its laser cannons on *her*! Brilliant shots streaked out, melting holes in the deck plating at her feet.

The warrior girl danced from one side to the other, using her attunement with the Force to second-guess where the bolts would strike. The high-powered weapons were too strong for her to deflect with a mere lightsaber. She stood all alone, unprotected—an easy target.

Grimly, she made up her mind. As the Imperial fighter roared overhead, Tenel Ka locked her lightsaber blade on, then carefully estimated the proper trajectory. Underhanded, she hurled her rancor-tooth weapon up at the craft.

She had spent a great deal of time practicing her aim, throwing spears and knives, striking her chosen target every time. But here the timing was rushed and the distance greater. Still, she never doubted her ability.

The TIE bomber arched upward, gaining altitude as it curved around for a final attack run.

Her lightsaber cartwheeled through the air and, with a blazing turquoise flash, struck the side of the TIE bomber. It did not slice off one of the power-array panels as she had hoped. Instead, the energy blade sheared off a stabilizer device and ripped open a hole in the bomber's hull. Her lightsaber passed completely through, then plunged downward into the jungle thickness below near the edge of the river.

Unable to articulate words, the Nightsister lunged back onto the command deck with a yowl of vengeful rage. Her black cape flapped like the wings of a raven swooping in for the kill. Tamith Kai's eyes blazed with violet fury.

Seeing the one-armed girl standing all alone without so much as a lightsaber, the Nightsister began to laugh. Her deep, guttural chuckle was filled with derision. "And now you are dis*armed*," Tamith Kai sneered, looking at the stump of Tenel Ka's arm. "You waste my time, child. Why don't you save us both some trouble and just lie down and die?"

Tenel Ka glared at the Nightsister coldly and moved a step forward, showing no sign of hesitation. "I may be disarmed," she said, "but I am *never* without a weapon."

With that, her left foot flashed out, swept around, and caught Tamith Kai just behind her heel. At the same time, Tenel Ka slammed her palm into the center of the Nightsister's chest and pushed forward, toppling her opponent to the deck.

She heard the stormtroopers shouting in panic—then overhead came the rattling whine of a TIE bomber in trouble. Tenel Ka flicked her glance up, and reacted instantly.

The TIE bomber she had struck with her lightsaber had managed to circle back— although its rear compartment was now in flames. Entirely out of control, wobbling and careening from side to side, the desperate craft came toward the battle platform.

Tenel Ka could vaguely sense the pilot's terror. He didn't know what to do and saw the platform as his last chance, a place where he might make an emergency landing. But Tenel Ka could tell from the speed of his descent and his total lack of maneuverability that a landing was impossible.

Seeing nothing but her own rage, the Nightsister lunged with one clawed hand to grab Tenel Ka's ankle. The dark woman didn't even notice the approaching danger.

Tenel Ka could waste no time fighting with her. She snatched her booted foot free and leaped over the black-clad Nightsister, landing among the stormtroopers next to Lowie.

The stormtroopers, though, had already seen the incoming TIE bomber and scrambled to clear the deck.

"Lowbacca, we must go now," Tenel Ka said, grabbing his hairy arm.

He roared, and Em Teedee chimed in. "Indeed. I believe that is a most sensible suggestion."

She and Lowbacca hurried to the edge of the hovering platform and looked down at the sluggish river below and the overhanging jungle trees.

Up on the command deck, Tamith Kai finally realized the impending danger as the TIE bomber came in, its engines building to a sputtering roar. The Nightsister screamed for the pilots inside the battle platform to start its repulsor engines and evade the impending crash.

They would never make it.

Lowie and Tenel Ka dove overboard, hoping for a safe place to land.

Behind them, the TIE bomber crashed into the Shadow Academy's battle platform and exploded in an instant. Its entire cargo of remaining explosives detonated along with the engines, blasting a hole entirely through the immense vessel.

Armored plates flew like metallic snowflakes in all directions. A gout of fire and smoke blasted into the sky, and the cumbersome battle platform plummeted, choking and rumbling.

The mass of unrecognizable wreckage exploded several more times as it plunged into the river. . . .

16

LASER BLASTS FROM the pursuing TIE fighters spanged against Jaina's stolen Imperial ship. One blast sizzled off a corner of the hexagonal power array, sending up a shower of sparks.

She fought to maintain control as her ship began to spin. She lost power, but still her ship flashed onward, propelled by its stealth drive. The silent engines had been made for covert action—not for all-out speed. Behind her, the furious TIE fighters closed the distance.

Jaina flew a frantic evasive action, up and down, diving toward the jungle treetops and then pulling up, hoping the Imperial pilots would make a mistake—slam into a tree branch or collide with each other or something.

No such luck.

The three pursuers had reached point-blank firing range, and Jaina had to take one last gamble. Using the mental speed given to her by Jedi training, she spun the TIE fighter about like a rotating ball, up and over, so that an instant later she headed not away from them, but straight *toward* them! The distance closed in a flash. Jaina had time for only a single shot.

And she didn't waste it.

The blast from her laser cannon ripped open the bottom of one of the TIE fighters, severing its controls, breaking the cockpit's airtight seal. The pilot fell through the hole and tumbled toward the jungle.

Jaina roared between the other two TIE fighters, heading as fast as she could in the opposite direction. They wheeled about, taking longer to complete a three-hundred-sixty-degree turn in the air, but within moments they were following again in hot pursuit.

Jaina flicked her gaze across the control panels, searching for anything that might help her, some secret weapon this TIE fighter might have. She doubted she would find anything that her pursuers couldn't counter.

Then her eyes fixed on a small button: TWIN ION ENGINE SHUNT. Suddenly she realized this would add the TIE fighter's normal engines back to the low-powered stealth drive her fighter had been using.

Without hesitation, she toggled the button off, deactivating the shunt—and with a screech of power, her TIE fighter leaped forward. The roar of acceleration slammed her back against the seat, jolting her lips into a grimace. The ship pulled forward faster than anything Jaina had ever felt.

If she could gain enough of a lead and head straight up into orbit, if she could swing around the jungle moon out of visual range, she could cut her engines for a while and drift out into black space. The stealth coating on this ship's armor would be an enormous advantage. If she could just get out of sight, she could make her ship invisible . . . and she would be safe.

Making use of the ship's acceleration, working with her hands against the increased gravity from the thundering flight, Jaina tilted upward on a straight-line course through the atmosphere, up into space.

The remaining pair of Imperial fighters streaked after her. She didn't know if her acceleration allowed her to fly much faster than the TIE's normal power, but she knew she had to gain distance and use all of her wits.

The atmosphere thinned to a deeper purple, and then the midnight blue of space. To her dismay, she saw that the remaining TIE fighters had closed the distance again, not as much as before, but to within visual range. Her plan wouldn't work—she could never dodge them and disappear against the silent blackness. Her stealth armor would be useless now.

She wondered if she should fight them head-on again. There was a chance that she could take out both Imperial ships before they shot her down . . . but she doubted it.

She was done for.

Just at that moment of despair, Jaina saw a glimmering in the blackness as new ships emerged from hyperspace—reinforcements! New Republic warships! Her heart leaped. It was a small fleet, but well armed, ready to take on the Shadow Academy. Her brother's distress signal must have gotten through.

With a whoop of delight, Jaina adjusted course and shot like a projectile straight toward the fleet of Corellian gunships and corvettes, the quickest bunch the New Republic had been able to muster for the Jedi academy.

Her stolen TIE fighter vibrated as she pushed the acceleration far beyond the red lines. She was still losing power from her damaged side array. "Come on, come on," Jaina said, biting her lip. The ship had to last only a few moments longer. Just a few moments.

The front Corellian corvette loomed closer and closer. But the enemy TIE fighters clung right behind her, still shooting.

Jaina spun and dodged until finally she came into range of the New Republic ships. They began firing huge turbolaser bolts that streaked so close to her ship that the crackling beams dazzled her eyes.

It took Jaina a moment to realize that the gunships were shooting at *her*!

She quickly understood her folly. Here she was in an Imperial ship diving toward the fleet with two more TIE fighters right behind her, laser cannons blasting. It must have looked like all three craft were on some sort of a suicide run.

She grabbed the comm system, toggled it to an open channel, and broadcast at full power. "New Republic fleet—don't shoot, don't shoot! This is Jaina Solo. I've commandeered an Imperial fighter."

More ships appeared at the side, heavily armed hodge-podge vessels bearing the insignia of GemDiver Station, Lando Calrissian's Corusca-gem processing facility that orbited the gas giant Yavin.

"Jaina Solo?" Lando's voice came over the comm system. "Little lady, what are you doing out here?"

"Turning into space dust, if you guys don't take care of the two TIE fighters on my tail!"

Admiral Ackbar's voice broke in. "We're targeting now," he said. "Do not fear, Jaina Solo."

"I'm in the *front* one," she reminded him nervously. "Don't hit the wrong TIE fighter! Well, what are you waiting for?"

A flurry of turbolaser strikes lanced out around Jaina in a pattern so dense that space became a web of deadly weapons fire. Dozens of bolts shot from the Corellian gunships and Lando Calrissian's private fleet. Within moments the two TIE fighters were vaporized, and Jaina let out a long sigh of relief.

Sending a signal from the front Corellian corvette, Admiral Ackbar guided her to the forward docking bay. "Please come aboard, Jaina Solo," he said. "We will offer you sanctuary for the time being while we combat the Shadow Academy. We believe that is the best way to protect personnel on the surface."

"Sounds good to me," Jaina said. "But as soon as it's clear, I want to get back down to fight next to my brother and friends."

"If we do our job well," Ackbar said, "there won't be much of a fight left."

After docking, Jaina climbed out of the stolen TIE fighter, perspiring heavily and glad to be free of the Imperial ship. She no longer felt a great desire to fly one of the craft. Her first experience had been exciting, but not necessarily one she wanted to repeat.

Greeting some of the New Republic soldiers, Jaina quickly ran her fingers through her long, straight brown hair and then rushed to a turbolift. When she arrived on the bridge, she stood beside Admiral Ackbar and watched the fleet attack the ominous spiked station.

New Republic warships pummeled the Dark Jedi training center in orbit over Yavin 4. The Shadow Academy's powerful shields remained up, but the constant bombardment took its toll.

Lando Calrissian's ships swooped closer, adding their weapons fire. Under the combined onslaught, the Shadow Academy would surely be destroyed before long, Jaina thought.

Ackbar sent out a transmission. "Shadow Academy, prepare to surrender and be boarded."

Jaina didn't have time to relax, though. The Shadow Academy did not bother to answer, and one of the tactical officers suddenly shouted, "Admiral Ackbar, we're detecting a surge in hyperspace, off to starboard. It appears that an entire—"

As Jaina watched the viewscreen, a group of terrifying Imperial ships appeared, Star Destroyers that looked as if they had been hastily assembled and modified. Hasty or not, their weaponry was new and lethal.

"Where did *that* fleet come from?" Lando squawked over the comm channel.

Ship after Imperial ship arrived, an entire, fully armed fighting force that owed allegiance to the Second Imperium. Before even orienting themselves, the Imperial ships opened fire on the New Republic fleet.

"Shields up!" Admiral Ackbar ordered. He turned to Jaina, his round, fishy eyes swiveling in alarm. "It appears that we may experience some difficulty after all," he said.

17

LUKE SKYWALKER ARRIVED across the river at the Massassi ruin known as the Temple of the Blue Leaf Cluster, a tower of crumbling stone blocks. He came alone, hoping to negotiate but ready to fight.

This was the site Brakiss had chosen for their meeting, their confrontation . . . their *duel*, if it came to that.

Luke listened to the jungle noises: the chatter of creatures in the underbrush, birds in the vines overhead—and explosions from Imperial fighters in the sky. He hated to be here by himself when he could be beside his students, fighting with them to defeat the forces of the dark side.

But Luke had a greater calling, a more important one—to stop the leader of these Dark Jedi, a man who had once been Luke's own student.

Branches parted in a thicket beside the carved pillars of stone. A man stepped out, moving as if he were made of flowing quicksilver, a confident liquid shadow. His perfectly formed, sculpture-handsome face smiled. "So, Luke Skywalker, once my Jedi Master—you have come to surrender to me, I hope? To bow to my superior abilities?"

Luke did not return the smile. "I came to speak with you, as you requested."

"I'm afraid speaking won't be enough," Brakiss said. "You see my Shadow Academy overhead? The battle fleet of the Second Imperium has just arrived. You have no hope of victory; despite your meager reinforcements. Join us now and stop all this bloodshed. I know the power you could wield, Skywalker, if you ever let yourself touch the powers you have neglected to learn."

Luke shook his head. "Save it, Brakiss. Your words and your dark-side temptations have no effect on me," he said. "You were once *my* student. You saw the light side, saw its capabilities for good—and yet you ran from it like a coward.

But it's not too late. Come with me now. Together we can explore what remains of the brightness in your heart."

"There is no brightness in my heart," Brakiss said. "I did not come here to banter with you. If you won't be sensible and surrender, then I must defeat you and take the rest of your Jedi academy by force." He withdrew a lightsaber from the silvery sleeve of his robe. Long spikes like claws surrounded the energy blade that extended as he pushed the power button. Brakiss heaved a quick sigh. "This seems like such a waste of effort."

"I don't want to fight you," Luke said.

Brakiss shrugged. "As you wish. Then I'll cut you down where you stand. That makes it easier on me." He stepped forward and swung his blade.

Luke's reflexes kicked in at the last instant, and he leaped back, using a touch of the Force to add power to his spring. He landed with legs spread, crouching, and pulled his own lightsaber from the belt at his waist. "I will defend myself, Brakiss," he said, "but there is so much you could learn here at the Jedi academy."

Brakiss laughed mockingly. "And who's going to teach me—you? I no longer recognize you as a Master, Luke Skywalker. There is so much more that you yourself don't know. You think *I'm* weak because I left here before I completed my training? Who are you to talk? You were only partially trained yourself. A short time with Obi-Wan Kenobi before Darth Vader killed him, then a brief time with Master Yoda before you left him . . . you even came close to true greatness when you went to serve the resurrected Emperor—and you backed away. You've never completed *anything*."

"I don't deny it," Luke said, holding his lightsaber in a defensive position. Their blades clashed with a sizzling sound. Brakiss's lips drew back in a grimace as he lunged again, but Luke parried his attack.

"You taught that becoming a Jedi is a voyage of self-discovery," Brakiss said. "I have continued that self-discovery since I left here. I abandoned your teachings, but I found more, *much more*. My self-discovery has been vastly greater than your own, Luke Skywalker, because you have locked many important doors to yourself." He raised his eyebrows and his eyes glinted a challenge. "*I* have looked behind those doors."

"A person who willingly steps into mortal danger is not brave," Luke said, "but foolish."

"Then you are a fool," Brakiss said. He swept his lightsaber low, intending to slice off Luke's legs at the knees—but Luke lowered his blade in turn and went on the offensive, clashing, striking, driving his opponent back. The Dark Jedi's silvery robes fluttered around him like nightwings.

"You can't win, Brakiss," Luke said.

"Watch me," the Master of the Shadow Academy said. He attacked with greater fury, opening himself up to anger so that his viciousness grew as he struck again and again.

But Luke maintained his quiet center as he defended himself. "Feel the calm, Brakiss," he said. "Let gentleness flow through you . . . peaceful, soothing."

Brakiss merely laughed. His perfect blond hair was tangled and plastered to his head with perspiration. "Skywalker, how many times will you try to turn me? Even after I fled your teachings, you pursued me. Don't you know when you have lost?"

Luke said, "I remember our confrontation at that droid manufacturing facility on Telti. You could have joined me then—you still can now."

Brakiss dismissed that with a snort. "Those events meant nothing to me, a diversion until I found my true calling—forming the Shadow Academy."

"Maybe you need to look for a truer calling," Luke said. He slashed sideways to deflect Brakiss's lightsaber again.

Now Brakiss took a different tack, whirling around. Instead of striking at Luke, he slashed one of the tall temple pillars, a cylinder of marble etched with ancient Sith symbols and Massassi writings. Sparks flew from the blow, and the lightsaber sheared the column completely through. Gravity, clinging vines, and the overhanging stone made it unstable.

Luke dove out of the way as the pillar split in two. The front lintel of the Temple of the Blue Leaf Cluster tumbled down. Stones and branches crashed from side to side, broken stone flew in all directions— but Luke danced out of the way, avoiding injury.

"You seem quite light on your feet, Skywalker," Brakiss said.

"You seem quite destructive to ancient structures," Luke said. He scrambled over the new rubble, coughed in the settling dust, then clashed again with Brakiss. "Perhaps you should check on how your Dark Jedi are doing. My students have been defeating them quite consistently."

He heard the battle continuing in the jungles and longed to get back to his trainees. The meeting with his former student had been no more than a distraction; it was leading nowhere. "This has gone on long enough, Brakiss. You may either surrender or I'll defeat you directly, because I have work to do. I need to get back to defending my Jedi academy."

Brakiss showed the faintest glimmer of uncertainty in his normally calm and peaceful eyes when Luke drove in, this time intending to win. Luke struck again with the lightsaber, always maintaining his focus and drive, not letting anger take control, doing only what he wished to do.

The Master of the Shadow Academy defended himself, and Luke saw his chance to strike. He altered his aim just slightly, not striking the energy blade itself. He could have swung lower to take off the hand of his former student, much as Darth Vader had cut off Luke's own hand—but Luke didn't want to maim Brakiss in such a way. He needed only to ruin his weapon.

His lightsaber struck across the top of Brakiss's handle, just below the terminus of the energy beam and above the knuckles of the grip. The top two centimeters of the spiked-claw end of Brakiss's lightsaber sprayed off, sheared away in a smoking, molten mass.

Brakiss shrieked and dropped his sparkling lightsaber to the ground, where it lay useless, smoldering, no longer a weapon, simply a hunk of components . . . none of which worked.

The Master of the Shadow Academy held up his hands and staggered back. "Don't kill me, Skywalker! Please don't kill me!"

The terror on Brakiss's face seemed all out of proportion to the threat. Surely the shadow Jedi knew that Luke Skywalker was not the type to strike down an unarmed enemy in cold blood. Brakiss clutched at his silvery robe, fumbling with the fastenings.

Luke strode toward him, lightsaber extended. "You are my captive now, Brakiss. It's time for us to end this battle. Order your Dark Jedi to surrender."

Brakiss let his robes fall away, revealing a jumpsuit and repulsorpack. "No. I have other business to attend to," he said, and ignited the repulsorjets.

As Luke stared in astonishment, Brakiss rocketed skyward, flying high out of reach. The Dark Jedi instructor must have landed his ship somewhere nearby, Luke realized, and he would no doubt head directly back to the Shadow Academy.

In dismay, Luke watched his fallen student escape once more—defeated, but still capable of causing further damage.

The pain of loss flooded Luke's mind, as fresh as on the day Brakiss first fled the Jedi academy. "Brakiss, I've failed to save you again," he groaned.

The other man dwindled to a small point in the sky and disappeared.

18

IN SPACE, THE Second Imperium fleet fired their weapons. Ackbar shouted, "All personnel, battle stations!" The

Calamarian admiral gestured with his flippered hands. "Shields up! Prepare to return fire!"

The two front-most modified Star Destroyers lunged forward, their turbolaser batteries blazing. Brilliant green streaks sliced out, zeroing in on Ackbar's flagship.

Jaina stood beside the Calamarian admiral and squeezed her eyes shut as the blinding flashes shattered against their forward shields. "The Second Imperium must have been building their fleet in secret," she said. "Those ships look like the construction was rushed."

"But they are still deadly," Ackbar said, nodding solemnly. "Now I know why they stole those hyperdrive cores and turbolaser batteries when they attacked the *Adamant*." He turned to his communications systems, bellowing orders in his gravelly voice. "Shift target from the Shadow Academy. That training station is a lesser threat than the new battleships. Target the Imperial Star Destroyers.

The weapons officers working at their command stations called out in alarm and dismay, "Sir, our targeting locks won't match! Those ships are broadcasting friendly ID signals. We are unable to fire."

"What?" Ackbar said. "But we can *see* the Star Destroyers."

"I know, Admiral," the tactical officer shouted. "But our computers won't fire—they think those are New Republic ships. It's built into the programming."

Suddenly understanding, Jaina exclaimed, "They stole guidance and tactical computer systems during their raid on Kashyyyk! The Imperials must have installed them in their own ships just to confuse our weapons computers. We'll have to change our targeting locks, or else we won't be able to fire. The 'Identify Friend or Foe' fail-safe systems will prevent it."

Lando Calrissian had been listening on the open channel; his voice now boomed over the comm. "Since my ships from GemDiver Station use different computers, I guess the first round is up to us."

Lando's hodgepodge group of independent ships swept in

on the Star Destroyers from all sides, firing a barrage of proton torpedoes at key points to dilute the overall shield strength.

"A little trick I picked up," Lando explained over the comm unit as Jaina stood beside Ackbar watching. "This whole thing reminds me of the battle of Tanaab." Then he gave a whoop of triumph as another volley of torpedoes detonated at once, two of them penetrating the shields and leaving a white-hot chain of flames along the side of one Star Destroyer. Lando's ships kept firing and firing, but now the Imperials began targeting the smaller craft, leaving Ackbar's vessels alone.

"Admiral," Jaina said, "if the Second Imperium is so clever that they can use our own computer systems to trick us, can't we turn the tables—use *our* computers against *them*?"

Ackbar turned his enormous round eyes on her. "What do you have in mind, Jaina Solo?"

She bit her lower lip, then drew a deep breath. The idea was crazy, but . . . "You're the supreme commander of the entire New Republic fleet. Isn't it programmed into the computers that they must accept some sort of override signal from you in cases of extreme emergency—like this one?"

Ackbar stared at her, his mouth gaping as if he needed a drink of water or a long breath of moist air. "By the Force, you're right, Jaina!"

"Well, what are we waiting for?" she said, rubbing her hands together. "Let's get reprogramming."

After destroying his own student Norys to rescue Jacen Solo, Qorl's insides felt deadened, as if the rest of his body had turned into a droid . . . just like his mechanical left arm.

After all his years of training and loyalty, he had betrayed the Second Imperium. Betrayed! He had allowed his heart to decide, rather than following blind obedience and cold ambition.

But young Jacen had been kind to him, had helped rescue

him, had shown him warmth and friendship, though Qorl knew he had done nothing to deserve it. . . .

He had taken the twins prisoner, threatened their lives, forced them to repair his crashed TIE fighter so he could return to the Empire. Since then he had made small, secret gestures to repay them, such as when he'd cautiously helped them to escape the Shadow Academy. But killing his own student to protect them . . .

Qorl had committed a grave mistake by making decisions on his own. He should have known better. It wasn't his place to make decisions. He was a TIE pilot, a soldier of the Second Imperium. He helped instruct other pilots and stormtroopers. His allegiance was to the Emperor and his government. Soldiers didn't have the luxury of making up their own minds about which orders to follow and which ones to ignore.

His mind in turmoil, he took his TIE fighter up toward orbit. Most of his squadron had fallen out of formation, attacked or destroyed by unknown defenses on Yavin 4. He should return and report to his superiors. He would have to decide whether to surrender or confess what he had done . . . and face Lord Brakiss's retribution.

Qorl's jaw clenched. *Surrender is betrayal.* How could he be willing to do this? His ship's engines howled as he tore free of the atmosphere and headed straight toward the looming Shadow Academy station.

He saw with astonishment that he had stumbled into the middle of an enormous space battle.

New Republic warships had appeared unexpectedly, firing and firing upon the Shadow Academy. But then came the newly arrived fleet of Second Imperium ships, cobbled-together Star Destroyers, Imperial battle cruisers assembled from leftover pieces in reclaimed shipyards. The new fleet used the computer systems, hyperdrives, and turbolaser batteries that Qorl himself had helped to acquire.

But seeing the Second Imperium's ships filled him with a sense of dismay. The new fleet lacked the grandeur and impressive presence of the original Imperial armada. Qorl had flown on the Death Star, served as part of Grand Moff Tarkin's Imperial Starfleet.

This new fighting force looked somewhat . . . desperate— as if people whose dreams stretched far beyond their resources had leaped into the fray.

Qorl saw the Second Imperium ships pounding the Rebel rescue fleet—but as he watched, the tide turned and clusters of nondescript ships attacked the Star Destroyers.

Then the Star Destroyers' defensive shields suddenly and inexplicably went down, as if their own computers had switched them off. As if they had agreed to surrender!

Rebel battle cruisers fired into the opening at full strength, ripping great gashes in the hulls of the new Star Destroyers. What was going on? Why didn't his comrades reestablish their shields?

As Qorl flew toward them, frantic to do something to help with the fight, fresh TIE fighters streamed out of the Star Destroyers and began to pound the Rebel ships, though they seemed no more than tiny gnats against Ackbar's great fleet.

Qorl suddenly saw his chance to redeem himself. He had already been a traitor to his rescuers and friends and to the Second Imperium. No matter which choice he made, he would be cursed—he would never be able to live with either betrayal.

At the moment, though, Qorl could join the fight on the side of the Second Imperium and cause whatever damage he could . . . perhaps even die fighting. He was a TIE pilot. He had trained for this. Long ago, he had flown from the Death Star on a similar mission—and now he would make everything right again.

Qorl powered up his laser cannons, weapons that had last been fired against Norys's ship to stop the bully's murderous frenzy. Qorl could now use the weapons against his assigned targets: the Rebel Alliance.

His TIE fighter stormed into the fray from out of nowhere, firing on one of the Corellian gunships, leaving black scorch marks as he strafed along its side. Other TIE fighters joined him, flying in a barely recognizable attack pattern. These fleet members were obviously untrained, having spent very little time even in simulators. But the chaos served the new pilots well as the ships flew around each other, blasting and pummeling with no set goal but to cause damage.

The Rebel fleet responded with heavy turbolaser fire, lancing out in all directions. With a blinding glare, one of the Star Destroyers blew up, its command turret in flames. Another Star Destroyer went reeling, its defenses down; it turned in an attempt to limp away. The Rebel fleet pursued, all weapons blazing.

The Second Imperium was losing. *Losing!* Qorl shot after the fleeing ships. Some of the TIE fighters sped off into space . . . though Qorl had no idea where they intended to go. Their flagships were destroyed and the Shadow Academy was under fire. Did they intend to give up?

"Surrender is betrayal," he muttered to himself—and flew directly into the Rebel flagship's line of fire.

Turbolaser bolts shot past, but Qorl dove forward, firing his insignificant laser cannons and diving down the gullet of the beast. He would never give up. This would be his final flash of glory.

The Rebels improved their aim—and the cross fire struck him. Qorl closed his eyes behind his TIE helmet, expecting to vanish in a bright puff of flame, a candle burning for his Emperor.

But the energy weapons had only managed to clip one of his engines and damage part of his power array.

Qorl's TIE fighter spun out of control, away from the battle fleet. Even in his crash restraints, he was thrown from side to side inside his tiny cockpit. Qorl held on, expecting his ship to explode at any moment . . . all the while careening farther and farther away from the continuing space battle.

Still spinning, he saw that gravity had caught him. He was crashing again, plummeting toward the jungle moon of Yavin. . . .

19

BRAKISS RACED HIS high-speed, one-person shuttle away from Yavin 4 and streaked back toward his precious Shadow Academy. He punched the coded controls that would automatically open the launch-bay doors and provide him clear passage back into the safety of the Imperial training station.

The space battle did not concern him. It was just one other event that had gone wrong today.

His heart still pounded from his lightsaber battle with Skywalker down at the temple ruins. His thoughts spun, filled with the resonating words of his former Master. Anger and despair swirled like an uncontrollable storm through his mind, through his emotions.

Every method he knew failed to bring his thoughts back to the cold, quiet levels he required to draw on his fullest powers. Brakiss even attempted to use some of the hated calming techniques Skywalker had shown him back in his incognito student days—but nothing worked.

Everything was crumbling. His grandiose plans, his carefully trained Dark Jedi, the troops of the Second Imperium—it all faltered here on the verge of what should have been his greatest triumph, the hammer blow that would shake the galaxy. The destruction of the Jedi academy should have been a simple victory.

The Emperor would destroy Brakiss for this failure, but for now he could think only that the Emperor himself remained their last hope. Their only hope. Brakiss would accept his punishment later; for now he needed to do everything in his power to bring about a victory.

He brought his shuttle to dock in the nearly empty bay of the Shadow Academy, where not long ago rows of TIE fighters and TIE bombers had prepared for battle. Tamith Kai had launched her armored battle platform, riding down from orbit with her stormtroopers and Zekk's squad of dark warriors.

They had been proud, confident, sure of crushing the light-side Jedi. . . .

Brakiss climbed stiffly out of his shuttle, straightening his silvery robes, trying unsuccessfully to regain his dignity. Not wanting to be without a Jedi blade, he armed himself from a weapons alcove in the wall with another of the mass-produced lightsabers.

But *how* could he defend himself? He had seen Tamith Kai's battle platform plunge into the river, a flaming hulk of molten slag. Zekk's Dark Jedi had been routed, the TIE fighter squadrons mostly destroyed—and now Brakiss watched the Second Imperium's powerful new fleet being trounced by Rebel battleships that had appeared out of nowhere and had somehow deactivated the Imperial shields!

Brakiss strode out of the docking bay into the near-deserted Shadow Academy. All capable troops had been sent to the surface. Only a few command teams remained here to keep the Imperial station secure.

The sterile corridors should have been hosting a victory celebration, but instead the place seemed like a tomb, an abandoned derelict. The Emperor *must* find some way to save them, Brakiss told himself, to turn the tide of battle so that the Second Imperium could rule the galaxy after all.

Palpatine had cheated death not once, but twice. After he had perished the first time aboard the second Death Star during the battle of Endor, he had managed to resurrect himself, using hidden clones to prolong his life. And though all those clones had presumably been destroyed, thirteen years later the Emperor was once again back from the dead—without an explanation this time.

Any man who accomplished such feats could surely manage to wrest victory away from a hodgepodge gang of Rebels and criminals, couldn't he?

Holding his head up, trying to summon Imperial pride and hope, Brakiss marched down the steel-plated corridors toward the isolated section of the station. He had to see the Emperor, and he would not be turned away. The fate of the entire war hung on the next few moments!

Outside the sealed doorways stood two of the four scarlet-clad Imperial guards. They wore sinister, projectile-shaped helmets with only a narrow black slit through which they could see. The two guards stiffened, crossing their force pikes to deny him entry. Brakiss strode forward without hesitating. "Move aside," he said. "I must speak with the Emperor."

"He has requested not to be disturbed," said one of the guards.

"Disturbed?" Brakiss said, appalled to hear the words. "Our fleet is going down in defeat; our Dark Jedi are being captured. Our TIE fighters are being shot down. Tamith Kai is dead. The Emperor should *already* be disturbed. Move aside. I must speak with him."

"The Emperor speaks with no one." They moved one step forward, holding out their weapons.

Brakiss felt fresh anger boiling within. It gave him strength. The power flowing in his veins tapped directly into the dark side of the Force. He could see why the Nightsister Tamith Kai had found the experience so exhilarating that she kept herself in a constant state of pent-up fury.

Brakiss had no patience for these meddling scarlet-clad obstacles. They were traitors to the Second Imperium—and he responded, letting the Force flow from deep within him.

His lightsaber dropped out of his billowing sleeve and fell firmly into his hand. His finger depressed the power button. A long rippling blade extended out, but Brakiss did not use it as a threat. He had grown tired of threats, of word games and diversions that prevented progress. He unleashed his anger.

"I have had enough of this!" He struck wildly from side to side. His anger narrowed his vision to a tunnel of black static that surrounded his two targets as they scrambled to use their force pikes against him. But Brakiss was a powerful Jedi. He knew the ways of the dark side, and the red Imperial guards had no chance against him.

In less than a second, Brakiss had struck both of them down.

He activated the sealed door mechanism. The security pass codes argued with him, so he used the Force to blow out the circuits. With his bare hands he wrenched the stubborn door aside, then strode into the Emperor's private chambers.

"My Emperor, you must help us," he called. The light around him was red and dim, hot. He blinked, finding it difficult to see—but found no one else around. "Emperor Palpatine!" he shouted. "The battle turns against us. The Rebels are defeating our troops. You must do something."

His words echoed back at him, but he heard nothing else: no response, no movement. He pushed on into another room, only to find it filled with a black-walled isolation chamber, its armored door sealed shut, its side panels held in place with heavy burnished rivets. This was the enclosed compartment the red guards had removed from the special Imperial shuttle. Bulky worker droids had lifted the heavy container out of the shuttle's hold and carried it here.

Brakiss knew the Emperor had secluded himself inside the chamber, protected from outside influences. Brakiss had feared that the Emperor's health was failing, that Palpatine needed this special life-support environment just to survive.

But at the moment, Brakiss didn't care. He was tired of having doors shut in front of him. He, the Master of the Shadow Academy, one of the most important members of the Second Imperium, should not be brushed aside like some civil servant.

He pounded on the armored door. "My Emperor, I demand that you see me! You cannot let this defeat continue. You must use your powers to wrest a victory from the hands of our enemies.

He received no answer. His battering noises quickly faded into the thick, blood-colored light that filled the chamber. Brakiss's heart froze into a chunk of ice, like a lost comet from the fringes of a solar system.

If the Emperor had forsaken them, they were lost already.

The battle had turned against the Second Imperium—and Brakiss had nothing more to lose.

He switched on his lightsaber again, held the thrumming weapon—and struck. The energy blade sparked and flared as it cut through the thick armor plating—nothing, not even Mandalorian iron or durasteel blast shielding, could resist the onslaught of a Jedi lightsaber.

He sliced through the hinges. Molten metal steamed and ran in silvery rivulets down the side of the door. He chopped again, hacking out an entrance, tearing open the wall like a labor droid dismantling a cargo container. He stepped aside as the thick chunk of armor plate fell to the deck with a deafening clang.

Brakiss stood waiting, frozen with indecision, as the smoke cleared. He held his lightsaber up . . . and finally stepped inside.

He stared in disbelief. He saw no Emperor, no plush living quarters, not even any complicated medical apparatus to keep the old ruler alive.

Instead, he found a sham.

A third red guard sat in a complex control chair surrounded on three sides by computer monitors and controls. Brakiss saw a library display of holographic videoclips taken over the course of the Emperor's career: the rise of Senator Palpatine, the New Order, early attempts to crush the Rebellion . . . recorded speeches, memos, practically every word Palpatine had spoken in public, plus many private messages. Powerful holographic generators assembled the clips, manufacturing lifelike three-dimensional images.

Brakiss stared in horror as it began to make sense to him.

The red guard lurched to his feet, scarlet robes flowing around him. "You may not enter here."

"Where is the Emperor?" Brakiss said, but as he looked around he already knew the answer. "There *is* no Emperor, is there? This has all been a hoax, a pitiful bid for power."

"Yes," the red guard said, "and you have played your part well. The Emperor did indeed die many years ago when his last clone was destroyed, but the Second Imperium needed a leader—and we, four of Palpatine's most loyal Imperial guards, decided to create that leader.

"We had all of the brilliant speeches and recordings the Emperor had made. We had his thoughts, his policies, his records. We knew we could make the Second Imperium work, but no one would have followed *us*. We had to give the people what they wanted, and they wanted their Emperor back— as you did. You were easy to fool, because you *wanted* to be fooled," the red guard said, nodding toward Brakiss.

The Master of the Shadow Academy stepped deeper into the chamber, his lightsaber glowing with deadly, cold fire. "You tricked us," he said, still in the grip of incredulous horror. "You tricked me—*me*! I was one of the Emperor's most dedicated servants, but I served a lie. There was never any chance for the Second Imperium, and now we are being destroyed here because of *you*! Because of poor planning. Because there is no dark heart to the Second Imperium."

Blinded by rage again, Brakiss flowed forward like an avenging angel, his lightsaber held high. The red guard staggered away from his controls, reaching into his scarlet robes to withdraw a weapon—but Brakiss didn't give him the chance.

He cut down the third Imperial guard, who fell smoking and lifeless onto the array of controls that had created the fake Emperor. The illusion had cheated Brakiss, and the Shadow Academy, and all his Dark Jedi . . . everyone who had devoted their lives to recreating the Empire.

"Now the Empire has truly fallen," he said, his voice hoarse and husky, his face haggard. He was no longer calm, like a statue, no longer a well-polished representative of perfection.

Hearing a noise outside the chopped-open door to the isolation chamber, Brakiss turned to see a flash of red—the fourth and final member of the group of charlatans. Brakiss moved slowly, feeling stiffness and pain, utterly discouraged—but he could not let this last one get away. His honor demanded that the deceivers pay. Brakiss rushed after him.

But the red guard had encountered his slaughtered companions outside and knew that Brakiss had seen all the video controls and holographic apparatus in the isolation chamber. The fourth guard, without hesitation, ran back the way he had come.

Brakiss realized with utter certainty that the glorious dream of a reborn Empire had already failed. His Dark Jedi had lost their battle down on Yavin 4. The Imperial fighters were being trounced—but he would *not* let this impostor, this traitor, escape alive. It would be Brakiss's final moment of vengeance.

With purposeful steps, Brakiss charged after the man. The red guard moved with astonishing speed, fleeing the restricted area and dashing down the empty corridors of the Shadow Academy. Brakiss ran, but the red guard knew exactly where he wanted to go. Exactly.

The last surviving Imperial guard reached the docking bay and dashed toward Brakiss's still-waiting high-speed shuttle.

Arriving at the docking bay door, Brakiss shouted, "Stop!" He held his lightsaber high, wishing he could use the Force to make the guard freeze in his tracks, to follow the command—but the charlatan did not hesitate. He dove into the lone shuttle, raised it on its repulsorlifts, and punched the code to release the magnetic atmosphere containment field.

Brakiss simmered with rage. He wondered if he could get to the Shadow Academy's weapons systems and blow the guard to frozen shards in the vacuum of space. But it would be too late for him.

He felt completely alone on the Shadow Academy. An utter failure. Everything he had tried had backfired on him. And this was the final insult: tricked by a . . . *guard*.

Unbidden, a memory came to Brakiss. When the Shadow Academy had been constructed—ostensibly under the guidance of Emperor Palpatine—as a fail-safe mechanism, enormous quantities of linked explosives had been implanted through the station's structure. That way, if Palpatine ever felt threatened by these new and powerful Dark Jedi Knights, he could trigger the detonation and destroy the Shadow Academy, no matter where it was.

Brakiss stood alone in the hangar bay, watching the tiny shuttle streak farther and farther away. It occurred to him that since there *was* no reborn Emperor, then the four red guards themselves must have kept the secret destruct codes.

As the escape ship fled from the Shadow Academy and the Yavin system, the last surviving guard acknowledged to himself that the military forces he left behind would be defeated utterly. With the success of the Rebel counterattack, there would likely be no Imperial survivors of this day's battles.

The guard had to preserve his secret and maintain the illusion that he and his partners had so carefully constructed as a way to restore themselves to power. He could not afford to leave the Shadow Academy intact if he hoped to cover his tracks. With luck, he might find a position among the many criminal elements insidiously working at the fringes of the New Republic.

The red guard sent a brief signal, carefully coded. He transmitted a dreaded phrase, a string of impulses, that he had hoped never to use.

Destruct.

As his tiny shuttle careened into hyperspace, the spiked ring of the Shadow Academy flowered into a fireball, an exploding blossom of flaming gases and debris.

20

AS HE PLODDED ahead, Zekk could barely see two meters in front of himself in the murk of Yavin 4's unfamiliar jungle. Dense underbrush tore at his hair and cape, and his breath came in ragged gasps. His ponytail had come entirely undone. Still Zekk pushed on. Occasionally he glanced back over his shoulder to see if any of Skywalker's Jedi trainees were pursuing him. He sensed no one following, but he couldn't be sure. Who knows? he thought. They might have light-side tricks he had never heard of, ways to keep him from sensing their presence.

He had seen many unexpected things today. Strange things. *Horrible* things. It hardly mattered that the winding path ahead was uncertain and difficult to see: he would have been blind to it anyway. His mind was partially numbed by the sights his eyes had witnessed today. Destruction, terror, failure . . . death.

Zekk's foot slipped on a patch of moldy, damp leaves, and he went down on one knee. Grabbing a low branch, he pulled himself back to his feet, then stood disoriented for a moment.

Which direction had he been heading? He knew he was going *toward* something . . . but he couldn't quite remember what. Finally some unconscious part of him remembered, and he set off again.

Suddenly, just ahead of him, a knee-high rodent sprang from the underbrush, its claws extended. Zekk's Jedi instincts automatically took over.

In one smooth movement Zekk withdrew his lightsaber and threw himself sideways out of the creature's path. His cheek split open as it smashed against the purplish-brown trunk of a Massassi tree; his thumb pressed the lightsaber's ignition stud at the same moment. Before Zekk could even blink or breathe, the blood-red blade sprang forth—and sliced through the rodent in mid-leap. With a shriek that broke off abruptly, the two smoking halves of the creature fell to the forest floor.

It reminded him of how he had killed Tamith Kai's student Vilas in the zero-gravity arena aboard the Shadow Academy station—not a memory that comforted him.

Blood trickled from the cut on Zekk's cheek, but the pain was too distant, too far away for him to feel. His ability with the Force had protected him just now—after all, he was a Dark Jedi. But what about his companions from the Second Imperium? What of *their* powers? Why had it all gone wrong? For today he had seen his Dark Jedi, one after another, lose their battles or be captured by Skywalker's trainees.

He had a terrible suspicion that only he remained.

Oh, the dark side had had its victories. The commando Orvak had obviously succeeded in destroying the shield generators and had no doubt moved on to the next step in his mission. And there had been other times during the day when Zekk had felt the Shadow Academy trainees achieve surges of victory. But each victory had been short-lived.

Brakiss, Tamith Kai, he, and his companions had all been so certain of a quick, decisive triumph. With their training in the dark side, they should have had no problem, Zekk told himself. Wasn't that what Brakiss had taught?

A few minutes later, Zekk emerged from the darkness into a broad clearing where the wide river ran sluggishly between the trees. His spirits rising ever so slightly, Zekk walked to the edge of the river and stooped to take a drink.

Despite the green color of the water, his reflection was clear. Sunken emerald eyes shadowed with dark circles gazed back at him from the rippling surface. Only the barest spark of his former confidence still lurked in his expression. Tangles of filthy dark hair framed a face as pale as the moon of his home planet Ennth. Blood still oozed from the wound on his face, contrasting nicely with the purpling bruises that surrounded it. It made him think of Brakiss and his finely chiseled features.

A wail of despair echoed through the young man's head, knocking him to his hands and knees in the mud of the riverbank. In a futile gesture, Zekk pressed his muddy hands over his ears. "Brakiss!" he screamed. "What went wrong?"

Hardly understanding what was happening, Zekk turned his face up toward the sky. For a split second he recognized the spiked ring of the Shadow Academy in low orbit above the jungle moon—

Then, without warning, the space station bloomed into a fireball high above him. Zekk's jaw went slack at the sight. He had not thought it possible to feel any more pain.

But he had been wrong.

Brakiss. The name whispered now in Zekk's mind. He knew that the Master had been aboard the Shadow Academy when it blew up. He could *feel* it. He had felt his teacher's despair—his mind crying out.

The silvery-robed Jedi had taken Zekk in when the young man had had no hope for his future and no purpose. Brakiss had trained Zekk, given him purpose, direction, position, and skills to be proud of. At the Shadow Academy Zekk had *belonged.* He had been its Darkest Knight.

Now what was left for him? All that he had trained for and lived for was gone. Pride, comrades, future . . . all gone. There was no doubt in Zekk's mind that the Second Imperium had been decisively defeated today, and now his mentor—the only man who had ever believed in Zekk—was dead.

No. Not the *only* man who had believed in Zekk. A fresh wave of anguish washed over Zekk at the thought. Old Peckhum had always believed in him, too. Zekk had promised never to do anything to hurt or disappoint the old spacer. Today, though, he had fought on the side of Peckhum's enemies. Despite all the faults that Zekk acknowledged he had, he had never in his life lied to old Peckhum.

Anger jolted through him—at himself, at having been forced to fight his friend, at having been forced to make such terrible choices. His muscles tightened until the tension inside seemed unbearable. With a cry of anguish he plunged his fingers deep into the mud. It was dark, slippery, treacherous. Yet this was what he had chosen: the darkness.

Today he had stood and watched as his comrades blasted the *Lightning Rod* out of the skies. For all he knew, the only other man who had ever believed in him might also now be dead. Zekk's hands clenched in the ooze and he jerked up fistfuls of mud and smeared it on his face. The mud stung his cut. Now he could feel pain again. But he didn't care. He deserved it.

He had failed them all—Brakiss, the other Dark Jedi warriors, old Peckhum . . . himself. Silent tears dropped unheeded from his eyes as he scooped up more mud and rubbed it into his hands, his forearms, his neck. Dark mud.

This—*this* was what he had become. Darkness. He had chosen it, immersed himself in it. He was *stained* with it.

There could be no turning back for Zekk anymore. He had made his choices, and he was what he was: a Dark Jedi. That could not change now. Though his comrades were defeated or captured, and Brakiss dead, Zekk would never be able to cleanse himself for as long as he lived—however long that might be.

Not even Jaina and Jacen, if they were still alive, would be able to forgive him. Considering the space battles above, the destruction of the Shadow Academy, the attacks here on the ground, Zekk himself was responsible for a hundred or more deaths today. Maybe even Peckhum's. The twins would know that. They had never believed Zekk's decision to join the Shadow Academy was the right one, had never believed that he could become anything.

But he had made his choice and he had done his best. He had even warned Jaina on Kashyyyk not to return to Yavin 4, hoping to keep her away from the fighting, though he doubted she had listened.

He pushed himself to his feet and caught sight of his reflection again in the slow-moving water. His once-beautiful cape hung in tatters from his shoulders, its scarlet lining shredded. Mud covered his skin. And the sunken emerald eyes were now bleak and hopeless.

But he wasn't finished yet. It might not matter anymore what happened to him, but he still had choices. He would show the twins what he was made of. Turning, he headed along the riverbank toward the Great Temple.

Zekk still had one card left to play.

21

"DOWN THERE," JAINA said, pointing at the jungle clearing that Luke had chosen as a rendezvous point.

From the pilot's seat of his personal shuttle, Lando Calrissian grinned, flashing his beautiful white teeth. "Sure thing, little lady," he said. "I'll take 'er down. Looks like they're waiting for us. The fighting must be done."

As Lando brought the ship in for a landing, Jaina used Jedi techniques to relax, but it did her no good. Her muscles remained as tense as if she were still in the tiny TIE fighter flying for her life. For some reason, she just couldn't loosen up. For the first time, today, she had fought as a Jedi, with other Jedi, against the dark side.

It was what all her training had been about.

When Lando's shuttle touched down, Jaina wasted no time on formalities. She scrambled out of the ship as quickly as she could, ran to her uncle, and threw herself into his arms. "You made it. You're alive!" she said, feeling a surge of relief and jubilation.

"Luke, old buddy!" Lando said. "I came to offer you some help, but it looks like you've got things pretty well under control."

"We could still use your help, Lando," Luke replied. He hugged Jaina back and said soberly, "I'm afraid many of our numbers were not so lucky."

Realizing that she had no idea how the ground battle had gone, Jaina bit her lip and looked around wildly, hoping to spot Jacen, Lowie, and Tenel Ka.

What she saw shocked her. As far as she could tell, no student from the Jedi academy had escaped unscathed. Several trainees limped. Tionne's right arm hung in a sling and the hair on the right side of her head was singed. Others sported scratches and bruises, as well as more serious injuries.

Jaina stared in surprise when she saw Raynar, his face

muddy and his bright clothing torn and covered with filth, moving among the wounded and offering assistance wherever he could. He seemed subdued.

When she noticed the patient Raynar was currently tending, she blanched and dashed over to where Tenel Ka lay, looking feverish and bleeding heavily from a nasty gash just above one gray eye. Another shallower wound ran along her thigh and ended at the knee.

Raynar was already tearing strips of cloth from his relatively clean inner robes. Jaina made a pad of the cloth and pressed it to Tenel Ka's head wound to stanch the flow of blood, while Raynar bandaged the leg cut.

Jaina looked around, still searching for Jacen. Only a few meters away, though she hadn't noticed him before, Lowie lay flat in the grass, moaning quietly and clutching his side.

Around the edges of the clearing, Tionne, Luke, and Lando helped the injured stragglers. There was still no sign of Jacen, though.

"Lowie, are you all right?" Jaina asked. The Wookiee rumbled something noncommittal and waved a hand, as if to tell her to finish caring for Tenel Ka first.

"Oh, Mistress Jaina! Thank goodness you're here," Em Teedee cried. The little droid's voice sounded strange, and Jaina noticed that the speaker grille was bent. "You have simply no idea what the three of us have been through today. Master Lowbacca and Mistress Tenel Ka were forced to dive from the battle platform in order to avoid being blown up. Which was a good thing, since the battle platform crashed only moments later.

"When we fell to the trees, Master Lowbacca was able to catch himself, but Mistress Tenel Ka struck her head on a branch. She nearly fell all the way to the forest floor, but Master Lowbacca dove after her, caught her arm, and broke their fall by landing stomach-first on a wide limb. Oh, it was bravely done, I assure you, Mistress Jaina. I'm no medical droid, of course, but I'm afraid you'll find that Master Lowbacca has a dislocated shoulder and at least three broken ribs."

Raynar pressed a fresh compress over Tenel Ka's head wound and began winding a bandage around it to hold it in place. "You go ahead," he said, nodding toward Lowie. "I'll finish here."

When two more wounded Jedi students staggered into the clearing, Jaina looked up hopefully, but neither was Jacen. "Have you seen my brother?" she asked Raynar as she went to Lowie's side and knelt to examine his injuries. "He went in the *Lightning Rod* with old Peckhum to call for reinforcements. He should be back by now."

Raynar frowned and shook his head. "Well . . . well . . . I saw the supply shuttle—the *Lightning Rod.* I . . . think one of the TIE fighters hit it."

Jaina gasped. "Did they crash?"

Raynar looked away. "I don't know. The ship seemed to be going down, but . . . " He shrugged uncomfortably. "Anyway, it was hours ago.

Jaina bit her lower lip and closed her eyes, reaching out with the Force, searching for Jacen. "He's not dead," she said at last. "But that's all I can tell. Can't feel old Peckhum— don't have a link with him like I do with Jacen—but my brother's definitely out there somewhere."

A genuine smile broke out on Raynar's face. "Well, good," he said. "That's good."

"That's the last of them, I think," Lando said, striding up and kneeling beside Jaina. "How are you doing, Lowbacca, old buddy? You look like you've seen some hard action."

Lowie gave an *urff* of agreement.

"I think we got everybody who's in the neighborhood now," Lando said. "We did find one more," Luke said, coming up to join them. He pointed toward the edge of the clearing, where Tionne was tending a treelike Jedi with a broken limb.

Jaina looked up at her uncle. "What about Jacen?"

"He's alive . . . ," Luke said slowly. "We don't know any more than that."

"Yes," said Jaina, "but where is he? Shouldn't we go look for him?"

"We need to get the injured back inside the Great Temple first," Luke said. "If old Peckhum and Jacen managed to get the *Lightning Rod* going, the first place they'd head is the landing field. They wouldn't be able to land in a small clearing like this."

Jaina's spirits brightened. It was true. She looked at Lowie. "Can you walk?" she asked. Lowie groaned an affirmative reply.

"Master Lowbacca believes himself to be quite capable of perambulation with only minimal assistance," Em Teedee supplied.

"Okay then," Jaina said, "let's get back to the Jedi academy." She was anxious to see her brother again, eager to know that he was all right.

It was close to an hour later when the band of hobbling, limping Jedi trainees finally emerged from the jungle near the Great Temple's landing field. To Jaina's dismay, the flat patch of cleared ground stood empty.

"Don't worry, little lady," Lando said. "I'll help you look for them."

Jaina heaved a sigh and nodded. Even though she knew that Jacen was alive, she had a feeling of foreboding, of impending danger. "All right," Jaina said. "Let's get the wounded inside first. They'll be safe and protected in the temple. We'll have to take them in through the courtyard door, though. The hangar bay's blocked shut."

Crossing the landing field to the flagstone courtyard seemed to take longer than Jaina remembered it, but finally the entrance was only ten meters away. Seeing her goal so close, Jaina smiled and sped up.

Suddenly, a ragged figure lurched out of the shadowy doorway. His face was bloodied and bruised and covered with a thick layer of mud, but Jaina would have recognized him anywhere.

Zekk raised his chin proudly and stood barring the doorway.

"No one goes inside the temple," he said.

22

FACE-TO-FACE WITH HER old friend Zekk again, Jaina could find no words. Her breath refused to move in and out. It seemed to have frozen in her lungs like a chunk of winter. Her heart raced, and her palms grew sweaty.

Zekk didn't move.

Luke came forward to stand beside Jaina. On her other side, still partially supported by her, Lowie voiced a soft growl. And behind her, Jaina suddenly felt the presence of all the remaining Jedi trainees—people who had never met Zekk before today when he had led the attack against the Jedi academy. They saw him only as an enemy, without a glimmer of his being anything else.

Her eyes still fixed on Zekk's mud-covered face, Jaina said, "This is up to me, Uncle Luke. I need to handle this alone."

Luke hesitated for a moment. Jaina knew that her request was difficult for him. His voice held an undercurrent of warning when he spoke. "This isn't a broken machine that you can tinker with and fix."

"I know," she said softly. "I'm not sure he'll listen to me, but I know he won't listen to anyone else."

"I remember thinking the same thing," Luke said, "when I set out to turn Darth Vader back to the light side. It's a dangerous thing to attempt . . . and success is so rare." He sighed, as if thinking of Brakiss.

Jaina tore her eyes away from Zekk and turned to look at her uncle. "Please let me try," she said. Luke studied her for a long moment and then nodded.

Jaina focused her full attention on Zekk now, shutting out all other distractions as Luke took Lowie away across the courtyard. She drew strength from the Force, but was at a loss as to what to say to the young man.

Where did one start when talking to a Dark Jedi?

Zekk, she reminded herself. This was her friend. She took a step toward him and raised her voice, though only enough so he could hear. "The fighting's over now Zekk. We just need to get inside to tend our wounded."

Zekk shuddered from an inner chill. He backed up a step and spread his arms across the temple entrance. "No. There'll be a lot more injuries if you don't stop where you are."

Jaina balked at the threat. She would need to try a different tack.

Zekk's eyes darted from side to side, as if he were assessing the strength of the Jedi trainees, with their various wounds, wondering how many he could kill before they took him down.

"Let me be your friend again, Zekk," Jaina said. "I miss being your friend." He flinched as if he had been struck. "Let go of the dark side and come back to the light. Remember the fun we always had together, you and Jacen and I? Remember the time you salvaged that old slicer module and we tapped into the computers at the holographic zoo?"

Zekk nodded warily.

"We reprogrammed all of the animals to sing Corellian tavern songs," she went on. A wistful smile tugged at the corner of her mouth at the memory.

"We got caught," Zekk pointed out quietly. "And the zoo restored the original programming."

"Yes, but so many returning tourists requested it that a few months later the zoo added our singing animals as a separate exhibit." Jaina thought she saw some flicker of acknowledgment in his emerald eyes, but then they became hard as chips of green marble.

"We're not those children anymore, Jaina," he said. "We can't go back to the way it was before. You don't understand that, do you?" His gaze darted around the courtyard and he rubbed one hand across his forehead and eyes, smearing the mud there.

Jaina said, "All right, I *don't* understand. Explain it to me."

Zekk took a deep breath and began to pace in front of the dark doorway, like some wild creature trapped in an invisible cage. "There's no place where I belong anymore, Jaina. The Shadow Academy became my home. It's gone now—completely destroyed. Where can I go? The dark side is a part of me."

"No, Zekk," Jaina said. "You can give it up. Come back to the light."

Zekk laughed, a sound filled with anger and a touch of madness. He clawed at his cheek with one hand and held out his fingers so that she could see the mud there. A wound on his cheek seeped blood, but he seemed not to notice. "The dark side isn't like this mud," he said. "You can't just wear it for a while and then scrape it away—wash it off like some child who has finished playing in the dirt."

Zekk wiped his hand on his tattered cape. "I'm a different person now than the uneducated street kid you knew on Coruscant. I don't belong there anymore. Where *could* I belong? I've been trained as a Dark Jedi." His expression turned bleak. "And now my teacher is dead, too. He taught me and believed in me, gave me skills and a purpose."

"Peckhum always believed in you, too," Jaina said in a gentle voice.

Zekk put a muddy hand to his matted hair, and a wild look came over him. "But he's dead, too—he must be. I saw the *Lightning Rod* go down."

Jaina felt as if she had been rammed in the stomach by a mad herdbeast. The *Lightning Rod* had crashed? Then Jacen could be badly injured.

"I failed my teacher, Brakiss, and he's dead," Zekk said. He gestured as he spoke. "I led the Shadow Academy into battle, and all of my comrades were killed or captured. And if Peckhum's dead, then that's my fault too." Zekk's eyes looked glassy and feverish; his breathing was fast and shallow.

Jaina set her jaw in stubborn determination. "Well, Zekk, I don't want to see any more people die because of you. Just let me into the temple so we can take care of our wounded."

Zekk stopped pacing and whirled to look at her. "No! Stay back."

Jaina took a step forward. "Zekk, there's nothing left to fight about. What can you possibly hope to gain?"

Zekk shook his head. "You never did listen to my advice. You always thought you knew better." Despite his obvious agitation, Zekk's movements were eerily smooth as he drew his lightsaber from his belt and ignited the glowing red blade with a *snap-hiss*.

Then, in a move so instinctive that a moment later she couldn't even remember it, Jaina found her own lightsaber in her hand, its electric-violet beam humming and pulsating.

A feral grin spread across Zekk's face, almost as if he was glad that it had come to this.

"You see, Jaina," he said, taking a step toward her and twitching his energy blade from side to side, "once you let it in, the dark side is like a disease for which there's no cure." He lunged toward her, and their two blades met in a sizzling struggle of red against violet. "And the only way to remove the disease"—he lunged again and again and Jaina parried—"is to"—*thrust*—"cut"—*thrust*— "it"—*thrust*—"out!"

Jaina spun away and kept a wary eye on Zekk while she circled, waiting for his next move. Out of the corner of her eye she could see Luke watching the battle with calm acceptance.

At that moment Jaina realized that she had been trying to force Zekk to turn to the light side. She had been trying to fix him. But she couldn't. It had to be *his* choice. She drew a deep breath, letting the Force flow through her, and backed away from Zekk.

"I won't fight you anymore, Zekk," she said, switching off her lightsaber and tossing it to the ground. "There's still good in you, but you'll have to decide which direction you want to go—starting now. It's your choice, so make the right one for you."

Surprise and anger and confusion chased each other across Zekk's face. "How do you know I won't kill you?"

From the corner of her eye, Jaina saw Lowie step forward as if to protect her, but Luke put a restraining hand on the Wookiee's shoulder.

Jaina shrugged. "I *don't* know that. But I won't fight you. Make your choice." Jaina pushed back her straight brown hair and looked directly into Zekk's eyes with calm assurance— not assurance that he wouldn't harm her, but assurance that she had done the right thing.

"Well, what are you waiting for?" she whispered.

With slow deliberation, Zekk raised his glowing red lightsaber over Jaina's head.

23

IMPERIAL COMMANDO ORVAK finally awoke, feeling thickheaded and groggy. He fought away nightmares that were filled with serpent fangs and invisible predators slipping out of cracks in the wall. When he shook his head, a wave of dizziness and nausea pounded through his skull.

Orvak couldn't remember where he was or what he was doing. The stone floor felt hard beneath his sprawled body. He had fallen in an uncomfortable position and apparently slept there for some time. His hand throbbed, and he saw two small wounds there—punctures—before his vision blurred and lost focus again.

He must have taken his gloves off, and his helmet. What had he been doing? Where was he?

He heard no other sounds of combat around the Jedi academy. What could be happening?

Then Orvak remembered creeping into the ancient temple, his important mission for the Second Imperium . . . and the invisible glistening snake that had struck at his hand. For some reason, its venom had knocked him unconscious.

He brought his hand close to his eyes, but clarity of focus continued to evade him. Some kind of poison . . . he had been drugged, but now he was coming out of it. Was he a captive of the Jedi sorcerers?

Orvak heaved himself to a sitting position, and the universe turned in giddy circles around his head. He clutched at the cool, smooth floor for support. He had come here to the temple to plant explosives, to wipe out the great stone pyramid. Then everyone would see the weakness of the Rebellion and its Jedi, and they would make room for the Second Imperium.

But something had gone wrong.

Now he heard something. A clicking. Shaking his head again, he looked in the direction of the strange sound. It came from the timing device across the stone platform from him—

Timing device!

He blinked and finally managed to bring his vision into focus. His eyes burned, but he could see the string of descending numbers on the clock display.

Twelve . . . eleven . . . ten . . .

He launched himself to his feet—but too quickly. Dizziness swept through him again and he fell into black oblivion.

Nine . . . eight . . .

24

THE BUZZING HUM of Zekk's lightsaber filled Jaina's ears as her former friend brought it slowly down toward her neck. "You never understood, Jaina. . . . You can't understand.

You've always been so protected. The dark side is like a scar that's on the *in*side."

Zekk's eyes locked with hers. His hand remained steady, and he began speaking in a low voice, his words barely audible. "But these are scars that can't be healed," he went on. "You can try to cover them up"—*hum, buzz*—"but they're still there . . . underneath."

A swarm of angry insects buzzed near Jaina's right ear—but it was only the lightsaber, no longer above her head but continuing its excruciatingly slow descent.

Then, as if from a distance, Jaina heard new sounds: a crackle of static, and then a booming voice coming from a comlink.

"This is the *Lightning Rod*, callin' anyone who can hear me. Better clear everyone from the landing field real quick. We're comin' in. Oh, and if you got any of those energy shields back up, you better put 'em down now—we've had more'n our share of problems already today. My arm's broken, so the young Solo kid is flying—but our wings're clipped, and I'm not sure how maneuverable this baby is."

In that moment of delight and surprise, Zekk's lightsaber wavered and lifted away from her. A droning sound caught his attention, and Jaina glanced back over her shoulder to see the *Lightning Rod* coming into view above the treetops, sputtering and wheezing.

"Come on in, *Lightning Rod*," Jaina heard Luke say into his comlink. "You're clear to land." Zekk stared in amazement to see the battered old ship still intact, then shook his head. He reached out his free hand toward her. "Jaina, I didn't mean to—"

Just then, a concussive boom split the air, obliterating all other sounds. The ground vibrated beneath Jaina's feet, lurching with tremors and shock waves.

"Get down!" Zekk shouted.

She dove toward the courtyard wall and hit the ground, gasping at the jolt of pain that speared through her. She rolled, looking upward to see the gouts of smoke that erupted from a huge explosion inside the Great Temple. The crumbled remnants of massive stones tumbled down its sides in an avalanche.

Zekk ran for cover, too, but the hailstorm of rock moved faster than he could dodge. A large chunk of stone struck him in the head, while other fragments pummeled his body As Jaina watched the dark-haired young man sink to the ground, it came to her in a flash: he had known.

Zekk had *known* the temple was going to blow up.

And he had saved them all.

25

OUT IN THE unexplored jungles of Yavin 4, on the far side of the moon from where Luke Skywalker had established his Jedi academy, the wrecked TIE fighter smoldered after the crash.

The cockpit hatch opened, and Qorl crawled out, coughing and wheezing. With a heave from his human arm, he raised his shoulders, then worked the rest of his body free. His droid arm sparked and sizzled from damage it had received in the crash.

Qorl felt no pain, though. He was still functioning on adrenaline as he hauled himself out of the ship. His legs were numb and stiff, but they still worked. He dropped down from his ruined TIE fighter, then staggered into the protection of the trees just in case the craft exploded.

Alone in the jungle, Qorl watched the TIE fighter smoke until he was confident that none of the engines would go critical. The wrecked ship gradually heaved its last sigh and died.

The damage to his craft was severe: its outer hull had been punctured by iron-hard Massassi tree branches, its two planar energy arrays ripped askew; one had even been broken off.

As he had flown in, pummeled by the Rebel forces, dodging turbolaser bolts until the fatal strike that had caused him to reel out of control, Qorl had seen the Star Destroyers defeated. While wrestling for control of his TIE fighter, he had watched the Shadow Academy explode behind him.

He knew now that all hope for the Second Imperium was gone. The Emperor himself had been aboard the Shadow Academy, as had Lord Brakiss. The remaining Dark Jedi fighters on the surface would no doubt be rounded up and taken to Rebel prisons.

Qorl had much to regret. Rather than let one of the Solo twins die, he had made the choice to sacrifice his twisted student Norys. That had been a betrayal, and he was ashamed of it. Surrender was also betrayal. . . .

But Qorl had never surrendered.

He found himself stranded in the jungle again. His ship was beyond repair. The Second Imperium was defeated. Qorl had no place to go, no orders to follow . . . no reason to do anything other than search for a new place to live.

Perhaps it was best this way.

He could make a nice home for himself here. He knew this jungle, the fruits that were good to eat, which animals were easiest to hunt. Qorl realized that, despite the glory of returning to the Second Imperium and fighting once more for his Emperor, he had enjoyed those years of solitude, the quiet peace of living alone in the jungle.

In fact, he decided that this fate was not so bad, after all.

Qorl trudged off into the jungle to search out a new home. This time, he intended to spend the rest of his life there.

26

THE MORNING AFTER the great battle on Yavin 4 dawned cool and clear. Within hours, the bright sunlight dispensed with the lingering tatters of lacy mist that clung to the rubble-strewn base of the Great Temple and to the trees around it. Overhead, the giant orange planet Yavin filled much of the sky.

Waiting with Lowie and Jacen on the landing field, Jaina marveled at the difference a night's rest and a good meal could make on her perspective. After Luke, Tionne, Lando, and a couple of GemDiver engineers had determined that the lower two levels of the Great Temple were structurally sound, the remaining trainees and staff had made their way back into the pyramid, retrieving an ecstatic Artoo-Detoo, who had been waiting below. Admiral Ackbar's transports had evacuated the most seriously injured students, while those with only minor wounds had been treated and returned to their own chambers in the temple.

Jaina felt fortunate—and a bit guilty—that she had emerged from the battles almost completely unscathed. She had a few cuts and bruises from where stones had hit her after the explosion, but that was all.

Jaina ran an appraising eye over her friend Lowbacca. His shoulder was back in position again, his arm supported by a wide cloth strap, his broken ribs wrapped. The Wookiee normally wore only his webbed belt made of syren plant fibers, so the sling and the thick white bandaging around his midriff seemed oddly out of place.

She heard a warble and bleep behind her, and turned to find Artoo and her uncle Luke coming across the landing field to join them. The Jedi Master's face held a look of serenity and determination, but his eyes showed a glint of humor.

"I think *I* looked even worse than that," Luke said without preamble, "after my encounter with the Wampa ice creature on Hoth."

"Yes, but Lowie's looking a lot better this morning," Jaina agreed.

Luke chuckled. "Actually, I was referring to the Great Temple itself."

Jaina turned to study the ancient Massassi pyramid. The topmost level had collapsed where the detonators had exploded, and part of the sides had slumped downward. The broken, jagged walls of the grand audience chamber could have been mistaken for crenellations atop the battlements of some ancient fortress.

"At first I thought we might have to move the academy to some other temple," Luke said, "but now . . . I'm not sure we need to."

"You mean we could rebuild it?" Jacen asked with a groan. "Great—more practice exercises, lifting rocks, balancing beams . . ."

Artoo-Detoo twittered and beeped, as if excited at the idea. Lowie rumbled thoughtfully, then growled in pain, holding his aching ribs.

"Yes," Luke said. "In one way or another we've all been hurt through our encounters with the dark side. I think rebuilding the Great Temple might be a part of healing each of our wounds."

"Like Zekk," Jaina murmured, feeling her heart contract painfully "He needs a lot of healing."

"That reminds me, Uncle Luke," Jacen said, "what will you do with the Dark Jedi trainees we captured?"

"Tionne and I are working with them. We'll do our best to turn them back to the light side, but if it's not possible . . ." He spread his hands. "I'll have to discuss that with Leia, and—"

"Oh, Master Lowbacca, look!" Em Teedee interrupted from his clip at Lowie's waist. Jaina noticed that the tiny droid's speaker grille had been straightened and meticulously polished.

"Hey, they're back," Jacen cried.

Lando's shuttle, with Lowie's battered T-23 in tow, arrowed toward a corner of the landing field well away from the blaster-scarred hulk of the *Lightning Rod*.

Uttering a joyous howl, Lowie gave Em Teedee a grateful pat.

"Well, what are we waiting for?" Jaina asked as the shuttle and the T-23 touched down.

Jaina, Jacen, and Lowie hurried forward. By the time they reached it, the shuttle's landing ramp had extended, and Lando Calrissian strode down it with Tenel Ka on his arm. Lando's cape swirled behind him and he flashed his most charming grin. "Your friend here is quite a tough young lady," he said approvingly.

"This is a fact," she said, without the slightest trace of humor.

"I could have told you that," Jacen said. "Did you find it?"

Tenel Ka nodded, a satisfied look on her face. She pulled her arm free, plucked something from her belt, and held it out to show Jacen. It was the rancor-tooth lightsaber that she had lost during her clash with Tamith Kai on the battle platform. "It was not as difficult to locate as I had feared," she said. "Perhaps because I knew the rancor whose tooth this was, I was able to sense its location."

Tenel Ka no longer appeared feverish, and Jaina was amused to note that the warrior girl had braided her red-gold hair carefully around her face so that her bandage looked like a primitive warband across her forehead.

"I've invited Tenel Ka to come and visit GemDiver Station, since she missed it last time," Lando said. "We have some good bacta tanks there that'll fix up that cut on her head no time. Lowbacca, looks like you could use a few days in one of our tanks, too."

Lowie barked his acceptance and a thank-you.

"Oh, that would be exceedingly kind of you, Master Calrissian," Em Teedee said. "Master Lowbacca is most anxious to complete his healing and begin repairs on his incapacitated vehicle."

"His little skyhopper ain't the only vehicle that's incapacitated."

Jaina jumped when Peckhum's loud voice boomed out behind her.

"I know just what he means, though. The boy and I can't wait to get started fixing the *Lightning Rod*. But I think Zekk is going to be laid-up here for a while recuperating." Old

Peckhum stood by the damaged *Lightning Rod*, one hand on Zekk's shoulder, the other arm heavily bandaged.

Zekk's face was as pale as the dressing that wound around the base of his skull. His eyes seemed curiously empty, his face expressionless. He did not meet Jaina's gaze.

"I think you've got two more candidates for your bacta tank, Lando," Jaina said. "Can Jacen and I go along with them, Uncle Luke?"

Artoo-Detoo twittered.

"Oh, indeed! That's a marvelous idea," Em Teedee said.

"We promise not to get kidnapped this time," Jacen added with a lopsided Solo-style grin.

Luke chuckled. "All right, I think that would be good for all of you. You young Jedi Knights are stronger together. If you have some time away to heal, then you'll come back ready to help us rebuild . . . ready for a new beginning."

"Thanks, Uncle Luke," Jaina said.

"Jacen, my friend," Tenel Ka said. "Perhaps we had better leave soon. We do not want all of the injured students to come away with us and leave Master Skywalker here alone."

Jacen gave Tenel Ka a quizzical look. "What do you mean?" he said. "Why would you worry about that?"

"Because," Tenel Ka said solemnly, "a Jedi *must* have patients."

Jacen blinked at her, uncertainty written on his face. Then a shy grin lit Tenel Ka's face. It was the first time he had seen her smile so broadly.

"I don't believe it . . . ," Jacen began.

Jaina shook her head in wonder. "Sounded to me like she just told a joke."

"This is a fact!" Jacen said.

Lowie chuffed with delight. Jaina giggled.

Soon the entire clearing rang with laughter.

About the Authors

KEVIN J. ANDERSON and REBECCA MOESTA are the authors of all fourteen volumes of the *Star Wars: Young Jedi Knights* series. Working together, they have also written for *Star Trek*, *Titan A.E.*, *Starcraft*, as well as original short stories. In addition to many other *Star Wars* novels, Kevin is the author of an epic science fiction series, which begins with *Hidden Empire* and *A Forest of Stars*, and original novels *Captain Nemo* and *Hopscotch*. With Brian Herbert, he has completed six prequel novels to the science fiction classic *Dune*. Rebecca has written three volumes in the *Junior Jedi Knights* series and *Buffy the Vampire Slayer: Little Things*. More information can be found on their website, www.wordfire.com.